THE GREATEST ADVENTURE EVER

BY

J STEPHEN PROCTOR

Glory to God

The book is dedicated to my parents and godparents, who lovingly guided and guarded me through those perilous years of childhood and the daily reiteration of that little prayer, 'Forth in thy name O Lord I go'

To the hundreds, probably thousands of sermons I have heard Sunday by Sunday from dedicated ministers and preachers each one honestly trying to portray a little bit of God.

To 'the cloud of witnesses', the friends colleagues and casual acquaintances who, mostly unknowingly have contributed to my poor understanding of God.

To the authors of the various commentaries that have added greatly to my understanding, to William Barclay, to Tom Wright and to the authors of the Bible Speaks Today series

Most importantly to my wife, Veronica, for all the support she has given me. The enthusiasm for the story as it was unfolded to her, her constructive, critical comments that have helped to shape this offering. The loving patience extended to me as I spent many hours reading, writing and re-writing.

Thanks be to God

Index

Foreword

This book started out as a Life of St Peter but quickly became something bigger than an attempt at a biography. Peter is mentioned more than any other of the Twelve Apostles, the references portray a man of great courage, enthusiasm, loyalty and action. They also expose to us a man who can fail and fail spectacularly to understand the relationship between God and man being revealed to him through the life and work of Jesus. It is through his very weaknesses and failures that we are taught about this amazing revelation.

The book is not

- a theological treatise, it is a novel, intended to be enjoyed and engaged with.
- an impertinent attempt to write a gospel although it is a message of Hope.

The book is

- an attempt to portray the apostles struggling with the reality of living day-by-day with the Son of God. No other group of people has been so privileged and challenged. We are, as they were, challenged to find the reality of God.
- a story full of surprises, as all the apostle's preconceptions about God, their humanity, their taboos, and their expectations of Emmanuel are continually challenged.
- a story of the task of bringing God's urgent message that cannot be delayed. It is packed with energy and action.
- a story of growing understanding of man's total dependence on 'God with Us', of the agony, fear, lack of confidence that is separation from God.
- a story of growing faith that God is with us and really does care for us when, and especially when, things are going badly.
- a story of growing acknowledgement that the infinite power of God, that is available to us all, will be used through us to fulfil his plan.
- a story of growing awareness that God has a plan, a plan that starts with Adam and is being worked out through the ages.

5

Even when things are going wrong in men's eyes, God is still working his purpose out.

- a story of growing understanding that God is Love and that we can only be his true disciples if we are also personifications of his love for his creation.
- a story of growing recognition of our total dependence on God and that it is through prayer that God's purpose is revealed to us and God's strength is made available to us.

The story is told as the lives of very ordinary people doing very ordinary things and that their very ordinariness is extraordinary when seen as part of God's plan. I hope that reader will enjoy meeting new characters, farmers, rope makers, foresters and many others that they will respond positively to the message to faith and power frequently repeated, Just as it is today to open eyes and open ears.

We all struggle with our faith this book is, I hope, a help to all Christians and non-Christians alike who are searching for God's peace that passes all understanding.

Introduction

This first four parts of this story starting about the year 0 AD and finishing at about 30 AD, it is written by Jonas a Galilean fisherman, the father of Andrew and Peter. These, imaginary, papers were found after the death of Jonas and consist of 4 documents written at intervals covering this 30 year period. It sets the social, political and economic environment in Galilee during this man's life and how he and his family took advantage of the relative peace of the Roman occupation.

Part 1

About 0 AD

My name is Jonas, I am a fisherman, as all my forefathers have been before me for as many generations as anyone can think, and we have fished the Sea of Galilee all that time. We know the waters and the weather better than most and we have an eye for where the fish are, day and night, summer and winter. It is a hard life, you have to be strong and keep your wits about you. The Sea of Galilee is really a lake, its water is fresh and sweet and its full of fish, the only problems are finding them and catching them. The Sea is very good to us but you have to always have a weather eye out because there is always a danger of sudden ferocious storms. Round the sea there are boats lost with the men every year, good men too.

There are many fishing towns round the sea very like Bethsaida, where I work. My grandfather told me that before the Romans came, in his father's time, life was even harder than we have it and that's hard enough. In those days all the boats had to be hauled up the beach after every trip and the catch was sold on the beach with each boat owner getting the best price he could from the locals and the merchants, everyone was at each others throats. The only result was that fishermen were poor and everyone else seemed to be making a good living, salting, pickling, smoking and drying and then selling to the rich people in the cities. Well then the Romans came and built the harbours we have now and since then the whole industry has changed, I suppose its always the same some of the change was good and some was not so good. The Romans didn't really build the harbours we built the harbours but they showed us how, they didn't just show us they forced us to do the work. At the time we thought we were being enslaved, the overseers were cruel, demanding men who treated us just like slaves we were all forced to work three days each week, they collected all the fishermen from up and down the coast to this "voluntary" work. They also collected up as many people as they could from the farmers and the hired labourers and made them help. Nobody believed it could be done, "How can you build a wall out into the sea? Was the question! If it was that easy do you think we wouldn't have done it years ago? The really frightening thing that we learnt and are still learning just how ruthlessly efficient the Romans are when they have decided that something has to be done. Well they built seven harbours round the lake, five on our side and two on the eastern side. On our side there are Bethsaida, Capernaum, Ginnosar, Magdala, and Philoteria, on the east side Gergesa and Hippos. They were all built in two winter seasons!

Out of all the beatings and discontent came many good things. The demand for good stone for the breakwaters was supplied by opening new quarries up in the hills and the men who were made to work there have continued and sell cut and dressed stone to the Romans and the wealthy Jews and Greeks for their houses and palaces. Of course we can't afford the stone and our houses are still made from mud bricks just as always, its said we learnt how to do that when we were slaves in Egypt, so some good comes out of bad! To get the stone down to the sea we were made to build roads, nobody knew what a road was, now they are being built every where, but then we only had tracks through the hills and mountains. Of course that was all we needed everything was carried on asses and camels, the great blocks of stone needed for the harbours had to be dragged on carts pulled by asses, camels, oxen and men. Nobody had ever seen such things, the only thing that had wheels as far as we knew were war chariots. Well a new business started from that some of the local carpenters were drafted in to copy the one cart the Romans brought up from Ceasarea, and now there is a good business running building carts of all sorts for moving heavy loads like the stone, posh carts for wealthy ladies, less posh carts for the rest of us that run regularly to places like Sepphoris, and, very important to us special carts for carrying our fish! Everyone said it was daft starting up making carts the only roads were to the quarries and back, but we were still learning about the Roman way of doing things. Once they had taught a few people how to build roads they wanted roads everywhere, they used the Jews to oversee the vast hoards of slaves who came here from all over the empire. The quarries of course, in cutting out usable blocks for buildings, produce a lot of waste; the Romans knew that this was ideal for road construction. It is still going on so we all know that a road has to be just so wide. It has to have a solid foundation, it has to have well-cut and dressed stones on the top and it has to have strong kerbs to keep it all together. I know all that and I'm only a simple fisherman!

The Romans seem to know everything they make sure that it is never too steep, to do this they cut through solid mountains. They want the roads as straight as they can and instead of going round things as the donkeys did they go straight though them and over them. The first time they built a bridge nobody would believe it people came from miles around just to see a bridge! Another thing they did, which we thought was quite daft, was that at every Five of their Roman Miles they built a resting area. Travellers could stay here for the night, there was always food and water, for people and animals, it was a brilliant innovation it was now safe to make long journeys, the robbers would not attack these "service stations" as there was nearly always some Romans staying there. People are so impressed they are asking the Romans to start building roads all over the place.

As I said every silver lining has a cloud! As soon as you get a road you get droves of officials coming to inspect you and to insist on their way of doing things and that means taxes. It's terrible they tax absolutely everything that they can; we can't escape everything we do they tax, they'd tax the very air we breath if the could think of a way! To start with we thought the harbours were a sure way for us poor fishermen to become wealthy like the land owners, we could come and go as we pleased we could not be picked off by the buyers, our boats were safe from the storms there were many, many advantages. What we had not expected was that the Romans could now count our catches as well as we could and we were taxed, to have a boat we were taxed, to put to sea we were taxed, to buy new nets or sails we were taxed; there was nothing that was not taxed and there was nowhere for us to hide. There are stories from when the harbours were first built that some fishermen would not change their ways and wanted to continue to fish of the beaches. The Romans stopped that at once, after only one month to get used to the new ways any beached fishing boat was broken up. They only had to do it once, boats are very expensive, and everybody knew they were serious.

The other thing that surprised everyone was how the towns expanded. It seems incredible now that the tiny little village of Bethsaida which only two generations ago had twenty boats and about one hundred families is now a prosperous town connected to the highway, more than seventy boats and all the crafts any town could need and two new synagogues. It's the same in the other harbour towns and all because of a harbour, some roads and the taxes. We don't know where the fish come from, but we trust in God that there will always be more. We used to know where they went but now we don't even know that, but we trust in God and the Romans that the demand will go on and on!

Well, those aren't all the changes, when we saw how the system was working with all the taxes and things we had to change our ways of doing our business. The first thing that happened was that all the fishermen now met every day we saw what we had all caught. Very quickly we decided that we would sell together, the buyers would be offered one price and all the fishermen would stick to that price. The only differences were on quality, a price for pickling quality, a price for smoking quality, a price for salting quality and of course a price for fresh fish for the local people. Then we found that we could do deals with the net makers, of course the demand for nets was increasing and they all got together so that we couldn't pick them off as we had done. So we negotiated, guild to guild to set the price for nets, we were satisfied and they were satisfied, guild fishermen only bought from guild net makers! The next deals really changed the world round here for the fishing industry, boats are expensive and all round the lake there were only about three reliable boat builders in those days and it was not long before they couldn't make enough boats for the expanding fleet. They tried the old trick of putting up the prices but that just accelerated the big change, and that was and is that the fishermen became boat builders. By a few well-arranged marriages we got boat builders into our families. The harbours are ideal places for boat building, the beach inside the harbour is protected, launching is into quiet, calm water, all the things needed are to hand or can be and we the fishermen can influence the design of the boats. At first the changes were very small useful things that the boat builder didn't know about that would help the fishermen, then much bigger changes. Boats are now being built for allsorts of uses. Special boats for moving the different types of stone found round the sea to the building projects in the ever-expanding towns. Special boats for moving grain and other foodstuffs, special boats for moving cattle, sheep and goats. Special boats for moving people and all this traffic and business are new opportunities for fishermen and their families. Some of the 'one-time' fishermen are now making a living out of transport and do no fishing any longer. All the fisherman and other boatmen are in a guild and we decide what boats we will build and who will run the new service. We all contribute to setting up the new venture and we all share in the profits, or losses, there doesn't seem to be anything we can't tackle.

So the next thing was to control the selling of the fish, the big buyers were the picklers, and the salters, driers and smokers. There were lots of problems between us all, as one accused the other of making all the profit and not having fair prices for each product. What was worse was that the tax collectors were getting a major slice of the revenue by taking a percentage at every transaction. So again, after a few well-chosen marriages, we started to include them in the total system. Once they were part of the fishermen's guild they of course got better prices for their fish than the others, as you can imagine very quickly there weren't any others. We combined together and built special purpose buildings on the quayside, along side the tax collectors offices, for the mass production of salted fish, pickled fish, dried fish and smoked fish. The quality improved dramatically, the costs fell and the prices increased and the market size grew. Then we realised that the people who seemed to be making all the money were the merchants who bought from us and distributed the fish round the country so they came on board and we now have an interest in the fish from building the boats to the fish being sold to the final customer who is going to eat it. Amazing all in two generations and all because of a harbour, my great grandfather would not recognise the place or the business. It goes without saying that all these changes have spread right round the lake and we have regular contact with the guilds in the other harbour towns to make sure that nobody breaks ranks. I'm sure we haven't exploited all the opportunities yet in fact for a little fisherman in a small town on the Sea of Galilee life is pretty good, even exciting!

We have to pay our taxes but as I was saying to Zebedee the other day "You've got to have it to be taxed on it".

We did have a short respite from the tax collectors, it took them a while to work out how to tax the fishermen when they stopped selling any thing and the fish stayed in the business until the final sale. It didn't last long they soon invented ways of making sure they got their cut.

I thought I would give you a short introduction, but once I get talking about the business I can't stop, so the introduction is quite long. I hope you have not been bored! I decided to write some thoughts because we are going through a very upsetting experience. What's happening has never happened before and I hope it will never happen again, only God knows why it is happening at all!

The whole district is in a state of excitement, the Romans had issued orders that a population census was to be taken. This was alarming, it had never happened before, there was no explanation and the rumours were all frightening. Was it so that people would be moved, or that the demand for slaves for Rome or other cities could be fulfilled? Could it to be able to demand higher taxes? Perhaps it was to draft more men into the Roman army? Was it to be able to identify troublemakers and criminals? Maybe it was to know who the wealthy men were, and to find out who owned the land? Was it to find out who owned the fishing boats and the fishing rights? What about lists to define who was responsible for the maintenance of the harbours and roads? Perhaps it was to find out where the fish were sold? Everyone you spoke to had a different rumour. The rabbis were just as much in the dark as any one else, even though they seemed to have fairly good relations with the Romans. The scribes who usually knew exactly what was going on were useless the letters they were writing for soldiers were just the same as ever, letters to families and friends usually complaining, as soldiers do, about the food, the weather, the officers and the local population; but nothing, absolutely nothing, about counting of the population. After what was almost a rebellion the Romans had finally conceded that the timing should be moved from the middle of the harvest to the quiet time after the harvest, but even that presented difficulties. They insisted that everyone went to his hometown; by hometown they didn't mean where he was born but the principle town of his tribe. There was no explanation why, but the rumour was that the Sanhedrin in Jerusalem had suggested this and then insisted on it. They hoped to be able to use the information to exclude any family who were not "pure" from the traditional rights and access to the Temple without paying for even more sacrifices. That's what was being said, everyone agreed that this was most likely, the Sanhedrin would find every possible way of filling the Temple coffers and their own pockets.

So now the orders had been given and the whole population was moving round the country. The idea that the tribes still lived in the land that Moses had designated was incredibly stupid. People had moved for all sorts of reasons but when the 'Remnant of the Tribes' who had been banished by Nebuchadnezzar returned from Babylon hundreds of years ago they stayed just where they could find somewhere to live. Of course they knew where their traditional tribal lands were but they had no way of demanding land in particular places just because of their name. The population was thoroughly mixed up. Then, after the Greeks had been defeated by the Maccabean family, a large population was forcibly moved from Judea to Galilee to ensure that the Jews dominated the Gentiles who had been living there since the times of the Assyrians, and that was a long time even before Nebuchadnezzar.

May be that was the reason, so the whole idea may have come from the Sanhedrin so that they could move people back to their tribal homelands. The Temple kept detailed records, going back to times of the slavery of the Hebrews in Egypt, concerning the descent of every Jewish man. It was the law, for as long as we were a nation that the first-born son of every family must be registered at birth with the authorities. For us that authority was the Temple in Jerusalem and that meant to all intents the powerful Court of the Sanhedrin. This Court exercises absolute power over the Jewish population; the Romans delegated this power to them when we were conquered. My father was alive then and he told us terrible stories of cruelty and mayhem, of massacres and summary executions, usually by crucifixion, an awful slow agonising death. The only sentence that the Sanhedrin cannot hand down is the death sentence; the Romans have retained this for the Military Governor alone. There are however unfortunate stonings still carried out without the Roman authority for things like blasphemy and adultery; there is then an enquiry by the Romans but it never comes to anything and the poor unfortunate can not be brought back. If you have ever seen a man or a woman stoned to death you will not want to see it again, it certainly keeps people in fear of falling foul of the Law. The enquiry is always about our Law that was given to us by God through our greatest ever leader, Moses. The Romans don't pretend to understand that so the matter is usually allowed to conclude that there is no action to be taken. We had hoped that the Roman insistence on overseeing the application of the death penalty would stop all the gossiping and tell-tailing, and nosiness that goes on but it hasn't. Everyone is watching everyone else so that they can be reported to the scribes and Pharisees; there are many punishments that can be exacted like having to make more sacrifices or being excluded from the synagogue. There was no way of knowing who were your friends or your enemies, even your relatives can accuse you of some infringement of the rules and there you are in trouble for nothing. It doesn't make you feel particularly religious when everything you do seems to be wrong, our God must be a very angry and unforgiving God. You can't avoid all this spying either, we know it's awful but we have to keep an eye on our neighbours just in case any of them dare to accuse us, our defence has to be the guilty behaviour of the accuser. The result is everyone is watching everyone else and we are all frightened of our own neighbours.

Now back to the census. So the Jewish authorities seem to have cashed in on the idea and will undoubtedly use the information to suit their own ends. To us, normal mortals, it seems a typical madcap idea from those high-class administrators, they had no understanding about the property problems, the disruption to businesses, and the chaos in the whole of society. I'm sure that the winners will be the lawyers and the scribes sorting all the problems out! Nobody seemed to have thought out any of the real problems. Where were all these people going to stay? Who would be responsible for all the empty houses? What about security, somebody had suggested that visitors should be housed in the homes of people who were away, but what about thefts, breakages and worse what if they wouldn't leave? Any way it wouldn't work, nobody had any idea how many people would end up in any particular place; some towns would be so crowded there would be no room for anyone. Some places would end up totally deserted and a golden opportunity to thieves and burglars. What about the sick and the elderly? What happens if you die while on this forced journey? People do die unexpectedly! There is no use complaining, there are no excuses allowed, the scribes are in charge of telling people where they have to go if they don't know, so that's no excuse. People have tried every possible excuse and none are accepted. Of course the journeys vary some people have long journeys and some short, a few lucky ones are able to stay where they are, but only a few. Most people are making up groups for safety's sake, there is no security for travellers, the countryside is full of dangers from robbers and from wolves and bears and lions and wild dogs so you don't go on your own!

We heard that the rabbis had asked for military escorts to take groups through the worst areas. The Romans just replied that a few dead Jews were not their concern! They didn't have enough men and any way with this number of people on the move they had enough problems themselves at the census points. These are the men we have billeted on us all the time, we care for them, and we feed them we try to make friends with them despite their pagan habits! When we really need some protection we are just abandoned! We asked for protection from the Jewish army. We thought that King Herod would help us in our difficulties but no; they just laughed and said they were far to busy escorting important people and we should look after ourselves, We have heard of some people tagging on to these escorted "special" people but they travel too fast and never think about the train they have collected, so they just get left behind as prey for the robbers.

The exploitation of the travellers is dreadful, there is no friendliness at all everyone is willing to provide a bed and a meal to strangers but only at a price and what a price! Travellers are being charged a week's wages for a roof over their head for a night in some places. Of course they will be charged in the same way when it is their turn to travel but you might have thought that being Jews looking after Jews there would be an attitude of generosity and care; not a bit of it! The result is there are people living rough in the open air in every town, hoping that they won't be robbed or worse during the night. Of course I have had to put up my prices for fish the demand just exceeds the supply and you can't let a chance like this slip by! All the locals of course get their fish at the proper price but the travellers have to pay. After all our people are being fleeced on their journeys. I've been told that in the Jordan Valley even fresh cool drinking water has trebled in price. The Samarians, as usual, are attacking any Jews that have tried to take the route south through Shechem and on to Judea. They are dreadful people; they all know that there are very few of them who will have to go outside their own territories for the census. It's a good job we threw them all out

16

generations ago!!

I feel sorry for the craftsmen you see them with their donkeys loaded down with their tools and their stock, taking it with them, nobody will risk leaving it behind in case it is stolen while they are away. Because there are so many fishermen round the sea we have worked out a system among us; a sort of common property system and we care for each other's boats and nets and all the other gear we need. We have extended this property protection to the salters and driers and picklers after all we will depend on them to keep our sales going when this is all over. The other serious problem is that we just can't catch enough fish to meet the demand; the buyers are furious, they say the price of fish in Jericho and Jerusalem has gone through the roof, but we just can't catch enough to meet the normal demand let alone the inflated demand from these travellers. The tax collectors couldn't be more greedy and are exploiting the situation, they say that the Emperor still wants his taxes and has no interest in the census so taxes have nearly doubled in the last three months; that's partly why the prices have had to be hiked up. Everyone is sure that most of the increase is going straight into the tax collectors pockets, they are just leaches working for the gentiles, nobody even speaks to them now they were ostracised before, now we make sure that they pay the very highest prices for their fish. The 'guild of fishermen' is holding; we have not found any of our group making special deals to get more trade. The agreement we made at the start with the men from Capernaum and the other ports to keep to our own patch is holding. Otherwise there would have been a price war and nobody would have made anything out of this "opportunity"

Well, I'm one of the lucky few, I suppose. I only have to go to Capernaum to register, so we are making it a bit of a holiday. I have agreed with my partner Zebedee that he goes this week and I will go next week. We will both have to take our family because all males have to be counted no matter how young or old. We will be a ship full, there's my mother, my two uncles and they're wives and families and my family and my brother Simeon's brood. Uncle Joseph has four children my cousin Jonah and his wife Sarah and her two babies, then there's cousin Reuben, he's married with three children neither of his daughters are married so they staying at home to keep an eye on things for us. Uncle Daniel has four boys and one daughter who is married. She is going with her husband and his family to Ashcalon!!! Seems like the other end of the world, but she says the sea fishing is good down there. The eldest of his sons, Daniel is very religious and is training to be a rabbi, so he is making his own way. The other three are all married and have twelve children between them, six and six, all the boys are in the fishing business with us and generally are doing the shore jobs while the rest of us go out in the boats, that's not to say they don't sail it just seems to work out that way. Three of the girls are married, two of them married local boys in Bethsaida and as good fortune would have it Jessie lives in Capernaum and her family have very kindly offer to give us all lunch it will be a splendid party with all her new family there will be more than twenty of us. Of course there's my family as well, That is my wife Marianne, Jenny our eldest, then Andrew who is only three but a tough little fellow and of course Marianne is expecting our third any day now hopefully not until we get back. She is a strong wife and has had no problems when the other children were born. I only wish my Dad was still alive he would have enjoyed the party though he would have kept on about loosing two days fishing and worried about people falling overboard and the weather and any other possibility of disaster, he did enjoy a good worry. He's been dead now for five years, he was still young and it was very sudden, I only have one sister and she was married a long time ago seven years I think and she lives in Sepphoris, her husband is our agent for selling fish there and in the countryside around. They did a good deal when Herod was rebuilding the town after its complete destruction and the selling of the population into slavery by the Romans only seventy years ago. Of course he wanted new people there and provided new housing and tax-free businesses for the first five years! It is now a very good business indeed and the whole family benefits from it.

Zebedee's family is still small he was only married three years ago, their first child was a girl but his wife Mary is expecting again so like us all they are hoping for a son. They don't expect the baby will be born for about two months so we all hope the journey won't upset her too much. They have a big family too; between them and us we have a real quiver full!

I don't really mind this census thing that Quirinius has ordered, its got to be good for our business, it's a bit of a holiday and any way the Romans have given us peace and security to get on with our lives. Far better than the stories we are told of the rebellious period of the Maccabees and before that those Greeks who did nothing compare with the Romans, if we can't be free my vote goes for the Romans! and I'm sure I'm speaking for nearly everyone round here.

Well there was not too much excitement when we made our trip to Capernaum, for the census. We had a splendid party with all the family and all Marianne's family. These infrequent family get-togethers can be a strain but it all went off well. The trip there and back was uneventful, in the end we had to take two boats as we had agreed to supply the goat and lamb for the feast. You know what wives are like they take everything as if we were going to Damascus and nobody else would produce pure Kosher food. We got home having a remarkable easterly it only took two hours and Zebedee and his family were there to welcome us. They'd had a really good catch and were convinced that this was God's hand at work and blessing our trip.

The Zebedee family made their trip and returned safely later that week and everything had been done between Sabbaths and with full respect of the Law. Heaven alone knows how people making long trips get on, hopefully for them they can manage everything properly and don't have to be purified continually on the way. Then within only two weeks Marianne had her baby, a boy!

What excitement a brother for Andrew and he is already showing that he will be strong and big. Compared with Andrew his hands are big, his shoulders are big and he has sturdy legs. Of course he is only a few months old yet but he already shows he will be a strong lad and will be a great fisherman. I'm not being critical of Andrew but already at just three years old he is a bit of a loner he sits and thinks a lot, now he can talk he comes out with remarkable things, only yesterday he asked why the fish were only in the sea, well I'd never thought about it so we gave the stock answer that that was the way God made it, but he was not satisfied with that and quizzed us why sheep and goats don't swim and why we have to learn to swim and why pebbles sink and all sorts of other things that were clearly bothering him. There aren't any answers either! I suppose all boys go through this 'Why?' questioning. Andrew doesn't seem to just ask 'why?' for the sake of it, you feel he really is interested and has thought about the question and wants a proper answer. He loves his little brother and is happy to rock the cradle to put young Simon to sleep. We called him Simon after his great grand father; we have been told that he was a good fisherman too. Marianne and I sit of an evening trying to think what sort of world these two boys of ours will grow up into, there's no knowing, we only have to think of all the bewildering changes we have seen to in the last thirty years!! Hopefully it will be a better world, certainly ours is better than our parents!!

Now we have to do our best to bring them up as proper sons of Abraham respecting the Law and in the Fear of God.

Part 2

About 6 AD

King Herod, the tyrant and murderer, some call him "The Great", died, just about five years ago, and after a lot of trouble, things have finally settled down. Here in Galilee we try and avoid trouble, so all the terrible things that have gone on in Judea are far enough away to not be of any direct concern. The stories and rumours we hear are a further confirmation, if it was needed, of the dreadful Herodian Family, they murder their sons, they murder their wives, absolutely nobody is safe! They are not truly Jewish, if it wasn't treason you would say they weren't Jewish at all. Everyone thought that when the old tyrant died instead of the Romans respecting his dynastic ambitions they would have put the government back to the priests but with a garrisoned army to keep the peace. In the end they split the country three ways. Judah and Samaria was to be ruled by Archelaus; Galilee and Perea was to be ruled by Antipas; Philip was to rule the territory to the north and east of the Sea of Galilee. Archelaus was so tyrannical that the Romans deposed him. He was replaced by a direct military governor ruling under the authority of the Roman Governor in Syria. To ensure that Antipas did not become a threat to the Romans, his territory was divided by the Decapolis. This is a strange archaic set of ten Greek towns, as the name implies, that have been allowed to retain their independence from Rome, they are distributed mostly in the eastern desert and act to some extent to keep the wild desert tribes under control.

So we got Antipas, he is known as Herod and we all have to treat him with respect not because he is a good or a great man, quite the opposite, but if he is angry he does the most dreadful things, like his father he is a tyrant. But he does do some good things, things that are good for the working man as well as good for himself and his clique of courtiers.

As long as anyone can remember Sepphoris was always the capital of Galilee, but it has a tragic past. Only a few years ago when Herod died some hot heads thought this was the moment to rebel against the Herod family. While the three contenders, that is, Archelaus, Antipas and Philip were in Rome trying to persuade the Emperor who should inherit the kingdom there was mayhem in Judea, they say 2,000 were crucified on the orders of Archelaus. Nobody now knows how it started in Galilee but the city was attacked by a Roman general called Varus. The result was that the city was burnt it to the ground, there was nothing left. They killed most of the people there and those they didn't kill they herded up in the main square, surrounded by the corpses of their friends and families and, after killing all the old and the very young, they marched the rest off to Sidon. Nobody really knows what became of them but the rumour is that they were shipped to Rome and sold as slaves. The ruins laid deserted for a few years nobody went near the place but then after Antipas had established his power in Galilee, by the usual Herodian brutality, he announced he was going to rebuild the city and it would be more glorious than before and that it would once again be the main city in the area. Well he did it and the new city is dramatic, it is of course Greek in style everything has to be, it has open squares, it has wide straight roads with purpose built shops on both sides, there are bathing houses, there are pagan temples but they have also built three beautiful new synagogues. There are fresh pure water fountains on every other street corner and all the waste is carried in water washed, covered, gullies in the middle of the roads. The roads are all paved with limestone flags and there is a pavement on both sides for people to walk safe from the traffic of camels and donkeys and carts. The houses are all built of stone and have awnings to protect everyone from the sun or the rain. The whole town is surrounded by a massive, totally impregnable wall. There are watchtowers and a wide walkway on top for soldiers and defenders and there are only four gates. May it be God's will that it never suffers the fate of its predecessor but if it does it will at least be able to defend itself.

Of course Sepphoris is at an important crossing of the road from Ceasarea on the shore of the Great Sea to Damascus through the hills and plains of Galilee going roughly north and the other main route from the Sea of Galilee and the Valley of the Jordan to Tyre going roughly west so most of the traffic has to pass through the town. We all know that Herod really had self-interest at heart because this is the ideal spot to extort even more taxes from the goods and people passing through. Of course he also knew that there would be a lot of business to be done in feeding the travellers, in making and selling to them every possible artefact, in providing accommodation to men and animals and where there is business, to his avaricious mind, there are taxes to be had. He is as cunning as his father before him. It's been a huge success and he is making a lot of money from the venture. The town is so splendid, with all its modern ideas, that people flock there just to see what can be done and of course they spend money. Through our family outreach we are, needless to say, making a profit by distributing our very high quality fish products, hand selected, carefully prepared and packed according to the Law of Moses, long may it last. Sorry for the advert it comes naturally!

As Jews we have our promise from God to Abraham, that one day we will be rewarded for our dedication and obedience to Him and that reward will be the restoration of the Jewish kingdom of the time of our ancestors and particularly King David. I would like that time to come too but not with the risk of revolution and bloodshed which we have witnessed in the last few years. We all know that Herod was an absolute tyrant he was hated everywhere, but for most of the time he kept the peace and stopped any hot-headed revolutionaries from causing trouble. His technique was brutal but it was only very stupid and determined people who stepped out of line when they saw what would happen. When he died he left a power vacuum and his three dreadful sons all wanted to be king, the result was that there was rebellion everywhere. In the end either the Romans, as in Sepphoris, or the Jews as in Jerusalem and Judea put down these hot-heads with terrible cruelty and loss of life. It's all very well having ambitions to overthrow the present system but people have to understand just how powerful the Romans are. There is just no point in opposing them and everyone should remember that the peace they bring, "Pax Romana", has given us an unbelievable improvement in all the things that make life worthwhile and enjoyable. I won't join in any of these hair-brained schemes and say so every time there is any sort of discussion that might lead to a confrontation. I hope that there is peace for me to see my children flourish and my business to prosper, now Andrew and Peter are my insurance for the future and I shall have nothing to do with any thing that might upset that plan. Not even for the Rabbi!!

Part 3

About 20 AD

Well doesn't time fly! I've just looked up those old papers and I have a lot more to say now.

The peace that I was talking about has been maintained, Herod Antipas who is our Roman Puppet has busied himself in raising more and more tax revenue, rather than persecuting the population. His policy is that he will be more prosperous if the general economy is more prosperous. To achieve this he has invested heavily in the infrastructure he has built miles and miles of roads, he has built new towns, Tiberias, and rebuilt old ones, Caperaum, and rebuilt destroyed towns, Sepphoris. This has brought in skilled artisans who need housing and feeding and it has brought in a huge amount of trade in the transport of supplies. It takes a while to see another thing and that is that he is spending his money locally by employing people who live locally and spend their money locally so we all win! I suppose we are paying the taxes to fund his projects and so we are just getting our own money back! It's a funny old world!

Despite all his brutality and tyrannical behaviour Antipas has brought stability, peace and security, his methods are not soft or forgiving, if you step over the line you are executed usually after horrifying torture. After a while petty thieves, brigands, bandits and political or religious agitators realised that they were not welcome where the power of Antipas held sway.

I can well remember that census, nearly twenty years ago now, when the main worry for people was whether they would be murdered or worse travelling to Jerusalem or anywhere in Judea from here. Now a-days the annual Passover Pilgrimage is a holiday with no problems of robbers or bandits or only very rarely and then never where the rule of Antipas holds sway. The result is that people will travel with confidence and will do business with confidence. The change is dramatic; we can send consignments of fish products not only to Damascus but also all over the Roman Empire with absolute confidence of its safe and timely arrival at its destination. We have already set up a chain of agents throughout Israel, Syria and Asia this has been possible only because of the rule of 'Pax Romana' and that is what Antipas is determined to maintain. We are planning to extend this side of the business into Egypt and onwards to Africa. We are just one of hundreds of businesses who are thriving in this climate of confidence and all the time Antipas is reaping bigger and bigger tax revenues from the trade. The result is, we do it and so does everyone else, the area is booming. It's a win, win system. I hope everyone remembers that the prosperity we are enjoying now is due to the peace and security that the Romans provide and that somebody doesn't think he could do better without them and start any trouble.

We moved from Bethsaida to Capernaum when Peter was four years old. It was a real wrench to leave the town where we had been born, where we had grown up, where we were married and where the children were born and where all our family have lived for as long as anyone could remember. There were several reasons all of which were in hindsight good enough in themselves but together they were indisputable.

The first was the business, it was quite clear that the prospects were far better in Galilee on the western coast of the lake, with Antipas in control. The eastern seaboard was far less secure or prosperous. Antipas' brother Philip was in control of the northern part of the coast and the southern end was under the control, if that's what it is of the Decapolis. Neither of these powers had any of the drive and determination of Antipas with the result that they quickly began to look very backward. The differences were clear, little or no investments in roads and harbours and in rebuilding for one thing. Then security was as bad as it used to be here, it was just not safe to travel except with an armed escort, and the risks are too high to send goods they just disappear. Then having to send all our product west meant either a road journey or a sea journey either of which just added un-necessary costs.

But really I think the most important thing in the end was the re-building of Capernaum, of course the cost of living here is higher that in Bethsaida but that is offset by the comfort and beauty of the new town. We all live in stone built houses, the roads are paved with flag stones, there is a pavement for people to walk on safely separated from the wagons and camels and donkeys and out of the mud when it rains. There are lots of specially built shop premises and we are able to extend as we like within reason. The harbour is now magnificent, I had no idea what the end result would be when I talked about it before. I have to keep reminding the boys, well they are men now, that all this has happened in my lifetime, they have no idea how hard life used to be. The town's buildings are magnificent and easily compete with what was done at Sepphoris, though the new capital, Tiberias, is just mind blowing in its magnificence. Anyway, just like Sepphoris, we have sewers and running water throughout the town. Once Marianne and her mother and my mother saw what was being done they overcame all the difficulties they had raised about moving when I suggested it would be good for business, it took about ten seconds, so here we are and very happy. Most of the family are here now and we don't feel strangers at all!

The Zebedee family decided to stay in Bethsaida, this was partly for business reasons our co-operative partnership needed a base in Bethsaida just as much as we needed to expand into Capernaum to take advantage of the developing economy in the area and the infrastructure developments that would allow further expansion of trade into the hinterland. Of course the Zebedees had the usual problem of moving a family not least because of the support they had received when their sons were born, James and John, shortly after our Peter was born. The Zebedees went on to have another 5 children. Anyway the JJ's as we call them are fine lads and are totally absorbed in the fishing world and will make very good businessmen, God willing! Well they perhaps did the right thing by staying put in Bethsaida because Herod Philip has now started rebuilding the town and extending the harbour. We all say that he has learnt a few tricks from his wicked half-brother Antipas. Philip seems to be a totally different character, he accepted his portion of his grandfather's kingdom and is mild and considerate, nobody could accuse him of being a tyrant, we sometimes wonder whether he really is out of the same stable as Antipas. He has built a beautiful new town just below the source of the Jordan in the foothills of the Mount Hermon range. It is magnificent, but not too opulent, it has incredible views to the south and west, it is not too cold in the winter but has a cool climate in the summer. Everything you can think of is grown on the slopes of those hills they want for nothing except fish so we have developed a solid business through our agent, another good marriage, and send a caravan of mules every week or so to replenish his stocks of the best cured fish in Galilee! Part of the deal we have in the area is to bring the mules back from Ceasarea Philippi loaded with timber, oak, ash, beech and cedar which we either keep for our boat building enterprises or we sell on to joiners and carpenters for their use. There is one chap in Nazareth who seems to have an insatiable demand using it for all the building work in Sepphoris and his furniture making business. Most ordinary people could not afford such wood for their needs so he must have wealthy discerning customers.

Going back to Zebeddee, the business developments we have undertaken here are now being repeated in Julia, that's Bethsaida's new Roman name. Initially we thought it would be on a much smaller scale than Caperaum but having once started to put our products on the market and given the merchants a far more reliable supply than ever before that market looks as if it will be as big as Capernaum. The fish and fish products market in the Decapolis has never been exploited but we can now see really exiting opportunities.

Education is a good thing! We all agreed that the boys should learn to speak, read and write Greek and how it has paid off, they are always involved in any deals with Greek speaking businessmen and are now expert at the business of negotiating supply contracts. The buyers are at first amused that our small sons are brought in to the discussions but later go away very impressed with the business acumen that they have already developed. The next generation is already helping the old generation, just as it should be!

Andrew is 22 years old now and very mature, there is nothing rash or demonstrative about Andrew. He always takes time to think things out, when we are discussing business policies or investments or any other matters he is always the steadying influence. He will not be hurried, he will always sleep on a problem and usually allowing some more time is very sound. Many of the problems that other people are getting excited about have disappeared by the next morning, and if they haven't people have had time to consider the various options quietly and in the end we make better judgements about what to do. Sometimes though we wonder if he would ever decide anything if he was left to himself! He says he will not get married until he is at least 30, he says that he is sure that there is some big adventure or test that he has to undertake before he settles down. He says it is important that he has no ties to stop him doing what will be needed. He is absolutely adamant, nothing will move him, Marianne is very upset with him, she wants as many grandchildren as she can! He has no idea what this task is that he will have to do; I just hope he is not going to be a rebel against the Romans, that would really be bad for him, the family and the business. I just hope that he has understood the advantage we all derive from "Pax Romana". He does take the "writings" very seriously and spends a lot of time discussing the deeper niceties of the of the predictions of the prophets and the history of Daniel and the Macabees, he talks for hours with the Rabbi and then comes home and tells Marianne all about what he has learnt. He tries with me as well, some times, but usually I am either too tired or have my head buzzing with new ideas for the business to really take in what he is talking about. My impression is that it is all a bit airy-fairy and theoretical as it mostly revolves round the coming of the Messiah, my view is that if he does come I'd ask him not to upset the fishing business we have worked so hard to build!

Simon on the other hand is as different as chalk and cheese, where

Andrew is a calming influence Simon is an "Action this Day" operator. Everything is urgent! The solution to every problem is quite clear and simple and should be implemented immediately. Discussion is just time wasting and losing opportunities! He is the expert on every topic from buying salt to setting up an agency anywhere on earth. But he is a very good fisherman, he seems to know where the shoals will be, it's quite uncanny. He can go out with the other boats and nobody gets a sniff then he will signal he has found the fish and catches a boat load before the rest can join him. He knows whether to use nets or lines, he knows what bate the fish will take, he knows what net size to use to maximise the catch and minimise the damage. He can read the weather like nobody else he is only 20 but he can tell you when a storm is approaching before there is any sign at all that the rest of us can detect. He really is larger than life, everyone loves him, he has a reputation for good luck and success, and he is always cheerful. You know when Simon is about, there is always a crowd of young men around him, he stands head and shoulders above any of them, he is built like a giant, broad shoulders, a strong back and arms and legs like tree trunks. He will wrestle with anyone and win; the only person who can out run him is Andrew. He never tires, he works hard all day and sometimes late into the night, working the boats and the nets. His crew adore him and will go anywhere and do any thing for him, he oozes confidence and self-assurance nothing puts him down! The only person who can control his enthusiasm and his temper is Andrew. Andrew's calmness and patience might make some people furious, in other people it makes Simon furious. With Andrew he sits and listens carefully, even respectfully, he knows, from long experience, that Andrew's advice even though it is not instant is always the best. Oh Yes! Simon has a temper; he can explode like a volcano. If he thinks that anyone is not adequately respectful or is trying to short change us or is breaking agreements, there is no holding him. He will not be satisfied until restitution has been achieved. Sometimes this has already caused us real problems and he must learn to control his feelings otherwise he will fall foul of some authority and end up in serious trouble.

Of course being so big and confident has attracted the attention of the authorities already. First the Jews that is the Rabbis and the scribes have tried to fill his head with the idea of opposition to the Romans. Like me, he is sure that peace is worth a lot, anyway his interest is fishing not politics. The Zealots have tried to recruit him appealing to his national pride and identity but again he has shown no interest and he knows that they are really a set of terrorists in disguise and are watched very carefully by the Romans. All he seems to want just at present is a quiet life as a successful fisherman.

So Marianne is about to upset all that, he doesn't know yet, she has decided that he will be married and has chosen his wife. The negotiations are at a very delicate stage all about dowry and other contract agreements, Marianne is looking after the details but the principle is that the girl's family fit in with the business needs and her father is the most successful salt merchant in the region. To our business having a secure supply of salt is absolutely critical and we see this union as a very important contract to ensure continuity of supply. Andrew has been deeply involved in the discussions so I hope Simon likes the girl when he finds out all the plotting that has gone on behind his back!

Part 4

About 30 AD

I'm getting very old now, when I look back at all that has happened and all that we have achieved in my life I am proud that we have come so far. Of course it is God's will and we have to be thankful for all the blessings we have received. I am nearly 50 now and Marianne is 45, we have our children round us and a quiver full of grandchildren to keep us young. We have been healthy all our lives and it is only now that I find that I need to rest in the afternoons and am happy just to watch the young men at work with the boats and the nets. I don't go out in the boats any longer, they say I am not quick enough and I just get in their way but I think I could do as well as any of them; I certainly have done in the past! I like to sit here in the sunshine and count my, that is our, blessings. The most important blessing is our health that has allowed us to work, there are many folks who have suffered from illness or injuries and are now destitute and rely on the charity of the rest of us. We have also been very blessed that all our children have been well and grown to be strong young men and women we have four of each and they all give us great joy and pride. Of course Andrew and Simon are the best loved and they are the senior members of the business now, but the next two are good men too, they are quite a bit younger than their brothers Judas is 22 and Benjamin is 20. They have both learnt the fishing business well and have been important in developing the many sides of the business empire we have created. In fact, I think, they could run it on their own now if they had to! I wouldn't dare to say that in Simon's hearing, he is sure that the world would stop and crumble if he wasn't around. Andrew remains the steadying influence and makes sure that we don't try to run too fast. He really got very enthusiastic, just for once almost excited, when we decided that we would expand out of fishing and into farming in a small way. It was when our darling Mary was about ready to be married, 10 years ago, she's 25 now and has 4 children of her own. The business was thriving and we were in the position where families were approaching us to offer their sons as potential husbands. Just imagine that Jonas' daughters attracting that sort of attention! Well we had made some good marriages to support the fishing business as we expanded into fish processing and boat building let alone the distribution of fish and fish products and our transport business, sorry I am drifting off the point but it really is a big

29

business with tentacles like an octopus! Somebody suggested, probably Andrew that perhaps it would be wise to diversify into something else and suggested farming. We all laughed what do fishermen know about farming! But gradually we thought it through, of course Andrew argued that we weren't really fishermen any more, we were businessmen and that the skills we had developed could be used in farming. He explained that the distribution and marketing of agricultural products was in the same chaotic state as the fishing industry 25 years ago and look what had been achieved. He could see a similar development working, not for wheat or barley, but for high value products like figs, dates, wine, grapes, pomegranates, apples and many other possibilities. So we gave him the job of finding out all he could and choosing a good farm ready for a marriage contract! Within 6 months a deal was done we now have a farm! It is perfectly positioned facing south over the lake, it is only 3 miles from Capernaum, it is well watered catching the winter rains and snow. It is sheltered from the hot desert winds in the summer and has a well that never runs dry. From the terrace you look down onto the town and can see the boats and the factory.

After the first few years, which were hard work but very exciting, the family decided that Marianne and I should move up here. I wasn't very keen, I thought they were sidelining me, and they probably were, Marianne said it was what she wanted to do and so we are here. We built a nice house a little away from Mary and her family but close enough to be friendly and I can watch all the comings and goings in the harbour. It's a bit of a climb up here, so we don't go down to the town very often, but the whole family come here every week for the Sabbath. I suppose I have combined two blessings together our health and our children.

The next really important blessing is that we have enjoyed peace; there has been no bloodshed in Galilee for over 20 years, not since that terrible business at Sepphoris. I wonder what happened to all those poor people dragged off into slavery just because some hot-head decided to make their town his headquarters and then thought he could threaten the might of Rome. It was a lesson that the whole of the area took to heart. Antipas is a dreadful man but he has brought stability and security, he exercises his demonic pleasures on thieves and highwaymen, the torture chambers in the prison under his palace at Tiberius are not nice places! The result is that there is safety and security everywhere. There are always a few crimes of burglary and assault even murders, but generally nothing to compare with the almost total lawlessness of 40 years ago and I have been told it was worse before that. What has really made the difference has been the Romans. We all grumble about being occupied, of having a foreign army stationed on our fatherland, of having to obey their laws and worst having to pay their taxes, in my view it's worth paying for, and as long as we don't behave stupidly that's the way it will go on. Everybody I know just wants to be left in peace to get on with our lives and businesses and if the way is "Pax Romana" then so be it.

Well life is never quite what you expect, a few weeks ago we heard rumours that there is a new prophet, called John, he is living out on the fringe of the desert in Perea and declaring that everyone should repent and be baptised into a new life as the end of the world is at hand. He says he is the forerunner of the Messiah who will restore Israel to its former glory. Well you can imagine that has caused a stir, the last people who made those sort of claims were the Maccabeean family. The Herod royal family are not at all impressed; neither are the Pharisees, or the Sadducees or the lawyers or anyone else who has an interest in maintaining the continuing "status quo". They are keeping a close eye on his activities but are reluctant to do anything because he is attracting huge crowds from all over Galilee and Judea. People are coming from all over the empire to listen to him and enjoy the spectacle. Of course the Maccabees were a powerful family and had an army to throw out the Syrians and the Greeks and for a while they were successful. Like all these "royal families" though, after three generations they "lost the plot" and the result was that we ended up being conquered by the Romans!

Introduction

The next stage of the story, from part five to part sixteen, is written by Andrew, Jonas' eldest son, and describe in his words the experience of being caught up in a revolution that changed the lives of a group of ordinary young men. It was written as was the rest of the book at about 50 AD.

When my father died I found some papers he had dictated to a scribe; they told us about his life and the foundation of the family fishing business. They explain how exciting his life was and how he perceived the world and the realities of life in his eyes. I thought they are a great foundation for a personal history of the changes that have overtaken us, what can only be described as a great adventure. An adventure that is more, and more, exciting as time goes by; it is a journey of the soul towards eternal life. But I hope that in the end you will understand what that means and will be convinced of the message of Jesus Christ to all mankind.

I am Andrew, now a-days I am known as Peter's elder brother and have grown to recognise his remarkable leadership of the followers of Jesus Christ and his missionary work. Cephas or Simon, who we all know as Peter, the nickname that Jesus gave to him, has been so important in preaching the word. He has absolute confidence in God's power, his wisdom and perceptive foresight in handling a myriad of issues that we have had to resolve since we were left by Jesus at his Ascension, are a remarkable gift. I have done my own work too, but it seems insignificant when compared with my brother's achievements in his own spiritual growth and the way in which he has brought so many to believe. It was not always like that and I thought it was important to record my memories of those momentous few years in our young manhood that changed our lives and will, I am absolutely sure, change the world. Memory is a fickle thing and as I get older I find it difficult to be sure which bits are real and we understood before the Resurrection and the Joy of the Holy Spirit or which bits, on the other hand, are really the new understanding we all were given at Pentecost that once, what is now, many years ago.

I have tried to incorporate the memories of those of the original twelve who are left, but we are getting fewer each year. We all agree that it is quite remarkable, almost beyond human reasoning, that one man, in a short time, could raise the expectations, the personal commitment of such a mixed bag of twelve, unimportant, un-educated, ordinary men to such heights, that we have no fear of powers or princes or even death itself. Truly Jesus was the Son of God, no He was not, He IS the Son of God for all eternity.

I hope that by now you will have read or at least be familiar with the story that my father has recorded about the Jonas and Zebedee families and their progress. It is now nearly twenty years since he wrote that story and the family still prospers despite all the terrible tragedies that have overtaken Israel. The shock of losing four sons, to what must have seemed a wild cause, at the very peak of their energy was absorbed without a ripple. God provided another layer of brothers who were just as capable as we were to run the business and to cope with all the changes and chances of this mortal life. At the time you can perhaps imagine the reaction of the whole family as Andrew, Peter, James and John without notice walked off the job and left the family to pick up the pieces as best they could.

Now, many years later, when we visit them and talk about those times they all accept that we were called to do God's work in one way and they were called to do God's work in another. We have to recognise the great asset that having a prosperous family has been from time to time to help us to extend God's word, and I have to record our thanks to them for their sacrificial support to us all over the past twenty years or so. God will reward their service to us in His own way and in His own time. Suffice it at present He is protecting them and the industry they have developed and they are happy to support our efforts to extend His kingdom.

So now back to the start of this amazing story.

Part 5

John the Baptiser

I think my father mentioned John, called The Baptiser, who was preaching in the Perean desert, he was Jesus' cousin, but then none of us knew that after all we did not really know Jesus in any real sense. Peter and I were in our early thirties, or a bit younger, when the news came that a prophet was preaching in the desert east of the Jordan in Perea. For as long as we could remember we had been taught by the rabbis and the scribes of the synagogue that Israel's destiny was the promise made to Moses and before him to Abraham that a great leader would be sent by God to save Israel from her persecutors. They taught us all the references from the prophets of old, the predictions, the expectations and the portents of his coming, the stories from Isaac, from the psalms, from Isaiah and Jeremiah, form Daniel, from Enoch and many others. They all predicted not only the arrival the Emmanuel but also that there would be portents of disaster and chaos and war and bloodshed and cruelty and sinfulness, and there was and still is enough of that! But then, eventually, there would be a vanguard, a new prophet, who would confidently tell us that the time had actually arrived that God had sent his son to Israel to rescue her from her travail. He would pronounce to everyone that they must repent of their sins, seek God's forgiveness and lead a new life free from sin and ready to receive the Emmanuel.

Now I know better, but, at the time the implications were that, with the leadership of the long awaited Emmanuel, we would throw off the yoke of the pagan Roman domination by force of arms, there seemed no other way of combating their military might, that the "bad shepherds" of the Temple in Jerusalem would be overthrown and replaced by truly God-fearing, holy men. That the poor and destitute would receive justice; that the twelve tribes would be reconciled and Israel's position as a world power would be secured for ever. We could see that the arrival of this forerunner was a call to arms and that we all had a national, patriotic duty to dedicate ourselves to this man, to foreswear ourselves to the cause of national supremacy against apparently unassailable odds and military might. We would be the army that God's Son would need to defeat God's enemies, we were the young and the strong, we were the confident youth all we needed was a leader to show us the way. We knew that if God was for us who could

34

be against us. We had the examples of our forefathers of Abraham, of Jacob, of Joseph, of Moses, of Aaron, of Gideon, of Samuel, of Saul, of David, of Solomon, of Daniel, and more recently of the Maccabees they had all in their turn fought the good fight to remove tyrannies from our peoples and that in the end they had all failed through sin through pride and arrogance through forgetfulness that God held the power. We had the prophets who had warned Israel time and again of the wages of sin, we had the horrifying examples of the consequences of disobedience to God. The history of the desolation of the nation when they followed false gods, the punishment that this terrible God could impose on His chosen people when they refused to obey his commandments and his plan for the nations blessedness. Now it seemed it was our turn to obey or be destroyed!

Peter and I went down to Perea to see this man and to hear his words. We didn't very often get away from the fish but our family agreed, somewhat reluctantly, that we should go. We planned a trip for two weeks, it seemed a long trip but in the end we could have spent more time. We took one of the small boats with two crewmen and sailed south from Capernaum we didn't call in to any of the other ports but we were quite surprised to find that as we approached Philoteria where the Sea of Galilee pours out onto the Jordan River we joined up with quite a flotilla of boats full of young men all heading in the same direction. I suppose we could or even should have brought our wives with us but it seemed clear to us that this was men's work and it was men's decisions that were needed. After all this was the stuff of revolution and we would have to do the fighting. So after a day and a night of good sailing we arrived and this small army of men disembarked. We found we knew lots of them they were from most of the towns round the sea and many more from the townships in the countryside. Besides fishermen there were farmers and labourers, craftsmen, scribes, rabbis and even some Pharisees. We were surprised to meet many Jews from foreign countries who had got caught up in the excitement and wanted to be sure that they took the news of the fulfilment of the prophecies home with them to their communities. Everyone had come well prepared for the next stage of the journey down into Perea and out into the desert. We met others who had made the journey and were on the way home, their reports were amazing about this man, dressed in a goatskin, preaching the end of the world, baptising people to cleanse their souls and demanding repentance from everyone who wanted to be saved. These people were overcome with enthusiasm; the talk was of a new order being established, of revolution, of the revival of the state of Israel. As there were so many of us together we were not concerned about bandits and robbers and set off south our hearts and spirits on fire with expectations that Emmanuel was already with us and that this John the Baptiser would be our leader. After a two day journey along the banks of the Jordan we were told by returning pilgrims that we should turn east through the desert for another two days and John was to be found there. So we set off, by this time some people had already started to give up, it was too far, they didn't have enough food, the desert was a dangerous place and anyway they had the message from the people returning, the small army that had left the boats was by now just a small company of determined pilgrims to see this man in the desert. Peter, sorry he was of course Simon, was a great confidence boost to us all, he wanted to see this man, he wanted to be a leader in the vanguard of the action to restore Israel, he was very critical of all those people who gave up just because the path got hard, and dry and hot. At night round the campfire he harangued the backsliders "How can we possibly change the world if at the slightest difficulty we all give in and go home? Our forefathers had confidence in God to go on into the difficulties." He reminded them of the courage of our national heroes like Abraham and Moses and Joshua and Gideon, how they had not been afraid to obey God's command even though the task was difficult, if not impossible to human understanding. The replies were typical. There was the harvest, the children, the synagogue duties, the business and anyway it was alright for **them** in the old days things weren't so complicated then and then again **they** all tried and failed, so we would probably fail too and end up being captured and slaved or captured and executed. Peter persisted with his arguments about "Nothing ventured, nothing gained." or " You can't make an omelette without cracking eggs." He reminded them that even the heroes of the past had had doubts and fears before they started out on God's work, but with God beside them they succeeded in the task they were set. When the backsliders persisted he recalled the story of Jonah who tried to avoid the call of God but was sent back to his task after being swallowed by a great fish.

Eventually we found John, he looked a mess, he was unwashed, he was wearing a goatskin, straight off the goat, his hair and beard appeared to have never been cut, but he had a presence. He quoted Isaiah,

"I am the one sent before the Son of God to make his way straight";

"There is already one among you whose sandal I am not worthy to untie."

"Repent! For the end of the age is at hand."

It was very exiting; many people were swearing their lives to a new purity. When challenged John was able to predict the time of the coming of the Emmanuel! He knew it was now, that it was urgent, that tomorrow was too late. He also rebuffed the scoffers by reminding people that it was not for us to know the exact time or place of the coming but that we must be ready. The young men, and we were among them, pushed forward to register their support and enthusiasm, John seemed to be surprised and taken aback. He told us he did not want to lead an army that the Emmanuel of his prophesy was not a war lord but a peace lord and that our salvation was as individuals and that that did not need armies or swords or slings or chariots what it needed was a contrite heart willing to serve the lord and his fellow man and Emmanuel was here already to show the reality of this message. We all felt let down, we felt that we had made this pilgrimage to see the prophet in vain, after all the prophets of old had supported military action and civil uprising and that is what we thought should be done. It was interesting there were young men there from every walk of life, from the very wealthy to the very poor from the clearly well educated aristocratic priests, the sons of wealthy land owners to the peasant farmers and us, fishermen. People had come from all over the country from farthest south in Idumea to farthest north of Galilee from the coast of the Great Sea to the far Eastern Desert. In the evenings we sat around the campfires trying to understand what this prophet was trying to say to us. We had learnt from our rabbis, as we learnt the Holy Scriptures, how difficult it was to unravel the prophetic utterances, it was much easier to understand them in the light of some later happening. Nobody can be sure that even if the man is predicting the future just how it will be revealed. Could we interpret what we had heard as a call to revolution, even if John denied it, after all for him it would mean certain death if it was thought that he was proposing armed rebellion. We all knew only too well the swift and decisive action the Romans took at the slightest sign of revolt. One thing we all agreed was that we should be watching out for anyone who seemed to be ready to lead the restoration of the true religion of our forefathers and to stop the blatant exploitation of power that was quite evident in the behaviour of the Pharisees, the Sadducees, the scribes and the Sanhedrin.

We were quite sure, though there was some rabble with us, that we would support John's religious revival movement and that any call to arms was for that purpose only. The men who just wanted the opportunity to cause bloodshed for their own gain were not welcomed at all and in fact were thrown out as potential robbers and brigands. The other thing that was generally considered prudent was that when we went home we would covertly make sure that we had weapons to hand and that we would somehow if at all possible find ways of getting weapons training and practice.

The other discussions were about exactly what John had said. Could it be that the long expected saviour of the Jewish nation was really already here and if he was where was he? He should be able to be recognised, the scriptures implied that he would come as a great leader, a mighty king, a warrior destroying all his enemies before him, a righteous judge and a shepherd of the people caring for the poor and the sick and the widows. Well no-body recognised any of those admirable characteristics in any of the leaders that were holding sway at the time. In fact it was just the opposite they all were clearly in for what they could get out of the system, for power to control other peoples lives, for straight forward greed for money and possessions, for reputation that everybody looks up to them as important people, to have their interpretation of the legal disputes heard as they had the best way of arguing, to always be invited to the best parties and to sit in the best places, to be seen selling their heritage to be accepted by the Roman overlords. None of these in any way fitted to the saviour that John was proclaiming, so where was he? John says he is here but we can't see him, perhaps we are so sinful and misguided that we would not see him even if he were quite clear. Perhaps we would not see him because in reality we do not want to see him, after all quite clearly he is going to challenge us all and will cause a lot of trouble if he does only a small part of what the ancient prophets predict. Perhaps he will only be apparent to very few and his impact will not be seen as dramatic, but a gradual change in the way people see themselves. Certainly this seemed the least dangerous scenario, but it didn't seem to fit with the predictions, even though it let most of us sleep more easily!!

Peter was all for preparing for an armed rising on the basis that if the Son of God was with us he would immediately come to our aid and win the battle for the restoration of Israel. He made a very forceful speech to the group we were with; it was so impressive I can still remember bits of it. You should understand that at that time Peter was a firebrand every situation could be solved by direct physical action. On reflection I was not surprised that the words of John had really wound him up, but some of the people with us were clearly very nervous at what he was saying and moved away. We all suspected that the authorities had spies in the crowds to make sure that they knew what was going on, if there were we never had any repercussions.

What he said was something like this, "We have all been taught from our youngest memories that Israel is God's chosen people and that he will one day send his Son to rescue this chosen people from its persecutors. What is more he has told us that he will not just arrive he will forewarn us that now is the time! John is the new Isaiah he fits exactly into the description we have received from the prophets of old. The priests and the authorities want proof and then more proof because if it is true that the Son of God is here among us he will judge them and he will judge them harshly. They have shown no mercy or charity to the people, they have squandered the blessing that Israel has received, they have made the possibility of receiving blessings more and more difficult for ordinary people. It seems that they have changed God's message that it is now only the rich and powerful can approach our God. But we are all "Sons of Abraham" and the blessing he received was for all his seed. We have all accepted that we have to have rulers, our forefathers demanded that Samuel gave us a king and there have been many mighty kings since Saul and David, but there have also been some very bad kings sent by God to punish Israel for failing in its obedience to His Laws. So now we have the Pharisees making more and more regulations so called interpretations of the law and making God more and more exclusive to them, and the scribes and the Sadducees and the Sanhedrin, when really they are stealing our inheritance.

We are the young disinherited of Israel, Emmanuel is here we have to now do what we have been taught since we were children and support this new leader to rid our nation of its persecutors and its "bad shepherds". WE have to be armed and organised and ready to sacrifice our lives for the good of the nation."

Well lots of people cheered and supported the idea, I think that if we had actually had any arms things might have got out of hand, but it ended with groups swearing allegiance to each other and promising to be ready when the call to arms came. Everyone turned in for the night feeling very vital, certainly Peter had made a great impression on the group, "Despite being a Galilean", as some were heard to say. One thing that was interesting, looking back was that Peter spoke in Greek. Of course we had to be able to understand Greek and "get by" in negotiations with merchants and businessmen at home but I had never thought that Peter was so fluent, despite his accent. In the circumstances it was necessary because not many of the company there that night would have understood our North Galilean Aramaic dialect. For myself, I was very anxious at what Peter had said and tried to calm him down and make him realise the trouble he was courting for himself and for the whole of our family. If he was identified as a rebel the

Romans would not stop at executing him but the whole family would be imprisoned and probably sold into slavery. He would have none of it he was absolutely sure that our generation of young men was now called to fight God's last battles and that the rewards would be far greater than the risks.

The next morning I remember there was still an air of excitement, John had set off before first light going west towards the Jordan, we all hurried to break camp and set off to follow him. Eventually he stopped in a meadow on the bank of the river, the spot was tranquil and the water flowed smoothly past; a shepherd had collected his flock together and was patiently waiting for the crowd to disperse hoping that the grazing would still be worthwhile. The whole scene reminded us of the psalm, 'The Lord is my Shepherd, I shall not want, he leads me beside still waters, and he makes me lie down in green pastures.'

We were quite far back in the crowd, but were aware of something special happening close to John. Peter, being big and strong and having a "presence", elbowed his way forward to see what was happening. When he came back he was very different, he said that Jesus, that carpenter's son from Nazareth, was there and talking to John. We all knew Jesus he had come with his father for years to work on palaces being built be wealthy Jews and Gentiles, his father had died a few years before but he still came to get work with his brothers. He was a very skilled man and was much in demand as his work was of such high quality. He was also very impressive in his understanding of the Law and the Prophets whenever he was around he was asked to preach in the synagogue and people were spellbound by his words and interpretations. Well, Peter said, John and Jesus clearly knew each other and although he could not hear all that was said for the crush of people, Jesus was asking John to baptise him. Peter did hear John's reply it was amazing. John said in a clear voice for all to hear, that he was not worthy to provide such a blessing and that Jesus should be blessing John. Well Jesus insisted and John blessed him and immersed him in the river and as he immerged the whole crowd suddenly became silent, the air itself seemed to glow and there was a gentle noise like distant thunder. Peter was overcome he came back quite upset, firstly it was an extraordinary experience and then he couldn't understand why Jesus should have been at the centre of the happening. He told us that he had tried to find Jesus and talk to him but he had gone, nobody seemed to see him go but he had gone. We thought that perhaps he had found the experience too much. We were baptised, it was a sort of washing away the old and being able to start again and committing ourselves to a new way of life.

John's challenge to us, to prepare the way for the Son of God, was ringing in our ears as we set off on the journey home. We both said to each other that we had a feeling that there was something about to happen. The prophecy of John and his reference back to Isaiah's words and to Malachi, and the way we were taught by our father and by the rabbis about Israel's destiny. Were we really going to see this thing? Was it really going to be in our lifetime? How would we be involved? Would we become part of the new rulers of Israel like Joseph of long ago? Question, questions and more questions all generated from hearing one man's vision and perhaps Peter's witness of Jesus' baptism. Who was Jesus really? Had what John said actually identified him as the Emmanuel? How would John have known? We agreed that he was a remarkable man, we talked about the many times we had listened to him in the synagogue and the, sometimes, mind blowing analysis that he showed of something we had always taken for granted. But he was just a carpenter, how could he possibly be so important that John treated him with such deference? Nothing he had said or done had given any sign that he would be a great national leader who would turn Israel's society on its head and give the people back to God. Then we reminded each other that the prophets had said that he would not be recognised, that he would not arrive as a great leader and that the way he would rule the world would be different, his greatness would be seen by the impact he had on other people's lives. The example was continually used that he would be "The Good Shepherd", gently caring for his sheep and concerned for the well being of each and every one of them. We both agreed that not only did we have a great awakening adventure to tell the family but also that we would take a serious interest in Jesus of Nazareth next time he was working in Capernaum.

It took us two days to get home again and as we expected the family was all at the quayside at Capernaum to meet us. We were just a bit disappointed to find that we had not really been missed, we had been away for six days and nothing had gone wrong and what problems had occurred had been dealt with very satisfactorily. Jonas had of course come out of retirement to keep an eye on things; our younger brothers now had some understanding why we bought him a farm on the hill! But really all was well, the catches had been good and despite two rather violent early spring storms no equipment had been damaged and no deliveries of smoked and pickled fish had been missed. More importantly I remember we were very pleased that the youngsters had negotiated a very good contract with an export agent in Sidon, who would now become our second biggest export customer. Of course they didn't want to talk about the business all they wanted to know was about our adventures. We told them everything, including Cephas' late night speech, which alarmed Jonas. He started talking about losing everything he had given his life for! As usual it would be Cephas who would get us all into trouble and why could he not learn to think before he speaks rather than after. Well we gradually calmed him down and then talked for many hours about the prophecy of John and what it might mean and how it fitted with the ancient writings. It was agreed that it sounded absolutely reliable, as reliable as prophecy can be and we should prepare for what would eventually come as a violent disruption of society as we knew it. We didn't know what to do in detail but decided that at least we could start by stealthily buying some swords and other weapons with which to at the very least defend ourselves, and learning how to use them. We also started to think about how we might use our boats for either escape or attack. The women thought we were quite mad and made it clear that they wanted nothing to do with any such talk but in the end they agreed that they would make sure we had some stores of essential food and clothing so that we could escape into the hills and survive if the worst came to the worst.

After all that exciting talking and arguing and planning we told them what had happened at the riverside and the remarkable reaction of John to the arrival of Jesus the carpenter. Of course we couldn't explain the feeling of excitement and expectation that overcame the crowd neither could we explain the moments of complete serene peace and quietness as Jesus came out of the river. Everyone remembered how impressed they had been by his presence and by his interpretation of the scriptures. Even so, nobody could imagine him, the carpenter being anything more than a gifted man who had a slightly different slant on the old writings and a way of saying things that attracted your attention. It was agreed that as we had witnessed this event a the Jordan, or at least Peter had, we would invite him to eat with us next time he was in the town and perhaps we would get a better view of him to evaluate whether we thought he could possibly be Emmanuel.

The next day the Zebedee family came up from Bethsaida to hear all our news. After repeating the whole experience and talking through the possible implications John and James said that in their view the matter was so interesting and potentially important they would take a few days away, just as we had done, and go and see for themselves. So it was arranged and two weeks later they set off in one of the company boats with two crew and headed south to Perea.

So John and James set off on their pilgrimage to the desert to witness the prophecy of John. Perhaps one day they may write their own story, I shall do my best to remember what they reported to us when they returned.

They followed the same route that we had taken and joined a great crowd of people going down the river valley and other groups coming north. Every time they stopped for a meal or to rest the place turned into a meeting of people asking what they should expect and others explaining what they had seen and heard. It was quite surprising they said there were no signs of authority controlling the crowds, there was no need for any imposed discipline all the pilgrims were calm and well behaved those going south with great expectation and those coming north almost glowing with good fellowship and even holiness. There was no aggression, no pushing and shoving, none of the usual pompous behaviour of people who thought they were better than the rest, very little noise people were talking quietly together, but despite this an atmosphere of great excitement that something very special was about to happen and that they had to be prepared. John said it was quite remarkable, he felt that people were almost friendly and caring for each other, not a typical attitude we could recognise when large groups of people were together. It was noticeable that help was offered and accepted by the lame, the elderly, the young families and the poor, people shared their food with compete strangers and made sure that nobody was without some warmth during the cold desert nights. The other thing that they particularly noticed was that it wasn't just the poor and uneducated who were making this pilgrimage there were people from all walks of life but even the rich and powerful were walking there were no horses or carriages or chariots, there were a few donkeys, but as a rule everyone was walking. It was as if everyone knew that this was a time of penance, of self-sacrifice, of spiritual renewal and recommitment to the Law of Moses and the religious piety that was talked about so much by the Rabbis but not very often noticeable.

They said that there were landowners, and teachers and scribes and Pharisees, and judges and craftsmen and labourers and interestingly whole families and there were nearly as many women as men it was quite amazing. The thing that was missing was the travelling salesmen trying to exploit this crowd, there was nobody selling anything, no trinkets, no memorabilia, none of the usual touristy stuff that you are pressurised into buying even if only to show that you were there. Everyone was expecting a different fulfilment and certainly looking into the faces of the people coming north a very real fulfilment was being received. The other thing that was not noticeable, although they may have been there, was the secret police, those snoopers and taletellers who report almost everything that is happening to the

Pharisees and to the military. The arrogance of Antipas may well have blinded him to the real challenge to the established order of things that was being pronounced by this apparently wild man in the desert within his jurisdiction. People were talking quite openly and freely about a new age, a new ruler, and a new government and yet the existing powers were taking little or no interest, or so it seemed.

Because of the crowds their journey was much slower than ours it took nearly four days to find John in the desert, his habit was to preach in the desert for two days and then move to the river for a day where he baptised people who were sure that they wanted to dedicate themselves to a determination to hold to the Law and to be ready for Emmanuel. The two days in the desert were clearly to test peoples' real commitment; the environment is harsh, extremely hot in the day, bitterly cold at night and very often with a fierce wind driving clouds of cutting sand. It puts great physical, emotional and spiritual demands on people to stay there when they are used to a much kinder way of life, but reminds them of the forty years that their forefathers wandered in the desert after their escape from slavery in Egypt.

In the desert John preached, almost non-stop, from dawn to dark, his message was presented forcefully and directly he didn't pull his punches. When we were witnessing his mission he was almost entirely concentrating on the need for repentance so that his chosen people could receive God's coming blessing of Emmanuel. But when the Zebedees were there the tone had become more direct and severe. He berated the people for their sinful ways, he was overtly critical of the religious leaders and their avaricious behaviour, their luxurious life style their exploitation of the poor and needy. He was furious at their ability to pronounce God's ways and do the opposite; he challenged them to do as they said rather than to demand that others did as they said while they ignored their protestations of goodness and holiness. He accused them of making God so remote that he was unapproachable, their insistence on the observation of the most particular and ridiculous procedures of purification and "spiritual cleanliness". He reminded people that the God of Abraham and Isaac and Jacob had throughout the history of the Hebrews promised his blessing in return for their acceptance of him as their only God and to obey his law as given by Moses. He reminded them of the trauma they had suffered every time they went astray, of the disasters when kings and high priests forgot their duty as the guardians of the true religion. He recounted the consequences that had befallen them for their national disobedience as they followed other gods and as corruption spread through the leaders and the judges. He made no apology for accusing the present leaders of

44

the same sins, but he warned this time things would be different. This time God's Son had already arrived and would be the scourge of the sinfulness of the people; the only salvation was to repent. They must return to the right way and to obey God's laws in its spirit and not in the pathetic and impertinent attempts of the priests to decide what God would do in every circumstance. He assured them that the God of Israel was an inclusive God and not an exclusive God. For those who were prepared to make this commitment he was prepared to provide an outward sign of their spiritual renewal by washing away their sinful past in the waters of the River Jordan.

There was from time to time uproar as the priests and others realised just how critical he was being and how what he was saying would undermine their power among the people. Some times there were cries of heresy, but they were overwhelmed by cries of support, it was quite clear that some priests had come out to the desert intent on making John's message look stupid or irrelevant and to stop this mission. The crowds would have none of it. Some of the priests and lawyers questioned him very closely on why he was now prophesying this new order and he was never bettered by their attempts to undermine his sincerity and the absolute foundation in the old prophets to show that the time had come. It was quite clear that he was unsettling the established views, some priests and lawyers accepted what he was saying but most went away either furious at what they perceived as his gross impertinence or deeply troubled at the challenge he represented. It was quite clear that he was at great personal risk of being arrested and imprisoned or even being put to death. He was prepared for this and made every one aware that the way the Hebrews had traditionally dealt with prophets was to execute them and he expected no better treatment. He would not be silenced the message was too important and too urgent, he expected his mission to fail. Still he warned the people time and again that the one whose path he was preparing would not and could not fail because he was God's Son. What made it so urgent to repent and turn away from their sins was that he was already among them unrecognised and waiting his moment to turn the nation upside down.

Well, James and John eventually came home they were away much longer than they had planned but they were alive with the stories of all the happenings. I remember very well that their report to the families made us both enthusiastic and nervous. It was quite clear that eventually the authorities would take seriously what was happening and would crack down on this revival movement. It was probable that at the present time the crowds were too big and that there would be serious civil unrest if they attempted to arrest John. We would have to wait until the harvest time when people could not take time away to see what would happen to him. As two families we decided that we would take the call to obedience to the Law seriously and from then on we took special efforts to express our behaviour to the spirit of the Law and not to hide behind the priests dictates where they deflected us from it.

The business now took all our energies it was the spring and a very busy time, the demand for our processed fish products was always biggest as we approached the Passover and we had to make sure that all our distribution system in Palestine and throughout the Roman empire were well supplied before the festival.

One small aside is worth recording here and it relates to a tax collector. As fishermen and business men we were subject to taxation, it felt as if every time we breathed some authority would demand a tax payment, but that is how life is and since time immemorial everyone has complained about taxes. When the new harbour was built at Capernaum the Romans built a tax office at the very gates of the entrance. Nobody could enter or leave without passing through the tax office courtyard. What is more the office was so positioned that the officers could see directly down to the ships so that nothing escaped their knowledge. There were of course a staff of tax officials and they were themselves continually overseen by visiting tax inspectors from the various authorities. The resident permanent officers were suspect both from the taxpayers, that they were overcharging and from the authorities that they were pocketing the tax revenue rather than passing it on. In short, they were despised by everyone. From our point of view, as the local residents, they were also the most visible expression of the tyranny of Rome and Antipas. Mostly we got along pretty well, they knew we would try to get away with what we could and we knew that they knew, it was a bit of a game, and we all got some satisfaction out of playing the game.

One of the tax officers took a great deal of interest in both of our journeys to see John in the desert. Nobody would normally speak to the man because there was always the risk of letting slip something that suddenly became tax liable, but he was around and listened carefully to what he could, we thought that he might be spying for the authorities so we tried to shut him out. Of course he was a Jew and a Son of Abraham but the Pharisees, had specifically selected tax collectors as collaborators with the Romans and therefore publicly damned as sinners and made untouchables. This tax collector much to our surprise he enters the story of Jesus' mission as you will see later.

Part 6

The Ten Commandments

For a long time, it must have been at least two months; we got on with our lives running the business. We tried very hard to revitalise the way we lived out the Ten Commandments that Moses had given to the House of Israel. The Rabbi was very helpful, he really was a dedicated man who exercised his duty as a shepherd for his flock in Capernaum with great humility and love. He had been in Jerusalem in His younger days but had become revolted by the greed and avarice of the Jerusalem priestly set. Despite his high academic reputation he had foregone the wealth, comfort, and status that were readily within his grasp and opted to come as the simple rabbi in our small relatively unknown and certainly unsophisticated town. He was an elderly man and had given his life to the care and nurture of his rather unresponsive flock. He and his charming, delicate wife had always been good friends to our family and had been among the first to welcome us when we moved from Bethsaida. We regularly welcomed them to our home on the Sabbath for the weekly celebration of God's promise to the Jews. Now in his old age he enjoyed walking up the hill in the afternoon and sitting with Jonas watching the boats coming and going in the harbour reminiscing about the past and putting the world to right. Since all the excitement about John the prophet in the desert he had become a much more frequent visitor and had helped us all to think through again the Ten Commandments so that we could fulfil our commitment to start a new life that we gave to God through John. Jonas was just as involved as any of us and as head of the family, and the business, his opinion and understanding were more like education and instruction to the rest of us. Most of these understandings came from his discussions with our patient and forbearing rabbi.

When we looked back many years later at this short interval we felt sure that it was God at work in us to establish and reinforce in us our acceptance of the Law and of our Jewish inheritance. He knew that it was most important that the starting point of our journey was solid and secure. I will try to set down Commandment by Commandment the revitalising confirmations that we received by way of the written words, the interpretation of the rabbi and our discussions, all against the background of the urgency of John's announcement and prophecy that the time was NOW.

I am the Lord your God you shall have no other gods but me. You shall love the Lord your God with all your heart, with all your soul, with all your mind and with all your strength.

The first thing we were confronted with was that our God is a personal God, He is **my** God as **me**, **I** have a duty and a responsibility for **my** response to Him and **I** can not delegate this responsibility to anyone else, not the temple, not the synagogue, not the rabbi, not the Pharisees nor to any one else however powerful or demanding or coercive or convenient. What is more important is that **I** have to accept responsibility for **my** actions, for **my** obedience or lack of obedience to all the other laws. It is also important that **I** am not responsible for the actions of others however near and dear they might be if they failed in their adherence to the law. The order to have no other gods is to ensure that we only serve one master, but we must be careful this commandment forbids us to worship the polytheic array of Roman gods. It forbids us to worship any of the pagan gods of other nations and it forbids us to make gods of other things like the business, the family, our possessions or even our plans and ambitions. All these other gods are shallow and irrelevant to the well being of your soul. You shall love your God totally absolutely and without distraction or withholding any of your total being. If you do this there will be no possibility of having any other God. You do not need any other God, your God is infinitely powerful, your God, without your aid controls your very being and your destiny, your God will care for your every need and will never, never desert you. But if you disobey His laws then punishment and condemnation and retribution will be delivered, because He is a jealous and just God. Be sure that any judgement is against me, personally me! I, God, can see into your very soul, nothing you do or say or think is a secret from me and you are not able to pass the responsibility for your actions, your thoughts and your words to any other person, so beware, these are serious matters between your God and you, specifically and individually you.

You shall not make for yourself any idol. God is spirit, and those who worship him must worship him in spirit and in truth.

You must not allow anything that you can make or that any man can make to become an icon, to be come the focus of your worship and praise; if you do the icon will become more important than the Spirit of God which is within you, when I breathed life into Adam I breathed my

48

spirit into him and you are a son of Adam. You shall never have such an object of worship; if you do this it will very quickly take over your soul. Be careful the idol need not be a human or animal representation; the idol can be a building, and now the new Temple in Jerusalem, which is a beautiful building, has taken on the role of an idol. It is more important to the priesthood than what it may have been conceived to be. The ceremonial and rituals no longer are to do with love and respect for God but are about exclusivity and are barriers to true worship. You have by this means attempted to contain your infinite, all powerful God, within a box of stone made by man, be sure I can destroy it and I will destroy it because it is an idol. Be careful too about ritual, you treat the Sabbath as the day for God, the rest of the week you behave as if I did not exist, as if you were all powerful, as if you controlled your own destiny. You have tried to contain me in a man made ritual called the Sabbath, and then to give it more and more status you invent your own rules and regulations to make it as exclusive as you can. What impertinence! "I AM", do you not even now understand? After all the examples of my power shown to you and explained to you by the prophets I sent you and who forewarned to you of my power you still think that you can prescribe me or control me or contain me. The Law has become an idol in itself; there is more concern for obeying the detailed interpretation of the Law than in living your lives to approach God's expectations. The lawyers, the scribes and the Pharisees have made "The Law" more important than God. "I AM", there is nothing that "I AM NOT", nothing that you have or will ever have, nothing that you are or may ever be, nothing that you have made or may ever make has been without my power and my spirit at work within you. I can only accept the worship of a man's very being, his whole self, his very Spirit, nothing else is worthy to be offered if it replaces the worship of your spirit.

You shall not dishonour the name of the Lord your God. You shall worship him in awe and reverence.

Because I refuse to be contained within any human artefacts be it an idol, or a building or some ritual, you must be aware that I am always with you. I am all-powerful, I created the universe, I created the world and I created you. Remember what God has created God can destroy, I, and only I, will judge the world and everybody who inhabits the world. I will not be limited and I will not expose my plan. Judgement will be made and punishment or praise awarded as and when I see fit. My judgement is not your judgement and my sentencing is according to my righteousness that is beyond your comprehension. I AM to be feared, I

AM the great awful (full of awe) power, I demand reverence, I demand to be honoured above all else, nothing absolutely nothing shall come between you and me, not your own life, not your king, not your family, not your nation, not your status in society, not your ambition, not your reputation, nothing but nothing in heaven or on earth must you put between me and you. You can not hide from me, I AM "all seeing" therefore you shall be sure that if you dishonour my name I shall see it or hear it and I will be avenged. To dishonour my name is to use it without awe and reverence, my name is sacred and shall only be used in sacred settings and when the listeners are suitably prepared and fearful. My name is not one name it is the whole compass of holiness and Godliness it encompasses the universe, it is infinite, it is everywhere within you and without, it is majesty, it is power, it is presence, it is absence, it is things you think you understand, it is things you can never understand. When you, mere mortal man, invent a name for me, like Yahweh, you are making an idol for yourselves that you think is I, I have no name "I AM". Now the Law has set out the terms in which the Lords name may be used and the penalties for its improper use, but these are impertinences, God's command is that my name will not be used without awe and reverence. Now the lawyers try to encompass with petty regulation what is "awe and reverence", and worse than that they imply that there are circumstances where men can refer to my name without "awe and reverence".

Remember the Lord's Day and keep it holy. You have six days to labour and to do all your work. But the seventh day is the Sabbath of the Lord your God: that day you shall not do any work. In six days the Lord made heaven and earth, the sea, and all that is therein and on the seventh day he rested. Therefore the Lord blessed the Sabbath and made it holy.

The Sabbath is a day of re-creation, God knows how frenetic and care worn life is and his command is that all men should have a time to be re-created. Creation is a spiritual activity. It is as if God were giving a little bit of himself for man to use, He commands us to set aside one day of the week to make sure that we have time to allow Him to let this re-creation take place. To make the Sabbath a holy day is to make it a day when we are at peace with ourselves, our neighbours and most importantly at peace with God. This means that we must be free from the normal cares of our daily lives and responsibilities so that we can make time to listen to God, time when we can come to his presence, time when we can expose our reverence and awe to him. What we have to do is to worship him and the way we have accepted is the communal praise and teaching in the synagogue. The Lawyers and the authorities have continually defined what is "work", like all the laws, the obedience to these definitions is more rewarding than actually obeying the commandment. The interpretation of the law is impertinence, it sets man above God, and it is man telling God what God really meant when He said these things. It is used by the established authorities as a device to divide the "pure" from the "impure" it is a device to restrict the access to God. It is an invasion into peoples' souls; 'The Law' is more concerned with the counting the exact number of steps on the way to the synagogue than to be concerned for the spiritual needs of the man who is going to the synagogue to meet his God.

Honour your father and mother.

The marriage union of your parents is a God given blessing. Your very existence is due to the blessing God has poured out on them. The seed of your forefathers has been passed on through their physical union but their spiritual union is from God and therefore you exist only through God's work in your parents. Through them God has provided the security and love and nurture which has brought you from a helpless babe to a grown man. Your duty is to ensure that they are never abused or exploited or un-loved by you or as far as your power can influence the situation by any other power. Their knowledge and experience are part of the blessing that I have prepared for you and you must respect it and use it to build your own experience to pass to your children. When they become old and frail and are approaching death you must not neglect them, you must return to them the care and love and nurture that they gave to you as a baby.

You shall not commit murder

The gift of life is God's gift; it is part of His plan for the world. We do not know what contribution any individual makes to the world, we do know that in God's eyes and commands all men are equal and all have a duty to contribute to the common good and thereby to the glory of God. For one person to take the life of another is to contradict God's intention and is therefore a sin. The definition of murder is taken to be about the physical existence of a human being, but we must be careful in all our actions and interactions with others that we do not kill their souls. The demands of the scribes and the Pharisees and the other authorities which make God exclusive by condemning the slightest neglect of their man made rules are in fact committing murder. This murder is the murder of the souls of these people who are left rejected and in despair because they see no hope of any redemption. Murder need not be the physical killing of another being; it is just as easy for you to kill a man's soul. If you deny him the ability to use the gifts God has given him, if you deny him access to God, if you fail to allow him to take his place in society you are killing his soul.

You shall not commit adultery.

Your body is God given and as such is to be treated as sacred, what is more this applies to every person. Adultery or any other abuse of our own body or another person's body is sinful. A human body is the shrine of a human soul, our souls are not our own they are God's gift to us. If we abuse either our own or another's body we are desecrating God's gift. We always think of adultery as the sexual intercourse between a man and a woman, it is much wider than that, it includes all sexual acts not part of a union blessed by God, it includes the abuse of our bodies with drugs, the abuse of our bodies by decoration. It includes action and behaviour that replicates actions intended to titillate others and to encourage them to adulterous behaviour by purporting it to be acceptable. The sacred nature of the union between a man and a woman in marriage is spelled out very clearly it is; for the mutual love and comfort of the two, it is for the mutual security of each, it is to ensure that there is a secure environment for the care and nurture of children and it is to show God's glory to the world. It is the whole of societies responsibility to protect and respect this contract. It is critically the responsibility of the two partners of the marriage contract to ensure that no actions of theirs are adulterous and damage the sacred purpose of the union.

You shall not steal.

All that you have comes from God, he gave you your health to work, he gave you your wits to earn your livelihood from your surroundings, he gave you the opportunity to succeed and he expects you to use these assets he has provided to make your way in life. He provides everything that you will need. Stealing is a rejection of God's love and generosity, it belittles the thief into thinking that he can live without God, that he has better ways than God, he becomes self confident and arrogant in his relations with God and God will be avenged. Society depends on individuals struggling to succeed; success is seen as the accumulation of assets, society has to provide security so that these assets are not to be stolen. We have to be careful that the accumulation of assets does not in itself become an idol that separates us from God. We have to be careful that the accumulation of assets is not at the expense and disadvantage of our fellow men, that in our personal endeavour to accumulate wealth we are not putting obstacles in the way of others particularly obstacles that exclude them from God, allowing us to ignore their needs in our selfish search for material wealth. We must be careful in our dealings with our fellow men whether Jew or Gentile that we deal fairly and honestly and honourably otherwise in our hearts we know that we are stealing.

You shall not give false evidence against your neighbour.

God is both Just and Righteous and he commands us to be the same. Justice can only be achieved if the evidence presented to the authorities is honest and true, everybody wants to be treated fairly and justly we must all then ensure that when we have to testify we do so honestly. The decisions of the systems of justice must also be honest and righteous.

The reliability of the system is only possible if the whole system is free from bribery, coercion and corruption and this will only happen if we obey this law. It is not uncommon for the leaders of the nation to act outside the law and then use whatever means are to hand to prevent justice being made available to the offended. The offended plaintive can be both man and God. It is not unusual that the time for a dispute to come before the authorities is too long, that the cost of coming to the authorities is too high, that the support to plaintives in presenting their case is inadequate. These techniques used to disadvantage people is a way of making them feel excluded, it is transparently seen as a way of protecting the leaders of society from being confronted with their sins against God and society. We as individuals are charged with not bearing false witness against our neighbour; our neighbour is anybody who needs our support. Bearing false witness is not just about courts and the formal administration of justice although this is critically important because it establishes the attitude in society towards justice. Our daily responsibility is to avoid gossip, to avoid character assassination, to avoid bullying, to avoid lying, to avoid swindling, as all are false witnesses. We are also to be positive and to come to the aid of those who are being falsely treated to protect other people's reputations and to guard against coming to conclusions on the basis of inadequate or incomplete evidence. We have to give the benefit of the doubt to the accused until the evidence is clear and beyond dispute remembering that, first, we are all guilty before God, second, we are there, as the accused, but for the grace of God, and third who are we to cast the first stone.

God is the final judge, His ways are not your ways and His words are not your words! Judge not lest you are judged!

You shall not covet your neighbour's possessions.

Jealousy is a cancer in society. Jealousy is like a great burden on our souls, we can always find someone who has more than us, more wealth, more possessions, more children, more success, more status, more and more and more. If we look with envy at our neighbour we will gradually come to hate him, we will bear false witness to him; we will do our best to reduce his advantages. All the bad characteristics that God's laws are set to control are set loose once we allow envy to invade our spirits. We separate ourselves from God, we become blinded with aggression, envy and hatred towards our neighbour, they absorb our spirit and our souls by imagining the wickedness of our neighbour, by imagining the evil that he has committed to achieve his advantages, we distort our own souls and become remote from God.

What God really wants us to do is to rejoice at the success of our neighbour and much more importantly we must rejoice in the great benefits that we have received from God. Our attitude must not be: "How little we have compared with our neighbour." it must be: " How great are God's gifts to us." Furthermore it must also be "How can I use the gifts God has given to me to help other people?" The world will only become a better place if we look to maximise the use of the assets that God has provided for us and then actively find ways in which we can help each other. The world becomes a worse and worse place when we are jealous of other peoples "Good Fortune" we are forgetting that his "Good Fortune" is God's blessing and it is not for us to question God's wisdom in His distribution of His blessings. It is important to remember that everything we have or our neighbour has comes from God and is not of our making, if we assume that another man's "good fortune" is of his making then we are being impertinent to God, we are setting ourselves up to think that we can make better decisions than God.

We were all very surprised by our rabbi's progressively developed analysis of the fundamental requirements of God's Law as it was given to Moses. He didn't mention any of the rules that we are usually told we must keep about washing, about eating, about praying, about charity, about chastity or any of the other daily parts of living What is more he didn't tell us about the punishments for breaking the law that were demanded by the Pharisees and the scribes and the priests and he didn't rehearse for us the penance that has to be forfeited to cleanse our souls. What he did show us was that our souls were our own individual responsibility and that if we obeyed the meaning of the Law we would lead a just, upright and righteous life and that we would together produce a society which was as God wanted it, not how man wanted it! He showed us that all the detailed regulations invented by man and based on a human interpretation of the law separated us from God because it allowed us to hide behind these interpretations and forget the great truths, God's truths that are the real basis of the Law. He taught us that in all our doings we must continually judge our behaviour against the spirit of the Law and not the letter of the Law. He re-emphasised time and time again that our relationship with God was an individual, unique, personal relationship and that we had no need for any go-betweens. He strongly criticised the Pharisees and the other established authorities for their determination to insist that it was only through their disciplines that anyone could approach God.

At the time he made us very uncomfortable, what he was saying seemed to be dangerous and even revolutionary. We argued with him and between ourselves about the fundamentalist view he was putting forward. The main thrust of these arguments was that the strict adherence to the Law of Moses was the principle characteristic of the Jewish people; it was the very essence of their Jewishness. The Law controlled every circumstance of our daily lives, even the most insignificant matters had regulations attached. If and when any situation came up that was not covered by the Law there was a body of expert, professional lawyers who would decide what the interpretation was to be. The lawyers were well occupied with disputes between individuals who disagreed about a decision and disputes between lawyers about the relevance of particular decisions to specific circumstances. The way to God was through exact adherence to the Law and it was very disturbing to people that the law could be re-interpreted. There was a general acceptance that what ever you did you would be wrong and that God operated a universal, all-embracing "catch 22". That was a bad way of approaching God. It was actually socially very bad as well, because the outcome was that everyone was watching everyone else to be sure that any, however insignificant, failure to observe the Law was noticed and made public. Personal security was almost non-existent, society was full of spies, there were no people you could really trust even closest family members would betray other family members when and if it suited them.

But we all accepted this as part of life, the advantages always seemed to outweigh the disadvantages. The advantage was that, despite being persecuted almost continuously for hundreds of years, the great strength of the Jews was the absolute conviction that through the Law they had access to the protective, avenging, might of the one, true, infinite, all-powerful God who would preserve them for ever. And now we had come full circle because this same all powerful God has promised, and repeatedly promised that he would restore Israel to a position of world power and domination, John was here and now declaring that the time had come.

I think that the Rabbi had seen that the message John had given to us and the impact it had had on us needed to be tempered by a revitalising of the Law. He was sure that we four young men had witnessed something extraordinary and that he had a duty to God to be sure that we understood where we were coming from even if he had no idea where we might be going. What he taught us was in fact a sound platform from which we would one day be able to understand why Jesus came to earth and the importance of his fulfilment of the Law.

Part 7

Jesus arrives and calls the Apostles, Andrew and Peter

Following on from these discussions we were convinced that we had to stand on our own two feet and consider our actions against the Law as it was intended and not to rely on the Lawyers to tell us what to do. We got into difficulties almost continuously with the Scribes and Pharisees and were labelled as "sinners" despite our careful attention to the law. Our "sin", it seemed, was to argue with the authorities, particularly Peter who took to openly questioning the teaching in the synagogue on the Sabbath. We all tried to dissuade him, or at least to get him to enter discussions with a less confrontational stance, to just ask his questions in a way that implied his wanting to learn rather than to criticise. We were very concerned that he would really overstep the mark one day and be accused of blasphemy for which the penalty was stoning, but fortunately it never came to that. I think it is quite probable that the old rabbi acted as a protector. It is certain that the synagogue elders were very agitated by his almost weekly interrogation of what they were teaching; it never was the style of the meetings that they were intended to be a two-way exchange of views!

So our life had become somewhat a routine of the fish business all week prompted by a Sabbath of considerable anxiety as we anticipated what Peter would say next. Our anxiety about Peter was not unfounded, the news had spread very quickly that John, the prophet, had been arrested. Antipas had been greatly embarrassed and angered by his overt condemnation of his marriage to Herodias. The details of the affair were a bit sketchy it was, of course well known that he had divorced his wife after a visit they had made to Rome. His first wife was Arnon the daughter of Harith VI the king of Petra and Nabatea; she was, therefore, not only a princess but also her marriage had been arranged by Herod the Great, with the active support of Rome to forge a diplomatic tie to the desert Arab State to the East of Perea in the mountains overlooking the Jordan Valley. This was the Eastern extremity of the Roman Empire and was for them a critically important hostile frontier. As might be expected Rome was mighty displeased with Antipas' marital infidelity, effectively tearing up a valuable treaty and causing great affront to the Arabs. It wasn't long before the Arabs attacked in force they marched north and threatened the Decapolis, who had a protective alliance with Rome. Antipas had to hurriedly put together an army to defend the frontier and was defeated when the two armies joined battle. The Romans then had to set up an expeditionary force of two legions led by Vitellus to quell the enemy. The campaign was abruptly halted by the death of the Roman Emperor Tiberius while Vitellus was in Jerusalem, in the end a truce was agreed but Rome was most displeased and this incident must have contributed to Antipas' eventual removal from power. (Not many years later Antipas and his wife were banished into Gaul, modern France, and died there in disgrace.)

Herod Antipas did not have John executed, which would have been the normal penalty for such open, personal, criticism and condemnation of the king, he was imprisoned in the desert fortress palace at Gadara in Perea East of the Jordan where he could no longer publicly berate Antipas, his wife Herodias and their daughter Salome. It was quite clear that Antipas was very concerned that John really was the messenger foretold by Isaiah and that he should be careful not to fulfil the other prophecy that the rulers of Israel "have tortured and killed all the messengers I have sent to them." We were disappointed, we had all been very impressed by our experience in the desert and at the river with John, and we were convinced that here at last was the forerunner and that we had to repent to be ready to accept the Emmanuel. Now it seemed that it was all for nothing that John was probably as people said, a demented "seer", who was convinced that he had a special communication with God. But God had not saved him from the vicious, cruel powers of Herod Antipas. Perhaps John was misguided in choosing to preach in Perea that was controlled by Antipas. Perhaps John believed he was safer there than in Judea or Idumea or Jerusalem where the power base was Roman and they were brutally repressive to any one who could possibly be thought to be stirring up any sort of rebellion. Of course Jerusalem was a doubly dangerous place to preach repentance right in the face of the same powerful priestly clans of the Temple, he was after all openly accusing them of being the "bad shepherds".

It was about now that we started to hear rumours that Jesus, the carpenter from Nazareth, was preaching in the towns and villages in the region of Sepphoris, and not only preaching but also healing the sick and working miracles. We remembered what Peter had witnessed at the Jordan and agreed that this was a remarkable turn of events. Had he waited until John was arrested so that "The Messenger" had finished his task? Was he trying to divert attention from John to perhaps persuade Herod to release John? Were the rumours of miracles true? The prophesies talked of supreme power and of dramatic happenings, but why should "The Messiah", if that is who he was, be wandering about in the countryside of Galilee, surely if he was going to bring about great changes he would be in Jerusalem. But then John had said in Peter's hearing that this Jesus was the one who was in our midst and yet we did not recognise him. It really was very disturbing and very strange.

Then we heard that he had been to Cana and Nain and now Magdala, every day he turned up somewhere different and every day he was getting nearer and nearer to Capernaum. The people were in great excitement, as soon as it was known where he was people streamed out of the towns and villages taking their families, their sick and their picknicks. It was like a holiday! Everybody wanted to see this man and to listen to his messages, to his stories of God and His people, to witness the amazing miracles and to witness the curing of the sick. He was the only topic of conversation, all work seemed to slow down, everyone was discussing the latest tales of teachings and miracles, most of the teachings were difficult if not impossible to understand clearly, there were always several ways to divine what he might be saying. The cynics, began to put it about that he was a magician and that he was in league with the devil.

As he got nearer to Capernaum and on a day when James and John were with us on business, the four of us decided to visit the old rabbi and ask him for his reaction to all the speculation and to ask his advice on how we should react to this man and his message. The old man was very polite and I think impressed that we should seek his advice, after all there were other rabbis much more our age who we could have talked to, and would have a more up to date point of view. We had a real confidence in this old man after all he had taught us new understandings of The Law after our pilgrimage to John and had helped us to change our life style to suit John's prophesy. What surprised us was how short he was with us. He asked us one question, "Do you really believe that John was Emmanuel's messenger? We all replied as one man that we did. His instruction then was very short and simple. All he would say was, "Watch and Pray, and be ready to be called!" We asked him what he meant and he would say no more, we left somewhat confused and not a little disappointed. When we got home the family's opinion was that we had spent too much time worrying about John and Jesus and we would be better occupied concentrating on the business on which so many livelihoods now depended!

The next day John and James went back to Bethsaida. Peter and I did a thing we very rarely did, we were up very early and took a boat and a couple of men and went fishing. It was a beautiful morning with a light breeze to take us to the best fishing grounds as we sailed totally at peace with the world we watched the sunrise and glisten on the water and then it picked out the little white houses on the shore, we all agreed that this was a most tranquil and satisfying life a man could lead. We were all very experienced fishermen and thought we knew the waters well but we caught nothing. What was worse was that the nets got tangled and somehow the sail got twisted in the rigging and we could neither raise it or lower it, there was only one thing to do we would have to beach the boat on the shore and sort the mess out. We all felt very stupid and knew that we would be teased terribly by everyone back at the harbour when we eventually got back and the tale was told, you can imagine we were not best pleased.

We had just beached the boat and were carefully trying to disentangle the nets without breaking them when there was Jesus. We didn't readily recognise him, we had no reason to expect him to be there that early in the morning and even more so when he asked, " Who are you?" A funny question! Everyone knew who we were and Jesus did too, in the past we had talked to him on several occasions, so Peter said, rather gruffly, " We are Andrew and Simon the sons of Jonas the fishermen from Capernaum". By now Jesus had come much closer, he was alone, there was no crowd following him, he had an air of calm confidence and we felt that there was a sort of power around him that made you concentrate on him and only him. Nothing else seemed to be of any consequence, everything, the boat, the nets, the rigging, the beautiful morning, our business, our wives and families were absolutely insignificant, the only thing that filled our whole beings was Jesus' "presence". He looked at us with a concentration that you felt pierced you through, for a moment or two he said nothing, and then, as if he was now sure about something, he said, "Come with me and I will make you fishers of men!" so we did. We just picked up our coats and without a word to the men we walked up the beach, as we approached, he turned and led us off the beach and out of one life into another life.

Looking back now it was quite extraordinary, there we were successful businessmen with every possible worldly responsibility and we just left. Put yourself in the same situation and realise that we were not religious fanatics we were just ordinary folk with a minimum of education, recently enhanced by the old rabbi, and just Jesus presence and the insistence in his calm appearance and voice was enough to give up every thing. The only promise we had was that he would make us "Fishers of men" whatever that may have meant, and we didn't question anything. There was no reason to even think of the questions that would normally fill anyone's mind, Why? When? Where to? When shall we come back? Where shall we stay? What shall we eat? Should we get money or clothes or sandals or a staff? Shall we tell our family where we are going? The thousand other questions that a rational thinking man would ask, were never asked. It was really as if we had totally left the world of those worries and entered a different world where this Jesus, the son of a carpenter, had absolute control. We accepted his challenge without any hesitation and we now know of course that this Jesus, the son of a carpenter was actually the Son of God and he did have everything under his absolute control!

We had taken the first small step on an adventure like no other mortals have experienced before or since, an adventure that would change the world forever and would fulfil the predictions of the prophets of old. Others have and are and will continue to take up the challenge but we were the privileged few, just twelve of us, who lived day and night with the Son of God. We were the privileged few who witnessed God's infinite power at work in the world through his Son, to see the miracles, to see the healing of the sick, to listen to the parables and to be taught just what the Kingdom of God is like. We also now know what He meant when he said "Follow me!" our lives have, ever since that day, been dedicated to the extension of the knowledge of God's Kingdom and that Emmanuel has been fulfilled "God is with us!" now and forever.

Part 8

Jesus calls James and John

So we followed, neither of us talked, we were, I seem to remember, confused and surprised to find ourselves walking along behind a very ordinary looking man just because he had "commanded" us to do so a few minutes before. Instead of turning left when we reached the road he turned right and set off at a determined pace eastward towards the Jordan River and Bethsaida. After a little while Peter asked me if we should catch up with Jesus and ask him what the plan was or at least to let him know we were there on the road behind him. After a while of silent trudging I suggested that Peter does the talking and I will try and make sense of why we were there at all. Peter quickened his pace and shortly we caught up with Jesus, Peter asked him straight out "Where are we heading for?" after a silence that seemed to imply that he wasn't sure he said very quietly and gently, "We are doing God's work and he will decide exactly what we will do, but I think we have a task in Bethsaida." We knew that Bethsaida was a long walk and would mean staying overnight somewhere on the way and there weren't many places, so Peter asked whether he had any plans for the night and added that we had come with no money or food. Jesus again replied very quietly and gently "We are doing God's work and he will ensure that all these matters are taken care of, do not worry!" So we walked on for a while trying to understand how he had such confidence that he could set off on a journey with no planning with apparently no money and assume that all these matters would be satisfied. Peter started to mumble about how did we get into this expedition, I reminded him of the power that we had both felt when Jesus commanded us on the lake shore and that was why we were there. Jesus was we thought out of earshot and we were horrified when he suddenly stopped in the road, turned round and waited for us to catch up and said, "You are here because God needs you and you cannot disobey. God has been preparing you for this work for some time and now the work starts. God will take care of everything, you have my promise that he will protect us and provide for us until this work of his is done. It is not for you to understand. What is to be done will be unveiled to you as God's will is unfolded and not before." He was not short with us in fact we felt warmth spreading over us from him, as if his task was to guard and comfort us.

Having said this he turned on his heal and set off at a cracking pace along the road as if he had to make up the time he had lost when he stopped. By now it was about midday and the sun was very hot, Peter and I had been up since before dawn, we had had nothing to eat and nothing to drink, we were beginning to feel tired and very thirsty. Much to our surprise almost out of nowhere there was a shady olive grove off to the side of the road, we did not remember it from the many times we had made the journey, but there it was, Jesus did not hesitate he turned off the road into the shade and there was a bubbling stream!! We couldn't believe it, apparently out of nowhere there was shade and water just when Peter and I were beginning to feel exhausted. So we joined Jesus who was already drawing water and enjoyed a welcome rest in the shade. In only a very short while a woman and her maid, it was actually her daughter, stopped off the road and joined us, much to our amazement they greeted Jesus and he them in a most familiar manner and produced a picnic from the baskets they were carrying, There was bread and wine and cooked chicken and apples and plums and cheese a wonderful spread and just enough for five people. In fact it was clearly planned for five people there were five beakers, there were five plates and five small freshly baked loaves of barley bread. Jesus invited us to join the meal and said a little prayer of thanksgiving and then moved a little away as if he wanted to eat by himself. Peter and I were hungry and thirsty and made short work of the food and then waited for Jesus to be ready to move off. He seemed to be totally absorbed in his own thoughts as if none of the rest of us were there. So we decided we should talk to the two women, they were sitting patiently a little way off and had to be persuaded to come and talk. It turned out that the older woman was Jesus mother! The younger woman his sister! They told us they had walked all over Galilee, that there never was a plan, that they had no money but that every day it seemed that things worked out. There was always somewhere to sleep, there was always food to eat and water to drink and they met lots of very kind people, and a few not so kind. We had only just exchanged these few words when Jesus came and joined us and said we should move on as we had a long journey before we got to our rest and evening meal. The women just accepted this but Peter asked again how far we were going, because he didn't know of any hostelry between here and the Jordan crossing and that was still a long way. Jesus just replied that everything was in God's care and we have to trust him! There didn't seem any point in asking more so we set off again, very quickly the women fell behind until they were out of sight. Jesus didn't notice and kept going at a good pace. Out of deference we stayed a little way behind him and it gave us some chance to talk. Both of us were completely confused, we had walked for about two or three hours in the morning and were totally unaware that the women were on the road behind us, then how had they known to prepare a meal for five people when they set out there were only three. Then there was the olive grove and the water, we had travelled that road more times than we cared to remember and neither of us had any recollection of the place. It would have been well known but not to us, very, very strange. And then there were the women themselves, they implied that every day was like this, they didn't have any of the bundles of possessions which women seem to find necessary even for the shortest journey. Jesus didn't take any real notice of them even though they were his mother and sister; the journey was the all-important thing and nothing was to get in its way. By late afternoon we were approaching the crossing of the Jordan where there is an inn which does a good trade serving as a resting place for travellers using the main route from Ceasarea and Sidon inland and north to Damascus. Both the ancient camel caravan route and the Roman road take the same route and after crossing the river the road turns north to Damascus but also continues east round the edge of the lake and then south almost hugging the shore to Bethsaida. Herod Philip has since these times built a new harbour and town even further down the coast; he called it Julias, in honour of the Roman Emperor's wife. You will remember that Antipas had established a new town on the west side of the lake and called it Tiberias in honour of the same Roman Emperor. The inn is always busy and has extensive accommodation but it is usually full. If a caravan is stopping the chances of getting a bed or even food is limited. When we arrived we could see that in the courtyard there was already a caravan and a large Roman military escort for some important dignitary on his way to Ceasarea Philippi. Jesus just went up to the "major domo" and talked to him very quietly and there we were with accommodation and a good meal set well away from the gentiles. The next day we heard that he had been offered a part of the stable as the only available space and when he readily agreed to this the inn keeper relented and found he had some space in proper rooms. This was to be our first experience of a meal with Jesus and it was extraordinary. Of course after the journey we were dusty from the road and so we washed, but Jesus did not make a great ceremonial as we did, he just washed the dust away. When we went into the dinning hall he did not look to sit separate from the other travellers although they were clearly "sinners and publicans" as the Pharisees would have it, you only had to look at them to tell the sort of people they were, normally we would not have had anything to do with them. Jesus made for them directly and asked if he could join them for supper, they were astounded, it was clear to them that not only was he a Jew but that he was at least a rabbi and they all knew that he should not mix with the likes of them. They "hummed and ahhed" a bit but after a few ribald comments about their language and jokes, "of course he and we could join them and welcome". We felt very uncomfortable, we knew we would have to report to the priest at the next town and be cleansed, we did not know what to talk about, we did not know what to eat or how to share the food with these people. They didn't seem to be in the least discomforted, they were enjoying their food they talked about their journeys, their business, their prowess at getting good bargains, they found they had friends and acquaintances in common they were just ordinary people doing ordinary things. We on the other hand were amazed at ourselves we had never experienced anything like this. Here we were, having abandoned our business, our families, our friends and all that we knew and understood. In its place we had walked about 10 miles following this man who had hardly spoken to us but was a fount of confidence and peace. We found ourselves sitting at dinner in a house frequented by gentiles and sharing a meal with sinners and publicans whose language was profane and who blasphemed against God with every other breath. It was unbelievable and he had told us he would make us fishers of men!

Quite suddenly the room went quiet, Jesus was at the other end of the table and we over heard the last few words of his comment to the man he was seated next to, they were "-----think God wants from you?" There was no answer, so Jesus told this story.

"There was a shepherd, tending his flocks and it was evening time and he went and collected the flock together and led them to the fold where they would be safe from the wolves and lions and bears who would otherwise molest them and scatter them and kill them. As the sheep entered the fold he counted them and he found that one of his one hundred sheep was missing. So he left the ninety-nine with his faithful dog and went out into the hills to find the one that was lost. He walked carefully because it was getting dark but he whistled and called and eventually he heard a sheep calling from a thicket, it was a young lamb not more than six months old and it had fallen and got caught in a bramble thicket. So he released the lamb from its captivity and torment, picked it up and carried it home on his shoulders to the fold. This shepherd was a good shepherd, we all know what a hired shepherd would have done he would leave the lost sheep to its fate to be killed by the wolves or eaten by the lions."

We were not just listening to Jesus but were watching the men round the table, they were silent, some men were crying others could not raise their heads, they knew they were the lost sheep, they also knew that nobody really cared what happened to them. They were Jews, the Sons of Abraham, but because of their work or their life style or their sinfulness they had been excluded, some for generations, from the promised blessings that that was supposed to bring. The Rabbis and the scribes and the Pharisees made sure that these sorts of men were "untouchables". Jesus said in a quiet, confident, comforting voice

"I am that Good Shepherd. I bring you salvation; I bring you a new promise of forgiveness of your sins and the promise of eternal life. All that I ask from you is that you confess your sins to God and repent and promise to reform your lives and have absolute faith that God can restore all. What is more God is concerned not for the house of Israel but for the souls of each individual lost soul!"

Jesus got up from the table and, after a moments pause left us all to try and take in what he had said. Some of the dinners went back to their eating and drinking as if little, if anything, had happened but a lot of them went very quiet said nothing and slowly left the room. We were absolutely amazed and not a little frightened. Jesus had told us that we were doing God's work and that God would make all things possible but never in our wildest dreams did we think that we were about saving the souls of the "untouchables". We sat outside, under the stars, and talked about his story. Well if he was the Good Shepherd did he really mean that the religious powers of Israel were Bad Shepherds? Why should God be concerned about one person when so many were, in the story, sheep who followed their master? Who were the wolves and lions he had spoken about when the story is transposed into human terms? Most of the answers we came up with seemed to be radical and dangerous. We thought about the teaching of the old rabbi in Capernaum that we needed to re-examine the Law of Moses. Suddenly as we mentioned Capernaum we were filled with anxiety, sadness, and guilt. What were our families doing? They must have got over their surprise but were now probably angry and judgemental, how dare we just walk away, we had responsibilities that we could not just drop people, lots of people who relied on us for their very existence, we must be mad!! Both of us were nearly in tears as we contemplated the pain and disappointment we had caused, the sorrow, the bereavement, the desertion we had brought onto our wives, our children, our brothers and sisters and our parents, we had not even said goodbye properly to any of them, and for what? Today had not been in any terms we could think as other than a bit of a disaster. Perhaps tomorrow we should cut our losses and go home!

We were just at this depth of depression when Jesus was there with us, we don't know whether he had heard us talking but he was there! Even before he said anything, things seemed to be all right, he sat down with us and said, "God has chosen you to be part of a very special band to do His work. He has sent me to bring salvation to the world; I am the fulfilment of His promise to Abraham and to Isaac and to Jacob. I know your very inner feelings but God will make all things right, you have to be confident, as I am. God will care for your family, God will be there with them to ensure that they do understand and support you, because you are chosen by God and you cannot refuse. Remember how Elisha tried to avoid God's command, remember how Jonah tried to avoid God's command, you cannot avoid it. If you turn and go back now God will find a way of making you join his final visitation to Israel, the matter is out of your hands!"

So we went to bed, very disturbed but much less anxious than we had been. In the morning we got up early and came down to the eating room. There was Mary and Ann they were talking most earnestly to Jesus and clearly making him have some breakfast. When they saw us the women withdrew and Jesus welcomed us most heartily and said that before we ate any food we should pray for God's guidance and his power to face the challenges of the day as we did his work. He told us that every day must start with prayer, that he had already started the day and had been out in the hills to rededicate himself to God and to the task he had to fulfil. To pray, he said we must be quiet and private and relieved of the distractions of the world and to do this we should go outside and away from this very congenial but busy and noisy place. So we three went out into the beautiful freshness of the morning and walked just a little way down to the banks of the River Jordan before it enters the Sea of Galilee. There was an air of serene peace and security, Jesus stood and looked round and then talked to us.

"God has made the earth to be like this, it is the sinfulness of man that makes it ugly and cruel and full of wickedness and vice. He has sent many prophets and messengers to the House of Israel to tell them that it is their sinfulness that is separating them from God. None of the prophets have been heard and Israel has continually turned away from God's purpose. Because they have been given a promise they assume that they can behave as they wish, they can break his laws, they can kill

67

his prophets, they can ignore his warnings but still God will keep his promise and they will be saved. They will be saved if they repent but now the message is final and it is directed to every individual however great or humble he or she may be. You heard my little story last night about the shepherd, well our job is to find and save the lost sheep and remember God's promise was to Israel and all the people upon earth. I saw you at the Jordan with John the Baptiser, he proclaimed the coming of the Messiah and commanded Israel to repent and to turn from their evil ways and many did. When you heard what John was saying you were greatly disturbed and since then you have tried to improve your closeness to God, the old rabbi has told me about the lessons he has given you and your family. His last challenge to you was to be ready, and when I called you, you were ready. I am the one for whom John prepared the way and my task is to save Israel and you are chosen to help me.

Today I hope that two more men will be ready to hear the command and respond to the challenge and we will collect more in the next few days so that there are enough workers for the task now and later!

Now you understand a little, gradually you will understand more and more and eventually you will understand enough for the greatest test of all, but that is not now."

After a pause, when our minds were trying to take in what he had said Jesus continued. "So now we will pray to God for his strength and guidance, because this is new to you pray with me; Our Father who art in heaven, today we need your strength to help us to complete the next stage of your plan. We ask you to give us the power to convince our next recruits to join our mission to do your work. We ask you to guide our words and actions to help us to complete the task. We are a small band but you showed us last evening that your words can bring about great change in people's lives, give us those words when we need them to bring your blessing, and peace to men on earth. Amen."

With that he got up and said "Right breakfast, it should be ready now and then we have a lot to do!" he marched back to the inn and there were Mary and Ann waiting to serve us. Jesus thanked God for our food and we all ate heartily, and without any hesitation we set off, the "major domo" was at the door and wished us a safe journey and hoped we would visit again, there was no question of paying a bill or any such thing. The man seemed almost honoured to have had our little party to stay the night. Quite extraordinary, considering that when we first arrived he had suggested the stable as accommodation.

We passed the road to Ceasarea Philippi on our left and followed the road that was now more a track than a road, round the north coast of the Sea towards Bethsaida. We all knew the area well, we, that is Peter and I, were borne and brought up in the town and knew all the surrounding countryside as you would expect from our boyhood adventures and Jesus knew it as well he had come before with his father, the carpenter Joseph, doing contract work for Philip Herod's building projects. We were still surprised that we were clearly going to Bethsaida; it is after all the last Jewish settlement before the desert and the control of the Greek Decapolis towns. It was hardly a Jewish town any longer, Philip had developed and extended the town and many new people had come to live there, mainly Greeks and Arabs, escaping the harsh climate of the desert. After what Jesus had said we felt sure that the band of helpers he was intent on collecting together must all be Jews after all the Messiah was to come to Israel not to the gentiles. One thing was certain at Bethsaida we could be sure of a welcome and a good lunch from the Zebedee household.

The little town of Bethsaida, the morning we arrived, looked more like a building site than a fishing village, Philip's reconstruction work was in evidence everywhere. There were stonemasons and carpenters busy preparing materials that were arriving by road but mostly by ship into the newly completed harbour. There were construction gangs building houses and civic buildings, the style was Hellenic as required by any town rebuilt by the Romans or in this case their puppet ruler. The town would now begin to prosper just as Capernaum had done when its harbour had been built twenty years previously and provide more prosperity for the Jonas/Zebedee fishing interests. It all had the air of action and confidence!

As we walked into the town Jesus took a casual, almost professional interest in the works but was clearly intent to get on with his task. On the way we had talked to each other about whom he could possibly be intending to collect. We knew pretty well everyone certainly all the Jews and nobody sprang to mind, one or two we remembered had been particularly diligent at school in their learning the Holy Texts. But nobody seemed to be outstanding.

Of course we knew that most of our discussion with the Zebedees, if there were time, would have to be about the business and their families. Just how would we explain what we were doing to our business partners it was like resignations without notice and an expectation that we might want our jobs back at any time! We agreed that the initial meeting could be very awkward, but we had known the family for all our lives, we had grown up together, we had worked together and most recently we had shared a remarkably similar spiritual experience in the desert with John the Baptiser. They might understand, but it was unlikely we agreed that they would be best pleased, and it was certain that their father would be furious. Jesus was a little ahead of us as usual but as we got down towards the harbour he stopped and waited for us to catch up, he looked at us very seriously and said, "Remember, this morning we prayed to God for his strength to see his work done. You must have faith in his power and you must not be anxious for the future, I tell you all will be well!" If you want to make somebody nervous that is about the best way, neither of us could imagine what He was about to do but we now expected it to be something dramatic. And it was.

With out further ado he walked onto the harbour wall and straight to one of our boats and said to James and John "Come with me!" Well it was dramatic they were mending nets and without looking round or speaking to the other crewmembers they got up climbed onto the sea wall and waited for Jesus next instruction. We were amazed how could God want the four principles of a small fishing company to drop everything and set off after Jesus when there were so many responsibilities to be taken care of, we couldn't believe it! Neither could old man Zebedee, a man well known for his fiery temper and short fuse; he was speechless his mouth was opening and closing and nothing was coming out, his face and head had gone bright red, he was trying to jump up and down but his legs wouldn't work. Before he had time to pull himself together Jesus in that quiet but commanding voice we were getting to know said to him "The Lord has need of your sons, the Lord will care for you and your families but your sons must come with me." Zebedee was dumbfounded he sank down onto the gunwale and mumbled something about "never being able to retire."

Jesus turned and said to us all, the four of us "I know a very good place to eat and I think they may well be expecting us!" he seemed delighted clearly all the problems he thought he might have had were out of the way and we could move on to the next thing. We, of course, embraced our partners and had to admit to them that we were as surprised as them to be there and to have accepted the challenge that Jesus presented. Apparently one of the boats had come in from Capernaum and all the news was the sudden and dramatic departure of the Jonas boys! When they heard the story they had agreed that if they had the chance they would take it, despite the problems they might leave behind, they said that they decided that somebody would have to be around to take care of Andrew and particularly Peter. They both agreed however that even if they had not had some prior notice, when Jesus looked at them and demanded their support there was no way that he could be refused. We told them about our adventures of the last twenty-four hours, not least the amazing ability that Jesus had for stilling anxiety and commanding attention. But then there was the information that we had about the purpose of the band of God's workers that he was collecting together, that He was here to save Israel, that he was the one John had predicted, and then the way he had talked and prayed with us in the morning.

We were so busy talking that we merely followed Jesus steps and were absolutely amazed when he went straight into the Zebedee house. We were even more amazed when we found that Mary and Ann had already arrived, we hadn't seen them since breakfast, and that the table was laid for everyone, including Zebedee! To start with the atmosphere was brittle, Jesus on entering the house and after blessing it told the family the James and John were joining him together with Peter and me, to implement God's promise to Abraham and Isaac and Jacob and to bring about God's kingdom on earth. As you can imagine even with the preparatory experience we had shared when listening to John in the desert, this was a bombshell. Of course everyone knew Jesus was just a carpenter, they all knew that we four were just fishermen, who, perhaps had taken what John said too seriously. How were we going to change the world? The world was about power politics, about armies, about cruelty and about death, particularly the death of any body that attempted to challenge the power of the state. We didn't need many examples, almost in living memory there were the Greeks, the Seleucids, the Maccabees and the Romans. The sensible people kept a low profile and kept out of trouble and prayed that they would be left in peace. "So Jesus, why do you think we should willingly let you take the flower of our family off on a wild goose chase that will almost certainly end in their deaths?" You can see that Mrs. Zebedee was not very enthusiastic about the whole idea!

Jesus did not respond directly, he washed in the ritual manner and quietly sat where he was shown, next to Zebedee's seat and silently waited. I'm sure that he was praying for God's guidance and strength to answer the very real human emotions that the matriarch had delivered to him. Zebedee was not long in arriving and was still very upset, even angry, at his sons' desertion. He came in and shouted for his wife to tell her what had happened, he was very cross and it took a little while for him to become conscious of the guests at his table. He then huffed and puffed and mumbled an apology for his rudeness and inhospitable behaviour. When he took his place at the table, Jesus said the grace without being invited, everyone's' eyes were on Zebedee, would he explode again? He didn't and perhaps it was the words of the grace that stopped him, they were,

71

"O Lord God, bless this house and all who dwell here, we thank you for all the blessing and gifts you have piled onto this family, we thank you for their great generosity to us, their visitors, and to the community of Bethsaida. We ask you to give them the generosity of heart that they can return to God his greatest blessing of their two eldest sons to do His work, just as Anna gave up the young Samuel to God's work. We ask you dear God to provide for this family to care for them and to protect them and to give them faith in your power to care for their sons."

His voice was so confident, so calm, so assured that nobody stirred, it was as if they were waiting to hear more. Jesus clearly had said all he wanted to and so we all set about eating the splendid lunch that had been prepared. We four men talked among ourselves about the implications of our leaving for the business, we had no idea how long we might be gone, but Jesus comment about Samuel made it sound like forever. Neither James nor John was married but both Peter and I were and had children. However they were growing up fast and should be able to look after themselves, anyway in a short time we may be able to call them to our new world and the power that we might well exert, even as fisherman? I noticed that Jesus and Zebedee were talking quietly and closely together and that the old man's demeanour was improving as he listened to what Jesus had to say. At the other end of the table Mary and Ann were also in confidential conversation with Mrs. Zebedee and that she was also becoming less agitated. The day was getting on by time we had finished the meal and it was too late to consider returning to Capernaum that night so it was agreed that we would stay over and that Zebedee would send us off in one of the boats in the morning. We knew that if we left early there would be a steady easterly breeze off the desert to take us quickly and safely home. Jesus was a bit concerned he clearly wanted to be off as soon as possible on the next stage of his mission, now our mission. There was an air of urgency that, as time went on, we came to accept as a way of life for us all. After the meal was cleared away, Jesus excused himself and set off alone into the parched desert hills behind Bethsaida, he gave no indication of how long he would be but made it quite clear that he wanted to be alone.

Part 9

The Birth and childhood of Jesus as told by His mother, and recorded by Andrew

For the first time we had the opportunity to talk with his Mother and sister about his life and how they had coped with the extraordinary idea that he really was the Messiah The story was dramatic and quite amazing and by the end of the telling any doubts about his mission were dispelled the way in which his mission would be fulfilled was, of course still a great mystery which we could not even begin to understand. What we did begin to accept was the amazing even ridiculous idea that we four fishermen should have been chosen by God to be an integral part of this journey. The instruction that Jesus had given us that we should have faith in God's power was reinforced by the demonstration of faith that Mary had shown throughout the previous thirty years. I am sure that the story will be told time and time again all I can do is try to recall what Mary told us in the Zebedee house many years ago.

Mary sat very quietly and started at the beginning. She recalled that one day she was sitting her mother's house in Nazareth spinning wool when quite suddenly the room was filled with a sort of light, not the light of the sun or the moon or a candle, a light that was a source of power a light that had no source, a light that seemed not to just fill the room but to fill the whole world. There in the middle of this light was a man, but he wasn't an ordinary man, his whole being glowed with the same light that was lighting the room, but even he was not the source of this brightness. She said she was not afraid, not in the usual sense of fear; she was amazed that anything like this could possibly happen to her. She was just a simple girl for a small country town; she tried to be good and to keep the law. She was to be married to Joseph, the carpenter, soon, she did not know him well, the families had sorted out the marriage and had told her that she would be well cared for and that it was a good marriage arrangement. There was nothing special about that all her friends were getting married and that's the way it is done. "Well", she said, "You can imagine the shock when this man said that I was already having a baby. I could not believe it and I told him so and I told him that I was not that sort of girl and would he please go away and leave me in peace." But he replied, ever so gently, that I had been chosen by God to be the mother of his son who would be the Messiah.

73

By now you can imagine that my mind was on fire. How could I explain this to my mother? How would I explain it to Joseph? What would the neighbours say? What about all those terrible punishments that the Law demanded for people who broke the law of adultery? Nobody would believe my story of this strange alarming messenger! He could see that I was very upset and he must have been prepared for this reaction, again he very gently said, " Mary, do not be afraid! God will take care of all your worries. He will give you the strength you need! He will also make sure that people understand that this is to be no ordinary baby! He will not allow you to be put to shame! You must have faith in God!" So all that she could say was that she meekly accepted the situation and that she would do as God had decided. She then said that she now knew that what God had decided would actually come to pass and was actually coming to pass this very day! Just as Jesus had told us that morning by the sea, when he explained to us the command we had been given and that like Jonah and Elijah and many others we could not escape God's will or thwart God's plans. So we now understood that Jesus had been specially chosen even before he was conceived. All the problems that Mary had worried about, and we all were familiar with, were, in the end, only worries. Of course people wanted to point their fingers at her, you can't disguise the fact that you're having a baby for very long, but the rabbi put a stop to that. He said something one Sabbath in the synagogue and quite suddenly all the tittle-tattle stopped and people who had been tut-tutting came to visit and started knitting and sewing things for the baby. Many years later he had admitted that he had had a dream in which he was commanded to stop the gossip immediately, he remembered that he didn't know what to say but that when he started to preach that Sabbath the words poured out of his mouth without his preparation. He told the people that gossip was a poison, and quoted the Proverbs, he told them of other unexpected babies in the past, and quoted both Isaac and Samuel, he told them about love and forgiveness, and quoted Isaiah. He then challenged them as individuals that if they had no sin, absolutely no sin then they should come to him to discuss the matter of Mary's baby and they should not discuss it with any one else, not their wives, not their friends, not their family and that if they heard any one discussing the matter they were to immediately report the matter to him and him alone and he would decide on the punishment that a direct contravention of his instruction would entail! After that plain speaking nobody even breathed a word and the fact that Mary was having baby was not an issue. Even before all this happened there had been a big conflab in the family and with Joseph's family at first it was all very unpleasant and people got angry and critical, they had never heard such a tale and didn't believe it, in the end it was left to dear Joseph. If he accepted the situation then so would the families. He was very worried and went to his workshop and busied himself but everyone knew that he was pondering what to do. He didn't talk to Mary, maybe he talked to the rabbi but it took two or three days for him to publish his decision. He decided and told the families that the marriage should go ahead as planned and that the child would be brought up exactly as any other child the marriage may be blessed with and that he wanted the matter to be finished there and then. So that's how it was, they were married and set up home in an extension Joseph built onto his workshop and all was going well until Mary was eight months pregnant. Out of the blue the Romans decided that they wanted to know how many people lived in the whole of Israel, to do this they insisted that every man went to his tribal town to register himself and his family. Joseph was from the tribe of David and their tribal town was Bethlehem, Mary thought he meant the Bethlehem in Galilee that was only about fifteen miles from Nazareth and was horrified to find it was Bethlehem in Judea, near Jerusalem that they had to visit. Although Joseph tried to persuade the authorities that with his wife so imminently expecting a baby that he should go alone or that they could go when the baby had been born or could they just add his name to the lists in Nazareth, they would have none of it, they must go to Bethlehem. Well after all the fuss had died down and in view of the fact that Mary was so well and after mothers and mothers-in-law had had their say it seemed to the young couple that this was quite an adventure, their first trip to the Holy City as man and wife! Clearly Mary couldn't walk all the way so Joseph bought a donkey, they really started to feel sorry for the poor beast, it had to carry Mary, Joseph's tools as a carpenter (he had no idea how long he would be away and anyway they might get stolen if he left them), all the things for a new baby, their food and their clothes. So off they went on their adventure, by now they were very much in love, Mary could do no wrong and Joseph was so attentive she almost felt overwhelmed. It was fun there were lots of people travelling north and south. They had to go down the Jordan valley, the Samaritans would have been very aggressive to Jews trying to take the shortest route Jerusalem, but it was cool, the river was full the pastures were lush, there were plenty of places to stop on the way to camp for the night or to picnic for lunch. They met lots of friendly people who were so kind when they realised how imminent was Mary's confinement; she had more good advice from well-wishers than anyone should expect! The journey took about a week and despite the excitement Mary got more and more tired and more and more anxious as they travelled on, Bethlehem seemed to get further away rather than nearer. When they finally climbed out of the Jordan Valley and saw Jerusalem Mary was exhausted she wanted to stop there, there were plenty of places to stay, the city was geared up for the annual influx of Jews from all over the world who came as pilgrims for the Passover, the number passing through for the census was well below the city's capacity. Did they really have to go on the last few miles to Bethlehem? Well they did, Joseph knew that if they stopped in Jerusalem they would find it even more difficult to move on to Bethlehem, they stopped for a while to see the Temple and the palaces on the Temple Mount and then continued on to Bethlehem. They eventually arrived in the dark. They knocked on the doors of guesthouses; one after the other and there was no room. Mary admitted that she started to grumble at Joseph that they should have stayed in Jerusalem to the extent that eventually he agreed that if this last house could not give them a room they would have to go back. They didn't have room but there was a stable cut into the cliff-side at the back that they could use for a while until some of the visitors left. So they took it! The innkeepers wife was very caring and made sure that there was clean hay and that the animals were tethered away to give Mary and Joseph some space. She brought clean water and sat with Mary as the birth pains grew in intensity and frequency and she was there to help with the birth. She presented to Joseph his son, of course she knew nothing of any other matters, but when they were alone together Mary and Joseph talked together of the amazing adventure that had got them there. They wondered what was in store for them next and what this baby boy would grow into after the way that he was announced to them in Nazareth. They all slept well that night, Mary totally exhausted but serenely happy and content. At about three o'clock in the morning they were awakened by a group of rough looking, and rather smelly, shepherds who appeared at the stable. They were incoherent, spluttering with excitement and they were very frightened. Eventually when they had calmed down they said that they had been sent by angels who having suddenly appeared over the hillside off to the east of the road to Jerusalem where they were guarding their flock. The chief of these angels commanded them to go into Bethlehem to worship the Son of God who had been born there that very night. They were absolutely terrified but convinced that they must obey. They had been told by the angel, to find the baby in a stable of all places, then as they left the whole sky was filled with brightness and angels singing beautifully music they had never heard before. Anyway, here they were and here was a baby in a stable, so it must be true! The only trouble was that this baby looked like any other baby and didn't look at all like the Son of God. When they discussed it they didn't know what the Son of God would look like, but they did expect him to be a bit posh! Certainly it was extraordinary to find him in a manger in a stable and not surrounded by all the trappings of kingship. It didn't stop them admiring the baby with a sense of awe and trying to understand why the angels should have appeared to them and what was this baby really.

Within two days the innkeeper had moved them into the house and his wife was just like a mother to Mary and was so proud that a baby had been borne in the inn, she was even more impressed when she and all the town heard what the shepherds were telling of the night the Angels appeared to them. Lots of people, residents and visitors, came to see the baby and all went away wondering what this was all about. Joseph was extremely proud of his wife and his son. He had sent a message back to Nazareth, with a neighbour he had bumped into, to say all was well, baby boy, perfect, good head of hair, and that they had decided to stay a while so that they could present the baby at the Temple in Jerusalem. In the meantime Joseph had set up in business, first doing a few jobs for the innkeeper and then other people wanted this or that done. Joseph was pleased, Mary and the baby needed to have some rest to recover before they set out back to Nazareth. He really was at home in Bethlehem and found he had many near and distant relatives from the House of David who welcomed him and put business his way when they found just what a good craftsman he was. It all looked so good that he and Mary seriously talked about settling there and not going back to Nazareth.

According to the Law given by Moses the Sons of Abraham have to be circumcised on the eighth day by the rabbi, Mary and Joseph agreed that this special baby would not be presented anywhere other than the Temple in Jerusalem. So on the eighth day they set off with the faithful donkey, early in the day to avoid the worst of the heat. They told the innkeeper what they were doing, and his ever-caring wife put up a picnic for them and plenty of the things that the baby would need for this very special ritual. It is not so very far from Bethlehem to Jerusalem the road is almost due north and as the morning progressed and the sun came round behind them the city glistened in the sunshine, they could see why it was called the Golden City. The centrepiece was the huge Temple buildings, towering over everything else, and behind them the threatening Antonio Tower, the barracks of the Roman soldiers. When they had come through the city only a few days previously Mary had really seen nothing she had been feeling so tired and anxious, but Joseph had been agog at the magnificence and as they approached the city now he was confidently pointing out the other buildings outside the Temple platform. There was the Chief Priests Palace, Herod's Palace, that made a corner buttress and defence for the city wall, that stretched right round the city, it looked totally impregnable. The angel had told Mary the child she was carrying her arms would be the King of the Jews, and this was the holy city of the Jews! Could it be true? Nobody could possibly believe such a story, this tiny baby with his mother and father, simple people from far away Nazareth; was he really a king? Anyway it was certain that nobody was going to recognise them or him even if some rumours about the angels and the shepherds had filtered through to Jerusalem surely nobody would believe it. Even if they did they wouldn't connect Mary and Joseph with such a rumour they were just unremarkable, simple, people from Galilee. Or would they? Was the child at risk? Had this really been such a good idea? Wouldn't it have been better to present the child quietly in Bethlehem? So a little apprehensively they entered the city at the Genath Gate at the foot of one of the massive towers of Herod's fortified palace. Herod clearly was a frightened king he had built his palace fortified all round as if he were just as much afraid of the citizens of the city as any possible invaders! Then they tumbled into the narrow streets that were a veritable labyrinth, the streets were teaming with people and animals. There were donkeys laden with every imaginable goods but mostly firewood. As there were no trees in the area firewood had to be imported from the countryside. There were camels laden with sacks and bundles driven by men who looked strange in their dress and spoke in dialects that neither Mary nor Joseph recognised. There were sheep and lambs and bulls and chickens and doves all being driven or carried east so they followed them, they were sure that the animals would be sacrifices for the temple. Progress was slow and punctuated by delays due to important people being carried through the streets on litters so everyone had to get out of the way, or as companies of soldiers marched through blasting the air with their warning trumpets. People were polite they must have known the purpose of this little family making its way towards the Temple and made way for them when they could. Eventually they passed The Hasmonaeans Palace and proceeded across the bridge that had been built to give access to the Temple Courtyard from the south-east, crossing the Valley of Tyropeaon. They entered through the colonnaded Royal Porch and then into the courtyard of the Gentiles a huge expanse of beautiful paving. The atmosphere was frenetic. There were people selling souvenirs and sacrificial animals and changing money from all over the world into temple currency, there were jugglers and clowns but mostly there were pilgrims, Jews from all over the world. They came, not only from the Roman provinces where Jews had set up communities, but also from cities and countries to the East outside the control and power of Rome, many would be making a 'once-in-a-lifetime' pilgrimage to the very centre of their spiritual and cultural homeland. There were guides taking groups of these "tourists" round the sights, there were touts offering "good deals" on almost anything. They crossed this courtyard and then Mary dismounted with the baby and they entered The Courtyard of the Women. Through the gate it was suddenly cool and quiet, there were not many people about but eventually the found a junior cleric who directed them to a building on the south wall. He was a charming young man and explained to them that this was a very special day as very infrequently the high priest officiated at the presentations and to day it was Simeon who was taking this duty. The young man told them to wait in the room he had directed them to and he would find Simeon and send him to them there. So they did as they were told, they were of course apprehensive they knew full well the ritual of circumcision but they also knew its risks and they prayed together that God would be merciful and bring their baby son through this ordeal safely. They were sitting quietly together deep in thought when the door opened and in came an old, old man, he was bent and frail, his hands were long and thin, his face was wrinkled and at first sight he looked a bit frightening and severe, but then as the light picked up his face it was clear he was a kindly, caring, old man and they immediately had confidence in him. He took the child in his arms and blessed him and then talked to his parents about who they were and where they came from and who their parents were and lots and lots of details. They had not noticed as they entered the room that there was a desk in one corner the occasional scratching noise told them that a scribe was preparing the necessary records for the presentation. It seemed to be taking a long time and Mary was getting worried that the child would need to be fed before they got to the ceremony proper but eventually the old man had finished with all his enquiries and the clerk indicated that all was in order. There was a little blood and a lot of screaming from the baby, as there should be, but Mary quickly quietened him and they called his name Jesus, just as the angel had told Mary nine months before in Nazareth. When they had calmed the baby they noticed that Simeon, who must have circumcised hundreds of boys in his long life, was quite overcome with emotion and through his tears and smiles and laughter he made this prayer.

"Lord, now lettest thou thy servant depart in peace. For mine eyes have seen thy salvation, which thou hast prepared before the face of thy people Israel. A light to lighten the Gentiles and the glory of thy people Israel"

Mary and Joseph were very surprised and asked the old man what he perceived about their son and he predicted that

"This child will be a sign that many will reject and that your Heart Mary will also be pierced. Many in Israel will stand or fall because of him and the secret thoughts of many will be laid bare."

This sounded a very frightening prediction and they wondered how this could be when the angel had said he was to be the saviour of the nation. Simeon would say no more, he seemed to be almost ecstatic as if suddenly all the anxieties of his life had been removed and that his work was fulfilled. He could not take his eyes off the baby and his parents and he went from tears to smiles to laughter and back to tears time and again but his mood was one of great joy. As they were leaving the room a very old woman approached them as if she knew who they were, she came straight up and asked if she could see the child. Mary was a little anxious but also quite naturally proud to show the baby. The old woman, whose name was Anna, was overcome with emotion, just as Simeon was. She told them that she was eighty-four years old and that she never left the temple precincts, she said that she had been told in a dream that before she died she would see the saviour of Israel and she, like Simeon, was sure that this baby was the one sent by God. Both Mary and Joseph were now becoming worried, this well meaning, very holy, old woman was beginning to spread the word that the Messiah was here and that she had seen him and crowds were gathering round her listening to what she had to say. Joseph and Mary became very concerned that the temple guards might get hear about this and would come looking for their son; anything might happen! So they decided to leave and as quickly as possible, they had hoped to have time to visit more of the Temple. Joseph would have liked to enter the inner sanctum but it was more important, they knew, that the baby must not be put at risk, if they could avoid it. The donkey was patiently waiting for them, they un-tethered him and led him out of the Temple precinct and as quickly as possible out of Jerusalem. Once they were outside the walls away from the crowds, they felt they could relax a little and found some shade in an olive grove where they enjoyed their picnic, Mary fed and washed the baby. When he was settled they talked through the amazing things that had been said about this tiny child. The story seemed to be coming together and being confirmed and if it was true it was extraordinary. God had a very unconventional way of doing things and that just as they were very surprised by the happenings of the last few months, a lot more people were going to be very surprised as time went on. They agreed that the less they talked about these things the better, God had chosen them to care for the child and look after his upbringing and clearly his security depended on the very minimum number of people being aware of any of the story. They agreed that they would never let anyone see that they thought he was special other than that he was their firstborn son and therefore in Jewish tradition a special child. They set off back to Bethlehem where the Innkeepers wife was delighted to see them back safe and sound, she wanted to hear all the details of their day and this was their first practice at being "Economic" with the truth. For a few more months life went on well they were establishing themselves in the Bethlehem community and becoming more and more convinced that they really would stay. Joseph had borrowed a small workshop from a distant relative and was making enough money to satisfy the innkeeper, his wife didn't want them to leave and the valuation of little jobs that Joseph did round the inn seemed somewhat inflated, they seemed secure and although the climate was much more severe that the balmy atmosphere of Galilee there were lots of attractions. One of the attractions which weighed heavily with Joseph was the question of the child's security, he knew very well that when they went back to Nazareth the tongues would be wagging and also that it would be difficult to stop the rumours about his early life. Against this was the fact that Nazareth was much further away than Bethlehem was from the dangerous megalomaniac Herod, whose reaction to the possibility of a challenge to his power, even if it was only a baby, would be swift and final, however all seemed quiet for the time being! It is probable that the excitement of Anna in the Temple courtyard that had so upset them, had, in the end, been assumed to be the ravings of "a silly old woman" and ignored. Then the next extraordinary thing happened, in the middle of the morning there was a great to do, people were running out of there houses and lining the street all looking towards Jerusalem. Clearly from the amount of dust that was being thrown into the air there was a large caravan coming into town. This was not that unusual, Bethlehem was on a main caravan route from Arabia and from the sea. We took little notice of what was going on we were, as you can imagine, more concerned with our baby. To our great consternation this large and clearly wealthy caravan turned into the courtyard of our inn. The innkeeper and his wife rushed up to us to explain that the three leaders of the caravan were asking to see the boy child. She said they really did look like kings, their entourage was huge there must have been about one hundred men mostly mounted on camels of the highest quality and the rest of them on Arabian horses, whether they were kings or very wealthy merchants she could not tell.

They did not speak Aramaic or very much Greek or Latin, but they had made it clear that they had come to see a great prince born to this nation and what is more they were convinced that he was not only in Bethlehem but in this very inn. In view of all the other things that had happened we decided quickly to welcome them into our room and hopefully send them on their way before too much excitement was generated. So with a great deal of pomp they came in, one at a time, the room was too small for more than that because each one brought about six courtiers with them. In turn they bowed very low to the ground and then presented us with gifts, one was gold, one was incense and the last was myrrh. It took quite a while for us to understand their reason. They said that they were astronomers and that about four months earlier they had seen a new very bright star suddenly appear in the sky. All their knowledge and learning told them that this must be the announcement of a very important occasion, something very significant to the whole human race had happened and that the star would tell them were it had taken place. The three of them decided that they must try and find out what this great happening was and the star led them every night until eventually it came to Israel. They had been to see Herod, clearly he had no knowledge of any such happening but his advisors said that the prophets of ancient time had predicted that Bethlehem was a likely place. So they had arrived at our temporary dwelling and were convinced that our baby son had been the instigation for this heavenly happening. They were, I have always thought, a bit disappointed that they found just a small child living in a very humble inn with very humble parents and none of the usual wealth and opulence that surrounds kings. I think that they had perhaps come with the aim of making some agreement with the king so that this new great king would favour them in the future. What is absolutely true is that they only stayed in the town for one night and then disappeared towards the desert, we didn't know what to make of it. Joseph and I talked about the visit after they had left us and gradually as we thought about the possible implications all the anxiety we had felt at the temple in Jerusalem came flooding back. The fact of Jesus was becoming too well known and this was dangerous. Herod had just had both his sons and his wife murdered because they were putting it about that he was mad and they ought to take over. It was clear that he would stop at nothing to destroy any threat to his power however unlikely it may be. He may or may not believe the prophets, he may or may not believe in God's plan for the recovery of Israel, but here were these three men who had travelled for months because they were convinced something extraordinary had happened. To add to this when he questioned his experts and advisors it is sure that he would find out what Anna had been saying, what Simeon had said and probably what the shepherds had experienced. As we thought about Herod we became very frightened. We went to bed very disturbed and in the middle of the night, it was pitch black with no moon, Joseph woke me and said, he had had a dream, it was just like the dream he had had telling him it was alright to marry me, but this dream was a warning that we must leave Bethlehem right now. I told him that we couldn't go in the middle of the night, the baby was asleep and we had to pack things up and what about thanking all the people who had been so kinds to us, but he was adamant we had to go now there was no time to loose, it was an angel that had told him and it was God's instruction and was desperately urgent. So we packed what few belongings we could, crept down to the stable saddled the donkey and left. We didn't wake anyone and I felt terrible that we never said thank you to those kind people who had taken us in and cared for us and befriended us. But we were sure that if there really was a threat it was better that nobody knew where we were heading, in truth we were not sure either, what we did know was that somehow we had to get away from the influence of Herod and his murderous ways. We set off south and went as fast as the donkey could go we paid our way either with the little money Joseph had managed to put aside or by his doing little jobs in return for kindnesses provided. In this way in less than a week we crossed the border into Egypt, we had hardly stopped but now we felt safe, it was common knowledge that Herod and Cleopatra, the queen of Egypt were enemies and that his spies would find it difficult to find us particularly if we stayed totally anonymous and were just a Jewish couple who had left home and wandered to Egypt. There would surely be no questions and no difficulties. Well of course it wasn't as easy as that, we were questioned by the police, Joseph was arrested several times as an illegal immigrant but eventually we were admitted to a local Jewish Synagogue where we found many Jews who had escaped Herod and did not want anyone to know who they were. This community at the northern end of the Nile where it joins the sea was almost self sufficient they traded with places all over the world but they kept themselves separate from the local population and they were delighted to welcome a highly skilled carpenter into their midst and didn't ask any questions. We stayed there for eight years; we made a lot of good friends. Jesus learned to speak Aramaic and Greek and Hebrew, he went to the local school run by the synagogue and was an excellent pupil, he also learnt his father's skills as a carpenter and his work was greatly admired and sought after. He and Joseph, in the time we were there, completely re-fitted the synagogue with beautiful furniture and fittings. Three more children were born there and we all were thriving. Joseph and I often talked about the stories about Jesus, the predictions of the angel and of Simeon. As he was growing up he seemed such an ordinary boy, he was bright and quick-witted but he also loved doing boy things like exploring and adventures and rough games with the other boys. He was a great help round the house, particularly with his younger brother and sisters and never seemed to give us any worries. He did enjoy listening to the rabbi and discussing the ancient writings of the prophets with him. Joseph's view was that God had sent us into Egypt, God had made sure that Jesus and we were safe here and God would tell us when he wanted us to go back to Israel and until then we would stay where we were. He said God had already done amazing things and we had never understood the whys or wherefores so why should we expect to now. We had to have faith that our living in Egypt was still part of God's plan even though it seemed ordinary and routine. He said he was quite happy to live an un-exciting life and that all the excitement in the first year of our marriage would be quite enough for him if that were what God wanted from us. We had very little news from Galilee, our families must have thought we were dead, we daren't get in touch because we didn't know what threat there might still be to Jesus' life. Through all the traders passing through the town we knew that Herod was dead and that his kingdom had been divided among his three sons; that Judea was governed direct from Rome; that Antipas governed Galilee and Philip governed the north eastern province. His third son, Archelaus had been removed by the Roman authorities after continual uprisings against him that he had put down with great cruelty, including the mass crucifixion of 2,000 so called rebels. After he had been removed the situation calmed down gradually although there was a continual under swell of resentment against the Romans who had set up direct control from Damascus the Roman provincial capital, but it rarely came to open confrontation. The Roman system of law and order had actually made the country much safer to live in and although there were still highway robberies they were less frequent and the robbers themselves were dealt with severely when they were caught. I think that gradually as we talked about home we both began to think that perhaps God was ready to send us back to Galilee, we dare not talk to any one else that we were feeling un-settled but I think they sensed it. One day a neighbour told us that a Phoenician ship was in the harbour and was intending to sail direct to Ptolemais, which is only about fifteen miles from Nazareth. We went down to the harbour and talked to the master, who seemed an honourable man, he said he had room for our family and all the other stuff we wanted to take with us and that he would be leaving in two days! As usual we were now disturbed, was this God's plan or was it our selfish satisfaction of a moment of homesickness? We talked it through for hours, and were still as perplexed so we went to bed without a decision but hoping by the morning we would be surer. During the night Joseph had a dream, he didn't dream very often so when he did we took notice of it, this dream was not as direct and urgent as the one he had in Bethlehem but he was just as sure about its meaning. In the dream he was standing on a road, he couldn't make out which road it was or even which country he was in: and there was a five ways junction all the ways looked as good as the others, he remembered looking at the hills and the pathways; there was no signpost to direct him and he started to feel lost and alone and to panic, he knew that he had to move on going back or staying where he was did not seem to be options but how could he decide what to do; then into his dream came the family all looking to him to decide, and he couldn't; then he saw coming towards him up one of the roads were his brother, his father and many friends from Nazareth, they were all smiling and with arms outstretched in welcome; and there the dream ended. He woke up still very confused but perhaps more confident that going to Galilee was the right thing for them to do. So he got up before anyone else was awake and went down to the harbour, the ship's master was pacing up and down the quayside muttering to himself. He was mighty relieved when he saw Joseph; he told him that since they had talked he had been unable to get out of his mind that if he didn't take them with him some disaster would overtake him and his ship. Joseph told him that when they had talked it had only been a fancy and any way they probably couldn't afford the fare, the master said he would take whatever they could afford but they must come with him, it was a matter of life or death. Well you can imagine Joseph's confusion, he came home and over breakfast we talked again, Jesus was listening very intently to the whole story, I remember he did not take his eyes off Joseph and he once or twice asked for bits of the dream to be repeated to make sure he had heard it right. We didn't decide what to do and Joseph went off to his workshop while I busied myself round the house and with the youngest child, Jesus stayed sitting at the table very quiet and clearly thinking about all that had been said. Eventually he said very quietly, "You and my father have to finally decide, that's your duty, but if it helps you decide, I think God is calling us home and we should obey!" I looked at him very seriously and said that sea journeys were very dangerous and he said if it is God's will He would protect us and if it wasn't God's will He would still protect us to do His will later when He was ready.

Well I couldn't think of any counter argument to this so I went through to the workshop and told Joseph what had happened. Joseph looked so pleased, he said that we knew that Jesus was God's son and we should thank God that He had used Jesus to help us understand what we had to do. So now we had one day to get ready, to pack up all we wanted to take with us, to sell and give away all the things we did not want to take with us, to say goodbye to all the dear friends we had made. The children were very excited at the thought of the journey which to them was just a great adventure but they were also sad to be leaving the friends they had made and promised that one day if it was possible they would all meet again. The local rabbi was very kind and prayed over us and blessed us and gave us letters of introduction to friends he had in Ashkelon and in Ceasarea just in case we had to make a stop over on the way! Eventually all was done and we joined the ship, it seemed that the whole town had come to see us off and wish us well, we were all very tearful, parting is such great sorrow; so they went back to their mundane life and we set off on the next stage of our adventure.

The crew were very kind to us and got us settled down, out of harms way and then we were off. We had a gentle breeze off the desert and very quickly Egypt had slipped out of sight over the stern. The sea was very calm, the crew assured us, but we were all sea sick, the movement of the ship was so unexpected and the strange noises, creekings and bumpings, were alarming. We were already regretting our decision and wishing for just a small piece of dry still land to appear and we would be willingly get off, we all had a pretty miserable first day but then the next morning after we eventually got to sleep things seemed better and the sickness had gone, The sailors told us we had now got our "sea legs" and that we would manage the rest of the journey without any more sickness. The children looked at their legs very carefully to see what had changed! Of course by the morning we had no idea where we were but the master said this was one of the easier journey's he made. There was generally a fresh northerly breeze off the desert at this time of year and so we would use this as long as we could, then when it began to fail we should pick up a special wind that blew to the west in the morning and to the east in the evening and that by tacking in this wind we could continue our northerly passage. We might have to tack eastwards to find this wind as the desert wind began to fail. He said he did not want to get too close to the shore because there were always pirates on the lookout for laden merchant ships to attack, a very comforting thought! Sea journeys are boring, the daily routine, there is nowhere to go there is nobody to talk to or nothing to talk about the sea looks the same all the time. Preparing meals was a new experience but even that quickly became routine, one thing was there was always a good breeze to dry the children's clothes. Jesus was very good and set up school to teach his brother and sisters to read, he had brought a slate and stylus for them to use. He had remembered to bring some of the board games he had made, as exercises under Joseph's tuition, so that most of the time they were well entertained. When they got fractious we sang songs and invented games like I-spy or we told them the stories of the history of the people of Israel. It was difficult to maintain the strict eating disciplines particularly as the whole crew were gentiles. We managed the best we could and hoped God wouldn't notice where we failed, after all this was his idea! And so for four or five days the routine was established and it seemed that we would have a safe and uneventful sailing, the winds were just as the master had predicted and we didn't see any other ships, who might have been pirates! In fact the master told us that we had made such good progress that he now expected to be in Ptolemais in six days rather than the seven he had allowed which cheered us up. He casually said "So I need not have worried and been so determined to have you on board. The trip was OK anyway!" Joseph looked at me and we both said "You shall not take the Lord's name in vain". It was quite uncanny within an hour the wind changed direction and grew stronger and stronger. The crew were clearly very alarmed they put out sea anchors and lowered the sail so that we made less headway, they said it was a good thing the wind was off the shore and it almost immediately turned to an on-shore gale. It was terrifying, unless you have experienced it you cannot imagine how frightening it is, oh, sorry, I forgot I was talking to sailors and I know you have bad storms on Galilee. We all prayed, we, to the one true God and the crew to their various pagan deities. The storm just got worse and now night was coming on and we had had no food for hours, not that that mattered because we were all seasick again. The waves were so big that the water came over the side of the ship, we all got wet and cold and everything in the boat was soaked. Our confidence disappeared we were convinced that we would all drown, what a way to end so much endeavour! Jesus had been sitting very quietly and when he saw how panic stricken we had become he said to us, "Remember what I said to you in Egypt, God will protect us when we are doing his will and he will protect us if this is not his plan so that we can fulfil his plan eventually. You must have faith and you must not be afraid." Truth to tell he didn't look afraid; he looked absolutely calm and confident that all would be well. The sailors were sceptical and didn't see any reason why our ship should be saved in a storm when many others were lost and it was part of the risk business of shipping. If they were to drown here then that was that, end of their story! Jesus left us in the belly of the ship and went to the prow, he sat there apparently just watching the sea and not long afterwards the wind started to abate. The sailors laughed and got on with the job of sailing the ship again, the master seemed to be confident how to steer the ship and we were all so tired we went to sleep, but I knew that Jesus had been praying to God and that God had answered his prayer and that we would all be safe. So in a few days we came to Ptolemais without further incident but we were all very relieved to once again feel the firm earth under our feet, in fact, I remember we found walking difficult for a while as the road did not rise and plunge in front of us.

Well that is the longest sea voyage I have ever made and I shall not be disappointed if it is the only sea voyage I ever make! As soon as we had disembarked and said farewell to the crew and the master all of whom had become friends during the storm if not the voyage. Joseph set off to buy a donkey to carry our little possessions and the smallest children. In less than an hour he came back with a donkey and his younger brother Jonas whom he had met in the market, he was in Ptolemais doing business, selling olive oil on the "Futures Market" whatever that may have been. We were so pleased to see a friendly family face and he was absolutely overcome with pleasure, surprise and shock at finding us there, the last he had heard was that Jesus had been born in Bethlehem and nothing afterwards. Every one had assumed we were all dead! It took us two days to make the journey back to Nazareth, it was slow because of the donkey and the children and all the folk we met on the way some going west to Ptolemais and some overtaking us and going east. We had forgotten just how many people we knew and of course I had really only been a girl when we left to go to Bethlehem all those years ago. Joseph kept meeting his old friends, business acquaintances, fellow carpenters and even relatives and every time it meant a delay of an hour or so. When we eventually arrived in Nazareth; the whole town had heard we were coming and they were all out to greet us. We were celebrities, after all they had thought we were dead and there were not many of our neighbours who had ever had such adventures as we had. Joseph's mother had died in our absence but my mother was there and full of concerns for all these grandchildren she had suddenly been presented with. She had prepared a magnificent feast to celebrate our unexpected return, all the town was there and we talked and talked and laughed and cried until the night was dark and then they took us to our old house! They had kept it clean and tidy they had never let anyone work in Joseph's shop or live in the house. They said that although they had heard nothing for years they were sure that one day we would come home! They provided us with all the things we had had to leave behind in Egypt and we went to bed very tired but very, very happy it truly was a happy welcome home. Life quickly settled into a routine, there were two more children, it was a happy home and probably the happiest time of my life, so busy but so rewarding and we felt safe and secure. Joseph always had work. Some times it was contract work anywhere in Galilee. There were building works for the Romans and "important" and wealthy Jews enjoying the peace and stability of those years and spending their money on new houses and palaces. The stone masons, blacksmiths and carpenters were in great demand for the basic structural work but there was also a band of artists working to provide the final touches in the way of plasterwork, wall paintings, lead work for fountains and pools and then the very skilled mosaic artists. There was so much work that Joseph was able to pick and choose what he would do, he made sure that Jesus and the other boys all became skilled craftsmen and took them, in turn, as his apprentices to wherever he was going to work. He even sometimes chose particular jobs to make sure that they all had the right experience, he was not a hard master but he demanded that they all learned their trade and the business so that, as he said, they could use their gifts to God's good purpose in the future. He died quite suddenly when Jesus was 22, he was not ill but he went from being strong and healthy to his last breath in a few days. Jesus of course took care of everything and was then responsible for me and all his brothers and sisters, the elder boys were part of the business so in fact we were well positioned and there was never any real problems.

There was one surprising trip to Jerusalem, we went up for the Passover several times but we had one scare. I remember we had set off to come back and you all know just how chaotic it is to get a group of pilgrims together for a journey. The day before everyone agreed that we would leave at about mid morning so that we could get well on the way before nightfall. In our group there were about 30 families, a lot of people to get on the move together and we actually left, despite everyone's best endeavours at three o'clock. So off we went, Jesus was not actually with us but we were sure he was with one of the other families. It wasn't until we stopped at about five that it became clear that he was not with the group. Joseph and I both panicked, we felt negligent after all we had gone through for this child and knowing that God held us responsible for his safety. We left the rest of the family and all our belongings with friends and raced back to Jerusalem, our hearts were in our mouths, we couldn't imagine what had happened to him but we thought of every disaster possible. We even thought that somehow he had been recognised as a threat to the power of the priests or the Romans, and was arrested. When we got back to the city we had no idea where to start looking, fortunately because the main holiday celebrations were over the crush was thinning out, we went first to the guest house we where had been staying, but they assured us he had left at the same time as us and they had not seen him since. We went to the local synagogue where we knew he had made friends with the local rabbi, then through the markets asking if anyone had seen a 12 year old wandering about on his own, most people were very kind but a few said that most of the 12 year old boys they had ever seen were wandering about on their own! Of course they were right but that just made us feel more desperate to find him. By now it was dark, what were we to do? What if our paths had crossed and he was already on his way to join us? Should we go back to the group? Where should we look next? Then Joseph said "Come on, we'll go and look in the Temple, if he is not there we will have to assume that he has set off and so shall we, the matter is in God's hands and he will look after things, he always has done." Brave words when your firstborn has gone missing! We made haste to the Temple, the Courtyard of the Gentiles was almost empty, so was the Courtyard of the Women and Joseph then went on into the inner sanctum and returned in only a few minutes with Jesus firmly held by the hand. You can imagine how relieved I was, and not a little cross but when I remonstrated with him all he said was "Why should you be anxious? You must have known that I would be about my Father's business." Joseph was absolutely calm and just said, "Come on we have to hurry; we have other children to look after as well." without another word he set off almost running to catch up with our group and our family. Nothing more was said, but later when we were quiet and it was just us two Joseph told me that he had found Jesus surrounded by a group of obviously learned men discussing the Law. They were surprised when Joseph called Jesus away and several of these grand old men said what an advanced grasp the youngster had of these things! Mary said that that was nearly all that there was to say, about 6 months ago Jesus had come to her and announced that he had to start his real work. He told her that things would not be easy and that some great important destiny awaited him, he told her that she and the family would be cared for, but now he had to go to do other things. Without more ado he went he took no money nothing except his staff and he was away for all of four months. When he came home he stayed only for a few days and then set off on his journey. Somehow he had become remote but had an inexplicable presence, when he was there everyone had their eyes on him, when he spoke they all listened and were amazed at what he said. He was never condescending, never critical of people but always confident and always making people think about themselves and their behaviour and their belief. Then he started curing people and since then the crowds have followed him wherever he goes. She said that she and her daughter Ann had decided that he needed somebody to care for him and so they had left everything and followed him. Wherever he went, they went, they never asked for a plan, they never expected to be consulted, they were always now absolutely sure that although each day was an adventure with no security, every day ended that they were not hungry, they had a place to sleep and people were very friendly. They had got used to the idea that sometimes Jesus just took off into the hills by himself, he wanted nobody with him and he always came back full of energy and enthusiasm however tired and warn he may have been when he set out. This trip to Bethsaida was completely unexpected and much to their surprise the crowds had literally disappeared so that he had some space to himself. This was most unusual; the norm was frenetic activity always on the move, always crowds of people and Jesus stopping quite unexpectedly to cure the sick, to comfort the unloved and to use everyday situations to teach about God. Clearly he knew he needed help in his work and somehow he knew who would help him, so here we were.

There was a long silence while we absorbed what this loving patient mother had told us, it took a while for us to begin to understand what we had got into, this was revolution! Serious stuff! Did we really have the stomach for it? The old rabbi in Capernaum was right we had been called and we did believe what John the Baptiser had said in the desert "This is the one!" The afternoon was wearing into evening and there were very encouraging noises from the kitchen and then quite suddenly Jesus was back with us. As Mary had said he was full of energy and wanted to be off there and then. It took not a little of Mary's motherly persuasion that he should stay the night as had been arranged.

91

Part 10

The calling of More disciples

The next morning we were all up early and breakfasted and loaded the ship but Jesus was nowhere to be found. Mary said that he would normally have gone out early in the morning on his own into the countryside to pray, but she had not heard him this morning. We saw him coming up the beach from the far side of town and with him was another man. When they arrived he introduced us to Phillip, although it was a Greek name this man was a son of Abraham, we never did discover what he did "before Jesus" but I think he was probably in trade, you know buying and selling all sorts of commodities when he had the opportunity. Bethsaida was a very good place for an enterprising entrepreneur as a seaport and on the Arabian caravan route to Damascus. His face was familiar, and he said he came from Bethsaida but James and John didn't know him though they admitted they had seen him about, they only knew the people in the fish industry. I think he had been born in Cyprus, hence his Greek name and his fluency in the language and had come to Bethsaida when he had grown up. He was married and later his wife joined our party when we went to Jerusalem, his children two boys and two girls were grown up and they took over his business when he accepted the call and the family prospered just as Jesus had promised. His wife, whose name was Marion, told us that her husband had been sitting outside the warehouse with the two boys looking through the business accounts, when Jesus approached him and challenged him to follow Him. Phillip was very surprised by this approach and tried to object, and to explain that he was not worthy to be God's servant and that although he understood business he had never seriously thought through fundamental religious beliefs and how could he possibly preach to others about the power of God. The boys witnessed all this monologue of excuses and Jesus patiently let him finish and then said "Phillip, do you think that I don't know all that and more, do you think that God doesn't know that and every inner thought and anxiety that you have? No this is all known to me as it is to you but I tell you God needs you, He needs you now this moment there is no time to be wasted you have to obey." Phillip was astounded, how did Jesus know all this? How did he have such confidence? There was no aggression in his manner only an intense urgency. The boys, who had listened to all this conversation, told to their father, "We are sure this is what you should do, we are also sure that we can run the business and care for all the family while you are away however long that may be. This is the chance of your life, how many times have you said to us all that you thought that trade was really a waste of time that you would never leave your mark on the world, so go and join this adventure and perhaps you will be remembered as one of the ones who did change the world, or contributed to changing the world, if you don't go you will never know what might have happened, good or bad." So Phillip had then wanted to explain to his wife what was happening, they stopped him and agreed that they would break the news so that he did not have to deal with all the objections she would raise. They told him, "Listen to this man, he says there is no time to be lost so go, and go now, just give us your blessing and we give you ours but if you are to go you must go this moment!" Jesus was very quiet and said to the boys, " If there was only a tiny part of your faith in all Israel then Mankind would be saved." and he blessed them with this blessing "Father in heaven, bless this family, and these two young men, May the Lord bless you and keep you, may he protect you and all you love and care for from this time forth and for ever more." Then he turned to Phillip and said with a tone of finality "Come on Phillip we have a boat to catch!" With that Phillip got up and left! And, said Marion "You know the rest of the story better than I do!"

At the time that he joined us he said very little about his being called but later he told us that his experience was very similar to our own, he remembered clearly the piercing eyes the kindly confident face but the intense sense of determination and command and urgency that forced Phillip to accept the challenge. Like us Phillip had witnessed John's desert proclamations, he had thought long and hard before Jesus appeared that morning about what he should be doing to further the "preparing a way" for the Emmanuel. He was convinced that Jesus was this God given prince after just one short meeting. This man had great presence and an air of calm surrounded him, we were to learn to respect him for his wise judgement and understanding as the next months rolled by.

Jesus seemed very pleased and relaxed; he had a quick breakfast and told us we should be off as soon as possible or we might miss the favourable morning wind! He didn't acknowledge that we had all been waiting for him for well over an hour! There was plenty of room for us all and very quickly we were speeding across the sea with a good wind behind us. In less than two hours we could see the harbour walls at Capernaum and then we were safely back to our familiar moorings.

Jesus spent the trip talking to us, that is the five of us, about what we would be doing, he warned us that we had a hard time ahead but that we should always remember that we were doing God's work. He said that he would be preaching and teaching and showing great signs to the people of Galilee and that eventually we would all go to Jerusalem where even greater things would happen. Our discipleship was to learn as quickly as possible because we would have to do our own teaching and preaching. We had to listen carefully to all he said and that if we didn't understand to ask him to explain. He needed a group of loyal dedicated people round him to manage the daily round, although he warned us, even then, that God would decide the plans and we would implement those plans however unlikely they seemed to be. He also told us very forcefully that we had to learn to trust God absolutely, without any reservations. God would look after our daily needs for food and shelter and rest, he knew our needs before we did and all we had to do was to ask and all our needs would be satisfied. He told us that the inner team would be twelve and that he would be collecting the remainder in the next few days. (Afterwards we agreed among ourselves that twelve would be to rally the remnants of the twelve sons of Israel.)

We unloaded the boat and set off to Peter's house, my Mother and father had seen us coming into port and guessed we would go to Peter's place, we were now a big party, and they wanted to catch up with our news. Jonas was horrified to find James and John had also been co-opted into this project. What he asked was going to happen to the business without, not just two of the senior members, but now all four of them! What, he repeated, did Zebedee think of this, how had he let it happen, how could they possibly run a business and plan their futures if the main people were just able to walk off the job? He took a long time to calm down but eventually, after Jesus had talked to him quietly and privately, just as he had one with Zebedee, he acknowledged that if it was God's will then he had to accept it.

Our party was now substantial, there was Jesus and us five, then there was Mary and her daughter and then Zebedee's wife and two servants. Peter's wife was very calm about the whole thing; although she had every right to feel abandoned and then overwhelmed with visitors. We couldn't possibly all stay there so we were distributed among our several houses. Jesus took no interest in any of these practical matters, he talked to Jonas and my mother for a while and then announced that he was going out for a while and would be back for dinner at sunset, with that off he went! Quite obviously, we five, that is James, John, Philip, Peter and myself, Andrew, were not needed and so we got on with the practical things and told the rest of the family the amazing adventures we had had and the story that Mary had told us about Jesus' birth and up-bringing. Every one was quite astounded and particularly when we combined those stories with what John the Baptiser had said in the desert when Jesus asked to be baptised. Mary was very quiet and said little except to give nodding confirmation as we repeated the story. I thought how simple and unassuming this woman was, who had already had an amazing life and heaven only knew what was going to happen next. The women organised the accommodation so that everyone had a bed to sleep on and were just working out how to feed everyone when Jesus reappeared and there with him was none other than Matthew the tax collector from the harbour!

We could not believe it, we were all good honest sons of Abraham and did our best to keep the law, we obeyed all the strictures that put on us, we were regular well respected members of the Synagogue, part of the established Jewish society in the town and were proud of our reputation. So here is Jesus with a well known publican and sinner, a man who we knew but who worked for the enemy, a man with a reputation, like all his sort, for extortion and dishonesty, a man completely ostracised by proper law abiding Jews, a man who would not be allowed inside the synagogue and who certainly would not be allowed into our house! What were we to do? Peter said to Jesus " Do you know who this man is? Do you know what this man is? He cannot come into our house!" Jesus replied very gently and quietly but very firmly, "Peter, Matthew has been called by God to be with me just as you and Andrew and James and John and Phillip have been. I have told you all that you have to have absolute trust in God however unlikely the situation may be in your eyes. In God's eyes Matthew is the same as you all and it is not for you to judge what God has ordained. You have to understand and to remember the story of the Good Shepherd I told you only two days ago, that I have come to save the lost sheep of the flock of Israel!" Well, Peter and all the rest of us were dumb-founded, we did not know how to react. How do you suddenly exchange greetings with a man who only a minute ago you would not go near or have anything to do with? Did Jesus expect us to eat with this man? Did Jesus expect us to have him stay in our house? Worse still did he expect us to publicly accept this man as our equal? We were horrified at the prospect, our families were even more alarmed they knew that they would have to live with a tarnished reputation in the town and might even become outcasts themselves from the very social group they valued most.

Jesus must have sensed the tension in the air, he asked us all to be quiet and calm and to all hold hands in a ring and then he prayed "Dear Father and master of all men, who gives us all our being, whose power is infinite, whose love is infinite, who understands our most private and inner thoughts. Help us to understand that in your sight all men are equal and that the distinctions that men make between themselves are against your will and show us how little real love we have for each other. You have chosen Matthew to be our brother, help us to share your love to us in our love to him, help us to make him a welcome fully appreciated and integrated member of our group to strengthen us all to fulfil your need."

There was total silence you could have heard a pin drop, nobody spoke nobody moved. I am sure that we all felt in an impossible situation. We couldn't reject the man after that but how could we not only accept him but with open arms to welcome him? Eventually Mary broke the silence and said to Matthew, "Please come and tell me about your family, and your work and I will tell you something about this son of mine although he does keep springing surprises on us all!" They sat together for quite a while, Matthew kept looking up rather sheepishly at us, but gradually the tension started to relax especially when the two of them burst into laughter. Clearly it had taken more courage from him to come with Jesus to our house than we could imagine, he knew he would be rejected and publicly shamed, but he told us sometime afterwards that Jesus had told him that God needed him and that he cannot escape, and that he must have confidence that all would be well. Of course it was and all the fears we had, and our families had were unfounded and disappeared like mist in the morning. There were some locals who gossiped and "wagged their fingers" but the local rabbi was pleased to support the family and to stop the tittle-tattle really before it had time to start. The rabbi confided in my parents that he had had many conversations with Jesus over the years when Jesus used to come as his father's apprentice and then later in his own right as a skilled carpenter doing contract work in the town. He did not know what we were to find out but he believed that Jesus had a very special calling and anybody who joined his mission was to be supported and not ridiculed. At the next Sabbath Jesus gave a homily on the love of God continually searching for the lost and sinful Israelites, and clearly exposed the hypocrisy of people who assumed to know God's judgement of who was lost and sinful; when all men were lost and sinful in God's eyes.

We were all desperately trying to come to terms with Matthew's arrival among us when Jesus said that we, that is the five of us were invited to dine with him at Matthew's house and some of his friends that evening. We had never faced such a test, how could Jesus ask us to do this thing, getting to know and trust and be open with one "publican and sinner" was as big a challenge as we could face in one day and we were all about to object when he turned to us and in a voice of command said "And you will all be very pleased to accept his most generous invitation!" So there was no possibility of not accepting the invitation but we were extremely nervous, not that we would be abused though there was some risk of that, not that the conversation would be coarse or blasphemous, no, we were anxious because the Jewish laws specifically forbade a Jew who wanted to be pure and acceptable in the sight of God to eat with any person who was not of the same "pure" condition. By definition and their own admission the people we would be eating with were "unclean". In fact there were many men who were unclean not because of their behaviour or religious scruples but just because of their work or even their father's work! We could be fairly sure that because Matthew was a tax assessor and gatherer the people who he would invite to his dinner would be tax men or other Jews who were working for the Romans and had by Jewish definition sullied their hands and their souls beyond redemption and were lost to any possible reconciliation to God. The danger we feared most, was not what other people might say about us, but that we believed that we were putting our souls at risk of eternal damnation by associating with these men. We knew Matthew, he was the tax assessor for the harbour who collected all the taxes that we paid to Caesar, to Herod Antipas, to the Roman governor in Damascus and to the tetrarch Herod Phillip and he was quite understandably a person we detested or should have detested, he was from what we knew about as straight as a taxman could be, but he was still a taxman. It was held to be an absolute truism that taxmen were all rich because they added their own percentage to the taxes they were charged to collect and this extra found its way into their own pockets. They were charged by the authorities to collect a specified tax revenue from the activity they controlled, it didn't matter for him whether fishing was good or bad, it didn't matter to him that we had to spend money on new boats, the only thing that mattered was the tax revenue and his percentage. You can see that these men were hated and ostracised, when times were good they did very well and even when times were hard they did very well!! To the man in the street they deserved the penalty of eternal damnation; no punishment was too severe.

We were very upset, but Jesus in his calming, way persuaded us that our souls were not in danger whereas their souls were in danger and we had to show them that they could save themselves if they so desired and

97

that was what we had to find out, and that was why we were having dinner with them. He was convincing and so we went, we had hoped to have the cover of darkness to cover our visit but it was too early and it was still day light as we walked together through the streets of Capernaum where we were all well known and respected. By the time we turned into the courtyard of the house of Matthew the tax collector we must have been seen by dozens of neighbours and we found it all very embarrassing and sinful. We were welcomed most graciously all the washing and cleansing formalities were respected; the placing of the guests around the table was properly done and respected the status of the guests. Jesus had not taken the seat of honour when he came in but was asked to take it by Matthew. The meal was sumptuous; we could see where our taxes were going! The thing that really surprised us was that these men were businessmen just like us; they were trying to make a better living for themselves and their families in a very competitive market. They talked about the things we talked about, like the harvest, the local politics, the national politics, the international politics, religion, wars and plagues and security and travel. They had a different relationship with Matthew, they teased him about his wealth, they teased him about his bosses but they made friends with him. It helped them and it helped him, he learned what was going on, he could feed this back to his bosses including views of anxieties about politics and resistance to taxes and he could help these peoples to minimise their tax commitment by avoidance rather than evasion. It was clear that they were all friends though they were clearly competitors as well, it was also clear that they did not behave like men whose main concern was that they faced eternal damnation. Most of the conversation was in Greek, surprisingly, although most of the guests were locals they seemed to be more at ease with this foreign language. We could all speak some Greek and mostly understood it well enough but we would never consider using it as a social language. In fact, because these men were so fluent, we began to feel the isolated group, and it was a great relief that at least Phillip could chatter with absolute ease and help us when we stumbled. When the dinner was coming to an end Jesus spoke and suddenly an expectant silence fell across the room. He didn't raise his voice, there was something urgent and sincere about his tone that made everyone stop and listen and he told this story.

"Matthew, our host invited me with my friends, to come to dine with you this evening, he has accepted God's command that he should leave his work, his family and his friends and to join me and our small band to do God's work. You have heard it said that a great saviour of the people has been promised by the prophets, that time is now and you will see and hear amazing things. You are ostracised by others as "publicans and sinners", you are all very surprised that I should come and dine with you as you know the rules of the Pharisees as well as I do, but the time has come when human rules will be pushed aside and God's judgement will be seen."

"The kingdom of heaven is like this."

"If one of you had an hundred sheep and loses one of them, does he not leave the ninety-nine in the open pasture and go for the missing one until he has found it? How delighted he is then! He lifts it on his shoulder, and home he goes to call his friends and neighbours together. "Rejoice with me!" he cries, " I have found my lost sheep." In the same way, I tell you there will be greater joy in heaven over one sinner who repents than over ninety-nine people who do not need to repent."

There was silence in the room; all eyes were fixed on Jesus. Then an old man who had been a "sinner" all his life and was despised by the Scribes and Pharisees; he was convinced that his soul would burn in Hell forever, asked Jesus, with tears in his eyes and a cracking voice, "Master, do you mean that there is still hope for even a man like me?"
    Jesus replied, "I have come to save sinners, to offer them forgiveness for their sins when they repent and to show them that God's love applies to all men."
    Then another man said to him " Why should we believe what you say, after all the scribes and Pharisees have been teaching the will of God for all time? What is so special about you that we should do as you say and completely change our way of life? We are considered by everyone to be so far lost; like the sheep you talked about, that it hardly matters how sinful we are now, we can never be saved."
    Jesus said to him, "It is for you to decide, I offer you redemption, that means that you can "wipe the slate clean" and start again, but you have to be true to yourself and to God. You have to be confident and to have faith that redemption means salvation and salvation means eternal life."
    Then another man joined in and asked him "We know who you are, you are the carpenter who has worked here and in all the towns of Galilee. We know you are a skilled craftsman, that you are honest and reliable and then suddenly you are giving us promises that only God can give. How can "you" promise "us" eternal life?"
    Jesus said to him "The time is now, the One who goes before has been to forewarn the world of the arrival of Emmanuel. There is no

time to delay, you, each one of you have to decide whether you will welcome the Son of God and seek his forgiveness or whether you will continue on the path which will lead you to eternal damnation. You will, in the next few months, see or hear of great happenings of wonders and of revelations of God's will. Many people will accept the challenge and many will not. But I will ask you this question in return for yours. Where else can you turn to put your soul at rest and to escape from the sentence that you now have to accept from the Scribes and Pharisees?"

Then another of Matthew's friends, who had been tut-tutting at everything that Jesus said took his chance in a gap in the conversation to address the company. He was not really asking a question but wanted to remind the guests of their Jewishness, he did not even look at Jesus, and the gist of what he said was, "You sons of Abraham, why do you listen to this man, don't you remember that we are the Blessed people chosen by God as his special people. We have been promised that we will govern the world, that we will be received into heaven that even when we are sinful we are worth more to God that any other people. Are you just going to forget all the promises that we have received from the Prophets and listen to this "carpenter"? Without our effort and despite our "sins", that the Pharisees keep reminding us of we are all saved, we don't need all this stuff about repentance and forgiveness it's already ours!"

Quite a few of the guests were nodding their heads and one said, "How do you think we stay sane? We know that we cannot obey all the rules the Pharisees invent, the only thing we have to hold onto is the knowledge that we are God's Sacred People."

Jesus listened very closely to these outbursts and then he told another story.

"There was a rich man who had two sons, he had many sheep and goats, he had vineyards and farms and his barns were always full, he and his family and their servants were never in need. The younger son became restless and dissatisfied with this comfortable life and wanted to become "his own man" not dependent on his father. These feelings of discontent grew and grew and eventually he went to his father and demanded his share of his inheritance now. His father was very concerned and alarmed for him but in the end he gave him his share and full of confidence he set off to make his fortune in a far country. Well for a while he prospered but then he fell in with bad company who led him astray and he led a debauched and sinful life, very quickly all his assets were squandered and he was left penniless, all the "friends" he thought he had deserted him and he was left destitute. To stay alive he had to take the most menial tasks, even feeding a herd of pigs and eating the food thrown out for them. He remembered the home and family he left and regretted what he had done after along time and with real anxiety that he would be rejected he plucked up his courage and determined to return to his father's home. In his rags and with no possessions he made his way home. His father had kept faith and every day he had searched the horizon for his son and then one day he saw him coming home, he was delighted he ordered a feast to be prepared to welcome him home, and then set off to meet him. His son, when they met, fell to the ground and asked forgiveness and asked for some sort of security in his father's house, he knew he could no longer be his son but perhaps he could be a servant. His father would have none of it and told him he was still his son and would be given all the privileges that a son should expect.

However when his elder brother, who had worked on the estates all the time of his brother's absence heard what was happening, he was angry and jealous. Why, he asked, "Can this 'ne'er do well' just walk back and carry on as if nothing had happened, and then be given a welcome and acclamations he, who had always stayed at home and worked for his father, had never received?" His father took him to one side and explained that of course everything was his. His situation had not changed but he should be delighted that his lost brother had returned."

After a few seconds of silence while Jesus allowed his words to sink in, he continued, "The father is God and the younger son is the people of Israel, they have left his household and have wandered away, they think they know better than God. But some individuals know how far they have fallen and are trying to find their way back to God's favour. God has come out to welcome them home, these wanderers who individually are repentant and seeking forgiveness and he promises them this forgiveness and his blessing. There are those who cannot accept the idea that redemption is available and make the return of these penitents impossible, I am here at God's command to make the return of sinners welcome, but I am also here to warn Israel that I am the only way to recover God's blessing. Being a son does not give automatic access to the fathers riches, it is only through repentance and forgiveness of sins that this can be achieved!"

There was now a long silence while the diners considered all they had heard, clearly many people were greatly disturbed and very uncomfortable with the challenge they were facing. Intimate conversations gradually started round the table as men talked about the issues.

One man said to me, "Well we didn't expect anything like this. Usually Matthews dinner parties are very light hearted, jolly times when we "put the world to rights", he did warn us that he was sure that tonight would be different and he wasn't wrong. But how can you all, the six of you just walk away from all your responsibilities?"

I told him, "When God called you, you could not refuse. I went to the desert to hear John the Baptiser and had thought about the Emmanuel, and had restudied the sacred word of the law as given to us by Moses so perhaps we were a little prepared. The reality was that when Jesus said "Come and follow Me." I did. I have had moments of doubt but he is very understanding but very persuasive." I finished by telling him that this evening may well be the start of his accepting God's call to him.

Another man asked me " Does he really mean that Jews are no longer a special people?" I was not sure what to say but Jesus seemed to have heard this challenge, he said, "The "special relationship" was not what the Jews had made, it was what God had made and God had not withdrawn from his commitment. The Jews had withdrawn from their commitment and despite his forgiving them many, many times they were still wandering away. God wanted to bring them back to his way and that when they did they would be the example to the world of the benefits that are derived from having faith in God, and the promise would be fulfilled!" On the other side of the table I could hear Peter saying the same sort of things to others. He emphasised that Jesus kept repeating to us that we had to have confidence in God, we were doing God's work and God would care for our every need and would save and defend us! The extraordinary thing was that it seemed to work out just as he said it would. Peter said that we had no idea where we would be going tomorrow or why but by time we went to bed tomorrow we would be able to work out some of the why's and wherefores. The Zebedee brothers were trying to explain how they came to be part of the Jesus band, but were not able to explain at all except that Jesus had such a persuasive confident commanding way that it was not possible to refuse. They were explaining that it could be that the Jonas/Zebedee fishery business had been robbed of its four most senior men on the other hand it could be concluded that the company was to be the support to us four as we did God's work and that because it was being used that way it would thrive. They were absolutely sure that that was the case and that the company and the families it provided for would be protected. It was interesting that so many people were interested in how we had responded; I felt sure that Jesus words had struck a point of stress or insecurity that was common to all these apparently self confident, arrogant, economically successful businessmen.

Peter and I had heard the story of the lost sheep two nights before when Jesus talked to the travellers at the inn on our way to Bethsaida. For James, John, Phillip and of course Matthew this was the first time they had heard Jesus teaching by using stories as parallels to the reality of life. When we all discussed the story later in the evening we found that there were many levels to the story and it was probable that everyone who heard it could have his own reaction and draw his own conclusions. We were sure that Jesus intended the story to be repeated and re-told and that the lessons may be learnt, but that did not reduce our anxiousness that the when the Scribes and Pharisees heard it they would see it as an overt criticisms of their stewardship of Israel. They would see it as a challenge to their power position in our society and would attack us, in whatever way they could and they had many possibilities.

The other very significant part of this parable was that the lost sheep was "lost" and the Shepherd, God went out to look for it, he didn't ask any pre-conditions from the sheep, the sheep didn't ask to be saved, the sheep probably didn't know that being saved was a possibility, the sheep may not even have known it was lost and yet God cared enough to go and seek this lost sheep (or soul) and bring him back to the care and love of God. Another aspect was that the other sheep in the flock took no trouble to save the lost sheep; their behaviour was typical of sheep. If he is lost it is probably his fault, if he is lost we have more important things to do caring for the other sheep and the other excuse, "it was all his own fault he didn't obey the rules that we had made quite clear, so we are blameless, oh! And by the way, this sheep had always been a nuisance more like a goat than a sheep and he had a funny smell about him." Then we started to talk about the rules that governed our society that in the light of this story, when you really thought about it seemed to be designed by the Lawyers and the Scribes and the Pharisees to exclude people from God, to force them to become "lost Sheep". What a terrible indictment, what a clear accusation that the rulers of the Jews really were the "bad shepherds" as opposed to Jesus claim that he is the "good shepherd". Then Peter reminded us that when Jesus demanded that we follow him he promised that he would make us "fishers of men" we thought at the time what a strange thing to say but perhaps saving the lost souls of Israel was what he meant!

By now it was late, we walked back through the sleeping town to our allotted sleeping quarters, Peter and I were lucky we were staying in our own beds, but it would not be many more times that that would happen. Jesus was very cheerful and talked and talked about the day, the interesting people we had met, what a splendid evening we had had, how pleased he was that Matthew had joined and how important he was going to be in the future. He didn't talk about plans for the next day and when eventually Peter had the temerity to ask whether we should go fishing in the morning, he was quite sharp and told us that our past lives were over, we were now God's servants and in God's loving care and that it was God alone who would decide what tomorrow would bring. With that he gave us a blessing, said goodnight and went to his bed.

The next morning after we had breakfasted in our various dwellings we all met together at Peter's house, Jesus and Mary had been sleeping there but as on yesterday morning Jesus was nowhere to be found. The conversation was very lively, wives and brothers and sisters and all the in-laws were putting every argument they could muster to try to convince us to give up this wild project. They talked about the risks to us and to them, they accused us of having no love for them, of deserting them and failing in our duty to honour our family. When that didn't work they recounted all the disasters that had overtaken people who had previously tried to save Israel from his sinful ways and why did we think we were different.

Suddenly Jesus was with us, he was standing right there in the middle of this crush of agitated people nobody noticed him arrive, we did not know how long he had been there or what he had overheard, perhaps we were all too busy to notice that he was there. The effect was dramatic, the first thing was that we all fell silent, for a few moments he said nothing. He just looked at us all. I felt that my very soul was being examined, His gentle perceptive eyes seemed to gather everything about me in an instant, I was ashamed that I had said some things that were not true, things that were selfish, things that were disloyal, things that were aggressive and things that I knew that I would regret. As his eyes moved round the group I could see others having the same thoughts, some people were in tears and could not look at his face. Without the slightest tone of judgement in his voice he said to us all, "I have to ask you for a great sacrifice each of you have to give up hopes and plans for the future, you have to give up the security of the present situations you know and understand, you have to see your loved ones take risks that neither they nor you can justify. But I say to you, your sacrifice is needed; God has demanded that these men, whom you love and care for, follow me. I assure you that you must have faith and confidence and that all will be well. The sacrifice that you are all making will be recognised and wondered at from generation to generation forever, many a tear will be shed when in future times this story is told. I only hope that one day you will see the great privilege and honour that God has imparted to your sons and husbands and fathers to be a part of Emmanuel and to witness the power of God at work in the world. In time to come it will be seen that their witness and loyalty have changed the world and that without your sacrifice this would not have happened." There was a pause, quite clearly, although everyone had heard his words there was still a high level of hurt, disappointment and disbelief, but Jesus, even though he knew this, had said enough and turned away saying, "This morning we are going to go to Nazareth, there is work for us there." and he walked away knowing that we would follow!

Part 11

Nazareth

Nazareth is at least 20 miles from Capernaum, and probably more, so we knew it would take more than a day and we would have to stop somewhere over night. There was no discussion about where we might stay and we had brought a little money with us but not enough to provide an overnight stay for our ever-increasing group, we were beginning to know the answer so we didn't ask "Where will we stay?" Matthew asked us quietly what arrangements had been made and we assured him that all would be cared for and we should not be concerned. He looked quite amazed that we could adopt such a laid back attitude. Jesus led the way and we, that is the six of us followed, and the women followed on a little later when they had collected a few belongings together. To start with we walked in silence trying to come to terms with what Jesus had said and to become accustomed to the enormity of the situation we had accepted. Jesus, as was the norm, was leading the way, he walked maybe fifty yards or so in front of us, he set a cracking pace and didn't slow whether the road was steep or flat, rough or smooth, on he went, he did not look round to see that we were still there. He spoke politely to other travellers on the road and wished them 'Good Day and a safe journey', whoever they were, Jews and gentiles all the same but he was not to be deflected from his intention of getting to Nazareth, his whole body language demonstrated here is a man with a plan.

The route from Capernaum takes you on the coast road towards Tiberias, it is about eight miles and there are fishing towns, like Genneseret and Magdala every mile or so along the lakeside and as we went along we saw many people we knew, mostly other fishermen working at their nets or filleting the catch or all the other routine jobs. We could not stop to pass the time of day with them as we would normally have done and had to call to them we were on our way to Nazareth and we were in a hurry. They all looked very surprised and not a little offended as we brushed past them and they called out after us "What ever could be so important in Nazareth?" We avoided answering because we didn't know the answer, but we did feel that we were making a spectacle of ourselves to add to all the other worries we were brooding over. The countryside is fairly flat. There are one or two ridges but nothing really steep, it was still fairly early and the air was fresh and sweet, most of the way we had shelter from the sun from the shade of trees. Everywhere there was the sounds bees and the perfume of the wild flowers, I had forgotten how beautiful the countryside is, our lives seemed to be just work and no time to relax and despite the anxieties as the morning wore on we all began to enjoy the fresh air and exercise.

Gradually conversations started among the six of us, we had all made the decision that had ended with us walking together this morning. There was no point in going over that again, the most significant thing we had to discuss was just what Jesus meant when he had said that people would wonder at the sacrifice we were all making for ever and ever.

Now Peter came to the fore, he spoke to us with confidence. "I think I understand what we are about. I am sure that what we have seen so far is clearly the start of a revolution against the Scribes, the Pharisees and the whole " establishment" of the Jewish religion. First of all the story of the "Good Shepherd"; clearly that is a direct criticism of the priesthood from the highest to the lowest that they had no care for people and in fact set about having a system of exclusion. Then there was last night's dinner with Matthew, wasn't this a demonstration that people matter more than the rules the priests have made. Again Jesus was saying, very publicly, that God takes no notice of human rules if they separate people from God. And then there was that story about the rich man's son to show us how far Israel had wandered from the true walk with God, with the challenge the he, Jesus, had come to show Israel the way to repentance and forgiveness. So it was quite clear that we were to be the vanguard of a revolution not against the Romans but against the Jewish authorities. To replace them with a new set of rules based on a new fresh interpretation of the Law. When Jesus had said that we were important in this work, clearly we would become the replacement authorities for the interpretation of the Law, we would become the replacement for the Scribes and the Priests and the Lawyers and the Sadducees and finally the ultimate Sanhedrin. That explains why he had said that we would be remembered forever! And that explains how we would be a party to changing the world."

That seemed to cheer everyone up for a while, perhaps we were all thinking about taking over all the power of the state and that we would all be rich and famous, which is why he could tell our families that all would be well.

Then James said, "I think that we should be very careful, revolutions are quite easy to start but not so easy to control once they had started and any way the Romans would hardly let a revolution take place however much we might protest that this was a change internal to the Jewish religion. We had all seen or heard, only too often, what happened when Rome felt her power was challenged. How a small band of ordinary people from the fringe of the Jewish state who know about fishing and things but know nothing about government could possibly expect to challenge any one!"

Phillip joined in, "Perhaps Jesus doesn't know either quite what was to be done or how things will work out. Already we had seen how he depended on his absolute trust and faith in God to decide what was to be done next. What I find most difficult is that there is no plan. Perhaps the plan is to convert the Jews or overthrow Rome. I would feel a bit less detached from everything if there was some plan."

Peter reminded us, "On the few occasions when we have broached this subject with Jesus the answer was always the same "We are doing God's work and God will decide, do not be afraid or anxious! But if we are to help we ought to be taken into God's confidence to tell us where we were going, so that we could see how we could help!"

Matthew had said very little up till now. He was still in a bit of shock, yesterday evening although he had accepted Jesus' challenge life had seemed almost normal.

He then shared with us what had happened after the dinner party last evening, "I think you all agree the dinner went off very well, after most of the guests had gone several of my friends had stayed behind and promised that they would care for his wife and family while he was away. Ruth, his wife, had been furious at his behaviour and he had not had much sleep while she went over and over his disloyalty to her and the children. She accused him of not caring if she and the children ended up destitute and begging on the streets. She agreed that the very presence of Jesus was disturbing but she was convinced that for "sinners and publicans" like them the best policy was to give him a wide berth. She really was very upset. Despite my love for her and the children I know that I can't refuse the challenge Jesus has presented to me. This morning she had calmed down completely when Jesus suddenly appeared when everyone was "going on", this morning. I keep hoping and praying that she will be all right by time we get home, whenever that might be." He was really becoming quite depressed and wondering about his decision making ability which he had always been quite proud of, so it was with some relieve that he found that the rest of the six seemed to be just as confused and insecure. When the chance came he told us that he had been incredibly impressed that Jesus and the rest of us had deigned to come to eat at his table last night and that if this was the sort of demolition of social barriers that Jesus intended to introduce to show that God cared for every one then that was a good thing as far as he could see.

I asked him, "How do you think a society could operate if there were no rules or sanctions against people who break the rules?"

He replied, "I don't think that that was what Jesus had said it was more that God's laws were very simple and straight forward, like "thou shalt not steal". Then the lawyers and the Pharisees make up all sorts of rules that make it almost impossible for people not to steal and then tell everyone "you'll all go to hell apart from us, because we make the rules!" All of you, have managed to keep clear of the system by not noticeably breaking all these nit-picking rules, and that he had failed and had been totally excluded from the comfort and support that the Law should have provided. I don't feel "bad"; I feel the system has made me wear a label saying "bad". I am willing to give up all I have to try to help Jesus, and God, help people like me to be reconciled with God again and to be able to make a worthwhile contribution to society as a whole!"

I remember that made us all think hard for a while and in the end we began to agree that the system could be grossly unfair to people and prevented them ever finding redemption and perhaps this was a necessary change to prepare the way for a revolution in the way power was operated in our society. Well it was all getting a bit deep and hypothetical, it was also getting hot!

We had gradually started to climb out of the lush lake side plain where the fields and orchards were abundant and onto the wooded slopes. Now the air was less full of the sound of bees and more of the sound of sheep bells and shepherds' flutes! We were all quiet for a while. I remember we had just past through Magdala, I was beginning to feel hungry when, as if he knew this Jesus left the road and walked up a side track and after a little while we came to a lonely farmhouse. The farm dogs had heard us coming and by time we came in sight the farmer and all his family were there to greet us. It was quite extraordinary, it was as though they had been waiting for us, the farmer's wife had fresh cool water there for us to drink a tent awning had been set up and there was lunch waiting for us. It was clear that Jesus knew these people, he had probably visited them with his father in the past, but how they knew we would be here today and how many, it was quite amazing, there was no way Jesus could have warned them! After a while the women arrived, I was surprised to find my wife, Ruth, with them, and was delighted to learn that she and Peter's wife, Judith, together with the other women of our extended family had decided last night that she and Judith would share the task of caring for their wandering husbands, "one month about" and that Ruth would take the first turn.

The meal was a simple farmers lunch enough to sustain us but not so much a to make us too tired to walk on! Jesus was delightful, he was cheerful and entertaining, he included everyone in the conversation. Even the women, who would not normally have been included in any discussion, were persuaded to join us and add their views to our adventure. The awning had been slung between two trees and we looked out across the sea, towards the northeast. We could pick out almost the whole route we had walked and there in the distance was Capernaum, even further away were the hills of the desert and we knew that tucked under them and on the sea shore was Bethsaida, we all hoped everything there that we loved so much was under control. Jesus talked mostly about his memories of these hills and the number of times he had walked them with his father and then alone as he grew older. He talked about how being alone in the quiet of the hills he always felt nearer to God. Seeing all the wonders of nature, the flowers, the trees, the wind in the grass, the wide blue skies, the perfectly formed birds and insects all made him wonder at God's great creativity and power and love for the world. He told us all that it was this caring concerned love that he wanted everyone to experience and that we had to demonstrate through our lives just how this great love applies to everyone. He explained that God's love would bring a sense of peace and joy into our lives born out of a confidence that God's power would take care of our every need as long as we were doing his work. Certainly he exuded this sense of peace and joy. He didn't talk like the rabbis and elders who made God sound threatening and repressive, he talked about a God who wanted to see his people successful and creative and involved in all the realities of life. Perhaps I am making it sound as if the meal was a sermon; it was not like that everyone was joining in, but somehow it was what Jesus said that stuck in our minds. Our hosts were delighted to have us there and were sorry that when we had eaten we had to set off again on our journey, we all thanked them profusely and Jesus blessed them and their family and their farm, they wished us a safe journey and a safe return when we would all be most welcome to lunch or more when we passed that way again.

So we set off, the same arrangement as before, Jesus leading the way, then us six following on and then some way behind the womenfolk. We didn't attempt to use the road which was to our left but walked on field paths up the hills of Hittim and then down to cross the roads at the junction at Golan. From there we could see Mount Tabor almost due south and we knew that Nazareth was hidden from view among the hills the west of the mountain. It was quite hard walking on the field paths but we had shortened the journey by several miles and it was quite clear that Jesus intended that we would make it to Nazareth without staying anywhere over night. Every now and then Jesus would stop sometimes to let us get our breath back, sometimes to let us catch up a bit, even sometimes to let us rest but always he chose the best views and told us what we could see down in the valleys or on the horizon and he always wetted our appetites with the next view he would show us as encouragement to keep going. As the afternoon drew on the shadows started to lengthen and we all began to think the journey was too long and that we should stop at the next possible place, there was some grumbling about 'biting off more than we could chew' and how tired the women would be after all Mary and Martha, Mrs. Zebedee, were quite elderly for this sort of hiking. Then we would breast the crest of the hill we were climbing and because we were going almost due west as we came out into the sunshine again. This happened two or three times and then we saw Nazareth as a silhouette on the top of the last rise and knew that our journey would be over soon. As we entered the town Jesus was greeted by everyone of course he had grown up there and worked there, but there was more than just the greetings of neighbours he seemed to be really liked and he was really warmly welcomed to his home town. Such a large party of people all arriving together from the field paths rather than the main road caused quite a stir and we felt we were 'a happening' in the town. We went straight to Jesus house and, as we were becoming used to, the whole family were there, the meal was being prepared and we were all made most welcome. There was cool water to refresh us, we were given comfortable chairs to sit at, we were brought little appetisers by the children who enjoyed the excitement of so many visitors. Of course when the womenfolk arrived the chatter increased and there was much laughter and giggling as they all got to know each other. Besides us arriving neighbours kept dropping in to welcome Mary and Jesus home as they had been away for more than two weeks, we were of course all introduced. Really all we wanted to do was to sit and rest, to have a meal and then to sleep, tomorrow would be another day and this one had been long enough! Eventually things began to quieten down and a splendid meal appeared, the family had made a great effort and lots of the neighbours had in fact been bringing dishes of food in towards the welcome feast. By time we had eaten it was late in the evening and we all went to bed without an after diner conversation, Jesus told us that tomorrow would be a rest day in Nazareth, we were all pleased that we didn't have to walk on again. We were distributed among family and friends for the night and everyone slept well after an exhausting day of travelling.

So the next morning, Friday as it happened, we all eventually came together at Mary's house, this was where Jesus had grown up, where he had learnt to be a skilled carpenter and where he had helped his father with his work and with teaching his younger brothers their trade. As in most craftsmen's houses the front of the place was the workshop, although it was closed off at night during the day all the shutters were taken down and passers by could stop to see the work going on. They could come and see how their job was going or they could watch, perhaps with envy the work being done for their neighbours. They certainly had time to admire the craftsmanship of Joseph and then Jesus when he became the Master craftsman, in due time. Behind the workshop was the home; this is where Mary ruled supreme. She was absolutely in charge, nobody, but nobody, gain said her, all the decisions about the running of the home were decided by her, all the matters of social, religious or finance were either decided or verified by her, nothing was done without her authority. And yet to the casual observer she was a dutiful obedient wife to Joseph and when he died she was the caring and self-demeaning mother to the new master of the house. The system worked to perfection, there seemed to be no stress or tension in the home, although she was in charge nobody felt that they were dominated, Mary had learnt from her mother that there was always a way to arrive without having a war to get there. Of course with six children running round the relatively small house there were tears and upsets but she had a way of calming things down without ever apparently resorting to punishments and threats. The house was not in any way ostentatious but as the family grew in number and in size Joseph had extended the building backwards from the road almost until the yard at the back was full of house! Now as the numbers were reducing as the children set up their own homes the pressure on space was reducing and strangely the house seemed to get bigger and bigger.

So this morning, there was an expansive breakfast for all the guests, as usual Jesus was absent. Mary said he had gone out early but that he would be back soon and then the day could start. The women folk set about the domestic tasks, if there was nothing to do and they had chatted for long enough they gradually drifted outside to sit in the sunshine and chat with the neighbours as they passed by. Then by some extraordinary group consciousness they all decided it was time to do the washing and they disappeared to the washing pool and peace and quiet suddenly descended on the household!

The young men of the household were busy at work in the workshop and clearly the six of us were more a nuisance than a help there, so when the coast was clear we went and sat in the sunshine and waited for our master and the start of our next adventure. It was not long coming! In many respects the next three days were the most dramatic we had witnessed. Looking back there was a day of being taught by Jesus on many things, then there was the wedding feast and the first miracle we witnessed and then there was the terrible row at the synagogue when Jesus was effectively rejected and we all left Nazareth never to return.

Jesus came back after the women had left, he then sat with us and started to teach us. First he said we had to be self disciplined, that we had to obey the Law of Moses he stressed particularly that His mission was not to undermine the Law but to fulfil the intention of the Law. We didn't really understand what he meant then, but he was insistent that all the requirements of the Law would be met. The next thing he demanded was that we learnt to listen to God and to understand and obey His commands; the most important thing was to pray to God for his strength and his encouragement and his instruction. He told us that if we prayed aright then God's will would become plain to us.

He asked us, because we had not asked him, "Where do you think I go and do every morning?"

Peter said, "Your mother has told us that you go to pray to God, but none of us know what that really means!"

So he started to teach us to pray, "To pray you must isolate yourselves from the distractions of the world, you must earnestly talk with God, you must ask for forgiveness and ask for guidance and you have to ask that your daily needs will be fulfilled. You must then give God the chance to talk to you, you must learn to listen, in quietness allow God to invade your souls and to show you what is to be done. You have to have absolute confidence that God will provide all the resources that are needed to undertake his work, he will never allow you to fail in his work from lack of resources, and so you should not be fearful of the work that has to be done. Finally you must ask God for the strength not to fall into the traps of the devil that were set all around you. These traps are pride, sloth, loose speaking, gluttony, immorality, drunkenness. You may think that these are easy to resist but the devil is a crafty operator and has found ways to invade men's souls. So I get up early every day before sunrise, just as the sky started to brighten and find a lonely, quiet place and pray. With constant practice you will find that you can isolate yourselves form the world and listen only to God. God is available to you all the time, in moments of difficulty God is there, when we felt unsure or lonely God is there, when you seem to be confronted with insurmountable challenges God is there, when we face persecution and rejection and abuse God is there and will provide the strength, physical and spiritual to deal with the situation. The most important support to prayer is confidence; with confidence or faith in God's infinite power and love, all things are possible. You must be disciplined and start every day with prayer. So now you know what I do every morning and what I charge you with doing every morning. You know how to pray and what to pray about, but you will only learn with practice. When you have practiced for a while I will teach you more.

Peter asked, "Why is this different from the prayers of the rabbis and the scribes and the Pharisees?"

Jesus replied, "The problem with the way they pray is that the prayers had become institutionalised. The words were beautiful, they were comforting and because they were old words people should really have to think about what the words mean. Very few people think at all, their minds were shut off, when the prayers were being recited. People are thinking about other matters, the clutter of the world and their lives and not listening to God, not asking God for help, real communication with God is impossible. The supplicant is neither speaking to God nor listening to God. The only possible use of these ritualised prayers is that it did stop people rushing about and sit quietly but it certainly is not what God wants and it is not surprising that the general view is that prayers never get answered."

Phillip asked, "Why is it was that people generally do not bother to pray?"

Jesus went on, "The problem is that because they are not in communication with God their experience is that their prayers are never answered. The truth is that prayers are always answered when you pray in faith. Most people don't pray in faith they state their problem and then tell God what answer they want, then when their solution doesn't happen they say to themselves, and those round them, that prayer doesn't work and they stop praying because they don't get their solution. The answer to prayers comes when you honestly and humbly admit that the situation that you face is too difficult for you to solve and you ask God's help, then you have to accept what he says or does to solve the problem. Be careful though sometimes the answer is not forth coming in your time. You have to learn that God is infinite, that means, that his decisions are made on a basis that a human being can not expect to understand, that the time scale for a solution can also be in the infinite and again human beings can not expect to understand. You have to learn and it is not easy, that God's ways are not the ways of men and that men have to accept humbly and obediently what God ordains. The result of such acceptance is not dumb accession to the world as we find it, God expects us all to endeavour to defeat evil wherever we find it and he will provide the power to ensure that with determination evil will be defeated. The other problem about prayer is just that because it has become ritualised it has become the sole province of the synagogue and the priests. Most people say to themselves "they" know how to pray so let "them" get on with it. God wants every individual to be talking directly and sincerely to him and asking for his solutions to the difficulties they face."

Matthew, who had said very little but had been very attentive asked Jesus about praying for forgiveness, " My life has been deemed sinful and I know that I fall far short of the standard set by the Law of Moses. I felt totally lost with nowhere to turn and no possibility of recovery unless through prayer I can find forgiveness."

Jesus took up this problem willingly and told us all, "Forgiveness is available to everyone but the pre-requirement of forgiveness is repentance. Repentance really means that we recognise and admit to our failures and when we do that God freely and without any other conditions will forgive those failures. It has to be that when we recognise our failures, it must be our intention to amend our behaviour so that these failures are not repeated, but God does not demand that we must not fail again, in fact God understands that the human spirit is not sufficiently strong to not fail again. What he does expect is that we struggle against sin and the devil, to support us in this battle he provides through prayer the strength to beat Satan if we will use it. So forgiveness is available, redemption is a gift of God."

He re-emphasised, "God answers prayers but it is only when God is convinced of true repentance and contrition that forgiveness is made available to us. Forgiveness was a part of the blessings that God has provided. Without forgiveness the first time you sin you would be condemned to perpetual exclusion from God, with forgiveness you can try and try again to reach God's perfection. You have to understand the discipline that this implies, that you know God's will and you have to sincerely endeavour to fulfil that will.

We reflected on the questions we had heard after the dinner at Matthew's house which confirmed that the way the Pharisees were operating a human form of judgement prevented people ever finding forgiveness and then persisting in their sinful ways as there was no possibility in that system of accusation and punishment for restoration into God's blessings. Jesus brought us back to the theme we had been thinking about, he told us that we must pray to God, that we must be absolutely convinced that God does answer prayer, prayer is a private personal contact between one individual and God and can not be replaced by any public showy ritualistic prayer, that when we pray we must put what ever our problem is before God and ask his solution with confidence that his solution will be the best.

Although what we had talked about was critical of the established authority it was not the stuff of rebellion and most of us felt less anxious about our mission. We also gradually had begun to feel a sense of power encircling us, somehow Jesus was providing an atmosphere of courage and confidence, perhaps we were seeing for the first time why it was that Jesus was so commanding of men's souls, because God really was with him!

We had all talked and talked we had hardly noticed the women come home and then Mary very quietly came out and whispered something in Jesus' ear. So when she had gone back into the house he told us that, firstly lunch was ready when we were and that on Monday Mary had been invited to a wedding at Cana and that she had arranged that we were all welcome as well. Tomorrow on the Sabbath of course we would go to the synagogue and we were all looking forward to meeting the men of Nazareth who must have had such an influence on Jesus spiritual up bringing. We had all concluded that Jesus perception of all things was so deep and extraordinary that he must have been taught by Rabbis who were far, far different from the ones we had experienced!

So we had lunch, it was an un-hurried affair, today Jesus had told us was a rest day so there was no urgency about seeing people or going places. It gave us all a chance to talk to each other to get to know Phillip and Matthew particularly, but also to let us become a team. It was quite clear that the women had forged close bonds of mutual affection and support over the washing and preparing food, Mary had been able to tell them about her life with Jesus and the absolute trust in God's love that she had learnt in the previous thirty years or so. I suppose the meal took about three hours and then after we had all eaten well the women started to clear away and Jesus suggested that we men went for a walk to help digest the splendid meal we had just enjoyed.

It was quite clear in only a few minutes that this walk had another, less physical, purpose. We walked almost due east through the town, it was the mid-afternoon and it was very hot hardly a soul was about and even the dogs took little or no notice of this group of men walking, with a sense of determination, out towards the hills we had climbed the day before. As we left the town instead of turning slightly to the north, which would have re-traced our steps of yesterday, Jesus took a southerly path that ran along the ridge of the hill towards Mount Tabor.

We didn't go very far when Jesus stopped and sat down under an olive tree, we all joined him, as it was clear that the discussion of the morning was going to be continued. The hill we were now on was in fact higher than the hill that Nazareth sat on and commanded a view in every direction. Jesus had sat down with his back to Nazareth looking directly at Mount Tabor. To his left was the valley we had walked up yesterday then further on were the green wooded hills of northern Galilee, in the distance just flickering in the hot sunshine was the Sea of Galilee and further on the mountains of the Arabian desert. To his right was another valley heading southeast down the Plain of Jezreel to the Jordan Valley; in the far distance we could just pick out the rooftops of the Decapolis City of Scythopolis. In the same way as we could look over Galilee, to the Arabian Desert, so in this view the distant backdrop was the same desert. Further to our right were the hills of Samaria and through the gap in the hills the road to Judea and then to Jerusalem. We all sat quietly admiring this panoramic view, all thinking our own thoughts. Some I am sure recounting the history of Israel that was so tightly bound up in this small parcel of land. Some wondering when we would be able to see it again and perhaps Jesus already knew how important the area was to be in the next few months and that eventually we would have to take that fateful road south to Jerusalem. After we had enjoyed the view and the tranquillity of the countryside for a while Jesus started to teach us again as he had done in the morning.

I will summarise what he said and perhaps it includes some of what we have learnt since then, we had all been so involved in the morning that we listened intently to what he said. When he spoke in his teaching, he spoke with an air of knowing and of authority that we had never experienced before and never since.

"Prayer and forgiveness are important aspects of communication with God and a demonstration of God's love for his creation. Now I want to tell you more about God's love. It is God's love that I have come to proclaim to the world, it is God's love that I shall demonstrate to the world and it is God's love that you will be charged with extending to the whole world in the future. You have to understand something about God's love before you can see it at work in the world; similarly you have to understand something about God's love before you can show it to the world. This morning we talked about prayer and forgiveness and I want to show you how they are part of God's love. We will start with forgiveness, it is easier and helps to later understand prayer as God's love."

"Perhaps you can already see that God's forgiveness freely available to the contrite heart allows every individual the possibility to fail and

117

then start again, to fail again and restart yet again. The human spirit is so far from God's perfection that nobody, born of man, can possibly come near to his ideal perfection. God knows this and instead of leaving men to flounder in perpetual failure he has provided through his love for this his greatest creation the gift of forgiveness. John came to Israel announcing the imminent arrival of the Messiah and calling everyone to repentance to receive God's forgiveness to be prepared for the coming of God to Israel. I am telling you that I am that Emmanuel and that through me forgiveness is available to all men. You have already heard me say that I am here to save the sinners and the lost sheep, to express God's love to his people through his all-inclusive forgiveness and many other blessings that he pours out to mankind. You must understand that man deserves nothing, if mankind had to rely on his worthiness he would receive nothing, it is because of God's forgiveness and mercy that his blessings are made available to mankind. Now we have received the blessing of forgiveness and have a little understanding of the importance of forgiveness it is our duty to show to others the reality of Gods blessing of forgiveness by forgiving other people. From time to time we all feel hurt, ill-used, exploited, injured physically and mentally, we feel belittled and ignored and we feel excluded, all these senses are due to the actions and words of other people in their dealings with us. They are the same senses that other people feel about the way we deal with them and it is the way God feels about the way we deal with him. He freely forgives us when we repent and we must freely forgive those who hurt us. We can not expect other people necessarily to repent, mostly people do things that are hurtful and unkind without "malice afore thought". Neither we nor they see or feel the damage they have done perhaps because of a lack of sensitivity, perhaps because they are only interested in themselves and not the people round them and be sure we are all the same. Of course there are times when people act specifically to hurt other people and both acts of commission and omission are part of our human weakness, we and they have to learn to ask God's forgiveness for those things we and they have done but we have to forgive them any way. If we don't forgive our neighbours we will harbour feelings of hurt and these feelings of hurt accumulate like a great load on our backs that we cannot put down. We will become distorted beings full of suspicion and hatred and will gradually fall into Satan's trap of plotting the down fall of people we consider our enemies and of anybody or group who might possibly become our enemies or be trying to hurt us. We fall victim to gossip and conspiracy theories and rumours our world becomes threatening and dangerous. The end result is the aggressive conflicts in society

118

which cause civil strife and wars, the exclusivity of all our organisations and the hatred that one people feel for any other. We have to be aware that hatred is the fruit of the failure to forgive and hatred is the basis of fear and fear is the basis of political power exercised by kings and rulers."

"Be sure that it is quite easy to forgive your friends when they hurt you, you can talk to them you can explain how you are hurt, but it is much more difficult to forgive your enemies. But I tell you it is more important to forgive your enemies, in this way you will show them God's love for them and they will realise how far they have removed themselves from that love. Forgiveness does not mean that the clock can be put back or that the consequences of our sinful actions can be reversed but it does mean that we are able deal with those consequences and avoid the outcomes of hatred, jealousy and bitterness."

"Peace among men will only be possible when men learn how to forgive each other, without forgiveness all is strife and aggression and warfare!"
Well that was a lot to take in!

After a lengthy pause while we tried to absorb what he had said, Jesus talked to us about the view and how we can see Gods power and love in the scenery around us and the beauty of his creation.

"Look", he said pointing down the Jezereel Plain, apart from the one hill of Hamor the land appears flat, of course we know that there is the steep, deep valley where the River Harod flows down to join the Jordan. Then to there are the hills of Gilboa to the south forcing the river to take its more northerly route. "God in his wisdom has made the land this way, he has provided the opportunity for man to exploit the land to grow food and to feed his sheep and cattle. When men become successful, they think that the land is theirs and that whatever they do the land will be fruitful. Their confidence makes them forget God and to grow in arrogance. When God sends good harvests men think that it is their good husbandry that has achieved a good result. Because they think they are successful in the fields by their own power they then think that they have to be successful at all things, they become proud and arrogant they lord it over their neighbours and anybody they consider their inferior. We have to understand that whatever men may achieve, in their turn on earth, it is God's will that it should be so, remember he threw up these hills and he formed the deep valleys and he can destroy it all and lay it flat and infertile. When he does so, in the storms and in the earthquakes man can only stand in awe and wonder at the infinite power of God. Then men turn back to God and pray for help and comfort and promise to amend their sinful ways. Our fathers saw this power in the flood, we should take care not to become over confident in our achievements, in God's eyes they are pathetically puny and he will show us how they compare to his power from generation to generation!"

He told us that he had sat on these hills above Nazareth many times and listened to God through the songs of the birds and the clouds in the sky and the flowers in springtime and the desolation in the high summer.

He then said a quite extraordinary thing, he said, "This hill is our destiny, to the north is Galilee where we will do great things, where men will begin to understand something of the power of God and many will be converted to the new way to God. There will be great confrontations with the Scribes and the Pharisees and we will send shock waves through their souls, there will be great alarm in Jerusalem. Now the Plain of Jezreel is the other part of our destiny that is the way to Jerusalem where we will all witness the final confrontation with the established power of the Jews and we will be successful because God is with us! And we will change the world"

None of us understood what he meant, Peter was about to ask him directly but I held him back, it seemed to me that Jesus was almost dreaming and that we should not interrupt this vision of the future that we were privileged to see if only vaguely!

After a little while he seemed to recover his spirit, he had been almost melancholy which was not like him at all, he was, it seemed, by his very nature confident, cheerful and positive, but we had seen just for a brief moment a different Jesus, brooding, insecure and even depressed with the prospect of things to come.

By now the sun was getting low in the west, there was that glow in the air as if it was almost on fire at the end of a hot dry day, we knew that shortly the sun would set over the hills of Samaria and Mount Carmel guarding the Great Sea. We knew that at Mary's house preparations were being made for the Sabbath and that we must be home for sunset to observe the strictures of the Law of Moses. Jesus didn't want to leave this enchanted spot, it was as if he knew he would never sit there again, as if he knew that this one day we had all enjoyed together would never be repeated, it was as if he knew that life for us all would become frenetic, exhausting, frustrating, frightening, exhilarating and that it would climax in high drama in Jerusalem.

Before we set off back into Nazareth he called us together and talked to us about God's love. "God's love is infinite, it is boundless, it exceeds the possibilities of human understanding, it is given without condition we do not have to ask for it, it never leaves us and it is the source of great joy and confidence and power. With God's love anything is possible and it was through prayer that we can see God's love at work not only within ourselves but also in the world around us. One critical part of our mission is to show God's love to the world, to those people who are blind to his love, to those who despair of his love or any other love, to those people who cannot appreciate the impact of God's love on their lives. To do this first of all we have to be confident that we know God's love around us. Then we have to treat every person we come in contact with as part of God's creation and therefore worthy of God's love, we must not prejudge people on the basis of their outward appearance, we have to treat people in the way that we would like to be treated. Remember always that we cannot hope to understand the soul rending problems that most people face, the disappointments, the remorse, the bereavement, the rejection, the loneliness and all the other emotions which mankind is subjected to by himself or his fellows. What we can be sure of is that by time a person has arrived at a situation where they are asking for help or are just prepared to expose their soul then they have problems that we cannot possibly understand. What we can do is extend God's loving comfort to them by never turning them away, by never being judgemental about their condition, by giving them hope, by confronting them with the reality of their situation and by showing them the way back to God's love through the forgiveness of their sins."

Then he went on to challenge us all, "You will see this happening and you will be empower to help people to find God, but you will also be tempted to assume authority that is not yours. You will see the sorrowful plight of mankind but you must not despair, you will see failure but you must not despair, many things are going to happen which will test your faith in God's love but you must not despair. You have to be confident that God's love is infinite it is with us always and that it reaches out to everyone. When things look bad and worse you must remember these few words I have given to you today, they will sustain you when you are most oppressed and when the situation seems disastrous.

Now it is nearly the Sabbath we will return to Nazareth, tomorrow I will teach in the Synagogue and you will see how men's hearts are hardened to the word of God. If God wills it on Sunday we go to Cana for a wedding and on Tuesday we will set off for Capernaum. As you see you are only yet six and I promise you that you will be twelve!"

The next morning at the appointed hour we all set off for the

Synagogue and there we joined a great throng, there seemed to be an air of expectation, of excitement, of anticipation that something significant was going to happen. It was quite clear that the whole town knew that Jesus was at home, they had all known him for most of his life and had watched him working with his father and watched him at his learning with the rabbis and they knew that he was no ordinary man. He had been away from the area for several weeks, and although he did not always read or lead the prayers or discuss the scriptures every week, now, when he was at home everyone hoped that he would read or teach this week. His way of reading and praying had always been different and more memorable than the other leaders of the congregation. And so it was that after the formal opening of the service with all the ritual prayers it came to the time of the reading of God's word. It was as if by his own right that the scroll was passed to Jesus to read, he could have chosen anywhere but he opened it to the prophet Isaiah and started to read. There was total silence the whole synagogue strained to hear not just the words, which they knew well but the slight inflections that Jesus was well known to add and which seemed to make the reading new. So He read as follows: -

The spirit of the Lord is upon me
because the Lord has anointed me;
he has sent me to bring good news to the humble,
to bind up the broken hearted,
to proclaim liberty to the captives`
and release to those in prison;
to proclaim a year of the Lord's favour.

Well you could have heard a pin drop, he passed the scroll back to the server and sat down, nobody spoke, probably nobody even breathed.

After what seemed an age, he said "Today and now this prophecy has come true in your presence. I say to you that you will see and hear great works and marvels that, through me, God will show to the people. You have heard John, in the desert, proclaiming repentance of sins in preparation for the coming of the Messiah, that time is now and I declare God's forgiveness of sins for those who repent and eternal life for those who believe on my name and follow my commandments."

A few moments of total silence were shattered by an unseemly uproar, the rabbis were saying, "We taught this upstart everything he knows", the Pharisees were saying, "This is blasphemy, how can he forgive sins?" the people were asking, "We have Moses' commandments, what are your commandments for us to follow?" Then people started saying, "This man is Joseph's son why should he start to preach to us why should we listen to him, how can he say these things and give a new interpretation of the word."

Jesus was quiet, we were alarmed and frightened for his safety, but he just sat and listened, gradually the hubbub reduced and one of the scribes said in a sneering voice, " Well, Jesus, son of Joseph the carpenter, if you are the messiah as you claim, show us some sign some wonder that will convince us, otherwise we will throw you out of the synagogue and pass you over to the authorities to answer the charge of blasphemy, and you know that the punishment for that is death by stoning. So you'd better look sharp, we don't want your sort of trouble makers in our town!"

What a terrible accusation from a man he had known all his life; the crowd were nodding their heads in approval of this challenge and were, I am sure, expecting some drama. The six of us had formed a sort of bodyguard around him but there was a lot of pushing and shoving, gradually a chant started up "Show us your power, show us your power, show us your power" Louder and louder! Jesus looked more and more saddened by the whole affair eventually he signalled for quiet and everyone seriously thought some great act was going to be performed.

He said to them, " Do you really think that God will perform magic for you? Has not Moses taught us "You shall not put the Lord to the test!" You are privileged; you have seen God and you are foolish because you cannot see God! But it is written in the same book I have just read to you that "a prophet has no honour in his own country" and I will trouble you no more, you are a people lost to God."

Now there really was uproar, people were saying, "How dare he criticise us?" "If he is a prophet let him show us, all prophets of the past have shown great signs." "He thinks he can judge us and condemn us, by what authority does he think he can do these things?" " He has brought six body guards to protect him, but if he is Emmanuel God will protect him!" Groups were forming to oppose him, there were the two or three Pharisees agreeing that they would make sure that their organisation knew about his outrageous behaviour, there were the scribes agreeing to make sure that wherever he or any of his adherents went they would be severely opposed and heckled, the rabbis were agreeing that within their power he would not be allowed to teach in a synagogue. These were the powerful people who controlled the way the masses were supposed to respond, they thought they had the power; they had not noticed that when they tried the same tactics against John in the desert they had clearly failed. Their failure was twofold, first the huge crowds turned on them and accused them of having no message for the poor of spirit, the sinners and the excluded, secondly they found that the John message was so convincing and persuasive that large numbers of the people they sent to disrupt his mission were actually converted by John's crusade. They also had to admit that actually putting any contrary argument in an open meeting with a large crowd of people hearing what they wanted to hear was not only difficult but also dangerous and not a few of their number had actually been assaulted. Some of those in the Nazareth synagogue that Sabbath also knew that Jesus was a much more serious and sinister threat to their hold on power as his intention was to supplant them as the only way to God, if he achieved this then they were finished. There were those among them who swore that they must be sure that the Sanhedrin knew the gravity of the threat and set about finding some way to contain this upstart "carpenter".

The meeting broke up in chaos, the women who could only watch from their gallery were just as upset and divided, Mary was ostracised by women folk she had considered her close friends for more than twenty years. She needed all her stoic resolve to believe that God's will was being fulfilled not to breakdown and cry, she was pushed about, she could see people gossiping about her and her beloved son, there were women wagging their fingers and turning away from her to be offensive. She remembered even in this crush what the chief priest had said to her thirty years previously that "a sword would pierce her heart", this morning she was sure she felt that sword. She took some comfort from the other women who had come with them from Capernaum who did what they could to protect her. They got her out of the building and away as quickly as they could, but she would not leave until she was sure that Jesus was safe. When she was satisfied she agreed to be escorted back to her house.

The men had not come back yet and the women started to discuss what they had seen from their vantage points, there was disagreement on the causes of the row and the outcome and even in Mary's house the argument became heated. There were those who said that Jesus had been unwise to generate such a conflict with the authorities, that a slowly, slowly approach would have avoided this crisis and in the end he would have got his message accepted. Then there were those who were perplexed that such a joyous proclamation could cause such an aggressive and belligerent response after all Jesus they knew was the Emmanuel, he was the one who had been foretold of old, unfortunately this was a small minority who had been involved in special conversations in Capernaum. Most of Jesus' brothers and sisters were very upset and were asking why their eldest brother should think he could just walk out of their well regulated and prosperous lives as the best respected carpentry business in the area and then come back and threaten all their customers with excommunication and worse. Their view was very clearly if he wanted to attack the synagogue and the scribes and the Pharisees and any body else they would be quite happy if he would go elsewhere to do it, and as far away as possible. They were very vociferous that he had in a few minutes undone a lifetime's work and that it was unlikely that tomorrow they would have any customers at all. Mary did her best to contain all the heated voices and found it impossible and was beginning to accept that this was the end of the family she had worked so hard to build when there was outside sort of rumbling noise. It was a noise none of them had ever heard before, it was like a grumbling excited cacophony of shouting, of cheering, of whistling, of laughter, and it was coming their way! Half the household rushed out to the front to see what was happening to their complete surprise came Jesus almost carried by an enthusiastic crowd, clearly these were well wishers, these people were the "humble and meek" who were ready to receive his message and to believe in him. This was the flock of lost sheep who heard the message and did not need the signs!

Interestingly these people were part of the congregation in fact they were the majority of the congregation at the synagogue, they had seen it all and recognised immediately the reaction of the scribes and the Pharisees and the rabbis was to protect their power. It was quite clear to them that they had no real interest in whether Jesus was the Emmanuel or not, their only interest was in defeating the threat that he represented to their power. The power brokers made all the noise in the synagogue the ordinary men watched in amazement at their reaction to the "Saviour of Israel". They had shown themselves in their true colours and once the crowd had disgorged itself from the synagogue they rallied to Jesus' support and the authorities realised they were defeated—this time!!

So Jesus came home with the six disciples to a household already in turmoil about the scenes in the synagogue. There was an embarrassed silence as he came in, he seemed to be relieved to be out of the limelight and gratefully accepted a drink of water, sat down and then talked to them all. He told them that he knew beforehand what would probably happen at the synagogue and although he was disappointed he was not surprised that he had been rejected by the authorities. He told them that they must not be afraid for themselves because they were doing God's work, yes, even the housework and the cooking, the joinery and carpentry, the buying and the selling these were all God's work and God would care for them. The support that they as a family had already provided was the outcome they had from doing God's work and was given to support himself and Mary and his sister in his mission to the people. He was sure he said that far from hurting them in Nazareth the outcome from today would be positive, the ordinary people had received the message willingly and had shown this clearly by their support on his walk home. It had not been surprising that the authorities had been resistant after all what he had said was a direct threat to their position if they wanted to see it that way. He was sure that when they thought it through even they would become less hard hearted and would want to hear and understand more. He told them that they must have faith that they should believe in him even though he was just the brother to some of them, they must not apologise for today's happening this was part of God's plan which had to be worked out. He told them that he would move to Capernaum and there he hoped that he would be better received, but he told them that he knew that he would be continually rejected and abused, but that through all that people would come to understand that he brought the message of God's love for mankind and through his reconciliation, eternal life was available. Some of the family started to ask questions but he stopped them and said to them "You will hear reports of great works at my hands in the region, you will begin to understand but it is too soon for you now to know what is in God's plan. Be patient, have faith, do not be alarmed or anxious all is in God's hands and he will protect us all."

So the atmosphere was defused but we six were feeling very unsettled having witnessed, for the first time, a direct confrontation with the clerical powers of the land, it was very alarming to us, after all we were just ordinary folk who had been plucked out of our lives for reasons we did not understand, and had then seen the overt hostility and anger that Jesus generated. We learnt to expect this response, and it became the norm. This first time, we began to ask ourselves and each other, "What have we got into? Is this what revolution is about?" Peter, in his usual dry humour, said, "You can't make an omelette without cracking the eggs." and I think we all understood what he meant.

The women folk were preparing the meal and we went outside with Jesus to talk, he seemed to know that we were unsettled and explained to us that what we had seen was but nothing compared with what we would see in the future. But he repeated we must not be afraid, God was with us and would protect us; we must have faith.

Peter said to him, "But they were threatening to stone you, they admitted that had we not been there as a guard they would have done so and what good would that have done?"

Jesus rounded on Peter and said to him and to us all, " Peter I have told you we are doing God's work and God will protect us, be very clear in your hearts and minds, you have not been chosen to protect me, you have been chosen to do God's work in extending his message of love and forgiveness and the promise of eternal life. I was not stoned not because you were there; I was not stoned because it was not God's will that I should be stoned. I will remind you that the Hebrews threatened to stone Moses and Aaron in the desert when they assured them that the Lord God would put the land flowing with milk and honey into their hands without a fight, and God protected Moses and Aaron from their rebellious people. You must trust God, as I do."

Jesus said that the proof was that nothing had happened and we should recognise that was not our doing or their doing, it was God's doing. God had ensured that there would be no harm to anyone, that is physical harm, the confrontation had been important to us six because it was part of our learning. It was important to the elders and others governing the synagogue because they had seen God and perhaps on reflection some of them may recognise that it was God they had seen. It was important to the ordinary people because they also had seen God, perhaps they also did not recognise him but they had seen "hope" and the possibility that the future would be better. It was important to the family because it had helped them on the first step of their understanding of Jesus as something other than their brother and finally it was important because it confirmed to Jesus that he had to leave Nazareth, his home town, and move to Capernaum as God had commanded him!

"So you see", he said, "today was very important. What you have to learn is that every day is important what happens is not accidental it is part of God's intention and he will have many levels of intention some of which we can unravel and today is especially one of those days. You will learn, as we work together, to think about God's purpose and it will help you to confront the powers that you will face in doing God's work on earth. You must have faith and confidence that we are in God's care and he will provide the courage and the strength to go on when it all seems too difficult and even pointless. He will be there to support you, each individual, when you need the support, he will, I assure you, be there even when you think you don't need him. The most difficult thing to do is to know with any certainty just what it is that God is doing, as I have shown you, in analysing today's excitement, there are many things that he is doing because he wants to maximise the possibilities of every individual and every situation."

Just as we were about to ask questions Marion came to the door and said the meal was ready and the sun had set. The meal was a very happy feast, I thought how awful the day had been in the synagogue and how Jesus had first of all comforted the family and then given us a lesson in being faithful to God and seeing his hand in the things that go on around us, sometimes big things, sometimes small things but he is always there with us. It seemed that an air of relaxed tension had descended on us, how much worse things could have been, and perhaps we had to learn not to be pessimists!

Tomorrow, it was already arranged, we were to go to Cana to the wedding; it was Mary's cousin's daughter who was to be married to a young man who was the son of a local vigneron, who owned some of the best vineyards in central Galilee on the south facing hills to the north of Nazareth. The lesson we had from Jesus about looking for the many purposes that God has in every situation was to be dramatically demonstrated during the next two days.

The walk to Cana was one of the most memorable of all the walks of the whole memorable visit to Nazareth, the air was like crystal when we left Nazareth and as the sun took hold it was warm and then hot. We walked along the ridge of the hills and then dropped down into the town. The views were magnificent, east across the hills towards the Sea of Galilee and west towards Sepphoris and the hills rolling on towards the Great Sea and Tyre and Sidon. Everywhere had a sense of fruitfulness the fields were dressed overall with wheat and barley, the orchards were full of apples and olives and figs, bubbling streams tumbled down the hillside from unseen springs. In the distance there were villages of glistening white houses, occasionally we heard a dog bark or a cock crow but mostly it was quiet except for the buzzing of insect wings and the singing of birds, the larks soared into the sky singing what seemed to be exotic hymns of praise to God the creator.

It was interesting that as we walked through Nazareth we were greeted politely, even enthusiastically by the townsfolk, Jesus striding out in front the six of us following on behind and then the women folk bringing up the rear. Somehow we had now accumulated a donkey that carried the various bundles of clothing and bedding that seemed to be necessary but I can never remember actually being used. We must have looked a little daunting like the vanguard of an army, set on a determined march. Several people joined us and walked along for a while. Apart from wanting to know where we were going, they really wanted us to know that we were welcome to Nazareth and the confrontation in the synagogue had not been about the ordinary people only the clerics. The message that we heard was that these people knew that they needed the redemption that Jesus promised and also knew that they were separated from God and needed a reconciliation that the Rabbis were, it seemed, incapable of providing. We made no promises, we had no idea what we would be doing or where we would be going except, we told them that after Cana, we would be going down to Capernaum. Jesus kept his own council, he did not talk very much and then only to tell us of his boyhood memories or to take in the view across the countryside otherwise he seemed to be deep in thought. His face had an air of concentration almost of rehearsing, we knew he was working something out in his mind because he occasionally smiled to himself, sometimes he was reciting something to himself, clearly he was getting real satisfaction from his private contemplations. We marvelled at his concentration. Nothing distracted him, he did not want to join in our conversations, he was having his own, he didn't want to teach us as he had the day before and we were reluctant to interrupt him. Along the way we crossed a stream of fresh pure cool water and He stopped to drink. We all gathered round him and eventually Peter plucked up the courage to ask him why he was so remote from us this morning. He immediately apologised profusely and sincerely, he said he was in prayer to God and that his prayer was so sincere it was like a conversation and he was learning Gods next intentions. Prayer, he said, is not a thing that is only done in the quiet of your room or in the early morning or late a night or only when the rabbi prays, God is there to listen and to teach all the time and he said, it seemed that this walk was an ideal time to pray. "Make use of every minute of every day for God's work!" He reminded us of his first lesson in praying and said that perhaps we should, like him, practise what we had learnt as we walked along. He helped us to begin to pray by suggesting that we should bring before God our families and our friends and all the people who one way or another were supporting us, that we should pray for a deeper understanding of yesterday and for His strength and guidance today and tomorrow. So we set off again this time the buzz of conversation among us was hushed as we all tried to pray and, as we had been taught, to listen as much as to talk. I have to admit that I did not find it easy, in fact I don't think I really prayed at all, not in the way that I now know, but we all have to start somewhere and we started on the hill path between Nazareth and Cana. We discovered that it was only with almost continuous practice that you learn to hear God, to begin to understand his purpose and to see his hand in finding the way through life's difficulties.

It is not really very far to Cana, so by about lunch time we came in to the outskirts of the town and people came out to see us. Jesus was well known, and talked to people as we passed to the bride's parents house, but it was quite obvious that the news of the row in Nazareth had already spread to Cana. I heard one man ask Jesus why he thought he was so special and claimed to be the Messiah. Jesus reply was quite surprising and the man had nothing more to say, Jesus said to him "If you have eyes to see and ears to hear you will see and hear the evidence you are seeking!" the surprising thing was that we thought the man was being aggressive but Jesus assumed that he was sincerely looking for guidance. The questioner was also surprised because we all agreed that he had not contemplated that what he really was looking for was guidance, but his spirit was stained with the expectation that he would get no real answer, and this showed through as anger. We all arrived at the house together, there was a degree of alarm among the bride's family to see such a large group. They were of course delighted to see Mary and her family and after the rest of us were introduced and welcomed everyone busied themselves with the setting of the table for lunch. It really was a jolly affair there was a lot of banter and teasing and remembering of other times and other people, of talking about expectations and plans, of telling us all about the family that was being joined with them tomorrow. It went on for hours and it was almost sunset when we finished and Jesus took us outside to be quiet with him. Instead of sitting outside the house as the sun slowly sank behind the Hills of Samaria in the far west, as we expected, he suggested that we should perhaps walk round the town to help our feasting digest. So we set of ambling along looking at the houses occasionally stopping to talk to people we passed or who were sitting out enjoying the end of the day. Eventually we came to the town square, it was a large flat area and was used for the weekly market it was here that produce of all sorts was bought and sold and where animals were auctioned. It was used for town celebrations and was always the centre of the annual round of Jewish holidays. There seemed to be little if any overt presence of the Romans and Cana was far enough off the "beaten track" that even the Greek influence was not so noticeable as it was in most Galilean towns. The square was edged in large ancient fig trees that provided shade for people to set up their stalls and to sit with some protection from the sun. There were groups of men sitting around gossiping and laughing under most of the trees but Jesus focused his attention on one in particular where a man sat by himself quite obviously deep in thought. Nothing was said and we progressed round the town until eventually we had worked our way back to our host's house, by now all the clearing up had been done and sleeping quarters decided for the guests. We were all

130

ready to sleep and were just taking leave of each other when Phillip announced that he had remembered that a friend of his had come to work in the town. He thought that, despite the late hour, he would go and find him as he was sure that tomorrow would certainly be too busy. The rest of us wished each other a good night and went to our beds. We were not really surprised that the next morning started early, when there is a wedding there is a lot of final arrangements to be made a lot of excitement and a lot of coming and going. We took our breakfast early and then vacated the house to let the women get on with the final preparations. Jesus was absent as usual so we talked about our adventure so far, by now we had confidence in each other and we exposed our inner thoughts. Some were anxious after the scene at the Synagogue and the rest of us tried to comfort them by reminding them what Jesus had said. Others were confused about our real work, and questioned where it was all leading us. Some of us said with greater or less conviction that we must, as Jesus had told us, have trust in God. Others were concerned that we had given up our livelihoods and our security and for what. We still had to learn that the security that God provides for every one of us is far more valuable and reliable than any security we may try to provide by our own efforts.

Then someone, probably Peter, quite out of the blue, asked Phillip whether he had found his friend the previous evening. Phillip then recounted the meeting he had with his friend Nathaniel. This man, he told us, was a deep thinker he spent most of his spare time studying the scriptures and trying to understand God's message and intentions for the Jews, he was a devout religious man but was very concerned that the way religious practice had now been established did little if any thing to help to bring individuals nearer to God. After Phillip had explained this background to us he told us that he had pronounced to Nathaniel what we were all doing and told him about the extraordinary man, Jesus, who had called each one of us individually to come with him to "do God's Work". Apparently Nathaniel's immediate response was to ask "Has anything of note ever come out of Nazareth?" to which Phillip had replied, to his credit, "Well don't just take my word, come and see for yourself." So he told us we might expect a visitor. In a little while Jesus arrived, I think most of us had practiced praying before we met for breakfast but none of us had thought of venturing out doors to try and talk to God.

Jesus looked radiant, his smile was so warm and comfortable, he exuded confidence clearly nothing we or anyone else might say or do was going to upset him. We all thought that the pleasure of being at a wedding was the motivating expectation, we only realised later that he knew that today he would demonstrate, in a way that will be re-told for ever, the incredible, unexpected and unfathomable power that God has over nature and the human mind. It was still mid-morning and as we sat and drank the sweet juice of the pomegranate Jesus asked us of our understanding of what was happening. We already had such confidence in him that all the anxieties we had came pouring out like a torrent. Six men, who until very recently were "important" in one way or another, who would have never dreamt of admitting to any sort of weakness were suddenly exposing their very souls to Him. He listened to each one of us, it was as if to Jesus the particular speaker was the only person in the world, his attention, his whole being was focused on the speaker, it felt as if nobody else existed let alone had any call on his attention. For each of us his words were of encouragement, of confidence, of determination, of courage and of faith, "you must have faith that God is with us and will protect us, that God will answer our prayers although sometimes we may be surprised by the answer."

We had all confessed our worries and anxieties to him when Phillip got up and brought his friend Nathaniel to join us, he had been waiting within earshot for a while and when he came forward to be introduced he was already emotionally charged having listened to many of the things that had been said. Jesus looked up and, as if he had been expecting him, welcomed Nathaniel, as if he had known him always he introduced him to us with these astounding words, "Here is an Israelite worthy of the name, in whom there is no guile." Nathaniel was completely taken aback and asked him, "How do you come to know me?" Jesus said to him "Last evening I saw you under the fig tree." Nathaniel replied, "You are the Son of God; you are the king of Israel." Jesus replied "Just because I said I saw you under the fig tree you are convinced, I tell you, you will see greater things than that and you will, I assure you, see the gates of heaven open wide and the angels ascending and descending to the Son of Man." Nathaniel became the seventh of the special disciples of Jesus and left everything and followed Jesus until the end.

The wedding feast was about to start and we all were invited into the tent set up for the celebration. It was important that all the law should be observed nobody should ever be able to say in the future that "so and so" ritual had not been observer and therefore there was shame on the family and the groom and the bride. In particular there should be nothing unclean about any person at the feast. We were, of course, well versed in all the requirements of The Law and the interpretation of The Law by the Pharisees, we had all made sure that all the sacrifices required had been made and that we had not been involved in any "unclean" activity. When we arrived there were servants to wash our hands and feet before we entered the tent as was required, during the feasting the servants brought us bowls of water to wash our hands so that no foods could become contaminated, a wedding is a very important ceremony and everything must be "just so". It was a sumptuous meal, there was course after course of delicious food; the wine, as you might expect considering who the groom's father was, flowed like water. It was the best wine from his cellar and his cellar was the very best in the area. Of course nobody became intoxicated but the guests really did enjoy the open handed generosity of the host. It was perhaps because there were so many unexpected guests from Nazareth that as the afternoon wore on, Mary became aware of a flurry of anxiety around the top table. As an aunt of the bride she was an important guest and signalled to the Master of Ceremonies to come to her, on enquiring she was horrified to be told that it was likely that they would run out of wine. This would be a tragedy, the family would become the laughing stock of the area, the shame would be to hard to bare, she felt for the bride and groom and for the parents, she knew only too well what was likely to be said by the gossips, and she had to find some way to remedy the situation. She called Jesus to her and explained the difficulty and Jesus then took control. You will have heard the story many times, this was the first time that anyone had witnessed the power of God over the physical world but there are some other significant aspects of the occasion which we, the seven of us discovered as we talked with Jesus and among ourselves about his dramatic transformation of water into wine. It is not expected at a wedding that the guests will be asked to help, they are to be waited on and their every whim indulged, Jesus commanded the young men to fill the water jars, and they did. There was no question about it, he didn't use a commanding dictatorial voice he just said quietly to them "Can you please refill these jars with water." It was no mean task and they had to work hard to do it. The important thing was that the other guests knew what was happening and they witnessed that it was water. He didn't make any issue of the transformation, he didn't for instance bless the vessels, or like Elisha call upon God to produce a spectacular demonstration, like rain in a drought, or fire from heaven. All he said was, "Draw out the wine and offer it to the Master of Ceremonies." The effect was awesome, the man could not understand and it took a while for him to realise that the power of God was at work right there. The groom and his father had to explain that the wine that they made was not to be compared with the wine that God had prepared. The bridegroom's father had to admit that although he made very good wine, he had been shown that he should not be over-proud about his prowess as God had shown quite clearly that he was a far better vigneron, what is more, it had all been done in seconds rather than months! It was astounding how much wine God had provided and Jesus explained to us later that what we had to recognise was that God's blessings are magnificent they are over and above anything that we can ever ask for, they are totally unexpected and undeserved. He also explained that God knows the fragility of human relations and will use opportunities like this wedding to show people just how he is intimately involved in our lives and can help us even, as in this circumstance, to be saved from the shame of public humiliation. It is now many years since the wedding at Cana but this example of God's power and God's love and God's understanding is always recounted in the marriage ceremony among faithful Christians to this day.

The whole day was a great success and Jesus reputation as a great leader of the Jews was enhanced here, unfortunately there were people who began to expect miracles all the time, but Jesus told us that these great works were to turn men's hearts and souls to God and were not to be stunts to impress their minds.

Part 12

Capernaum and healing the sick and the parables

We spent a very happy time with the families and their friends and we were all accommodated in various houses in the village for the night and next morning, as planned, we set off back to Capernaum. We were all still overcome with the power we had seen at work the day before that it wasn't long before Peter summoned up the courage to ask Jesus about it. So as we walked along the Roman road from Sepphoris to the Sea of Galilee Jesus said to us, "The power of God has been given to me to control all the forces at work in the world, I am empowered to show to sinful man the power of God. But the purpose of the demonstration of such power is not to impose obedience through fear but to give men confidence that if they have faith in God, if they really trust in God, if they really accept his love and forsake themselves for him he will ensure that all their physical needs are met, that they will have spiritual peace on earth, which passes all human understanding and that they will have eternal life. What is more, they will have the power of God beside them to change the world, not just the simple business of changing water into wine." Peter then asked him if we would have this power and he told us that we would receive power as much as we needed to fulfil God's work and that eventually we would change the world.

We were amazed, we did not understand, as we do now, how that power would be given us but we started to discuss among ourselves how we could possibly defeat the power of the Sanhedrin let alone the power of the Romans and their legions. We agreed that we had no knowledge of government or military matters and all the organisational skills that such matters required. Jesus overheard enough of what we were saying and told us, very severely, "You are misguided, you must not think like that, it is the way men think but you have to try to understand God's plans. These do not include the Sanhedrin or the Romans or any other work of man as being of any real significance, they have a part to play but when that is done God will dispense with them just as he had created them!"

That made us all think a lot, none of the things that we took for granted, it seemed, had any real permanence. They were real enough to us but to God they were transient, all the things which man had done, or would ever do, were temporary. These great sources of man's arrogance would all disappear with time the only reliable permanence was the spirit of God. What we had been shown by the changing of water into wine was just a small example of this infinite power that God has over man's puny endeavours.

As we left the hills and Cana behind us we came to the junction of the west to east road we were on and the north to south road. Here we left the road and took the field paths to go to the lakeshore without having to pass through Tiberias. As we walked Jesus told us that he would not go to Tiberias, it was the dwelling place of the devil. He instructed us that it was not our business to go looking for trouble there would be plenty of trouble without our searching for it. He was absolutely frank and told us that the people who lived in this city would be destroyed, they had no interest in God or in redemption or forgiveness, their hearts were hardened and they were the children of the devil. If, he told us, any individual wanted to repent and ask for forgiveness then he would happily help them to find their way back to God. While they were determined to continue their headlong dash to purgatory then he would use his energy to help people who really wanted to be helped and recognised that Jesus was here to help them.

We were now walking towards the farm where we had stopped on the way up to Nazareth and sure enough it soon came into view and we were very surprised, if not a little disturbed, that there lunch was laid out for us. It was as if there were some sort of thought transfer taking place, some sort of telepathy, we knew absolutely that nobody had gone ahead of us to warn the farmer and yet he was expecting us. When we asked him how he knew, he just said it was a hunch that we would be passing that way. We asked him what he would have done if we had not turned up.

"Oh," he said without any hesitation, "if the guests had not arrived he would have invited all the neighbours in for a feast!"

Jesus said we should not be surprised, "How many times", he asked us, "did he have to repeat that, "God will provide".

We set off again after a splendid lunch and promised the farmer that if we passed that way again we would call in, he said, "Yes, I'll know when you're coming I'm sure!" We then dropped down the very steep hillside to the lake shore, it was late afternoon when we got to the lake and already the shadows of evening were spreading across the lake as the sun set over the hills behind us. Jesus said, "I think tonight we will stay in Magdala, and I am sure I know where." We knew a lot of Magdala people through the fishery business, it was here that the first fish processing business had been set up when the harbour had been built by Antipas to bring in the stone needed to build his new capital,

Tiberias. Although we were competitors we were also friends, the demand for the products was so huge that there was plenty of business for both of us. The customers liked it as well because they could get competitive prices. Most of our discussions were about managing pricing situations as they arose so that we didn't cut each other's throats! You see even now after all this time I can't help being a fish businessman! Jesus avoided the sea front and walked into the town, he turned into a street about three roads back from the shore and without any hesitation went to a house apparently at random and walked in through the open door. The rest of us stood in the road waiting to see what would happen, expecting Jesus to come out with a red face and an irate housewife after him. Within a minute or two he came out with a beaming smile and called us all to come in, at least fourteen and a donkey!

We were all made very welcome Jesus introduced us to the family and their twin sons, one was Thomas and the other was Theo. The family business was in the trading of flax products. They imported finished products from as far away as Egypt and Cappadocia. They bought raw product from the local Galilean farmers and had spinning and weaving shops and a rope walk to manufacture as wide a range of local produce as was possible. When we talked to them we discovered that all the ropes, the fine twisted yarns for the nets and even the sailcloth for our boats came from this family. Our agent had always been very cagey about his sources and we had all assumed that the supply was in Egypt. I am sure that he knew that if we knew he would quickly be out of business, after all it was only a short trip from Capernaum to Magdala. After we had promised not to give away their trade secrets and that we would continue to use their agent they agreed to show us round their premises, we were very interested in the way ropes and twines were made. (Well at least four of us were and the others came along.) We must have spent well over an hour on the visit and when we got back the sun had set and the women folk had the evening meal ready. We were now getting used to the idea that meals were Jesus opportunity to relax and he was in high spirits that evening. The first thing Jesus did was to recount how he knew this family, it was all to do with the weaving looms. Jesus reputation as a skilled craftsman had spread far from Nazareth so that when the families looms were in need of repair it was Jesus they called on, in fact he had built brand new machines for them based on the original designs but we were told by his very complimentary customers he had incorporated some major improvements. Our hosts told us that when Jesus came to stay with them he spent hours and hours watching how the machines were operated and where the joints took most strain, where the moving parts caused most wear and used this to try out alternatives to increase the efficiency of the machines to the delight of his customers. There was a lot of chat about how the machines had been working and it came out that they were still buying machines from the business in Nazareth. By time the meal was over it was dark, Jesus took us down to the seashore, the water was like a mirror, the air was heavy with the scent of bougainvillaea and broom, and the stars were twinkling all over the great dark bowl of the sky. We walked slowly down the harbour wall and it was a little while before we realised that neither Jesus nor Thomas were with us. We made nothing of it and looked at the boats and criticised their rigging and tidiness and then when we returned, passing the tax office which Matthew recognised, we found Jesus and Thomas engrossed in conversation. Jesus looked up and said, "Here is our next companion, Thomas is joining us to help in God's work." So now we were eight! We went back to the house all wanting to talk to Thomas and he wanting to ask us questions, Jesus walked behind and left us to our chatter, by time we arrived he was nowhere to be found, we were not concerned, we were now quite used to the idea that he would want to be alone to pray. Our beds could not have been nicer, instead of putting us up in the neighbours houses we slept in the warehouse using the coils of rope as mattresses and fell asleep among the familiar smells of rope and canvas.

At breakfast, Jesus was absent, as we had now expected, Thomas asked us many questions about the mission we were engaged in. Our answers were not very helpful but I think that our confidence in Jesus was infectious. We were surprised that the miracle of the wine was already common currency and people were all asking who this man could be. We told Thomas about the way we had all been summoned, about the amazing way in which everything turned out all right, that Jesus kept repeating to us, "God will provide". We told him about Jesus' instructions to pray, and that the way he prayed was so different from the ritual or rote praying of the synagogue. How Jesus was always cheerful and positive, how he had this quite disturbing ability to look right into your heart when you talked to him and could turn aggression into understanding and teaching. Thomas asked many questions as we went through these things and we began to see in him a quality of needing a full clear explanation of things before he could accept them. Having talked about all the positive, comforting things we then went on to some of the disturbing things. The reaction to him in the synagogue for instance; his determination that he would change the world but would not talk about tactics or revolution. We told him that we were all very concerned that there seemed to be no plan, we did not know what we would be doing today or tomorrow let alone next week and that when we challenged Jesus about this he replied that we were doing God's work and that God and only God would decide. Another aspect was that we were encouraged to have faith in God's infinite power it seemed very vague if we were to confront the power of the Sanhedrin and Rome whose power was very real and dangerous. Then out of the blue as it were he shows us God's power dramatically at the wedding at Cana, but then when we were beginning to think that a few demonstrations like that and even Rome might be impressed, he told us that his purpose was to bring men's hearts and souls to the love of God and not to impress their minds with dramatic exposures of his power. That may well have an impact, he told us, but it would be short lived and would become a titillation to stimulate their excitement just like the Roman games. We told Thomas that Jesus had promised us that God would empower us and that our work was to change the world, when we almost laughed at this idea and asked how that could possibly be, he looked very severely at us and said, "This is your work, God will give you all the power you need, I will show you this power at work and teach you to accept it. You are the means by which God will change the world" He didn't say when this would happen but he was absolutely sure that it would happen and that we would succeed. None of us, we admitted, could understand this command and assurance but although we felt very nervous when we talked about the possible implications we were also unable to ignore the attraction of the confidence that Jesus showed all the time. Peter who had joined in all these discussions then had a bit of a revelation. He said that perhaps we should listen more carefully to Jesus actual words because when he had heard Jesus say we would change the world, his own immediate understanding was that we would rule the world. Now, as we talked about it, we should all understand that changing the world has nothing to do with ruling the world. This led to a lively discussion and we were all in full flight when Jesus came in, he looked radiant, he greeted us all warmly and asked after us closely and said, just as if he had been a part of the conversation and with a knowing twinkle in his eye, "Well come on then we have to get on with changing the world, and the next place is Capernaum where there are some problems we have to deal with." We all noticed the slight emphasis that he placed on the word "changing". Almost within a few minutes we had all said our farewells and thanks and were on our way, Thomas despite his overt need for detailed confirmation of everything had accepted what we had said and like us left his family and all he had and knew behind him and stepped out with us along the coast road, north towards Capernaum. None of us knew what to expect but now we knew that whatever lay ahead Jesus would cope with it and what ever his solution was it would be impressive.

Quite clearly Jesus was in a hurry to get back to Capernaum, although he had said that we were needed there he didn't say why and was more vague than usual when we asked him, we concluded, without him saying it, that all would be revealed when we arrived. So we didn't stop along the way, people stopped to see this troop of marching men pass through their towns and villages. We saw many of our acquaintances but could not delay to exchange news with them, it was just the same as when we passed by a few days earlier in the opposite direction, they must have thought our behaviour very strange, if not offensive. It was a strange experience because people stood by to let us pass, we overheard one or two say, "That is Jesus of Nazareth the new prophet of Israel, born to set his people free!" The news of the wedding would be here as quickly as it had got to Magdala, and people would be very impressed although nobody had any knowledge of the message of repentance and forgiveness, of God's love and compassion for his people that was for later.

The women and the donkey had disappeared in the distance behind us and we were a little anxious that they may be delayed with questions by the locals and end up very far behind. Jesus was not concerned he was confident that they would come to no harm from locals or from robbers or anything worse. We covered the eight miles or so in just over two hours, as we entered the town Jesus turned left away from the sea and much to our surprise made straight for Peter's house. As we got close we could see a small crowd of people outside in a very sombre mood and before we could get to the door we were told that Peter's mother-in-law was sick and close to death. Jesus was very quiet, he didn't ask what was wrong or how long she had been ill, he stood in the doorway as if he was riveted to the spot, gradually the noise subsided and when it was all quiet Jesus went into the house. Peter's wife was in tears as were our mother and father and all the children. As Jesus came in they looked at him and we could see over his shoulder that look of despair, of disdain, of accusation, of disappointment, a look that we would all get to know only too well as time went on, it was a look which could easily turn to hatred and abhorrence and total distrust and disbelief. We knew that Jesus' eyes would be filled with love and caring that he was sharing in their grief, their anticipation of imminent disaster, he could sympathise with their natural antagonism to him. He, after all, had taken their son, their husband, their father the very centre of their whole existence, they had listened to him, they had understood the urgency of his command and had submitted to his need. They had their own hopes and expectations for the future but now the only compensation for the total destruction of their lives was that they were to be visited by death. Not just any death but the death of the one person who was there able to help Peter's wife to deal with the distress of loneliness the feeling of desertion and rejection which must have been the lot of all our women folk. He said nothing and they parted a way for him to go into the bedroom where she lay fighting for her life. He took with him, Peter, his wife and John. Later John told me what happened, he said that Jesus went into the room and sat beside the bed for a short while, everyone was quiet and watching every movement, then Jesus took the woman's hand and said, "Now everything will be alright!" with that the woman sat up and after a few minutes stood up, washed her face and hands and muttered that she didn't know what all the fuss was about, she thanked Jesus and went through to get on with preparing the meal. You can imagine what we saw, this woman who was deemed to be dying suddenly recovers and is not just getting better but is fully well. So, our Jesus was not only able to change water into wine but could make sick people well!

Some of us went outside and told the distressed and curious that everything was all right and the woman was well again so they could all go home and we thanked them for their concern and that they had seen the power of prayer at work. We hoped that they would not ascribe the recovery to Jesus, he had told us only the day before that he wanted his power to be carefully used and that we had to win peoples hearts and souls and not just their minds and emotions. It was a vain hope, the news went round the town that Jesus could cure the sick, and there now started an amazing period which did not stop until the final moments of the mission, there was all day and all night, wherever we went, crowds of people, most bringing with them their sick. The sick of mind, the sick of body, the disabled, the blind, the deaf, the mad, those possessed, the broken in body and the broken in soul. It was heart rending, every day there came this mass of the sick they came in the hope that something might be done to relieve their suffering and to allow them to lead a meaningful worthwhile life, to be accepted once again as valued members of society rather than being rejected and excluded. For us, his close friends, we saw what nobody would normally see. Most of these people were not seen in public, their families kept them hidden away, ashamed to have to admit that one of their family was not whole, to have to face the accusation that this disgrace was the visitation of the wrath of God for their sinfulness! Mostly the pleading for a cure came with desperation from the parents or the siblings and very quickly as Jesus powers became broadcast the pleading was not so much in hope as in absolute faith that God could and would give them the comfort they searched for.

The particular instance of the curing of Peter's mother-in-law had another dramatic effect, Jesus had shown to our families that they were not excluded for God's power and mercy, that they, who had given so much and would continue to give, were able to receive God's blessings. They began to understand just a little of the power that God had launched on the world through Jesus, and that this power was available to them as to everyone who has faith. Jesus stayed at Peter's house that night and next day before dawn a huge crowd had gathered in the street, somehow he had managed to slip out unrecognised and had walked into the hills towards Chorazim to be alone with God. It was quite clear to us all that in two days he had changed the whole style of his mission, and now he really needed spiritual strength. We all found that we were praying too, we knew that we needed God's support to prevent the crowds getting out of hand and making sure that Jesus was able to have some peace, some rest and time to eat. This time was full of quite extraordinary experiences but it is a permanent memory that he never turned anyone away, even after a day of preaching, of healing, of travelling he would always find the time and energy to care for an individual who came to him for comfort. The evening meals we shared together were always lively discussions of the day's events, just being able to sit with us and talk, and teach, seemed to revitalise him and us. He taught us about the deeper meanings of what he had said or had done. He exposed us to the real love of God and explained how his work expressed that love through his compassion for the sick, the disadvantaged, the rejected and the excluded. Oh, yes and there were many times when he chastised us for our lack of understanding and our slowness at learning. We found we had to walk a very tight rope to protect him from the crowds and yet avoid his censure for keeping the needy from him.

Today was to be our first experience of the crowd attraction of Jesus, to most of the people who came that day the interest was in a spectacle, the word had circulated about Peter's mother-in-law and the miraculous happenings at Cana and people wanted to witness the next spectacular! Jesus was not unknown in the town, he had worked there as a contract carpenter from time to time, over the past ten years, the fact that he had now started to prophesy, to teach, to heal and to work miracles raised the curiosity of the town's people. The population was not exclusively Jewish, in fact the Jews were not the majority, there were many who were the descendents of Greeks, Arabs and Egyptians who had settled in the area following successive conquests and during the forced evacuation of the Jews by the Persians many, many years ago. It is true that the Jewish population would have been even smaller had it relied on the settlement of the returning remnant from Persia but during the Maccabean rule Jews from Judea had been forcibly resettled in this northern province.

The crowd that morning was by no means just Jews it was a mixture of many races and cultures, the language was predominantly Aramaic but you could hear a lot of Greek as well. Jesus had managed somehow to slip un-noticed into the house and had breakfasted calmly and un-hurried. All our questions and requests for instruction as to how we should behave were eventually greeted by "God will work it all out, today your real training in the propagation of God's will starts. You will see that God's love does cure people and that God's love changes people's lives. You will also see that there is real opposition to any change in the structure of worship and the access to God." and without more ado we went out into the sunshine! The crowd had been very well behaved and while they waited gradually the sick and the lame had been filtered through to the front, so we were faced with a wall of poor wretches in all sorts of conditions. Mostly there were cripples with withered arms and legs or distorted backs and then there were the mentally disturbed. To us they were all unclean, they represented to the Jewish mind God's punishment, to the third and fourth generation, they were in fact repugnant. Our immediate reaction was of revulsion; love and compassion were about as far from our emotions as they could be! We wanted nothing to do with them, we looked round for some way of avoiding them of conducting Jesus to a safer situation but we were surrounded, I remember feeling a sense of nausea and panic overcoming me just being close to these people. Much to our shock, Jesus stepped forward without hesitating, the crowd immediately hushed, the atmosphere became almost electric. He went to a man who had a withered arm and spoke to him, it was as if nobody else was there, he looked into the man's eyes and into his soul and asked him, " Why have you come to me?" to which the man replied through his tears, "I am unable to work, I have been cast out by my family and have to beg for food, but I am a Son of Abraham and I have feelings and needs just the same as everyone else. For reasons that I don't understand God has cursed me with this arm that is no use I need help and nobody is there to help, so I am here to ask for your help. You have already done great things and I believe that you are my only possible rescue!" Jesus was quiet for a moment or two he was still looking at the man intently and then he very gently put out his hand and stroked the ghastly deformed arm and as he did so it became whole. Jesus said to him " Your Faith has cured you!" The man fell to his knees, he mumbled something to the effect that nobody had ever soothed his arm as long as he could remember and now with one touch he was better. The crowd were overcome with amazement, they were totally silent, the man stood up and waved his arm to show them he was cured, his face was a picture of happiness, of delight and of relief. The crowd parted in front of him as he went away praising God for his dramatic healing and declaring to all that this Jesus was Emmanuel. The Crowd were now totally silent they cowered in front of this demonstration of God's power and were not sure how they should respond. Nobody moved! Jesus stood absolutely still, the perspiration was pouring down his face, it was as if he had undertaken some great physical feat, he was breathing deeply and seemed to be elsewhere. Then the moment was shattered, in one great movement a man threw himself on the road and in a convulsion shouted at Jesus, "You are a prophet and a healer, what do you want with us, we have seen your sort before, you come to upset us, to cause trouble for us. It will all end up in a disaster." The man was frothing at the mouth, he was jumping about and shouting at the top of his voice, everyone moved away from him. His family tried to calm him down but he escaped from them and shouted louder and louder that Jesus was not wanted here. Jesus stood his ground and eventually the man fell on the floor at his feet, Jesus looked down at him and said "Evil spirit be gone!" His voice was angry and commanding, the man gave one great, final convulsion and collapsed in a heap. His family rushed forward thinking he was dead, but found him breathing gently as calmly as if he were asleep. They lifted him to his feet and were about to retreat into the crowd but he turned to Jesus and said "You have given me back my life, only the Son of God could do this, for twenty years this devil has tormented me and my family and you have defeated it. I praise God for his loving kindness."

The crowd were now beginning to move out, away from Jesus. The power he had demonstrated was terrifying, here was a man who could repair withered limbs and could cast out devils from a man possessed. If he could do these things then what else might he do, and he might turn his power not on the visibly sick but on sinners generally and that could be anyone, perhaps it would be better to leave this man alone. There were murmurings and people were now not so sure that they wanted to see the spectacle they had hoped to witness. A Pharisee stepped forward and said to Jesus in an accusative voice "By what power did you command evil spirits to come out of a man? I will tell you by what spirit! You are in league with the devil and so have command over his minions. You are a charlatan, you are a cheat, you are an imposter, you can cast them out and so you can also curse people with the same devils! You would lead this people astray and you must be stopped!" Some of the crowd were starting to rally to this onslaught, the situation was becoming threatening and frightening. Jesus stood, looked at the man and his voice tailed away until he was quiet, and Jesus then said to the crowd " This man says that I cast out devils because I am in league with the devil. I ask you this. Would the devil cast out his own? He accusses me of being a cheat because I have healed the sick. Again I ask you this, When did he heal the sick who have always been with you? I tell you this, that the scribes and the Pharisees will do what they can to darken your eyes and to stop your ears to prevent you receiving the blessing of God's love which I bring to you openly and freely." The Pharisee turned on his heel and pushed his way through the crowd saying, "We will soon see who is in charge round here."

But the crowd was now calm and started to show some hostility to the Pharisee as he left. More people came forward and were cured; Jesus didn't just say "You are cured!" He talked with the sick and with their family, he always wanted to know why they were there, what did they expect, it was clear that he wanted the crowd to hear the answers and as he laid his hands on them he said "Your sins are forgiven, your faith has made you whole." We found this very strange he never took the credit for these amazing happenings, the onus for the cure was actually on the plaintiff, it was his or her absolute conviction that a cure would be achieved through God's power and presence that was the real source of the cure. If you believe you will be forgiven and cured! The process, if that is the right word, continued for two or three hours, the word had clearly gone round the town and although many people were cured the crowd never diminished, it just got bigger and bigger. They were quiet and still, they were patient and amazed, every time a cure was seen there was an audible gasp, the shock was felt by everyone most of the sick were known in the town, they were seen if at all as street beggars, as fleeting figures pushed out of sight at the back of houses. The courage and confidence of the relatives to bring these poor creatures out into public gaze was dramatic. They all looked round almost furtively at their neighbours as if to say "Please don't ostracise us, we have born this burden secretly and if a cure is not worked for us we will accept that we have to continue to secretly bear the pain and shame. We are sure that this is our only chance but it needs this sacrifice." It was quite clear that Jesus understood this and his comforting power was clearly directed at them as much as at the invalid. Their obvious relief that their heart's desire had been fulfilled was clear to everyone, their smiles, their joy was infectious and the crowd gradually became more and more light hearted as they saw that their town and the shame of their town was being put at ease. Jesus, however was becoming more and more weary, there seemed no way to stop the crowd presenting even more people in dire conditions needing his help, we became alarmed that he might collapse and eventually Peter called a halt. He told the crowd quite quietly and politely that as they could see Jesus must take some rest and some sustenance and suggested that we all disperse and perhaps meet later in the afternoon on the lake shore beside the sea wall on the western side of the harbour where the warmth of the sun would last longest. The crowd looked disappointed and then the women started to pull their husbands away saying that if he was their son he they would want him to rest and gradually they all dispersed except a determined few who stayed outside the house, some of them had received a cure and could not leave the place of their salvation.

Jesus had not moved from the threshold, as he turned to go back into the house he almost staggered with faint, the exhaustion was written all over his face, he looked at us and smiled weakly. Mary his mother was there to receive him and took him through the house to the bedroom and within a minute or so returned and signalled that he was asleep.

Nothing had been done in the house and the women said that they would prepare a mid-day meal, as quietly as possible, and suggested to us that we should go and prepare for the afternoon. It was clear that they were as spiritually and mentally shocked with what we and they had all witnessed and wanted to talk among themselves. We were in a state of almost total disbelief at the morning's events and needed to have time to try to put some sense into what we had seen. The women were right it would be appropriate to use the tranquillity of the lake to relax our battered senses! We walked through the town quickly and quietly we did not want to get involved with the town's folk now, most people it seemed had gone inside to perhaps talk through what they had seen, to relax and to get a meal, so it wasn't long before we arrived at the beach and the relative privacy that this provided.

Peter was by now very anxious that he had done what Jesus had asked them not to do, he felt he had taken matters out of God's hands and superseded Jesus' wishes. We all told him that it had to be done and that we saw this as God imposing his will on the situation which would have quickly led to Jesus collapsing and needing a cure himself. This raised an issue which has never been fully resolved it is to understand how we can be sure at any moment in time whether we are doing God's will or interfering with in his intentions. We talked about this for a while and eventually seemed to be going round in circles and then agreed that we would talk to Jesus about it if he didn't raise the issue himself. Peter had now recovered his self-confidence and when we were all quiet he suggested that we might pray, He led the prayer and it went something like this.

"Dear God, you find us in great anxiety, and we ask your guidance, Jesus who calls you Father, has called us to help him and to learn from him, show us how we can support him and protect him. We are trying to obey his instruction that we should trust you absolutely and that you will care for all eventualities but we have seen this morning the physical hazards that could overwhelm him. We took it upon ourselves to interfere and now we are unable to divine whether this was your will or our will. Help us to grow in faith that we can understand your will just as Jesus does."

Peter then reminded us that Jesus had told us that God would answer our prayers if we had faith and that we should not try to anticipate the answer. The conclusion he said had to be that now the matter was in God's hands and we should get on with something else while God sorted that matter out. There was a general air of relief at that, we were all very impressed with the way that Peter had thought out the prayer. We were also impressed that he felt able to address God as "Dear God" just as you would a friend, all our education by the rabbis was that God was to be feared and that He had to be approached with awe and in anticipation of some retribution for past sins. We decided that John and Peter would go into the harbour and bring a boat round to the beach, we felt that if things got too difficult at least we had a means of escape to separate Jesus from the crowd. Thomas, Nathaniel and Matthew decided they would join them; they were not sailors and thought it would be exciting to see how the boats were worked.

That left James, Philip and me sitting on the beach, the weather was warm and calm and we were soon talking about the past and how we remembered this beach and growing up and gradually the talk came round to what we were doing now. We all agreed that this was the most incredible adventure; in just over a week we had abandoned our pasts and accepted a challenge to be part of some undefined process to change the world. Then we had witnessed the man who issued the challenge, thrown out of a synagogue, change water into wine, heal the sick, forgive sins, fall out with the Pharisees, explain a new relationship with God and tell us that he was training us to do these things as well! Really if you weren't there you wouldn't believe it! While we were

147

discussing these weighty matters James' son Jude came down onto the beach, his uncle John had told him we were there. He had sailed over from Bethsaida during the morning and had only just heard about what had been happening in the town. We introduced him to Philip and then asked him how the business was and how the families were at home. He quickly answered all these enquiries and clearly wanted to talk about something else. So, after a pause he asked us how he could join with what Jesus was doing. We didn't know how to answer him, after all we had not volunteered we had been recruited, even commanded and it didn't seem to us that this was something you "joined". We explained some of the things that were happening and the feeling of uncertainty, of being exposed, of witnessing some amazing things that were mentally and spiritually very challenging and that probably if he was to talk to Jesus he must be ready to answer the question "Why do you want to join my work?" We suggested that he had better stay with us and see what happened in the afternoon and that might help him decide what to do. It was sure that Jesus would recognise him from the stay at the Zebedee home a week previously. So Jude said he would go back to the harbour, finish his business and warn the crew to wait for him to either join them or to send a message. When he left we all agreed that his determination was to be applauded, James and I wondered what his grandfather would say when yet another of his brood left home and family and responsibilities to follow Jesus. Philip said that he was impressed that such a young man had come to the conclusion that he should risk even suggesting that volunteering would be an acceptable way of recruitment. We all agreed that Jesus had emphasised to us all that we had been chosen, not by him but by God, so maybe this was another way in which God's choice would be shown. It was interesting that we were all beginning to develop a trust in God and that He would decide these matters. The boat now appeared round the end of the breakwater and we all went down to the beach to help land her and pull her up out of the surf. We decided that it was lunchtime and set off back to Peter's house hoping that there would be some food. On the way back we told Peter and John that we had talked with Jude and that he would be on the beach in the afternoon. The other three were discussing the niceties of sailing a fishing boat, from what we overheard they were almost experts already! Little did we, or they, know that their next trip in a boat would be a rather more impressive experience! When we got back to the house the meal was waiting for us, and so was Jesus. He looked well and refreshed, the women said he had slept for a while and had then slipped out by himself for about an hour, when he returned every sign of tiredness and concern was gone.

He had become the life and soul of the party and spent his time teasing the women and playing with the children, the house just bubbled with happiness and contentment. The table was laid and we all sat down to eat. We told Jesus what we had done and he was pleased, he thanked us for terminating the excitement of the morning and told us that he was praying to God at that moment to show him how he could possibly stop the crowd continually expecting more and more from him. We felt relieved and that Peter's prayer had been answered and that we had been doing God's work although it felt at the time very ordinary. The meal was a very jolly affair and after it was finished we set off back to the harbour and the lakeshore.

The crowd was huge most of the town was there, of course we knew nearly everybody, if not personally at least by sight. We kept being stopped or pulled aside by neighbours pleading that their needs should be met in front of the others. There were Jews and gentiles mixed up together clearly the news that there was a healer, a Jewish prophet, had attracted everyone and they had come with their sick to be healed. They had clearly also recognised that this Jesus asked for nothing other than the sincere belief that a cure was possible. He didn't ask for money, he didn't demand any ongoing commitment, he didn't demand any initiation ceremony, he didn't suggest cures that may be available, he had no potions and his cure was instantaneous. To us it looked over-whelming; we had no idea that there could possibly be so much suffering in our town! Much to our surprise and to the disappointment of the crowd, Jesus walked through them and climbed aboard the boat. He asked us to row a little out onto the lake and to anchor there, he sat in the bow of the boat and asked the crowd to sit down and to be quiet. Then he started to talk to them. His introductory question to the crowd we came to know well, he asked them " What have you come to see? A show of miraculous cures! or have you come to see the fulfilment of the prophecies of old? Many of you went into the desert to see John the Baptiser, I tell you he was the greatest of the prophets for he was given the task to announce the coming of Emmanuel! and now I tell you that that time has come and Emmanuel is here with you!"

There was total silence the only sound was the little waves breaking on the sand of the beach.

Clearly the crowd were anticipating some drama, but Jesus was sitting in the boat that prevented the sick being brought to him. The four of us who were fishermen stayed on the boat and the others were on the beach, the people sat down in the warm sunshine and Jesus started to teach. The effect from his very first words was impressive, "The kingdom of God is like this." Well nobody had ever taught like that, the teaching we all knew was about the Law and its application, all the "thou shalt nots", that seemed, in summation, to imply that anything that was enjoyable was sinful. He then described the kingdom through parables, it was very clever because the people really had to listen carefully as there was no knowing where the important part of the parable lay. Even then at the end it was not necessarily absolutely clear what the kingdom was really like. He told them the parables of the tares, the parable of the mustard seed, the parable of the yeast, the parable of the buried treasure, the parable of the immensely valuable pearl and the fishing draw net. Each time he started with the same introduction "The Kingdom of heaven is like this." He had finished these stories and was about to dismiss the crowd as it was getting towards dusk when there was a disturbance at the back of the crowd that spontaneously parted to make way for a Roman Centurion in full parade uniform to come through. He came down the sea; his air was not the haughty arrogance, overbearing pride and confidence that was typical of his like. He was known by the crowd who treated him respectfully rather than fearfully; he had left his guard at the top of the beach and was not seen so much of a threat. He carried his helmet on his arm and we could see his face was anxious and nervous he looked pale and tired, but we knew that any Roman was a potential source of trouble and were on our guard. It was at this moment that I noticed Peter uncovering two swords in the bottom of the boat, Peter had clearly prepared for any eventuality when he fetched the boat in the morning. I told him in our fisherman's slang, not to be stupid and to put them away, he looked a bit disappointed but heeded my advice, although he stayed near to the weapons, "Purely defensive he told me later!" After Jesus confrontation in the morning with the Pharisee we wondered with growing tension what would happen next and how Jesus would respond to this representative of the repressive dominant power of the invader and polluter of God's country.

He saw the soldier approaching and sat quietly in the boat. He did not stand up as everyone else did, he was watching the man carefully and the crowd who were now absolutely wound up for anything. Perhaps they were now going to witness the start of the defeat of Rome by the Messiah. Would Jesus destroy the man before their eyes to send a message back to his masters, what was going to happen? The man came on, perhaps the Pharisee who had been so angry in the morning had organised for Jesus to be arrested. The man came on, perhaps Antipas had decided that having arrested John that he must now arrest Jesus! When the centurion arrived at the boat he bowed politely to Jesus, he was standing in the surf but he didn't notice. For a moment or two these two men looked at each other, the one a resplendent representative of the worlds super power the other a rather humble looking common man; the one standing the other sitting. The one representing Man's understanding of infinite power confronting the reality of God's infinite power in the other.

Jesus said to him, "You have come to me! How do you think I can help you?" We were totally amazed, it was unthinkable that this humble man could possibly help the servant of Rome. It was unthinkable that any Jew would ever consider offering help to the representative of the hated oppressor, and further more this man was a gentile and therefore to be avoided at all cost as unclean and untouchable, having any thing to do with him would contaminate the Jew. Somehow Jesus knew that this man was in trouble and that he was seeking help that he felt only Jesus could supply. The Roman, we decided later had humbled himself to Jesus, he had humbled the power that he represented in front of the Jews and to God. He would have guessed that his meeting would be reported to his superiors and may seriously affect his prospects, but he had taken all those risks because he was confident that this man could provide the help he so desperately needed. The Centurion replied with the words that are now repeated among Christians everywhere and I will record them in full just as I heard them. "Sir," he said "a boy of mine lies at home paralysed and racked with pain." Jesus said "I will come and cure him." But the centurion replied "Sir, who am I that you should enter under my roof? You need only say the word and the boy will be cured. I know, for I am myself under orders, with soldiers under me. I say to one. "Go", and he goes and to another, "Come here" and he comes and to my servant, "Do this", and he does it." Jesus was astonished at what he heard and he said to the crowd "Nowhere, not even in Israel have I found such faith as this. Many I tell you, will come from east and west to feast with Abraham, Isaac, and Jacob in the kingdom of Heaven. But those who were born to the kingdom will be driven out into the dark, the place of wailing and grinding of teeth." Then Jesus said to the centurion, "Go home now; because of your faith, so let it be." and it was reported that at that moment the boy recovered and was cured. The centurion did not hesitate he bowed politely to Jesus, turned on his heel and walked briskly up the beach to his waiting escort. The crowd were spell-bound they had come with great expectations but none of them could have conceived what they had witnessed. The crowd started to disperse, it was almost dark by time they had all gone, some one produced a lamp and we sat around Jesus asking him questions about what we had heard and seen. In a little while Jesus noticed Jude who was standing just outside the circle and listening intently, he welcomed him, and said "Jude, I have been waiting for you. Are you ready to follow me wherever I lead and to forsake the world?" Jude stood silently in the midst of the group and said, "I have seen with my eyes and heard with my ears "God with us", I am sure that you are the Emmanuel for whom we have yearned for generations. I will do as you command, you are my master I am your loyal servant!" Jesus said to him " Very well, God has guided you to this decision and now you are with me and I am with you for ever. Come into the light and sit close to me." So Jude joined us, now we were ten and only needed two more to make the band complete as Jesus had told us.

Our discussion was first of all centred on the parables, and Jesus taught us how we had to grasp the meaning of these stories. He told us that the purpose of using parable in teaching was to use familiar situations and experiences to bring the listener to understand slowly, and then, to remember the deeper meaning of what he had heard. Because understanding a parable was difficult it needed an effort on the part of the listener, if the listener was not prepared to make this effort then he would fail to understand the message or its deeper meaning.

So taking these six parables in turn,

The Tares; the seeds are those people who hear God's word from Jesus and his disciples and accept it but among them are the tares, people who hear the word and half-heartedly accept it and then fall away, they may even tend to drag others with them. But it is sure that on the day of reckoning they will be separated from the faithful adherents to the word; who do God's will

The Mustard Seed; when planted this tiny seed produces a great plant, so it is with the people who hear God's word and follow it. They will achieve greater things than could possibly be expected.

The Yeast; the effect of a tiny piece of yeast on an apparently flat and inert piece of pastry is dramatic, it increases in size many fold and produces delicious bread. So it is that it only takes very few people who believe in God's word and do it, will produce great transformations in their world.

The Buried Treasure; the perfection of the soul that comes from doing God's will and the peace that gives that nothing human can approach has a value higher than anything that anyone has ever owned. So a man who seeks God's perfection will forsake everything just for that.

The Pearl of Immense Value; is another picture of the buried treasure, the value of a perfect relationship with God is worth more than the greatest riches we can imagine.

The Draw Net; many people will be attracted to God's word, as many fish are caught in a draw net, but only the quality fish will be accepted by God at the final judgement, those people who pay lip service to their discipleship will be rejected.

Apart from the parable of the shepherd and the father's younger son these were the first of Jesus' parable that we had heard and he took a lot of care to make sure that we understood the deeper meaning. He instructed us that we must listen very carefully to these stories because there would not always be time for Jesus to interpret them. It was also important that as we understood more he would expect us to be able to quickly understand the deeper meaning. He also made it clear that he expected us to struggle with the message as we had to learn to hear and to see the will of God.

This discussion took a long time with a lot of questions and answers but then we moved on to the experience with the centurion. We were right, Jesus had seen the huge effort that this man had made and the risks he had taken, the one we had not thought of was the possibility of rejection by Jesus. Jesus made us understand that God's blessings are given to those with the faith and confidence that if they ask they will be satisfied. This man had faith, he not only believed that Jesus could provide a cure, he recognised just how unworthy he was to receive such a blessing. The centurion's faith was such that he knew that Jesus didn't need to see or to touch the boy and yet that the blessing would be granted even if he only said the word. The centurion had rationalised this by comparing his power to command obedience from other men with his perceived recognition of Jesus' power to command the natural world and the spiritual world. Jesus explained to us that the miracle of healing was instantaneous, God having decreed that a change would take place it happened there and then. He tried to explain to us that these dramatic demonstrations of God's power "on demand" were sometimes needed to convince or to remind people of the reality of God's power. What we all had to learn was to see God's power at work in the world all the time, without these dramatic demonstrations, and that this realisation would only come when we truly accepted that God was the only controlling power in our lives. The centurion had shown by his submissive appeal to Jesus that he accepted that there was a greater power than Rome at work in the world. What is more he had shown that belief openly and publicly and therefore we did not have to fear Rome. Rome itself was subject to the same final judgement by God as was the rest of the world. We were all surprised that God's blessing had been extended to a Gentile what is more the representative of a hated invader and oppressor. We, the Jews, were God's chosen people how could God possibly extend his favours to any outsider, we had all seen the great need for healing among our own people but yet Jesus chose to help this outsider. Jesus response to our reaction, as we were beginning to expect, was totally unexpected. He told us that his message of redemption and forgiveness to those who had faith and were repentant was not exclusively to the Jews, it was in fact to all mankind. God had ordained that the messenger of His truth should come to the Jews because He had maintained a close, special relationship with them. If they accepted the message and changed their relationship to God and obeyed his commands then they would become the light of the world and all men would see God at work through them and would change their ways to receive the benefits that they saw the Jews were receiving. If, however, the Jews refused the opportunity they were offered then the task of changing the world was for us to carry the new message to all people. This gentile soldier had shown such faith, such humility, such understanding of the power of God that he had earned the blessing he requested. The Jews had to understand that they could not stand in God's way to prevent his plan for mankind being implemented. We were amazed, once again, as Jesus had shown in the parable of the father's second son, he was threatening the very foundation of the Jewish nationhood by stating that their special relationship had to be earned and was not to be assumed to be a permanent arrangement. We could all see that there would be a major confrontation to come, we were alarmed and frightened, we were so disturbed that we all had real doubts that Jesus was able to undertake this task and more to the point we wondered whether this really was a campaign we wanted to be involved in. Jesus as usual felt our anxiety and assured us that God was with us, that he had shown us his power over and over again that very day and that we must have faith that he would protect us through all the troubles that lay ahead. I'm not sure that we were quite ready to accept such an assurance at that moment, personally I began to wonder whether Jesus was blind to the enormous power of the establishment in Israel that would oppose everything that

Jesus was proposing.

It was dark now, the moon had risen and the reflection off the calm sea was awe-inspiring. We had experienced an amazing day and were all fairly exhausted, so we sat in silence each with his own thoughts, mine were mostly examining the short time that had passed and all we had learnt and then what would happen next; where was this project leading us? After a little while Jesus suggested that we should go back to the house as the women would start to worry about us all, so with some reluctance we slowly walked back to Peter's house. As soon as we arrived we were made to sit at the table to eat, everyone was very hungry and the meal was silent until the food had been eaten and the plates cleared away. The women then distributed the party among the various homes and left us to talk among ourselves.

Jesus asked us, "Well what did you think about this morning, the crowds and the healing?"

Peter set us off by replying, "We were surprised and shocked that there were so many sick people here in this small town of Capernaum. Even though Andrew and I have lived here almost all our lives we had no idea that so much unknown suffering."

Jesus pointed out to us, " Is it really surprising when there is huge, oppressive social and spiritual stigma attached to any sort of sickness or disability? The religious leaders have moved the Law of Moses, from some sensible and necessary precautions of a society to protect itself from contagious disease, to an open condemnation of any one who is sick and then by association to their whole family. The result was that people are ashamed that any member of their family should be sick and then to reduce the shame the sick individual was frequently abused by being shut away or actually driven away from the family disowned and forced into destitution, to beg for food and shelter. So should we really be surprised that these people and this social division were not usually on display? This was not God's will this was man's sinful exaggeration of God's will that has made the suffering of illness and disease an almost impossible burden for families."

Then Phillip asked, "Why is it that you can cure people with such apparent ease, when it was quite clearly not just difficult but actually impossible for any one else to?"

Jesus told us in reply, "It is not impossible, everything is possible when the power of God is involved. One of God's purposes is to use the healing of the sick to demonstrate his power and to make people notice that something very special had happened to their society.

Another purpose is to demonstrate his love for mankind and in particular to demonstrate his individual love for everyone and particularly for the outcast and downtrodden of society. These people had been ostracised all their lives! Nobody would have ever offered them any hope or any comfort! Nobody would consider them people deserving of human love, let alone God's love."

He continued to explain another less obvious reason, "Our purpose", he reminded us, "is to change the world. This will only happen if people are confronted with just how discriminating our society is. You were surprised and I'm sure so were all the people there when the invisible sick who lived in darkness were made visible by the light of God. What the population demonstrated to themselves was a severe criticism of their society. It showed just how uncaring society had become and how far they were from God's conception of love. The sin was worse, just think of all the talents that these people had been given by God that were being denied to them and to the benefit of society, such a waste was not any part of God's will."

Then somebody, I think it was Nathaniel asked, "Why can't we do it through the power of God?"

Jesus then made this amazing promise, but we didn't understand the significance of his reply, "The time will come when the power will be given to you and that you will cure people, that time would be when we had absolute faith in God."

Then Jesus had another challenge for us, "What was the common characteristic of the whole healing experience you witnessed this morning?" We were perplexed by the question after all people of all ages with all sorts of conditions had been cured, perhaps, we suggested it was that they were Jews.

Jesus reminded us, "But there was the Centurion, he was certainly not Jewish. What was it that I emphasised to each person?"

Nobody seemed ready to answer so he went on, "The most important thing was that the cure was not his special power, it came through the individual's clear faith that God could perform a miracle in his or her life and this allowed the power of God to work through me. This is an important matter. Our mission to change the world will only be achieved by the individual, personal commitment of people, one by one, to make their talents available to God to use them to fulfil his plan. There is no other way, God's love is unique to every individual and it is only each individual who can respond to God's love. What has to be understood in this mornings experience was the simple fact that these people had presented themselves publicly to Jesus accepting the risk of social exclusion, it was a dramatic demonstration of their faith and the depth of their secret suffering. They knew that only God could provide the comfort and restoration into society that they craved."

Then Thomas, who had been very quiet, and who we knew would be thinking very deeply about what was being said, asked Jesus, "How could the all powerful God allowed such sickness to exist if it was not the punishment for sin?"

Jesus replied, " Thomas, you have asked the question that will cause great anguish to multitudes of people that this problem would confuse people forever. One thing you have to remember is that it is not possible for man to fathom the mind of God and his plan for the world or for individuals. The forces of evil are real we saw that this morning when I cast the devils out of poor possessed people and that the Devil was partly to blame. He, the Devil, could drag peoples souls away from God by introducing sickness knowing just how quickly people came to despair, a definition of despair is giving up belief in a loving caring God, and therefore is a sin. Many of the sicknesses, on the other hand, were perfectly natural and were just a part of being, sometimes they are spread by people not taking sensible precautions like cleanliness and that the Jewish fastidiousness with cleanliness has grown out of just such an awareness. In time, I promise you, God will show mankind how to use his amazing, God given, talents to find cures for these diseases of the Body. It is God and only God, who can provide the cure for the Soul. This cure would only be available when all men were committed to love their neighbour, and to provide for his needs however demanding those needs may be both materially and spiritually."

Now it really was late, the moon had lit our discussion but now the night chill was upon us and Jesus said we had better go to our beds before we caught colds!

The next morning the assembly at breakfast was interesting, for the first time it was noticeable that we came together as individuals, and we all admitted that Peter's praying in the mid-day yesterday had convinced us to start the day with prayer and we had each found our own quiet bit of beach or hillside in which to try to talk to God! Jesus soon arrived clearly absolutely refreshed and "full of bounce" while we were eating, Peter's wife told us that it had been arranged that in the evening we would all meet together for the meal at Jonas' farm on the hill. They also announced that they had prepared a pick-nick for lunch as Jesus has told them, that is the women, that today we would be going to Chorazim.

Chorazim is a town set in the hills north of Capernaum and is on the main route to Damascus on the west side of the Jordan. The road was a new Roman road but there were field paths and mountain tracks that were well used and avoided the possibility of meeting with the Romans.

When we were ready to go we were amazed at the crowd and at their passive behaviour, they waited quietly and expectantly, they had with them the lame and the sick and the delirious. Jesus told them where we were going and that we would be back later in the day. It takes about an hour to walk to Chorazim, if you can keep going but the crowd kept delaying us, Jesus kept being engulfed by humanity and we had to try and extricate him so that we could make some progress. Sometimes he was forced to stop and then used the moment to teach or to cure or to dispute with people and then we would all move on. It was lunchtime when we got into the town and were met by a huge crowd, it filled the town square to bursting. The word must have got ahead of us because this was not just the townsfolk. The town is on the main road and as usual there were caravans working their way north and south, they had stopped to witness the day. Besides the hill route that we had taken, there were other tracks coming from west and east and north converging on the town, people seemed to be streaming in from every side. They were not just Jews there were Greeks and Arabs and Phoenicians as well as some soldiers and there were slaves. There were men and women, there were young and old, there were poor and wealthy, there were farmers, there were rabiis, there were scribes, there were Pharisees, there were shop keepers, there were artisans, there were small children in their mother's arms. But most noticeable were the sick, there were bodies twisted and distorted, there were the blind led by their friends, there were lame, there were crippled, there were imbeciles, there were the possessed; it was horrifying. I had never experienced any thing like it, far worse than the day before at home. I could see other people were moved by the public display of these poor wretches for whom there seemed no hope. Most people were clearly appalled but could not show any kindness or mercy for their conditions, they made way for them to pass not out of respect but out of fear of contamination. I think Jesus was as astonished as the rest of us, we almost automatically closed ranks round Jesus quite expecting a rush towards him, but the crowd was still and surprisingly quiet. There was a sort of murmuring but as Jesus turned and looked at them they fell silent in anticipation of some event, I remember looking at his face, he was smiling a gentle smile that was quite open and exuded comfort and confidence. He suggested that as we had all come a long way, that lunch would be the best thing, it appeared that this met with agreement and much to our surprise people sat down and produced pick-nicks. The atmosphere became very relaxed as we all enjoyed a meal together, as it was so informal nobody seemed to worry about the niceties of the washing rituals, not even the Pharisees.

During the lunch Jesus went very quiet, we concluded that he was praying, he knew that the afternoon would be hard work and needed God's support. After he had prayed he suggested to us that we could help by persuading people who were seeking cures should be brought forward to him, and that a clear area should be kept if possible so that others could witness the event. He told us that we must be careful not to give any possible criticism that either access was being denied to people or that miracles of curing of the sick were a circus act rather than the power of God at work through Jesus himself. Having given us this apparently impossible task he went out into the square and sat down under a shaded fig tree and people started to come forward! We found that we really had little to do except to help people and to encourage people who were becoming doubtful that any cure would be granted to them because of their sinfulness, or that they were unsure that perhaps their relative was so ill it was inconceivable that there could be a cure. We explained to people that the possibility of a cure depended on their personal faith and confidence, their belief in God and that Jesus was the Emmanuel, if they were not sure about this then perhaps they should consider. What we didn't realise at this time was that this confidence and belief was more than could be asked from people and that it was the reality of the cure that would finally convince people of the reality of God's Emmanuel. It was also important that people gained conviction that Jesus was recognised as the Emmanuel by witnessing the miracle cures before their eyes. We found that the revulsion we had initially felt quickly disappeared, we found that, not only could we look at these disfigured twisted bodies, we could see that these were people who had the same sort of feelings and emotions as us; the ultimate stage in our reconciliation was that we could actually touch them to help them forward. Every one of them was almost cured in their spirits just because we had recognised them as real people. For us the experience was a new vision of God at work among people, we were surprised that we received great spiritual comfort by helping other people. It was so rewarding to see these segregated, frightened, isolated people joyfully leave Jesus knowing that they could now re-establish themselves in the community and felt themselves worthy to worship God just like everyone else. The curing went on for a long time, eventually the queue started to subside, we could see that Jesus was getting exhausted. He put such effort into each individual who was presented before him. He talked to them quietly and directly, he did not make a public issue of their conditions or of the fact that he was providing them with salvation, there were no public displays of excitement, the crowd did not gasp or clap or cheer or any of the expressions of mass appreciation that might have been expected. We were just about to step in and send people away when some children who had been picking wild flowers while their parents were watching the cures, came forward to offer the flowers to Jesus. I am sure that Jesus was watching carefully and before we had time to turn them away he said, "Don't turn the children away! Children have a clear understanding of God, that grown-ups have lost and have to recover before they can be accepted into the Kingdom of God." So nervously they came forward to this great man that they had heard their parents talking about and who had miraculously cured all sorts of the sick. He made them welcome and comfortable and he blessed them and told them that the world they would live in would be very different just because he was there.

After this very touching and emotional interlude we were ready to return to Capernaum when a group of the Scribes and Pharisees who had been talking among themselves came forward to challenge Jesus. They were arrogant and aggressive in their posture, they clearly wanted to undermine the impression that was clearly now becoming established that this was the Emmanuel, so they had decided to rubbish the cures they and all the crowd had witnessed. In a loud voice that the whole crowd could hear and in a sneering tone their leader proclaimed, "We have watched this man working his so called cures here today and as your religious guardians we have to tell you that this man is an impostor. Only the Son of Beelzebub could cast out the devils from the possessed and so this Jesus, who we all know is a carpenter from Nazareth, with no training or education like us, is not God's messenger but the devils messenger and that the "cures" will only be temporary. You have been deluded, you have become hysterical you have been misled by his honeyed words but we tell you it is all a charade. We tell you all to go home now and have nothing to do with this man and tell your friends and neighbours the same. You will see that he will shortly be punished for his evil works." Jesus had sat through this tirade of lies and personal abuse without any reaction, part of the crowd were beginning to nod in agreement with the lawyer who had spoken, but clearly the majority were furious at the accusations that were being made and turned on the group of their religious leaders with angry looks and a general hubbub was about to start.

Jesus looked at the group of accusers and asked them, "By what power do you cast out devils? When did you last cast out devils? Would Beelzebub cast out his own? A city divided against itself will surely fall!" Jesus was clearly angry at the accusations and continued, "You brood of Vipers! You think that because you are the sons of Abraham you have a right to God's blessings, I tell you this, you have failed to execute the stewardship that God charged you to keep. You have made a stumbling block out of the Law of Moses that was given to you to be a stepping stone to God. I tell you all that unless you accept me and my words you will never enter heaven and will be cast out to where there is only pain and anguish and gnashing of teeth." There was total silence nobody had ever spoken out like that to such a powerful group of leaders; nobody knew what to do. The lawyer who had issued the challenge was dumbfounded his mouth opened and closed but no sound came out, he was purple in the face and his eyes were bulging, I thought he would explode, quite suddenly he turned on his heel and pushed his way through the crowd followed by the rest of his confederates. Jesus watched them go with a look of sadness on his face and then he repeated to the crowd his story of the Good Shepherd and the Lost Sheep, it took some of the tension out of the atmosphere and I am sure that a lot of people there worked out who were the Bad Shepherds.

So he then blessed the crowd and dismissed them, and we all prepared to set off back to Capernaum when a lawyer, who had separated himself from the group who had challenged Jesus, came to him and asked him "Master, how can I inherit eternal life?", we were all waiting to leave and were cross that this man should delay us, as far as we were concerned the lawyers had done their worst for that day and we knew that we had to get back to Capernaum that evening. We were also very concerned that Jesus had caused great anger among the leaders who had challenged him and that this lawyer was probably asking a trick question to be able to accuse Jesus of some crime. Perhaps Jesus had the same thoughts but he did not show any of these emotions, in fact he treated the question as a genuine enquiry from a serious enquirer. "You are a lawyer! How would you interpret the Law?" The lawyer replied "Love the Lord your God with all your heart, with all your soul, with all your strength and with all your mind: love your neighbour as yourself." Jesus said, "Quite so, go and do that and you will live!" Then we knew that it was a trick because he then asked, "Who is my neighbour?" The crowd had stopped moving away, they clearly were expecting another dramatic confrontation, and waited to see and hear what would happen next.

Jesus sat down and waited for the crowd to sit down and settle itself and then he told them the parable which is so well known I will not repeat it all, it was the Parable of the Good Samaritan. After what had gone before this emphasised the disgust that Jesus felt for the priests and the lawyers and the Pharisees and the Saducees. You will remember that it was these people who passed by "on the other side", to avoid the poor Jew who had been mugged and it was the Samaritan who had stopped to help. The criticism went home like a knife, the hated, detested Samaritan was better than the leaders of our society who were charged with setting an example on the application of the Law. The Samaritan was the example of a "Good Neighbour", the crowd and the lawyer were amazed, nobody could imagine that your neighbour could be other than a Jew. Jesus was advocating that no differences in race, in colour, in religious observance or of language or of country should be excluded from our duty to God to extend God's love to him. This was an almost unbelievable answer to the question posed, but the way it had been explained in the story made it quite clear and direct that our neighbour was any and all of the people that we came into contact with who were in any kind of need. It was our duty under the Law to do whatever we could to satisfy his need even the hated Samaritans!

Jesus' final question to the lawyer was, "You are a lawyer, you tell me who was the good neighbour to the Jew?" It was clear from his voice and his demeanour that the lawyer had to reluctantly agree that it was the Samaritan. Jesus said to him "Go and do likewise!" The lawyer turned in great confusion and walked away through the crowd. They, and we, had been so surprised by this exposé of God's law that we could hardly believe what we had heard. There seemed to be a lot of people in the crowd who could not accept even the idea that they might be expected to help a Samaritan or worse a Gentile or worse still a Roman where did this stop? After a while people started to move off, very quietly and deep in thought and very confused, they had witnessed a direct attack on the leaders of the society, that seemed OK, they should be criticised and brought to heel, but then this parable was a direct assault on their dearly held taboos of exclusion from God's kingdom, now that was very serious!

As the crowd thinned out we were able to set out for Capernaum, later perhaps than we should have but with just about enough time to be back for a meal at my parent's house. The walk was south and west into the setting sun, we walked along following Jesus with the crowd straggled out behind us. We were all quiet, what we had seen and heard was another frightening example of Jesus ability to confront people with the reality of their attitudes and behaviour and to overtly challenge the religious authorities who believed, most sincerely, that they were the guardians of the nations soul. Was Jesus there to destroy all that we understood about our nationhood? Were we to be his willing disciples to make this happen? Despite what he had said we had our birthright to God's blessing it said so in the holy writings, why should God renege on that promise? The risks were getting dangerous, rebellion against the authorities would be dealt with harshly, they had too much invested in their position of power to let it go easily. We had only met a few provincial lawyers and priests, when Jerusalem heard what had been said they would quickly demonstrate their power and send their best brains to control this rebellious Jesus. There was little discussion, Jesus was silent and absorbed in his own thoughts and it wasn't until we crested the hill behind the Jonas' farm, when almost all the crowd had left us, that he asked us whether we had understood this latest parable. To the man we replied that we had; but then added that it was a very high demand that God made of us and that it would cause a lot of trouble if we were seen to be Samaritan sympathisers. He told us that it was easy to love your friends, but God demanded that we love our enemies and those who hate us and persecute us and, yes, even put us to death, they were, he had shown us, just as much our neighbours as the family next door who fell on hard times. He then brought us up sharply by adding "---- and our next door neighbour who has a child possessed by a devil who you have all admitted to me are effectively excluded from society and any access to God!" Once again we fell into silence and reflected on this real direct and unanswerable criticism of our society, of us as individuals and by inference the people who set the examples and the rules by which we lived. We got back to the farm just as the sun was setting over the hills behind Tiberias, and beyond that Nazareth, the view was breathtaking, Peter and I congratulated each other that we had persuaded our parents to buy this particular plot of land. The air was like crystal and the silence was tangible, that was until wives, mothers, children and grandchildren were warned of our imminent arrival by the farm dogs. The welcome was so warm that we could feel that they had no anger at our having left in the way we did, they were just delighted to see us all again and they showed it.

We had had a long day and were tired, Jesus looked exhausted and as usual Mary was on hand to look after him, she gently shooed us all away saying that when he had rested for a while he would be with us for the rest of the evening. He was lucky, we had nobody to give us refuge just then, we introduced our new companions and then faced a barrage of questions about our adventures and about the reports they had received of the amazing works that Jesus was performing. Peter's family and my family had come up from Capernaum and had already heard most of what had been happening so we started by reporting on that day's events. In particular we told them the story of the Good Samaritan this led to a lot of heated discussion about the terrible things these fallen "Hebrews", the Samaritans, had inflicted on innocent travellers and started to catalogue all the grievances we had been taught from childhood.

It was Peter who stopped us all, "Don't you see," he almost shouted, "isn't that just what Jesus is trying to stop! None of us know the truth of these accusations but that doesn't matter, even if they were all true, Jesus told us that we have to extend to them the same caring love that we give to each other in this family. More than that we have to give them the treatment that we, each of us, would want to receive whatever from a friend, a stranger and an enemy whatever the circumstances. The way we are all talking will just continue the bad feeling that exists now, into the future. The truth is that if we want to serve God we have to serve each other and that includes our neighbours and that includes the Samaritans, and all the other strangers and people we ostracise from our society, and incidently, who ostracise us from their societies. We could start by showing Capernaum that they don't have to be ashamed that there are sick people in their midst and that these people have a soul just as we do!" Peter's wife retorted, "It is alright in theory but the Samaritans showed no intention of extending any care to us!" "Quite so" said Peter "and that is why we have to show them God's love. At the minute I think we should be thinking more about what we can do rather than what we can't do. I suggest that we find all the people who were cured by Jesus yesterday in Capernaum and invite them to lunch at my house?" There was a barrage of objections, "We don't know who they are", "We don't know how many will come." "Who will buy the food and prepare it?" It all sounded negative but gradually as the problems became less insurmountable the women became enthusiastic. Jonas was there and announced that he would pay the cost of the food, but added "Not every day!" It was very surprising to feel that a new spirit was invading people as they worked out how they could help other people. The discussion was very lively and came to an end when mother said if we didn't eat we would not be alive to help other people! So the women set to preparing the meal and the men went into the orchard overlooking the tranquil sea and sat down together to discuss what we had learnt that day.

Phillip started our resumé, " Don't you think it is extraordinary how many people Jesus cured? How can anybody possibly doubt but that this man had the power of God with him, and what incredible benefits must be available from God? He only had to heal one sick person to have created an impact on people's minds, if that was the sole intention. But Jesus must have cured hundreds of people it clearly demonstrated to me that God's mercy was boundless."

There was a general agreement but then, I think, Matthew said, "I am surprised, both today and yesterday, how patient the crowd had been. There was no pushing or shoving, there was no pecking order, the wealthy mixed with the poor, the proud with the humble waited their turn."

James joined in and added, "It was as if everyone accepted that, when confronted by this amazing demonstration of God's power, the differences between men was so insignificant that they did not matter! We were all equal before God! Even when Jesus was clearly exhausted and there was still an inexhaustible demand for his healing power, the people who were left disappointed did not make a fuss, they just accepted that their turn had not been now. What they had seen, and that they could take home with them was that God had not excluded them, God did not treat them as untouchables. God was aware of their pain and distress and it was men who created the barriers that excluded them and their families from the full participation of God's benefits. In God's eyes they were just as important as any other person."

Nathaniel continued, "We have been watching Jesus story of the Good Shepherd being played out before us and that it represented a challenge to our society. Just because we didn't understand them and their desparate needs we shunned these people when they were in fact the people who most needed our care. This was a serious challenge to our lawyers and the rabbis and the Pharisees. Maybe that is why they had caused a stir and accused Jesus of such a terrible crime as being in league with the devil! Perhaps we have to accept that we should expect to have this sort of reaction where ever we went."

James added a warning to us all, "Jesus has warned us that we have to love our neighbour even if he persecuted us and scourged us and put us to public shame and even killed us. We should be sure, that when Jesus said such a thing then it was sure to happen, each of us individually had to decide, was this what we were prepared to accept." The group nodded, but it was not clear whether they nodded assent that they accepted the possibility of death or that they accepted that that was what Jesus meant!

Somebody else said, "Of course there was a risk of being killed but there was also the prize of power and influence and wealth when we had completed the task of destroying the Romans and re-establishing the true honest God fearing state of Israel, and for him this was a worthwhile risk."

Peter was alarmed by this comment and told us, "I am not at all convinced that such a revolution was actually what this was all about, despite the attractions that it might hold for personal earthly pomp and recognition."

The subject then switched to the story about the Good Samaritan and how overtly critical it was of the "establishment" when we became aware that Jesus had joined our group. We didn't know how long he had been listening to our struggling with the problems he had given us, he looked at us very kindly and said, "Fear not! God is with you, who can succeed against you! Dinner is ready, and its time we ate!" After dinner most of us set off to our homes in the town, but Mother had worked out how many she should accommodate and had prepared beds for them all over the farm. A procession of lanterns would have been seen lighting the way from the Jonas' farm down to the town late in the night. The group were well fed and watered and were also filled with the infectious confidence and joyfulness which exuded from Jesus.

Part 13

The Sermon on the Mount

The next morning as arranged the women arrived from the farm to Peter's house and a child was sent to my house to tell us that Jesus was expecting us at the farm and that today would be a non-travelling day! We didn't know what that meant but we all assembled and set off up to the farm, we were surprised to find that there were many other people making the same journey. Jesus attracted people like bees round honey!

When we arrived at the farm we were told that Jesus had already left with the others and had walked north into the hills and we would find him there. It was not difficult to find him even if it was difficult to get near him. He was not healing people, although there were plenty of the sick in the crowd, he was sitting on a hillock where he could be seen and heard, the crowd were sitting themselves down round him and he welcomed us into the centre of the circle to join the other "disciples". When we were all settled he started to teach us about life and God and eternity. It was mind-blowing, nothing mattered except to catch every word and every nuance. It was obvious to every one that he was talking to us the "Disciples" but that everyone who was there was welcome to listen, and understand if they could.

This teaching has since been given the title of "The Sermon on the Mount", it has been repeated everywhere that the disciples have gone. It is the most dramatic explanation of the nature of God and his relationship with man that was ever produced it far outweighs the messages in the Pentateuch. But it is also enigmatic, superficially it is clear, but as we were beginning to learn, Jesus' sayings had very deep meanings for those who wanted to examine it closely.

The first part of the teaching was a series of eight recommendations to mankind stating the blessing of a particular attribute of personal nature or endeavour and the benefits that would be derived from such a nature. As an example one that springs to mind for instance is:

How blest are those who have suffered persecution for the cause of right; the kingdom of Heaven is theirs.

Then he told us of the importance of our mission and the importance of our keeping to his words. We have all used them many times, since then, to encourage each other and our brothers and sisters.

"You are the salt of the world; but you will be no use if you loose the will to teach people of God's will."

"You are the light of the world; so you must shine out and not hide the message of salvation from the people who need to hear it. Like a lantern you must shed your light on other people to show them God's will."

Then there followed an explanation of the relationship of himself to the Law of Moses, he told us that he had not come to replace the law but he had come to fulfil the law. He showed us how it was in a man's heart and in his intentions that the judgement of the law would be made and not by a man's outward behaviour. That this was the critical measure of a man's righteousness and not whether he had diligently obeyed the minute points of the law designed by lawyers and not by God.

Next he expanded on the command to "love your neighbour" which he had shown us in the parable of the Good Samaritan. Loving those who love you is not significant, it is only by loving the people who can and do damage you that you can show God's will for the world. If people demand service from you, willingly give them more than they ask. If people use you badly then you have to respond with acceptance even "turning the other cheek".

He then explained to us that we had to be sure about our real loyalties; that we had to decide whether we would serve earthly material things or to serve our spiritual God. In particular he warned us very strongly that money can become a dominant factor in our lives "You cannot serve God and Money, the love of money is the root of all evil."

The next lesson was on prayer he taught us to pray the now famous prayer, That starts with those intimate words "Our Father", that all followers of Christ are specially privileged to use, it is a special privilege because it confirms the loving relationship which God has for each individual. In its simple words it encapsulates the full beneficial relationship between God and man and between man and man, that God has ordained for everyone who accepts the reality of Jesus Christ as The Son of God. Of course none of us understood the significance of the words when Jesus pronounced them, it was only in the fullness of time that we saw the deep meaning and blessing that they expose. He told us that because our relationship with God was so special and so personal, prayer must be a holy, private intercession. God could see into the hearts of men and responded to sincerity and faith; he was unmoved by the hypocritical showy displays that had become the common behaviour of many. He expected secrecy and commitment, commitment to be totally concentrated and fixed on the act of penitence, of pleading and of worship, undisturbed by the distractions of the world and its affairs. He assured us of God's benefits that are available to us on request, he used such confident phrases as "Knock and the door will be opened" and "Ask and it shall be given to you" or "Seek and you will find" But he added that despite all these benefits the way to God was difficult, he likened it to a steep, narrow and rugged path, whereas the path to perdition was wide and smooth. He used beautiful parables and similes to explain the proper relationship with God and the absolute necessity to obtain this sublime state that could only be achieved through a proper relationship between men and men.

He had been talking for several hours and came to his final command, it is the bed rock command of a God fearing, loving society, the rule is simply "Judge not lest you are judged." This was another astounding clarifications of the reality of God's love and man's frailty, again he used metaphors to explain what he meant. He really posed a question to each individual that was "How can you possibly accuse, judge, or sentence another person when you are yourself so sinful? God has given you the Commandments to regulate your lives with God and with your neighbour. It is for you to obey these Laws not to accuse others of failing. And another question for yourselves, Do you know the real reasons and motivation for another's behaviour? You cannot and you never will, so your judgement is on the basis of bias, of hear-say, of learnt grievances, of pride and exclusivity and fear." The final question "Is it on this basis that you would like your actions and weaknesses to be judged?" So we come back to the real Law, " Love thy neighbour as yourself!"

I suspect that this teaching took five or six hours, you will understand what I have written is a very brief summary, during which time nobody had spoken, very few people had moved even the small children had sat patiently by their parents, if they didn't understand what was being said they were mesmerised by the calm, confident sympathetic voice. What was being said nobody had ever heard before. It was as though the whole of the history of the Hebrews had been laid out before us and an entirely new interpretation made of the real lasting relationship that God had looked for from his chosen people. We had not noticed but all the time more people were arriving, they came from the whole region, as they arrived they sat down and listened to the teacher. It was quite clear that what Jesus was saying was intended for our ears, this small band of disciples, but he had no problem with every body hearing what was being taught. The message was for everyone, but we had to learn it more and more certainly, so he talked directly to us. The experience was breathtaking it was as if the whole of life and everything that was and was to be were being explained with a certainty that we had never encountered before. We had experienced some of this sort of teaching in the private discussions we had with Jesus in the evenings after our exciting days, the most impressive feature was that although he was talking to a group of people each one of us felt that we were in fact the only person there. He managed to keep each individual totally attendant on what he was saying.

One man in the crowd was different, he did not sit he stood, he hardly moved as the lesson progressed he was very noticeable because even when the sun was high in the sky and it was very hot but he did not move, he hardly changed his balance, he was totally absorbed in what was being said, nothing distracted him, his eyes were fixed on Jesus and nothing else even entered his consciousness. We noticed his neighbours offered him water to drink but he did not seem to notice them. He was a tall man, handsome and fit, he was well dressed and clearly he was educated but he was not a Pharisee or a rabbi. There was something attractive about his person that we found from time to time almost distracted us from what Jesus was saying, I remember thinking that I wished he would sit down like the rest of the crowd.

Jesus had finished what he wanted to say to us, the crowd realised that there was nothing else to be seen that day and started to disperse. What had been said had gone home they were very quiet and small groups met together and then broke up, they were talking about what they had heard and they were very perplexed. Nobody had ever talked like this to them before, Jesus was challenging the very foundations of their belief. Worse than that he was implying that the accepted understanding of the specialness of the relationship between the Jews and the one true God had to change, the reality was that they were not any more special than anyone else. The special relationship, Jesus showed, was between an individual and God. Nobody could any longer hide their sinfulness behind the Lawyers and the Pharisees and the Rabiis, they were responsible personally and directly with no 'go betweens', or 'scape-goats'.

Jesus was very tired and although we had many questions we wanted to ask we decided that we should go back to the farm and let him rest. So we were collecting ourselves together when we noticed that Jesus had seen the man who we had all seen in the crowd. He was looking at him intently and the man was looking back directly at Jesus. It was as if some messages were passing between them that nobody else could receive, after a few seconds that seemed like forever, Jesus beckoned the man to come forward. When he came to Jesus he collapsed to his knees and was weeping inconsolably, Jesus was talking very gently to him, we never found out what they were talking about but from the look on Jesus face the matter was very serious. After a few minutes Jesus called us all to him and announced that this was the next appointed disciple, his name was Judas Iscariot, Jesus introduced him as, "A man whose deeds and name would be remembered for all time and that his actions would change the world." We were very impressed by this introduction, none of us knew the man, but he told us later that he had followed Jesus and listened to his preaching and seen his great works. He was, he said, absolutely convinced that this was the Messiah and that he was determined to do everything in his power to bring about God's Kingdom on earth. Much later, in fact it was probably years later, that some of us remembered this introduction from Jesus and wondered whether he knew, right from the beginning, the role that Judas would play in the great happenings in Jerusalem. There is no doubt that Jesus prediction about his impact was fulfilled and his name is and always will be thought of as the greatest traitor ever, but that was all in the future! Now we had a new friend and co-worker and he quickly became a stalwart support and enthusiastic disciple.

So the crowd had dispersed and we set off back to the farm, Jesus as was his custom set off at a brisk pace that the rest of us were hard pushed to keep up with, the way was not easy and although we were young and fit by time we got back to my parents house we were all feeling exhausted. I can still remember that day as if it was yesterday, you cannot imagine the impact that this great sermon had had on us all. We were almost numb with excitement and anxiety that we were expected to take in all these revolutionary ideas at the first hearing. As we approached the house Jesus stopped and said to us that we should relax before the meal and that he would talk to us afterwards under the stars and we should be able to examine the things he had said and that he would help us better understand. It was as if he knew we were confused and disturbed, even frightened, by the implications of his teaching and that we needed him to give us courage and faith to accept God's purpose and the new interpretation of the relationship between God and man.

After all the excitement of the day the tranquillity of the farmhouse and the domestic activities were a release of tensions that we were all feeling. Wives and children were all around us wanting to know what had passed during the day, giving us instructions and ordering us about, just as normal, but for us everything was abnormal. This practical "real" world seemed "surreal" while our heads were whirling with

171

Jesus words! Most of us managed to slip away and find a quiet spot to think and to pray. I remember using the first few lines of the prayer we had been taught by Jesus and repeated them over and over with ever growing intensity appealing for God's power help me begin to contemplate the enormity of what we were hearing and seeing "Our father who art in heaven, hallowed be thy name, thy Kingdom come, thy will be done on earth as in heaven", became more and more appropriate to the situation which was gradually unfolding. Jesus teaching was revolutionary, it turned everything that we held dear on its head, it demanded that we re-evaluate the whole of our being, not just our relationship with God but also our relationship with the world and with the people round us. It was a direct challenge to the political and religious establishment and demanded a response from them that would mean they had to admit that they were wrong in their way of governing the people. It stated a new vision of the interpretation of the Law that was based on only two principals, "Love God" and "Love your Neighbour". It was quite clear that everyone would agree with these "Laws", but it was also quite clear when Jesus explained their implication that they were generally ignored. I was still having problems accepting for instance that Gentiles and Samaritans were as worthy of my love as my brother Jews. I could not abandon the history of torment of the Sons of Abraham as they tried over many generations to satisfy God's will for them as His chosen people. It justified our national feeling of superiority and separateness, no other people had withstood so much and still maintained the belief in the one God, and although we failed and suffered his wrath, we did at least try, and He did at least let us try! But Jesus was telling us that this was not what God wanted, he wanted everyone of every race to come to receive His blessing, and that we were a key element in his bringing this to pass. Did this mean that the Jews would disappear as a race, they would after all these tribulations just be absorbed into all the other races of the world? The established temporal powers had not yet realised what was being proposed by Jesus, not just proposed but predicted and demanded, when they did they were certain to become very repressive and the work that Jesus had called us to do would become dangerous. Already we had seen the reaction of some local provincial clerics but we must expect to be challenged by the establishment in Jerusalem, in fact, to me, Jerusalem had ceased to be the place of great national certainty and comfort, it had become a dark threatening power which would have to be confronted one day. Yet Jesus must know this, he showed no anxiety, even when he was tired he was always cheerful and confident, he enjoyed the simple things of life. He did not continually

172

address the mission, he let things happen and then used them as examples to interpret God and to show how far our society had drifted from the Law. He made it clear that he would not criticise other societies for their wonted paganism because they had never been given any guidance towards God, on the other hand the harsh judgement he made of us was because we had been given the guidance and had continually contravened the Law. The other thing that was becoming apparent was the real urgency of the mission. We were a part of the whole endeavour but we seemed to have little or no time to absorb, or question or even just become used to the dramatic ideas and actions that seemed to be our daily bread! We seemed to be moving "helter-skelter" down a slide with no possibility to avoid what was becoming almost certainly a clash of power. From our perspective, at the time, the power of Jesus seemed little indeed compared with the power of the Sanhedrin in Jerusalem or the Emperor in Rome. Perhaps Jesus really did know what was going to happen each day, to us it seemed completely unplanned and that Jesus courted confrontation with the Pharisees, the lawyers and the scribes and relished in the challenge that they posed everywhere we went.

I was getting quite alarmed and depressed; it was a relief to see Peter walking towards me across the meadow, with his great confident smile and his strong gait. "Well", he said, "Andy, have you got it all sorted out now? I think that we will change the world; we will change it because at last we are going to get some planning. I have been talking to Judas, the new man; He has worked in the administration offices of King Phillip and knows a thing or two about organising campaigns. Most of his experience has been in military campaigns but he recons that what Jesus is trying to do is best seen as a military campaign. So now we will be able to work out where we will go and where we will stay and how we will eat and who we should meet to make sure that the people who matter know what we are trying to do!" I was totally amazed, I remembered the old Peter, or Simon as he was then, I had almost forgotten how excited he got when he saw a plan for action. A new venture for the fishing business always caused this almost tunnel vision that avoided all the real problems. Sometimes that was a good thing and he always made things happen. This time, however he and Judas seemed to have forgotten that there was a different factor to be taken into account. That factor was totally out of our control, that factor was Jesus, and I told him that try as they might they would fail to constrain Jesus to any man made plan, he was working to God's plan. Peter would have none of it, he complained that the situation that we were living in was best described as chaos. We really had little idea of

173

what we were doing! It was all right for Jesus to assure us that we were going to change the world but nothing was happening. Just look at it, we seemed to spend our time with the drop outs of society, we had had little or no contact with the people who held power and when we did it always ended in either a direct hostile confrontation or at best a stand-off. If we really were going to change the world we had to contact and involve the people who made the laws and controlled the money and could muster a military capability, that's the way things happen. Jesus didn't seem to understand the very basics of power politics and unless we started to manage this campaign it would all just fritter away to nothing! He almost exploded when he got to that part of the argument, he seemed very angry that he had, he felt, been swallowed up in project which was beginning to look like a waste of his time and heaven only knows what damage it was doing to the business. I tried to calm him down and reminded him of the feeling of electric awe which we all experienced in His presence, of the incredible powers He demonstrated every day to us and thousands of others, of His teaching to us today about the real meaningful relationship that God wanted to have with men, of the love that God had for mankind and Jesus' role in showing that to people. I told him that I did not believe that this mission to mankind was about power politics, and, whatever we may think, we had to recognise the incredible confidence that He showed in all circumstances. Peter gradually calmed down, fortunately he told me he had not shared his thoughts with any one else so the situation was contained. Then we began to talk about the lessons the old Rabbi had given us about the expected Emmanuel and the fulfilment of the prophecies and the re-interpretation of the Law that was predicted. We agreed that every day was an almost unbelievable experience and we were so privileged to be at the very centre of all these happenings. Who else had been chosen by God to be close to a man of such immense power over nature and the evils of disease. We were perhaps being small minded and overconfident in our role in this adventure when really we had no idea what we were doing or where we were heading except that Jesus had promised us that we would change the world for ever! On reflection that seemed to be a pretty good reason for staying the course and giving this extraordinary man all the support and protection we could and to learn from him all the lessons that he was daily teaching us. So in the end Peter and I agreed that it was unlikely that a military style campaign was appropriate and that we should take care to rein in Judas Iscariot's enthusiasm for "management techniques".

Gradually, as the evening began to draw in, the group coalesced and then Jesus arrived, until that moment every one had been quiet and pensive, what we had been taught that day was incredible this really was a revolution when the 'powers that be' heard this message they would be very alarmed, not only was this new prophet drawing huge crowds and working miracles and healings but he was forecasting the overthrow of the power base of the governing theocracy, dangerous ground indeed! Then Jesus came, he was bright and cheerful he said that today we had been shown the real plan that God had for humanity, all humanity and wasn't it amazing that an infinite God should care desperately about each individual soul. The fundamental message that we all had to understand is that GOD "IS" LOVE. For the next hour he talked to each of us confidentially and quietly. He clearly understood the fears and misgivings that his teaching of the day had generated, He moved gently among us and as usual when he was talking to you it was as if there was nobody else in the world. He answered questions and gave people courage and determination, I was so glad that Peter and I had talked together before hand and there was no temper in Peter to generate a confrontation.

By now it was almost dark and the sky was studded with stars which seemed brighter than usual, my eldest daughter came to tell us that the evening meal was ready and we all sat down under an awning stretched between the trees and enjoyed a meal that could only be described as a celebratory feast. My father Jonas had in the past been very reluctant to sit down to table with the group most of whom were, by man's classification, "sinners". I know Jesus had talked to him about his sensitivity but I am convinced that he could not stay away from the table when Jesus was there and listen spell-bound to the conversation. Well, we had a most entertaining dinner, Jesus was so positive, the conversation, as I remember it, centred on the role of the Jews in the great plan of God. This plan was to make his love and all its benefits available to all mankind, the Jews had a major role in this plan. Their role had been designated by God to be a window to the rest of mankind to see and to understand that the One True God provided the only basis for society. This would ensure the fulfilment of each individual's potential to contribute to the betterment of his neighbour by reflecting, on earth, God's eternal and infinite love for all mankind. We were shocked by the idea that our deeply held view of the special and therefore separateness from the rest of humanity was a complete misunderstanding of God's real intensions. The whole history of the Jews had been to isolate themselves from all other nations because they were the only ones to be saved and then only if they adhered absolutely to God's law. From this stance had grown the need that the Law was absolute and that lawyers had a duty to decide the minutest details of behaviour needed to stay within the Law. The result was that the Law had itself become and idol, a graven image, to the Jews. They had forgotten the real basis of the Law, that is to recognise the absolute superiority of God in all things and that this was demonstrated at all times and in all places not by the adherence to ritualistic patterns of worship but by the caring, selfless giving of every individual to satisfy the needs of the individual people that they had any sort of contact or dealing with. The problem was that although the Jews had been given this message, they had corrupted it. Now the message was being given again but this time it was specifically through the Jews to the whole world, and that was our task. We had all been listening attentively until now but we now asked questions some of which had been worrying us for a while.

Somebody asked, "So what is the future for the Jews?"

Jesus replied, "This race of ours, with its rich history, has failed in their chance to extend God's love to the world. They are determined to stay an exclusive, isolated and separated people. So now others have to be found to carry the message to every part of the world."

He warned us, "It will be far worse for an individual, or a nation, who had heard the word of God and turned away from it than it will be for the individual who had never heard the word on the Day of Judgement. Be sure that knowing the right way and choosing the wrong way was the certain route to hell."

At first we were quiet and listened without any comment or interruption, then gradually some of us started to question what he was saying, for instance,

"What about the promises to Moses, to Isaac and to Jacob? What about the prophecies of Isaiah and Jeremiah? Was all this of no consequence to God? Was He reneging on the deal he had with the Jews?"

Jesus replied emphatically, "No, He was not! God will never, never go back on his word! The special relationship was still there, the Jews could accept it if they chose, but they would choose to stay as they were, to maintain what they saw as their exclusive rights. In so doing they were disobeying Gods instruction and intention that the Jews should be a shining example to the world of the blessings that are available from the acceptance of God as their guide and inspiration."

To further underline the real plan of God, he continued, "To God", he said, "the accident of where anyone was born or by whom he was parented was of no importance. The only judgement God would make was how diligently each individual really adhered to God's two basic rules, love God and love your neighbour. "How", somebody asked, I think it was Judas Iscariot perhaps still wanting a plan, "How could we such a small band of simple men change the world?"

Jesus was very gentle and encouraging, he replied, "You 'small band' are the most privileged men who have ever lived in the world; and this is why, you were chosen by God, not by me, not because you have special expertise, not because you have been trained in the law or the testaments but because God can see in you a potential that neither you nor anyone else could possibly see. That potential will be realised as you witness to God's love over the years ahead. You are special because you are witnessing, as no other group of men has ever witnessed or will ever witness in the whole history of the world, God at work in the world. You will see and gradually understand the real majesty of God and the real majesty of man. You will be given powers that you cannot yet conceive, the spirit of God will be with you wherever you go and whatever you say or do. From the lessons you are learning now you will have faith to change men's minds, to change the events of history. You will be given the courage to preach the message of God not only to simple men, but you will witness to rulers, to kings, to armies and you will overcome the evil intentions of men. This will be done not by the force of arms but by the power of God that you will be witnessing. Your example will convince others, who will convince yet more and the end result will be that you HAVE changed the world!"

It was now getting late and Jesus could see that we were getting very tired and perhaps confused, so he suggested that bed was the best thing now and that as time went on we would increasingly understand what he was saying. He suggested that after such a day as today perhaps we should take the morrow restfully contemplating the things we had seen and heard today. So we were to take a walk together along the seashore after we had breakfasted and would perhaps have the chance to discuss the matters again! So we had a plan, not quite what Peter had wanted but at least tomorrow looked organised.

Part 14

Teaching and Miracles

We all slept well and rose early, as had become our way, to pray to God for his support in today's business. As it turned out we needed it and received it! We all met at Peter's house in the town and breakfasted together and then set off to the beach. We were amazed at the crowd that seemed to have been waiting for us, there were literally thousands of men women and children, all agog to see and to hear what this new prophet and teacher had to say and do today. Capernaum is at the cross road of the world, travellers, Jews and gentiles from all over the world passed that way and many, having heard about Jesus stopped for a day or so on the journey to witness his mission. When we talked to them we found that they were from all over the country and the world, from Syria and Asia, from the desert and from the coast, they told us that it was common knowledge everywhere of the miraculous happenings and the exciting teachings of Jesus. People were saying that this was in truth the Messiah and that He would lead The Jews to their true destiny and that they would follow Him wherever he would lead them, they were convinced that this was the long awaited new David. Jesus heard these protestations and wanted none of it, he asked for a boat so that we, the 'small band', could sail to the eastern shore on the far side of the Jordan where we might find the peace we were looking for. So Peter found a boat and we set sail, there must have been about twenty of us in the boat and with the wind light we made slow progress and had to row for most of the passage. The crowd on the shore could see where we were going and set off to follow us, their progress just about matched ours and after about two hours we met together again not far from Bethsaida. Jesus disembarked and set off at a brisk pace up into the hills just north of the sea, the weather had been unseasonably wet and the result was that he found a flat promontory covered in lush grass and wild flowers it was a beautiful place with wide, wide views over the sea and a backdrop of hills leading into the Arabian desert. Gradually the crowd gathered here, there was an air of expectancy, people were quiet and subdued but there was a tension in the air that you could almost touch.

So people began to bring forward their sick and disabled friends and relatives, Jesus as we had so often witnessed treated each one with compassion. Some of the illnesses and disfigurements were horrible and we were shocked at the open, sympathetic even sorrowful attitude that He took to each one. The cures were dramatic, diseased and distorted bodies were suddenly made whole again, all he asked of the sick was that they confirmed their belief that the power of God could make them well again. The reaction was almost always the same, a deep agonising gratitude, a shock almost amounting to disbelief that the burden that they, and their family, had struggled with had now been removed. People after they had given thanks to Jesus personally, went away rejoicing and praising God. Jesus always responded to the offer of thanks by telling the individual, "By the grace and power of God and by your own faith you are cured, may that faith in God to achieve the impossible, that you have shown and experienced today, stay with you for ever." It was very interesting he never claimed any power was his personal power. All the power he had came from God, this power, he continually showed was only released to become an active force in the world through the faith of individuals. There were lots of children running around playing games and making new friends, the parents tried to keep order but to the children this was a holiday and they were making the most of the freedom of the countryside and all the excitement that was distracting their parents. We 'small band' tried to keep some semblance of order and once or twice had to call the children to order when they appeared to be getting too boisterous. Jesus, despite his concentration at the time on healing the sick, heard the somewhat senatorial voice of Matthew, although it could have been any one of us, and stopped what he was doing and turned to us, "No" he commanded us, "let the children be and to encourage them to come to me." So then the whole atmosphere changed and families brought their children to Jesus to meet him and to hear him. He laid his hands on their heads and blest them, he told us and the parents that these were the future that they were the children of heaven and that they would tell their children and grandchildren that they had seen the Messiah, that they had held his hand and felt his blessing, and that from then on the world had changed. He reminded the parents that they had the responsibility to nurture and teach these children to understand the two great commandments, "To love God and to love your neighbour", and to remind them that they had been there when, through the faith of individuals great miracles were seen among the people.

The day was getting on and it was clear that the crowd had had nothing to eat and that they were far from any substantial town that could possible supply the needs of such a crowd suddenly arriving in their midst. Jesus was concerned for these people and wanted to be sure that they were not to be left stranded without food and having to make there way to their homes or accommodation tired and hungry. Some of us suggested that He should send the crowd away to find what food they could in the local villages, clearly Jesus was not satisfied with this suggestion. He pointed out to us that this was not showing the love of God to others just to send them away to fend for themselves with no knowledge whether there were any villages close by or whether they could possible supply the needs of all these people. He called Philip to him, knowing that Philip came from these parts and asked him whether there was anywhere where we could buy bread for this number of people. Philip confirmed His suspicion that it would not be possible anywhere in that locality. These people had come down to the beach in Capernaum expecting to see and hear Jesus, the town could have easily provided for their needs, but they had in their excitement and determination followed Jesus on a long walk around the North coast of the Sea of Galilee and now they were potentially stranded, nobody had really expected a day like this and had made no preparation for such an expedition. Later we discussed whether Jesus actually knew what was going to happen, we were always a little unsure whether he almost set up situations to be able to demonstrate God's power, we were sure that he had such faith in God that nothing was a problem always the answer was "God is with us and God will keep us safe."

Well the miracle of the feeding of the Five Thousand is well known and some people are tempted to put explanatory proposals forward, I was there and there were only five barley loaves and two small fishes and the boy was very reluctant to give them up. The people sat down as asked and they sat in groups of fifty and there were one hundred of these groups, so we knew there were five thousand of them. Some of us had witnessed the changing of water into wine at Cana and when Jesus took these morsels of food and blessed them we were ready for anything to happen and warned the others that we must do exactly as he commanded us. Well, having blessed the food he called James and his brother John and gave them some and said to them feed the people. So they did, it sometimes seems silly, now, to think of it but they had faith to take this small offering and present it to a group of fifty people and say here is your supper. We all did the same time and time again until everyone had food to eat, in fact they had more than they could eat because we collected up the wasted crusts of bread and filled twelve baskets, as you well know!

When the crowd realised what had happened, that just like the Hebrews in the desert who had been fed Manna from Heaven by Moses, so also these Jews had been fed real daily food from nothing by Jesus of Nazareth. The crowd began to stir and there were shouts of "This is the Emmanuel", "This is the promised Son of David", "This is the saviour of God's chosen people" Then the noise became louder and louder and the demand was, "This is our King, let him lead us to Jerusalem to restore the House of David and to destroy the gentiles in our midst, the desecrators of our Holy places", "Jesus of Nazareth, King of the Jews" Jesus become very ill at ease and said to us "You take the boat as quickly as you can and go back to Capernaum. I want to be alone in the quiet places near here, I hope that this crowd will disperse when they see the boat leaving and I can find some peace and quiet." He was very tired but also very agitated. This political adulation with its overt expressions of rebellion and power seeking was not what he wanted to hear and he knew that if he stayed visible to the crowd the situation could very easily get out of control and that the purpose of his mission would be jeopardised.

So, he managed to slip through the crowd northwards as we left southward to the sea, the diversion worked the crowd assumed that Jesus was with us and followed us to the sea it was only after we had boarded the boat and were setting sail that they realised that He was not with us. They were disappointed and some of them angry that they had been so easily duped, they realised that there was nothing to be done except to walk back towards Capernaum, or onwards towards Jerusalem or their other destinations. What a tale they brought to the city when they arrived a few days later and what a stir went round that the new King David was actually here among them now!

The twenty or so of us that had made the journey in the morning were greatly relieved to be away from the crowd in the relative comfort and security of the boat. We had no anxiety for Jesus we were already confident that he would be with us later that day or the next and we were sure that he would then be full of his old confidence and cheerfulness. We talked about the day's events and were amazed at the lesson we had received in what Jesus meant by "faith", we were beginning to understand that having absolute confidence in God's power resulted in situations being taken out of our control and solutions of dramatic proportions being made available. This power was available to us to transform insignificant human resources into unbelievable capability and always far beyond anything we could expect or even hope for, so a few loaves of bread and some fish fed five thousand mouths and there was food left over. We had to ask ourselves whether we could ever have such faith and confidence, we saw that all that Jesus did was to bless the offering in God's name and to leave the rest to God. He didn't attempt to tell God what the problem was or what he expected or wanted God to do. The "faith" was to allow God the total freedom to use his incomprehensible power to impact on peoples' minds, 'How great God is!' As I remember the discussion was very lively, everybody had their own impressions and sensations to add. We were not taking as much care of the boat as we should and when we noticed we realised we had been blown much further south than we intended and now had to work our way north again, against an ever strengthening head wind. The wind became so fierce that we had to drop the sail and take to the oars, for several hours we took it in turns to fight against the wind and were making little or no progress. The situation was getting serious as the boat was beginning to take in water and although we bailed out as hard as we could, it was clear that our situation was becoming dangerous. Some of us had years of experience at sea and were able to deal with the problems in a fairly calm way, however most of the compliment went from anxious to panic very quickly. Some one said we should pray for God's help, someone else said that God couldn't bail any faster than he was and what we needed was more discipline and less talk and shouting. Someone else said we should have faith that we were in God's hands and he would care for us, to which I remember a retort "The Lord helps those who help themselves!" and we should row harder. The whole situation was getting frantic there was nobody taking control, very quickly we were being tossed about like a cockleshell and were in imminent danger of sinking.

Then James said he was sure he could see something on the sea, we all looked where he pointed and there in the rain and wind was a ghost like figure moving towards us over the waves. Well there was now absolute panic. Everyone was convinced that this apparition was from the next life and had come to take us away and we were sure to drown. Total despair overtook us. I am sure that at that moment we did pray fervently for God to save us, we didn't explain the situation, we didn't suggest solutions but we did rely on his power to save us. Then to our total amazement the apparition spoke to us and there was Jesus saying "It is me, don't be afraid, you are in no danger, God is with us all the time, he will care for us in all situations." Almost immediately the storm abated and the sea calmed, our panic disappeared and we became confident that Jesus was in charge and all would be well. Peter who probably recovered most quickly called out to Jesus, "If you call me can I also walk on the sea?" Jesus replied, "Peter I have told you that if you have faith everything is possible! So come to me!" It was fantastic, Peter without any hesitation stepped off the boats gunwale and there he was walking on the water! He took three or four paces but then his courage and faith, left him and he started to sink, he cried out and Jesus caught his hand and brought him back to the boat. Much to our surprise when we had got over this shock we looked north and found we were in fact just off the beach and in a few minutes we were safely ashore. You will understand that we gathered round Jesus in great awe. We were actually quite frightened, here was a man of immense power who could, without any excitement or preparation, control the forces of nature, what would he do next? He told us that we had little time to discuss the matters of the last day and night as other evil powers were at work and that he had to confront them. He promised that we would understand what we had witnessed and he would help us with other examples that were all designed to give us that absolute faith in God that would help us to "Change the world" when he had gone ahead. We did not understand then what he was saying but we accepted it as our confidence in his power was growing and the latest demonstrations left us with a sense of wonder that would have made anything he said acceptable.

Unbeknown to us, but clearly Jesus knew what had happened, the remnant of the crowd from yesterday had seen us leave in the boat and having concluded that we would be making for Capernaum, had walked through the night to meet us. This crowd, of several hundred were different from any other crowd we had encountered, they were aggressive and belligerent, they were shouting phrases like "Where is the King of Israel?" and "Freedom for the Jews from the Roman tyrants!" and "Jesus of Nazareth, King of the Jews!" We decided that we should act as a body guard and formed a ring round Jesus to protect him, but he moved us aside and went directly to this crowd and addressed them, as he started to speak they became quiet and still, their ring leaders who had been so overbearing and over confident were silenced by his presence. The gist of what he said was this, first, you have remembered that Moses fed the people with Manna, that Elijah fed the people with bread and that because I have now fed the people with bread you think I am a re-incarnation of a long since dead leader. Secondly, you think that I can, and with your determination, satisfy your physical needs for food and shelter and security and power and that the might of Israel will be restored and you will have peace and freedom. Your whole hope and aspiration is self-centred, you have not listened to the message that I have given you that God's kingdom is a kingdom of love, that it is not of this world and has no ambitions political or financial. You have refused to listen when I tell you that I have come to save the fallen and to give hope and succour to the hopeless and despairing. I am not your king and unless you hear my words and believe them I will never be your king. Well when he had finished he turned on his heal and marched away from them. We were very concerned that they might become violent seeing their plans destroyed and their excitement turned to disappointment. One or two shouted out things like "Don't expect us to help you when the lawyers get you!" and "You won't get anywhere without a struggle of arms and don't forget it!" and "Think you're a King, you don't know what the word means!" Fairly quickly and without any serious trouble they went on their way. Jesus turned to us and said that his plan today was to go to Magdala, it's about a five mile walk west round the north coast of the sea. As far as we knew he had had no sleep and certainly we had had no sleep but he was determined that we should be off as quickly as possible. My house was nearest so all of us, that is about twenty of us, arrived totally un-announced on the doorstep and asked for breakfast. We were amazed it seemed like another miracle of feeding although not on such a grand scale, in a quiet moment my wife confided in me that all the women had got together and decided that the most likely place for breakfast would be my house so they had seen to the preparation.

Jesus used the time to talk to us about faith and God's power. He started by asking us a rhetorical question "How long must I go on showing you great works of healing, of control of things physical as well as things spiritual, by teaching and by parables, before you see that all is achieved by faith?" We were all very quiet, we knew he had been disappointed and even angry at the reaction of the crowd who were fed, but we didn't think he had reason to be disappointed in us. He clearly knew what we were thinking and explained to us the stages of our repeated lack of faith.

"When I challenged you as to how we would feed all those people you were defeated, it can't be done. There are no shops. There are no bakers. We don't have enough money, so nothing can be done so we'd better send them away to fend for themselves as best they can. When a small boy offers his morsel you almost laugh at him and then at me. You didn't even believe that I could use this offering. Even when I had blessed the food and given it to you to give to the people you were openly un-convinced that anything would happen except probably a ridiculous farce. Well, that's not really surprising! What happened will be talked about and taught about forever as one of those extraordinary manifestations of the power of God that will convince and confound the wise and the foolish. What you have to understand is that the power of God is with me and with you all the time if you have faith to completely rely on his power, and accept his solution. He will achieve amazing totally expected and inexplicable results. You are not yet able to have this faith, even Peter who showed such confidence as to leave the boat but then his faith left him and you saw God's power slipped from him. Interestingly he had enough faith to rely on my faith to rescue him. When you were tossed about in the boat you despaired. You were convinced that the end was at hand, you had forgotten the comforting words that I have given you and tried to show you that God cares for you. I have told you that your mission is to change the world, do you think he is going to let you drown when you haven't started the task? You were all concerned for my personal safety from the crowd on the beach this morning, you thought that your power was greater than God's power to defend me or that God was not with me then. You will face much fiercer trials than that in time to come and you will have no companions to defend you but I tell you it is absolutely true that God will be there to protect you. You have no reason to be afraid of any thing on earth, no powers of man can compete with the power of God. Your faith allows it to operate to defend you, and to resolve the difficulties that you face, if your faith fails you then it cannot operate. What God expects from us is the confidence to do what is right, knowing that God will make the outcome positive and progressive towards his intention. I know that it is difficult to put all your trust in God but you have to learn that this is the safest depository of trust that man has ever had, nothing else is so secure or ever can be so secure."

Having listened to this lesson and encouragement, we all talked about the situations we had experienced. The tenor of the conversation, I am sorry to have to remember, was generally attempts on our part to justify our behaviour. The message of faithfulness became clouded by our wanting to explain to ourselves and to each other why we had been sceptical about the boy and his fishes, why we were terrified of the storm, why we were frightened of the crowd. Jesus listened patiently and then gave us another lesson.

"First" he said "you all have to understand that you can never be justified before God, so making excuses for your lack of faith is a fruitless and worthless exercise. Worse than that if you go down this path you will begin to think you can justify yourselves and then you will begin to think that you have the right to judge other people. The Pharisees and the Lawyers have gone down this path and now they have lost any sense of God, because they have power over the Jews they also have lost contact with God." Then his second message was, "You have to be different, you must not judge others, you must rely on God to be the judge. You have to be different, you have to recognise your own failures and plead God's forgiveness and his redemption of your failures. You must be different, you have to rely on God's infinite love to forgive and to renew, to restore faith and confidence when it has failed, to understand your doubts and unbelief. You have to know that these failures are not unique to you they, rest assured they are the common lot of mankind and for this reason you must not judge others; their failures are exactly the same as your failures. People have to be convince of the greatness of God's love and mercy by seeing it reflected in your lives and words, words which are encouraging and understanding and not accusative and dictatorial. You have to remember my teaching to you of only a few days ago when I spelled out to you the blessing that God had bestowed on mankind." He then re-iterated the blessings to the pure in heart, the poor in spirit, the humble and meek, those who mourn and those who seek after righteousness.

Breakfast took a long time there was a lot of discussion, perhaps the way I have written the summary of what was said sounds like Jesus just talked and we all listened. It wasn't like that at-all, although Jesus presence was awe inspiring he always was approachable, he encouraged us all to ask questions to try to put our own interpretation on what he was saying. He always listened with total attention to what we were saying and then answered, very often with the most un-expected interpretation of what was being said. He managed to take comments, which were made sometimes only in jest, and often in ignorance, to further explain to us God's influence in our lives and God's will for our happiness and fulfilment. Some how he managed to make everyone feel included and although, Peter, James and John, were special in some way, we all felt equals, nobody was given or expected special favours or status. When someone made a comment which showed a growing understanding they were always warmly encouraged, when somebody clearly had misunderstood he was not admonished; the misunderstanding was used to restate the truth that he was explaining to us. The conclusion was that all our individual contributions were always welcome and were never met by rejection, our confidence in Him as our teacher and leader grew all the time. So finally, when breakfast was finished, Jesus bid the household thanks and farewell and off we set on the road to Magdala. In preparation, he told us, that we would see two quite dramatic demonstrations of faith and God's power during the day and that we should remember what he had told us over breakfast.

Then as we walked along the coast road, he changed the subject completely. He wanted to talk to us about the confrontation with the crowd on the beach when we arrived in Capernaum in the morning. He became very serious, his normal cheerful exterior gave way to deep concern, he talked quietly so that only those nearest to him could hear him properly, clearly he did not want to share what he had to say with the crowd who always followed us.

He told us that we should recognise the work of the devil, that this acclamation he had received was an attempt by the forces of evil to frustrate God's will. The Jews expected some political or military or economic messenger from God, they did not want a spiritual messenger, they wanted to see God's vengeance wrought on their enemies to show what a special people they were, they wanted political and military and economic power to be given to them so that they could rule the world and inflict on their enemies a terrible retribution for all the mistreatment they had received over the generations from Egypt to Rome. When they could see that the message he was bringing from God is one of personal sacrifice, to satisfy the needs of others, of loving your neighbour and especially your enemy, of loving God above and before everything else. They saw that this message undermines all their ambitions, it was an attack at the power structure of their society and when they recognised that consequence they wanted to destroy me and you. It would be easy for me to accept their self-centred adulation to become their leader and to become a second David but that is not God's will and it might change the world for a short time but my mission is to change the world for ever and this can only be achieved by changing men's spirits and not their purses. We were all alarmed by what we were being told and asked Jesus what he foresaw as the destruction of the Jewish nation. He told us quite firmly that it was not for us to know the time or the occasion but he assured us that the leaders of the Jews would attempt to destroy him. When we protested, he told us to remember to have faith, to have courage and confidence that however bad things may look God was with us. He then said the most extraordinary thing, which was that the Jews would think that they had rid themselves of this new prophet but would find out that they were actually fulfilling God's purpose to glorify His Son to the whole world. We would see for ourselves the infinite power of God to overcome the evil of the world.

We were now passing through one of the numerous fishing villages on the lake shore and the population came out to meet us, what a crowd, we had to make a circle round Jesus to prevent him being crushed. People were calling out the sort of slogans we were becoming used to and which Jesus refused to respond to; but when little children were brought to him he blessed them and their parents and charged them to bring them up in God's way and to understand the truth of the Law of Moses. The sick were also brought and many were cured of sickness of the body and the spirit. Then in the middle of the excited mêlée Jesus suddenly stopped and turned round looking sternly at the crowd, everything went quiet and in a severe voice he said out loud "Somebody touched me, I felt the power leave me!" Our immediate reaction was one of incredulous amusement, how could he possibly know that someone had touched him, the crush was so great that people were continually touching him, one of us said just this to him, and his eyes then became almost fiery, "I tell you someone touched me, this is no laughing matter. I want to know who touched me!" With that a woman came through the crowd, she fell to the ground in front of Jesus and begged forgiveness for her impertinence. She explained that she had been sick for years, that her sickness made her unclean in the eyes of the Law and so she had no comfort from worshipping in the synagogue, she was ostracised by her neighbours and excluded from all contact except from her very closest relations. She told how she had prayed and prayed for relief, she had consulted physicians and tried many, many so-called cures but nothing changed. Then she told Jesus that she had heard that he was coming and thought that if she could only touch just the edge of his clothing then perhaps God would have mercy on her. She babbled on so, she was very frightened and embarrassed having been caught and having to explain these intimate personal things in public, she was in floods of tears and trembling all over. We were all looking at her, most of us, disgusted at this unclean person disturbing our plans, we were just about to move her away when we realised that Jesus was looking at the woman, the expression on his face said only "Do not be afraid, I am not angry, there is no punishment!" The woman gradually calmed down, and Jesus bent down and lifted her head and looking directly into her eyes, and her soul, he said "Go home in peace, your faith has made you whole!" It was reported to us later that she was cured from that moment, her problem never returned and she became a very worthy member of the village community. Many years later on one of my infrequent visits back to Galilee I found her again and by now she was running a busy and expanding Christian community in the village.

Jesus turned to the crowd and said "My power comes from God, I can give it freely to anyone who has faith in the power of God but it cannot be stolen from me! The only people who can receive the benefits of this power are those who believe that I am sent by God to save sinners and to bring the lost sheep of Israel back to God!"

After this miraculous curing people did not crowd round us so closely, now people were in awe of this man, they were not a little afraid of how he might use this power. His last pronouncement hit home because they all knew that they were sinners and needed saving but clearly the need for faith to recognise Him as the Emmanuel was a huge step for many. So we progressed through the village and on towards Magdala.

Magdala was an important fishing town, it had shown the way to the rest of the fishing community of the Sea of Galilee what could be done and largely the prosperity that we had enjoyed for nearly thirty years was due to the risks and courage of the fishermen of that town. We knew a lot of the businessmen there and were looking forward to meeting them all again, but we were surprised at the enthusiastic reception that awaited us. You should remember that Magdala was very close to the new city, and capital, that Herod Antipas had built on the shores of the lake. Antipas had called his creation, Tiberias, named in honour of the Roman

Emperor. It was amazing that many of the citizens of this profane city had come out to see Jesus, the news of his approach had spread and many people including some very high ranking officials and their families were there waiting to witness what Jesus would do. The crowd was very large and many people had brought their sick and disturbed to ask for God's mercy on their plight. Jesus blessed people and cured many people but he seemed to be preoccupied as if he was waiting for something very special to happen. Then out of the crowd stepped an old friend of ours, Jonas by name, a wealthy fish merchant, instead of approaching Jesus he came to Peter and me and James and John. He asked us in an almost pleading voice whether we could persuade Jesus and his following to come to dine with him at his home that night. We were just explaining to him that last time we had visited the town we had stayed with the rope maker and probably it was already arranged for us to stay there again, he became very disappointed and protested that he had the accommodation and wanted to introduce Jesus to his many friends. Jesus saw us talking together and called out "Jonas can we stay with you tonight it is too late to go back to Capernaum. There will be about twenty of us, can you do that?" Jonas was totally spell bound his mouth opened and closed and no sound came out, he could not take his eyes off Jesus and eventually spluttered out that of course they were most welcome. He turned to us and asked us how could he possibly know what we had been talking about, we assured him that we had witnessed more astounding things than that and that it was likely that he would do so also and may be even at dinner tonight! So it was arranged. We spent the rest of the day with Jesus and the crowds as the day wore on Jesus took to a boat on the lakeside and taught the people and us with less crowding. He taught in parables, about shepherds and farmers and housewives and fathers and businessmen explaining for those who could understand about the reality of the Kingdom of

Heaven. He explained God's desire to save sinners and return them to a proper relationship with Himself. He warned us about the consequences of the failure of some people to actually hear the message of God and even those who did hear quickly forgot. He told us of the dedication needed to search for and to understand the treasure of God's word. He assured them and us of God's love for all humanity however sinful they had become, for those who repented and asked for forgiveness God's love was there to receive them back. He made it clear that we all, as individuals, had responsibility, each one of us, for the use we made of the resources that God had provided for us. The crowd were spell bound, Jesus relied on what he had seen as he grew up in Nazareth and in his family and with his father as a carpenter and then on his own as a carpenter just how the world ticked and used colourful living stories to try to help his audience comprehend the message of God's love. It was difficult to judge how many even began to understand, for Jesus success was that just one soul, one poor lost soul should be recovered to God. The crowd were very attentive and quiet, they laughed when they should, they nodded to each other in recognising the familiar situations and confirmed to each other the truth of what they were hearing. At the end Jesus stood up in the boat and blessed the crowd and said "Let them that have ears hear!" He turned to us and said "Surely dinner must be ready, come on, we cannot keep our host waiting!" and with that he strode up the beach and into the town.

Jonas had really put on a feast, the very best of everything, as we arrived he welcomed us most cordially and was particular that all the proper formalities were respected. Jesus was shown to the seat of honour at the head of the table next to the host and we all were shown to our places together with other notable business men and civic and religious leaders of the town, there must have been more than forty of us in all. It was quite clear that Jonas had worked hard to organise such a gathering at such short notice. He told us later that in fact he had had to restrict the guest list, it seemed that everybody wanted to meet with and listen to Jesus. All was prepared, and the meal was about to start when there was a commotion at the doorway. A woman was demanding to come in, she was a pathetic, dishevelled, unwashed, ragged woman, a woman cast out of society, her eyes were on fire and she screeched at the servants who tried to restrain her as she tried to force her way into the room. Jonas was horrified, he called to his servants to 'throw the baggage out', not only was this a woman, which was impertinence enough, but she was clearly a demented sinner who was contaminating the gathering! Jonas started to apologise to Jesus that his evening should be so disrupted, he was beside himself with embarrass-ment and was growing angry as the woman continued to protest that she must come to Jesus. As he was about to have the woman forcibly ejected, Jesus rose to his feet and to a hushed table said "Let the woman come to me." There was nothing to be done, this wretched, abominable person was permitted into the room. The clerics and several Pharisees all rose from their seats to leave. We twelve who were by now getting used to Jesus mixing with sinners were appalled that such a dreadful person should be admitted, she was the untouchable dregs of society, nobody wanted no have any contact with her what so ever. She looked at nobody, her weeping eyes were fixed on Jesus, she had to make her way past all the guests who shied away from her as she went, but she looked at nobody. When she got to Jesus she fell to the floor weeping uncontrollably, she gabbled away to him about her sinfulness, her hopelessness, her desperation, her remorse and finally pleaded with Jesus for forgiveness and the chance to start her life afresh. Jesus leant down very much as he had done to the lady who had been cured during the morning, he lifted her head in his hands and said, so that everyone could hear, "Evil spirits depart from this woman! Mary your sins are forgiven, you can start a new life, this evil spirit will trouble you no more. Your faith and courage are rewarded, you are restored as a daughter of Abraham". The room was silent, totally silent. The clerics started to move to the door to leave, muttering that no man was in a position to forgive sins, and how can he cast out devils? This man, Jesus, was making claims that were blasphemous, how could he claim the power to forgive sins, this was God's prerogative not man's. It was all right to preach remarkable insights into God's message to the Jews, it was almost acceptable that he should openly criticise the religious authorities, other people had been known to work amazing powers of curing the sick, but nobody, nobody would dare to declare the forgiveness of sins. This was blasphemy and the authorities would hear about it! Mary's reaction was dramatic, now she was clean and her self-confidence had immediately returned, she bowed graciously to Jesus, then to Jonas and then to the rest of the company and made her way to the kitchen. You can imagine that all the women in the house and our entourage had heard if not seen what had happened, Jesus' mother was there to greet her as she entered the kitchen. To everyone's surprise she put her arms round Mary (who was always afterwards known as Mary Magdalene) and welcomed her, she was given the most important job to serve the food to Jonas and Jesus. Jesus mother knew that this would emphasise to everyone that when Jesus forgives our sins nobody is to question the veracity of the forgiveness. His mother's faith in her son was again demonstrated, she had no doubts about his power, she remembered the predictions that she had received in his conception and childhood, she had already witness God's power being wrought by her son and she knew that he was changing the world.

All the Pharisees left the dinner, they did not apologise they just stamped out, one of the clerics stayed behind, the rest of the guests stayed, they, like us all knew only too well that we were sinners and needed God's forgiveness. The discussion during the meal was interesting, I think everyone was a bit embarrassed and perplexed by the scene with Mary, and so the topics ranged over politics and the power of Rome, We discussed the news that we all heard about, the in-fighting among the power mongers in Rome for supreme power over The Empire. There was news to talk about the expansion of the empire to the north to places we had never heard of. Then there was the usual discussion of "Pax Romana" and the terrible consequences to those who did not obey the rules. Being close to Tiberias and with important people at the table the gossip seemed more significant. Then we talked about the fishing industry, many of us had contacts directly or indirectly all around the Great Sea, in Greece, in Spain, in Egypt, in Gaul, in Asia and of course in Italy. Galilean fish products were well received, and good prices paid wherever they were distributed. Through these marketing contacts we knew a lot about the rest of the world, not just the Romans but also the other great power to the east, the Persians and their opulent capital in Baghdad. We talked about the cruelty of these super powers and their avaricious ambitions to dominate and subjugate all the land round them, their ever expansionist policies, their apparent need for confrontation with their neighbours. Then we turned to Israel and the Jews we discussed the recent past, the terrible cruelty of the Herod dynasty, the Roman tyranny, we all remembered the destruction of Sepphoris and the exile of the whole population as slaves, we had many friends who had just disappeared, never heard of again. Then we talked about the Sanhedrin, the Pharisees, the Sadducees, the scribes, the lawyers, the rabbis and the whole structure of power that had been constructed round the Law of Moses. Jesus was always in the middle of these discussions and used the occasion very carefully to show the company just how he saw the problems and what the real solutions were, solutions that would outlast all the powers and empires that man had ever created for his own glorification. He did not dominate the conversation he was seriously interested in what people had to say, he encouraged people to make their contribution. He never talked down to people, he never lectured or hectored, when he felt somebody was wrong in their view he put the counter argument in such a way that the proposer accepted the alternative view and learnt something about God's will, or love, or forgiveness. He didn't use parables to this assembly, he knew that they were men of some distinction in their own field, men who perhaps had a better than average understanding of the pressures and tensions of the society that they lived in. He probably sympathised with the continual reconciliations that they had to make every day, the balancing of the needs of their business and the Law, the responsibilities that they had accepted for the well being of the people they employed together with their responsibilities to their customers and suppliers. After all he had been a carpenter supplying a service to his customers but with the need to support his mother and brothers and sisters and their families. In his work He had to understand the way external social and political and economic forces dictated the limits of action that any businessman had to work within. He was absolutely adamant that the gravest risk that a businessman had to face was the "love of money". He reminded the assembled company several times that wealth in itself was not evil. Money was dangerous because whenever a man had money he wanted more and then progressively he became unscrupulous as to how he got more and fell into sinful soul-destroying habits. Wealth was a God given asset and should only be used to further God's kingdom, a wealthy man had a great responsibility to use his wealth for the good of others. Even if he did this then there was still the risk that he would enjoy the acclaim and prestige that he received from his good works and that this then became his aim not the true giving resulting from an expression of God's love for mankind. The law says quite clearly that "thou shalt make no graven images and worship them", money or status or honours or respect can, and often do, become graven images and are worshiped. When the worship of God takes second place to anything else then a man looses his soul. Beware, he told the company, the power seeking habits of the Romans, the Greeks, the Persians, the Egyptians and the Sanhedrin derive from the same risk that they faced, in this case the idolatry is the worship of power to control other people's lives.

"You," he told them, "are leaders among men and so you bear a special responsibility, as leaders others adopt the attitudes and standards of behaviour that you demonstrate not by what you say but by the way you behave. It is an awesome responsibility that you have to exercise all your waking hours. The members of your household, the people you work with, your customers, your suppliers and all your neighbours watch what you do and how you respond to every situation that confronts you and by this you are influencing the acceptable attitudes and behaviour in your society. In the great tyrannical powers

193

that govern the world, the cruelty of the emperor is copied by the governors and then by the senior officials and then by the petty officials to the lowest servant of all. The cruelty is physical by beatings and executions and torture and spiritual by lying and false accusation, by exclusion, by isolation, by denying people freedom to worship God. In the affairs of state what the great do the minions do also, in our lives what we do our society will do also."

His next statement was extraordinary, he said, "However we have to respect that the political powers that controlled our lives were put there by God, we as citizens have a duty to God to respect their ordinances up to the point where such ordinances put a barrier between men and God. The present age is full of such barriers, society was exclusive, the best example was the exclusiveness of the Jews who absolutely prevented anyone coming to God unless he was a Jew. Then within the Jews the Sanhedrin, the Sadducees, the Pharisees, the scribes and the Lawyers had made the whole society exclusive. Why had those upright and respected citizens who Jonas had invite to dinner with us left the dinner party? The answer was because their man-made rules separated them from that poor disturbed creature. Then when God's healing love provides a cure they considered the matter blasphemy, according to the rules they have made. So you can see by this example that you witnessed, here this evening, that people have almost forgotten that they should love, honour and obey God and their neighbour whoever he or she may be. They, and you, have been told, and now accept, that the way to God was to follow all sorts of man-made ordinances that effectively left men unable to even attempt to see God as he is and as he wants to be seen."

As the evening was breaking up he reminded them, "God only has two commandments," his words rang round the room like a clarion call to re-birth, " Thou shalt love the Lord your God with all your mind, with all your body and with all your strength, this is the first commandment and the second is this, thou shalt love your neighbour as yourself. Make no mistake all the rest of the Law are founded only in these two statements of God's ordinance to mankind. Any law made by man had to be measured in intention, in application and in implication against these two measures, if they failed they were bad law." He told them, "I have been sent into the world to show mankind, once and for all, what God intended for his creation, and that the result would be that the world would be changed for ever and that his influence would be felt for generations and generations to come until the end of time."

I think that everyone was exhausted, certainly we were, Jonas had prepared beds for us all and after we had said Good Night, we retired.

What a day, the crowds, the woman healed by her faith, Mary Magdalene's arrival and then the incredible discussion over dinner. Tomorrow, we were due to go back to Capernaum but we all knew now that the matter of tomorrow really was in God's hands.

Every morning we knew that Jesus was up very early and went off into the hills or the quiet places to pray to God. We twelve found that we started to meet together, away from other people, to pray together and to discuss the previous day's experiences. The coming together was totally informal, nobody said where we would meet or when we would meet or how long we would meet for, but it happened almost everyday. We always started by using the prayer Jesus had taught us and then we used each phrase to direct our thoughts. We always prayed for our families and friends. Then somebody would raise an issue relating to things that had happened and we tried to understand what the underlying teaching was that Jesus had been intended. We usually felt very dull and stupid that things that we were sure should be clear were shrouded in mysteries, it was very hard work but we found slowly that things were developing patterns and that the main threads of love and forgiveness and humility. The power of God to protect us we were able to devise in what he said or did. But as I remember we were usually left confused and not a little depressed at our inability to understand. However this always led to a very lively breakfast when Jesus came back and where the problems were aired. Jesus, in his gentle guiding manner, led us to a better understanding. He reminded us that on the previous day he had warned us that we would see some extraordinary things on the trip to Magdala, so he wanted to test our opinions on these matters.

First he wanted to talk about Mary. Why, he asked us, had we been so revolted by this woman? We replied that we were taught by the law that people with her condition of being possessed by an evil spirit should be shunned, that they represented things that were bad and not according to God's will and therefore we were taught to avoid them. He agreed that this was the way we were taught but he was teaching us a different way. Mary was a poor distressed individual all that she was looking for was some escape from her distress, she needed to know God's love was as real for her as for everyone and it was our duty to show her that love in the best way we could. He reiterated that he was sending us out into the world to change the world and that we would continually be faced with the prejudice of exclusion. The task we were to undertake was to break through these prejudices by extending God's love to all people even though the accepted norms of society said that some people should be excluded. The very process of our showing we

195

cared for all people would force our society to examine the injustice that it served to large numbers of its citizens. It was the exclusive clubs of Pharisees and the rest who would be most troubled by this demonstration of God's love because it would contrast directly with their attitude and it was their attitude that protected their perceived status in society. Every individual is worthy of God's love and it is not for us to judge who should share in his benefits. It is our duty to extend God's love to individuals who ever and where ever we see the need.

Then he turned to the woman who had tried to steal healing from him in the crowd, the import of this situation was not, as might have been inferred, that she had tried to steal from God, but that her disease had made her an outcast, she was excluded, she was ostracised. She was ashamed of her condition, she was so ashamed because of the guilt that society had forced on her that she could not bring herself to publicly ask for help, but she was sure, she had faith, she had confidence that even the slightest contact with the power of God would cure her, so she dared to risk being discovered. She showed to the crowd that this faith was justified, for she was cured but she had to publicly expose her faith. The other import was that although God is all-powerful he has to dispense his grace, it can't be demanded and it can't be taken. It is a gift, freely given to those who have faith in its power, to those who humble themselves to God. Jesus admitted that he felt that he was being robbed that someone was wanting his power without the necessary recognition of God's power as if his power were some sort of magic. We must beware that God's power is never contaminated with the occult which of its very nature is evil.

Then we talked about the discussion over dinner, he instructed us that the critical issue was that the actions of individuals do have an effect on great matters and that this was a weighty responsibility we all had to bear. We might not think that the things we do or say or indeed the things we don't do and don't say have a profound effect on the world we live in. It is not acceptable that people think that their actions and words are important unless they are people in "authority" the reality is that whatever we do or say they can and do affect the world. It is not for us to understand the when or the how this impact takes place, it is not for us to even recognise the contribution we have made but the accumulative effect of all the people doing little bits of good produces a good result, on the other hand the effect of all the people doing little bits of bad will produce a bad result. The powers that govern our world of emperors and governors can't withstand the power of good in the world exercised by the people that they rule but will be reinforced in their evil ways by the power of bad exercised by the same people.

As usual by time breakfast was finished, not only were the household totally absorbed by what Jesus had to say but a large crowd had gathered to hear his lessons. They had brought their sick and Jesus laid his hands on them and cured them, but shortly he said we must go because there was another matter that we had to attend to. He thanked Jonas for his hospitality, Jonas was by now absolutely dedicated to Jesus and was in tears as we left, we heard that he had changed his attitude to his business ethics and had become a caring loving master and prospered!

We set off back up the road to Capernaum, our little band, we had collected a few more dedicated adherents including Mary Magdalene so we were about twenty. We walked at a steady pace but there was time for us to talk and debate the matters we had been witnessing. We had just turned a corner in the road when we were confronted by a band of ragged vagabonds who were blocking our way. They looked aggressive, and we all, except Jesus, quite expected trouble. Although the Roman authority had done a great deal to curtail the bands of robbers who had, at one time, made journeys very hazardous there were still enough around in the hills and lonely stretches of road to make the traveller very cautious. Then we saw that these poor creatures were not armed and we realised that these were lepers. Leprosy, you will know, is the worst health scourge that any man could be cursed with, the only way we knew to deal with the sufferers was to exclude them from all contact with other people, they were simply sent out into the wilds and forbidden, on pain of death, from returning to their family or friends or communities unless and only unless the terrible disfiguring disease was cured. There was no cure and so these pathetic creatures had to live out what was left of their miserable lives in total isolation and abject poverty. People left food and clothing for them by the roadside, but the disease was so contagious that just touching the clothes they had warn could be enough to become contaminated. These men started to gesticulate to us and were calling out to us. The Law required that should warn us to keep away, but Jesus did not hesitate, then we heard what they were calling. "Jesus, the messiah, Jesus, the healer, have mercy on us! Jesus, the Son of David, have mercy on us! Jesus, we are unclean, cleanse us!" We were horrified as we watched Jesus go right up to them, he laid his hands on them and touched them, he blessed them and told them that their faith in God's power to heal had made them clean and that they should go to the town and present themselves to the Rabbi, as the Law demanded, to confirm that they were whole and cleansed. They were amazed they looked at their hands and feet and saw that the terrible white scars and the terrible distortions of their flesh was being remedied as they watched. They were so delighted they turned and raced down the road before us to show the authorities that they were able to rejoin society. Then one of the ten stopped and turned back he came to Jesus and fell on to the ground and worshipped him, tears were streaming down his face, his gratitude was immeasurable and was only comparable with the terrible deprivation that had blighted his life and his family's life. Jesus calmed the man and then asked him, "Were there not ten of you? Where are the others? You my son by your faith and by our belief in God's power are cured! Go your way and praise the Lord!"

Jesus didn't want to go any further on the road, he sat down on the grass and asked us what we made of this miracle of healing that we had just witnessed. Some said that this showed how powerfully God was working in Jesus to be able to cure this terrible disease, nobody could possibly doubt that he was God's messenger to the Jews. Even the doubters would have to acknowledge his power. Others said that with this ability we really could change the world and we wouldn't need armies. They asked if Jesus would teach them how to execute these miraculous cures so that they could expand the contact with the sick. There was talk about the probable collapse of all opposition to Jesus' reign when he could provide such protection against disease. Jesus just sat and listened to us all trying to see the import of this curing. After a little while he stopped our frantic chattering and taught us the meaning. He told us that these men were excluded from society, just as Mary Magdalene had been excluded from society and just as we had been because in the eyes of the Pharisees and other authorities we were sinners by association. Curing peoples' physical disease or infirmity or their mental distress was, for God, only of any purpose if it made those individuals and by their example the rest of society amend their ways. The great cruelty of society was its ability to continually invent new ways of excluding people and the worst exclusion was the spiritual exclusion from God. God's love is shown to people by breaking down the man made barriers that exclude individuals and groups from a full participation in God's world and God's love. Curing men's bodies was easy compared with curing men's souls and a much more profound demonstration of God's love would be needed to convince the world of its sinfulness and the way forward towards God's Kingdom. Mary, he said had known that somehow she had to find God, her frustration and spiritual distress had shown itself in extraordinary bursts of anger and distortion of her body. She was lucky because somehow inside her she knew what was wrong. She just could not find the way to put it right until she realised that I was the key that would open the door to God's kingdom for her. The lepers were also desperate, their desperation was of a physical nature born out of their exclusion from society which brought with it their exclusion from God, because the law, man's law, made it impossible to stay within the law which was understood to be the only way to God. The nine saw their miraculous cure as a gift from God to restore them to their families and to society only one of the ten realised that what had happened actually restored him to God and that was why he came back to give thanks and the others did not. All the happenings of the two days were a demonstration of God's infinite love for his creation, sometimes man does understand this great love and give thanks for it, but for most it goes un-noticed and un-appreciated and so men's love for God grows cold. God's love for men, each individual man, is available always and never diminishes, his great sorrow is that men do not see his power at work in their lives.   Jesus concluded, "That my friends is what we have to show them."

Then after a pause he continued. "Your attempts at understanding the import of what you have witnessed is still wrong, you are always thinking about a human kingdom of emperors and princes. The Hebrews demanded from Samuel a human prince and first Saul and then David and all his successors showed the weakness of human governance. The catastrophes that overtook the Hebrews and the Jews all demonstrate that human princes are sinful, that they become corrupted by the abuse of the very power that God has given them, they can't resist the temptations of the 'seven deadly sins' and all have failed. God promised the Jews another David but this time a David who would not fail who would not be corrupted by power, the prophets foretold his coming as a Prince of Peace, a Righteous Judge of the People, a Servant not a Master. The Jews, and you, are looking for a prince of this world. God has provided a Prince, who is not of this world, who will govern men's hearts and His kingdom will be universal and will last forever. He will fit the description of the prophets exactly but his world is a world of the spirit and it will fulfil the promise of peace to all men who believe in his word and walk in his ways. I am that prince but the world does not recognise me and men will do all they can to destroy me. What I am showing to you, and to those who can see and hear is that the power of man is insignificant compared with God's infinite power and whatever men may do or try to do to thwart the will of God, they will fail and God's Will will be done."

We were spellbound, the explanation was clear, the predictions were being fulfilled but we had not understood and it would be a long time before we did really understand. Always it seems we were tempted to our preconceived ideas that here was the Emmanuel who would restore the greatness of Israel and deal severely with her persecutors. We expected to have a share in this human earthly power and all the perquisites that we saw others in power receiving. Even when we accepted what Jesus was saying we still expected a material spin-off that would reward those who had helped him to achieve his Kingdom. Now we know how hopelessly wrong we were, it is almost impossible to think back to our state of un-knowing and disbelief which was really the result of our lack of faith in God's power. On that afternoon on the road to Capernaum Jesus spelt out for us, with absolute clarity, what was happening and we still failed to grasp the message.

So after this interlude we resumed our journey back to Capernaum, most of us were deep in thought, trying to unravel in our own minds what it was that we were involved in. Questions continually re-surfaced in our thoughts. How could we change the world without political or military power? When we thought we had an answer, 'That the healing miracles would convince men of God's power', then we were told very abruptly that that was not the answer. Every time we worried about the confrontation with the authorities, that Jesus seemed to relish, and interpreted this as the point at which we should develop some political strategy to ensure we gained the upper hand, we were told very abruptly that that was not the answer. When a popular movement to recognise Jesus as the Emmanuel started to gain any momentum Jesus made sure that it stopped immediately. All that Jesus seemed to concern himself with were the social outcasts and drop-outs, the people we had all been taught from our infancy that we should avoid at all cost and here we were fraternising with them and Jesus saying in effect "This is how you will change the world." The problem was that when he said it, it always sounded totally plausible, but then, when you thought it through, it just did not make sense. I suspect that Jesus knew what we were all struggling but he did not show any intention of helping us, he knew that we had to suffer the doubts and un-certainties, the bewilderment and disbelief before we could come to an understanding of the truth of his mission to the earth. So the group was fairly quiet, after a while even the women stopped chattering and we walked on with Jesus in the lead gradually becoming more and more depressed in our own personal misgivings. We must have looked a pretty sorry band as we came over the last rise in the road and there was Capernaum. It was late afternoon and much to our surprise there wasn't the usual expectant crowd, in fact the town was very quiet, to some of us it felt as if the people were already saying to us " It's all over, good try but it didn't work!" Before we went down into the town Jesus stopped us and said to us all, " In two days you have witnessed the power of God at work in people and you should rejoice at his love for mankind and his infinite power to change the world. He has changed the world for lots and lots of people, not just the woman whose faith made her well, or Mary, or the ten lepers but all the other people who may have just been bystanders or on-lookers. We will never know how many and we will never understand the eventual consequence of the changes he has made to their worlds, but we have been a party to actions that will change the world. This is our mission, we have no need of armies or political organisation, God's love is an irresistible force that will overcome all opposition. You must have faith, and from faith grows courage and from courage grows confidence. "Do you remember the story that I have told so many times about the Good Shepherd and how when he had found the lost sheep he came home rejoicing and invited his friends to join in with his rejoicing. Well here we are and we are sure that whatever happens for the rest of eternity, twelve lost sheep have been brought safely back to the fold and we, we should rejoice! So take off those anxious looks and let's show Capernaum that we are changing the world and that God is rejoicing with us!" We were back in Capernaum by mid afternoon and Jesus suggested that we tried to relax and take stock of what we had seen and learned on the visit to Magdala. The whole group split up and were accommodated by various members of the family and friends and neighbours. In the early afternoon most of the towns-folk were taking a siesta, escaping from the heat of the day and so we had managed to slip in without the people knowing and we were not surrounded by the crowds. It was a welcome respite, and gave us a chance to talk to our families and to further consolidate the friendships that had been growing up between the twelve of us. Jesus asked if he could stay with Jonas on the farm, he knew that there he would be isolated and that he could find solitude and peace, his mother and Mary Magdalene went with him but otherwise he was left alone. Mary told us that as soon as they got up to the farm and he had been welcomed, he excused himself and went up into the hill country behind the farm, they didn't see him again until the next morning at breakfast. When Mary had asked him how he had fared he told her that he had prayed to God for guidance and strength, that he had slept under God's firmament and that he had found food available along the way. He taught her as he had taught us that he was in God's care and God would protect him to enable his task to be completed.

Part 14

Sent as Missionaries

Later that morning we all met at the farm and Jesus instructed us on the next part of the mission. He told us that we had seen his works and had heard his message and that we now had to rapidly extend our contact with the people to convince them that the Kingdom of Heaven was upon them and that they must repent of their sins and amend their ways. He told us that we could use the parables he had used to explain God's love and compassion and forgiveness, to show God's justice, to demonstrate what he meant by love for your neighbour and even your enemy. He particularly emphasised that people should understand that he was the Emmanuel, that he had come to fulfil the Law not to change it, that the abuse of power by the established authorities had to be stopped. The critical issue was that this new message came to each and every individual, forgiveness was available to everyone, however unworthy he or she may feel or however unworthily he or she may be regarded by others. Faith in God's infinite power to forgive and to make good was the only prerequisite to enjoy the peace that is only available as a result of a proper relationship with God and with our neighbours.

Then he told us we were to go, in pairs, to visit all the Jewish towns and villages, in Galilee and in Judea, but not to the Gentiles or the Samarians. We were to go without encumbering ourselves with baggage or money or any of the things that you would normally take on a journey, he told us that God would provide for us. If, he said, we were rejected at a town or village we were to move on, the message was so important and so urgent that "Those who will hear, may hear, those who will not, may not." He told us we had to go now! He told us that we had the power to heal the sick and to cast out demons. He gave us God's blessing and sent us on our way!

Well, as you might imagine there was an air of consternation, this plan was totally unexpected he had never even hinted that we should have to do this sort of thing. When we tried to ask questions, like, who would go with whom, or which area any pair should cover, or how long we should be away from him, or how would we meet again. He told us that we were doing God's work and all these matters would be taken care of, we should only concern ourselves with doing the task he had given. He reminded us that Elijah and Jonah and many others of God's messengers, although they had got lost or tried to avoid the task they were given, they were directed and protected by God to fulfil his will, he had cared for them and he would care for us! So we set off, just as we were, somehow we sorted ourselves out into pairs, somehow we sorted out which direction we should take as we left Capernaum, Some of us walked and some took a boat which just happened to be going to the southern end of the sea. I joined up with Philip and we went back along the road to Magdala, round Tiberias and into the Jezreel Valley, we avoided Tabor and Nazareth because Jesus had already been preaching there, we concentrated on the towns and villages south and west bordered by Samaria and Phoenicia.

The valley was a rich agricultural area, it was heavily populated and the fields and orchards were well tended and cared for, we expected to find the people in good heart and prosperous but were surprised to find an air of poverty and dismay. When we came into the first village in the early evening we knocked on the first house we came to and proclaimed God's peace to the household, we were immediately welcomed and offered food and a bed. We were amazed; this was before we had even spoken of our mission. While the meal was being prepared we told them our message, just as Jesus had instructed us. We were not really surprised that they already had heard of Jesus and his great deeds, in fact they said some of their neighbours had made a pilgrimage to Capernaum to listen to Jesus and to witness his healing. Another family had made the annual Passover pilgrimage to Jerusalem and had heard on the way not only about Jesus but also about John's preaching in the Jordan valley. They told us that in Jerusalem there were many rumours flying about that the Emmanuel was here and that Israel would shortly be redeemed. They asked us many questions about the healing powers, about the claims of God's grace, who we were and why we were doing this work. So we told them about our experiences and showed them that we were convinced of Jesus' incredible powers and the miracles we had witnessed. Then over the meal we told them many of the parables and explained as best we could what these stories meant and how they showed that there was a new message to everybody to repent and be saved. The discussion was very lively and our understanding was continually challenged, some how we found that we could explain and answer their questions as if we were being prompted, it was an extraordinary feeling, almost as if Jesus was there in the room with us. We somehow remembered many texts from the prophets that substantiated the claims we were making, things we had not thought about ourselves until we were trying to convince this family. In the end they suggested that the next morning they would tell their neighbours that we were there and that we could talk publicly to the whole village, as they wanted everyone to hear what we were saying. We were disturbed to see how poor these people were, although the countryside looked prosperous they had very few possessions and looked undernourished. Gradually it became clear that although they owned their own land the demands from the authorities in the form of taxes for Jerusalem and for Rome were grinding them down into poverty. They told us that because they owned their land they were better placed than many of their neighbours who worked the land for wealthy land owners who generally lived in the cities, like Tiberias or Sepphoris or even Jerusalem; these land owners took everything they could and left the labourers in abject poverty. They were angry and frustrated that the whole system of food production and distribution was in the hands of the elite, that nobody cared for them and despite being essential to the livelihood of the nation they received no fair share of the country's wealth. They could see no hope of things getting better, even the Synagogue with its declaration of the Law showed no interest in their living conditions. So eventually we went to bed feeling elated, on the one hand, by the way we had received support as we spoke, but, on the other hand, feeling that the problems these people faced were insurmountable and that even God seemed to have forgotten them. Before we went to bed, I remember well how fervently Philip and I prayed for God's guidance and power to help us convince these people of the reality of His love for each and every individual.

So the next morning, after we two had again asked for God's strength and courage we met with the village in the square. There may have been fifty or so people, old and young, men and women, they all looked down trodden and dejected, they were poorly clothed and underfed and with them there were their sick. So we started, their faces were glum and unresponsive, we told them that the promised Emmanuel was with us, that Jesus of Nazareth had come to save sinners and to pronounce God's forgiveness. The people did not respond, one man said in a loud voice from the back of the group, "How can a carpenter change the world, nobody can help us we are just treated like work animals, we are not recognised as Sons of Abraham." There were general murmurings of agreement with this pronouncement and the crowd started to stir and looked as if they would disperse and we felt we had hardly started. Then Philip said to them " Jesus of Nazareth has come to save sinners, to support the weak and to heal the sick. We are his disciples and he has empowered us to heal the sick, those sick who have faith that God will forgive the sins of those who repent and intend to lead a new life, living according to God's law!" It was dramatic to see the interest that this statement produced. So we said to them bring your sick to us and we will heal them. Inside we were both terrified but we knew that God had the power, we had seen it operate so often and we were convinced that what Jesus had told us was true, "You have the power to heal the sick and cast out devils!" Both Philip and I placed our hands on these poor people who had all sorts of illness and we prayed and we asked them to pray and people were healed. The crowd was silent, awe struck, unbelieving, bewildered, they stared at us, could it be possible they were thinking that these two disciples had received this amazing power just because they had faith in God and Jesus and believed that his message was the salvation of the world. Then after the shock, there was great excitement; everyone wanted to learn more, to understand more. So now we really did have their attention we preached as we had heard Jesus preach that the Emmanuel was here and now that sinners must repent in the full assurance of God's forgiveness, that God was a God of Love and that he expected men to love each other, to care for their needs just as much as they cared for their own needs and that they should extend this love to their enemies. In this part of Galilee the enemy was close by, less than two or three miles south was the border with Samaria, to these people enemies were real and present, there were continual skirmishes, and blood feuds and sheep rustling and hostage taking. Life was dangerous! Jesus' message was not one of battle and military domination it was one of peace where men honoured and respected one another. We thought we had lost them at this point there were loud general accusations about the Samaritans. Then I remembered Jesus' parable about the "Good Samaritan" and we told them the story. They began to understand but were still very unsure, it sounded like 'pie in the sky' and anyway why should they start being nice to the Samaritans, they were never nice back. So we tried to help them see that this could only happen through forgiveness and that had to start with them. I think it was too much for them. They wanted to subdue the Samaritans and extract maximum penalties for all the evil things that had been handed out to them, they did not take into account that they and we knew that they had committed just as bad things on the Samaritans. Then they said, "What about all the taxes we have to pay, why weren't we talking to the land owners and tax collectors to reduce the continual squeezing of more and more tribute out of the peasants until they had nothing left and had to live in poverty and watch their children die of starvation if there was only a slightly worse harvest!" Philip and I were beginning to think we had no answer for these accusations, these cries of despair at the world. We were really at a loss, we felt deep sympathy for their plight we knew just how avaricious the land owners could be, they were usually absentees living in luxury in Jerusalem and every time they wanted more they just demanded that their agents took more from the peasants. The crowd could see that we were unsure how to answer their accusations, we knew that what they expected from Emmanuel was a powerful war lord who would sweep away the existing powers and allow them to extract vengeance on their oppressors and allow them to live in the same idle luxury as the land owners. Philip was brilliant he said to them that however bad things were God was still there with them. He told them that showing love to their neighbours was to care for the members of their community. That they were suffering from the sins that other people were committing but that did not give them the right to propagate those sins onto other people, God's judgement and justice would be shown on all people. Could any of them say that they were free of sin, the sins of envy, of greed, of false accusations? God looked at each individual he saw his inner soul and through the love that he had for each one of us he offered forgiveness. When everything looks hopeless it is most easy to strike out at our nearest and dearest, when we cannot strike out at the people who are actually the cause of our distress. When we do this we are just as much failing God's intentions as the landowners are failing by their sinfulness. The message that Jesus has brought us is that we can even in dire times show our love to each other by responding to each others needs, even if we cannot solve the problem, we can always find ways of easing the distress that we find around us. We must not, like the scribe and the Pharisee and the priest in the story, just pass by and ignore the needs that we may be able to relieve in some way. The world only gets worse if we all "pass by on the other side of the road, ignoring those in need". The change in the world that will result when we learn to love our neighbour will be dramatic because the power of good is more powerful than the power of evil. The little bits of good that each of us can do accumulate together to make the world a better place, alternatively the little bits of bad we do, including the "bad" of not doing the good we might have done, actually accumulate together to make the world a worse place. The crowd was subdued, nobody had explained things to them that way before, nobody said very much, even the men who had been aggressive at the start of the village meeting were now quiet. We were confused, usually when Jesus taught crowds there was a positive response and we could see that people did understand but with these people we were not sure. Perhaps we were expecting too much, perhaps we could not bring ourselves to have that total reliance on God that Jesus said we needed. Several of the families who had received a cure came to us and said that they would do anything to repay the miracle that had overtaken their lives. We told them to repent, to ask God's forgiveness for their sins and to show the whole community that they were changed and that the rule "a tooth for a tooth and an eye for an eye" no longer applied in their lives and that they would seek out ways to help their neighbour. The majority of the crowd were still grumbling that living so near to the arrogant, aggressive and belligerent Samarians was not the best place to be talking about loving your neighbour and that it was alright for prosperous fishermen and carpenters who lived well away from the border to have grand ideas about a new order, it was not likely to catch on! The crowd dispersed, many of them came and thanked us for our words and encouraged us to keep trying, but despite that we both felt pretty deflated that our first trial had been a bit of a flop. Looking back I think we were a bit ambitious to expect anything else. The square emptied and our hosts asked us back for refreshments but we both declined in unison and excused ourselves that we must get on! The hosts apologised that we had had a less than enthusiastic reception and excused themselves and their neighbours that life for them was very hard and insecure and there seemed to be nobody to help them. We repeated our message that God was there in the midst of all their problems, but we felt very inadequate.

We left the village and set off north-west following the course of the river until we came to the next township. On the way we both decided that we needed to pray for God's strength and guidance, so we left the road and found a small meadow beside a clear brook and there we rested and prayed. We really did pray, we felt we had failed that despite God showing his power by allowing us to heal the sick when we tried to extend Jesus message it just didn't seem to work, in fact we had started to doubt its truth ourselves, we realised that if we sounded unsure it was certain that our listeners would be unconvinced. We remembered what Jesus had said to us, those who have ears will hear and by contrast those who did not want to hear would be deaf to the message. The problem was that we were uncertain that we had promulgated God's message so that it could be heard, Jesus was so sure and confident that he could respond to every situation and turn it to project God's love, or to show man's sinfulness. We seemed to have got distracted by the problems the people had expressed and not been able to use their situation to show God's love.

When we arrived in the town we knocked at a door as Jesus had instructed us, this time quite by chance we had come to the home of the leader of the synagogue, this was not the Rabbi but was the man who managed the affairs of the synagogue and who was always well respected and was critical in establishing the respect for the Law and all the social as well as religious activities of the community. We offered a blessing on his house and his family but he was aggressive and asked us on whose authority we were blessing the place. We explained that we were disciples of Jesus of Nazareth. At this he became very alarmed, he told us that he had heard what had happened in Nazareth, and that he had been instructed to have nothing to do with this "upstart". He told us that he would not countenance our preaching in his village a message that was aimed directly at undermining the Law and the established forms of worship. He told us that he had been instructed to make sure that his "flock" were taught that the message was blasphemous and that no man could claim to be the Son of God, or the Messiah. We were unable to say anything, he was so determined that he, himself, would not be contaminated by having to discuss the matter with men who had broken the strict Jewish Law of not eating or socialising with "sinners". He told us that we had better clear out of town before he had us arrested and flogged or worse for advocating blasphemy. Clearly the peace we had proposed for his house was not available and we obeyed Jesus instruction and left the town, metaphorically shaking the dust from our shoes as we did so. When we were clear of the town we sat at the road-side and tried to evaluate this confrontation. It was quite clear that the religious hierarchy had decided that there would be no facilities made available for this Jesus mission, and that they would do everything they could to frustrate any attempt to explain the message to their people. We remembered that Jesus had told us of the urgency of the moment and that we should not hesitate to move on, when we were confronted with this negative, antagonistic reaction, to find people who would welcome the message. So despite the overt threat to our own safety and relying on God's protection we set off again. We had gone less than a mile when we came to an isolated farmstead, by now it was late afternoon and we had had an alarming and demanding day so we decided to try again despite the threats of the leader of the Synagogue, when we knocked at the door and explained what was our purpose we were welcomed as if we were expected guests. We blessed the house and family and were given water to quench our thirst, and were invited to rest while the evening meal was prepared and then we could talk to the whole household. They told us that they had heard, second hand, of the amazing works of Jesus and wanted to hear more: the farm kept them very busy and they had not been able to visit Nazareth or Capernaum or even to send one of the family. We were greatly relieved and took advantage of their hospitality, hoping that when we came to talk with them we would be able to convince them of the arrival of

Emmanuel in our midst. I know when I sat down I went to sleep and I'm sure Philip did as well, the next thing that I knew was that dinner was announced and we were all conducted into the courtyard of the farm, after the rightful preparations had been observed we sat down to eat. It was a large gathering there were great grandparents, grandparents, parents and children, while we had been resting neighbours and other relatives had been told of our visit and had come to listen and join in with the meal. The talk at the table was about the news in the country, a lot about Jesus and about Antipas, but then about the weather and the harvest, as farmers do! I told them about our fishing business and Philip told them about his trading company. They wanted to know why we had dropped everything to follow this "prophet" and so the discussion came round quite naturally to our experience of being challenged by Jesus to accept God's command to do his work. The meal was cleared away and all the household came to listen to what we had to say, even the servants and the slaves were there in the shadows at the fringe of the courtyard.

When everyone was settled and quiet Philip started, he reminded them that the prophets had foretold of the coming of the Messiah and that his coming would be forewarned by a last prophet announcing his imminent arrival. He told them that John the Baptiser who had preached repentance in the desert and baptised penitents in the River Jordan was the man who was to "prepare the way". Jesus of Nazareth had now shown himself to be the Messiah, his message was a message of love, the love of God for every individual. This love was expressed as the forgiveness of sins for those who repent and the promise of eternal life to those who follow his way. Jesus expressed his new message as the fulfilment of the Law, and that this fulfilment was achieved when we accepted that we must love God and love our neighbours. Then I explained as best I could that it was our sinfulness that separated us from God's love, that the sins we committed were not our inability to adhere to the man made rules of the scribes and Pharisees but were when we failed to respect the meaning of the Law as given to the nation by Moses. This law is a law of love it defines man's relationship with God and it defines man's relationship with his neighbour. The way the "Law" was now operated, through ritual and excruciating adherence to minute detail, actually put a barrier between individuals and God by allowing the responsibility for their own personal behaviour to be abdicated to the synagogue and the priesthood. Jesus message is that God is a loving God who cares for every individual person and that he promises us all a peace that we cannot achieve without him, he promises the forgiveness of our sins, if we confess them and promise to lead a new life, and he promises us eternal life. He only demands from us that we love him absolutely and have absolute confidence in him and we love our neighbours and treat them as we would want to be treated. The head of the house asked us how could this "man" this "son of a carpenter" make such pronouncements, he was behaving as if he were God and that is blasphemy. Philip and I looked at each other expecting to receive another explosion as we had seen in the afternoon. Philip answered, not accepting the accusation of blasphemy but as a genuine enquiry about Jesus' credentials. He told us all about the birth and childhood of Jesus and how that fulfilled many prophesies, then he told us about the way that water had been turned into wine and that 5,000 had been fed from five barley loaves and three small fish and that he had commanded the sea to be calm and had walked on the water. I took up the preaching and told them about his incredible presence, how he looked into peoples' souls and saw their real needs and hopelessness. I recounted some of the parables and gave them some understanding of the meanings as had been explained to us and we told them about the great acts of healing that we had witnessed day after day when the sick, the demented, the deaf, the blind and even lepers had been cured. These were the credentials that we had already witnessed and every day new marvels are shown to us confirming God's love for man. There has never been a man with such credentials to convince people that this is the Messiah. The time is now there is no time to delay the Messiah is here and has announced a new order! I suppose between us we had talked for more than two hours and it was now late, so we suggested that we all took our rest and that in the morning we could talk again. I felt a sigh of relief round the listeners, they were clearly tired from the attention and concentration that our words had demanded. Quite quickly the courtyard emptied, Philip and I were left alone, interestingly although we both knew the evening had been less confrontational we found it very difficult to gauge whether we had actually made any impact on our audience. Before we both went to bed we prayed to God, we thanked him for the guidance and skills he had provided for us and asked for his help on the morrow. It was noticeable that although we had suggested that we should meet with the family again in the morning we had no idea what we would talk about but it did not cause us any anxiety, I think we were perhaps just learning that God will take care of things in his way when we knew we were doing his work. We both went to the beds absolutely exhausted after a day of high drama; we slept like children.

The next morning we were up early before the rest of the house had stirred and like Jesus we went into the fields to be alone with God, all that Jesus had taught us about prayer was now put into effect. The quiet, the solitude and the concentration somehow worked together to allow God into our souls, I remember vividly that morning feeling that I was totally surrounded by a sense of peace and power, a sense that today we would be doing God's work and that it was his power which would direct and guide us. The critical sensation was that I really felt total and absolute trust in him. At the first meeting we held I could not summon this trust but today I felt such comfort and safety that I knew God was with us. Philip and I met up with each other as we returned to the farm and we both exuded confidence and joy. I could see it in Philip's whole body language, it reminded me of every morning how Jesus came to meet with us after he had been alone with God. For me, I knew that I had talked with God and that was enough! We had a cheerful and entertaining breakfast and then to our surprise lots of people began to arrive at the farm, it was clear that the word had gone round the area that we were at the farm and that we had cured people at the previous town. Most of the crowd seemed to be the sick and infirm and there was an air of expectancy that we could cure their sick. We decided that before we started our mission we should pray so we asked the farmer if there was somewhere quiet that we could use for a little while. He showed us into a small barn at the back of the buildings, inhabited by a cow and her calf and several sheep, we prayed just as Jesus had taught us we asked for God's guidance and strength to do his will and felt refreshed and empowered when we came into the sunlight to address the crowd.

We told them that we had been given the power to cure the sick but that this blessing depended on their commitment to accept the message we brought them and that they would accept that Jesus was the Emmanuel and that he preached God's love and forgiveness to all who repented of their sins and promised to follow his command to love God and to love his neighbour. For those who would accept this there was not just the blessing of forgiveness but also the promise of peace and eternal life. We told them the three parables, first The Good Shepherd, then The Pearl of Great Price and finally The Good Samaritan, and we told them that these parables showed them the love of God, the value of this love and the real meaning of man's love for his neighbour. As we expected there were immediately objections about the Samaritans, but we told them that for the world to become a better place we had to stop the rounds of injury and abuse and the only was that this could be successfully achieved was by our positive action to care for those who maltreat us and abuse us. Even if they could not see ways to show their love to the Samaritans they could change their neighbourhood by showing God's love by caring for their neighbours when they were in need or any sort of trouble by not withholding kindnesses that they could show if they really wanted to. We told them it was for them individually to decide if they could make such a commitment, God could see into their hearts and he would provide these blessings to those who had faith in his loving power. Several families came forward with their sick, Philip took some and I took others, we asked them if they if they had faith that God could cure them and that it was God's love for each individual that was working through us, that we had no power of our own. They were all clearly very anxious, they knew that they were being watched by their neighbours and they knew that they were publicly exposing what all Jews assumed was their sinfulness and the punishment that God had sent on them. They told us how they had tried everything that had been suggested but nothing helped, they had prayed every day for relief and no relief came, now they had heard that God had sent a new prophet and that he could cure the sick, their faith was such that even if Jesus couldn't come to their village himself they believed that his messengers could bestow the blessing of forgiveness and cure their sicknesses. We were amazed at this expression of faith after all we had claimed nothing except that we had seen these things and had been sent by Jesus to do God's work! We blessed them and saw cures happen before our eyes, we remembered that Jesus had told us that God's power was delivered there and then and the cures were instantaneous. The crowd was hushed, there was an air of wonder, of fear and of anticipation. Then there was a stir at the back of the crowd and we saw the leader of the synagogue, who had given us such a bad time yesterday, coming towards us. We did not know what to expect but we both kept on with our work for God, curing the sick, instead of berating us and publicly denouncing us to his flock he said nothing, he just watched. We could feel a tension developing in the atmosphere, after all he had told us we were blasphemers, he had told us to get out of town and he had told his flock to have nothing to do with us. Eventually he came close to us and said "Surely this Jesus of Nazareth must be the Emmanuel that such things can be done at his command!" The relief was tangible; we felt that God really was at work. Gradually the crowd thinned and eventually we were left just with the household and the leader from the town. Now the man came forward and apologised for his outburst of the previous day, he told us he had been in the crowd for the whole meeting, he had come intending to denounce us but had been over awed by the message we brought and then the gift of healing that we brought to show God's love to his people. He asked us to stay a while and preach this word in the synagogue, we told him that we had to get on, to spread the word as far as we could as quickly as we could. We advised him that as he had heard our words and as he knew the prophesies in the sacred books he should make sure that the rabbi taught this message to the whole population. This he promised to do, but again asked us to stay as he felt inadequate to the task, we told him that he must have faith in God to show him the way, just as we had to have faith and the people who had been cured had too and, what is more, that Jesus himself had to have. So he went back to the town, we never heard what happened, but we are sure that God would use the foundation we had laid there for his purposes. We thanked our hosts for their hospitality, excused our abrupt departure and after blessing them all and their farm we set off again. We had no idea what to expect next but we felt that this had been a successful day!

I think in total we were away for about a month, almost every day we were at a new town or village, sometimes we were rejected just as Jesus had warned us and then we straightway moved on, mostly we were welcomed. We always started our visit by proclaiming Jesus message of God's love, God's forgiveness and his redemption of sins. We told our listeners that the message was not to change the Law but to confirm the Law and to make people feel that they had a personal responsibility to obey the Law, that the Law was expressed most effectively that 'we should love God and that we should love your neighbours.' We used the parables that we had learnt from Jesus and we healed the faithful sick. Jesus had warned us to expect trouble from the authorities and we had some of that twice we were arrested by the Rabbis. On the first occasion we were able to show them that we were not blaspheming and were allowed to continue on our way proclaiming Jesus the Emmanuel. On the second we were actually taken out to be publicly beaten when an old Rabbi intervened and said that if we were doing God's work and we were ill-treated then God's judgement would surely fall on them, if we were not then his judgement would fall on us, his conclusion was that it would be better for them to send us on our way rather than ill-treat us. We were set free, but had found the experience of proclaiming God's love for mankind and being punished for it showed us just how far the people or at least the leaders of the people had fallen from a real understanding of God. We were getting to know this God as a loving, caring, forgiving and powerful God, a God with whom we could talk and in whom we had a growing confidence. After a month we seemed to gravitate back to Capernaum and found that we were not the last of the pairs to return. We all had tales to tell, Jesus listened to all our experiences and was delighted that we had done so much and that we had learnt for ourselves the meaning of God's power to fulfil his plans through us. He didn't try to ascertain what we had achieved by asking questions about how many people had openly acknowledged that he was the Emmanuel or how many people we had cured or were we sure that people had repented and asked for forgiveness. He was much more concerned that we had grown in confidence that we could project his message that God is love and that His love was available to everyone however sinful or rejected they may be by society or how lost they may feel. Philip and I had been lucky, our brush with the authorities had been mild compared with others, some had been imprisoned and publicly punished by beatings and excommunication particularly those who had decided to take the message into Judea. The reports were also clear that there was a strong support for the acceptance of Emmanuel, but a strong political, military Emmanuel, a revolutionary Emmanuel who would rid Israel of her oppressors.

These reports clearly worried Jesus, he shook his head and told us this was not the way and that such a revolution, if it were to happen, would be a repeat of the Maccabean revolt which had achieved nothing and that that was not God's plan. He confided in us when we all got back that after he had been baptised by John he had received God's blessing, that God spoke to him at that moment and promised him the power and resources he needed to complete the task. He told us that he was very disturbed by the experience and had sought isolation from the world to convince himself of the task before he set out on the path that he, and we, were now treading. He went into the hill country and desert area on the far side of the Jordan and stayed there for a period contemplating the possible actions he could take, he prayed fervently for guidance. The guidance he received was that the message had to be issued as a challenge to individuals to come to God, that God was wanting men to turn to Him, that when they came to him he would show them a new way to live which would change the world for ever. The alternative which might be a confrontational demonstration of God's power would not change individuals relationship with God and with each other and would become contaminated by man's sinfulness and would fail, as do all the man made power structures then and forever.

After we had told our stories he told us that he had travelled as well; he had been into the hill country in northern Galilee and out to the coast to the regions of Tyre and Sidon and then back to Capernaum. He expressed disappointment that he was received with acclamation and crowds wondered at his power but he was concerned that the expectancy was of a political Emmanuel and that this was becoming a serious and distorted consequence of the teaching and healing and miracles. The time had come for the final stage of his mission but we needed further preparation and training before we were ready for the confrontation to come. We were now very confused, we had hoped that he would see the support that was available to him from the people where ever we had been, but he told us this was not God's plan, and that political or military confrontation was not the way. We were used to not knowing what was next but now he seemed to be more confident about what was next, he even used words like confrontation but it was not clear what confrontation or with whom. He told us that God's plan was working itself out and that he would be "raised up", we all took this to mean that his power and authority would be recognised and somehow without a military revolution he would be established as the new King David. To us this was a very encouraging message we could see that the sacrifices we, and our families, had and were making would soon be seen to be have been worthwhile. I have given a summary of what took place over several days, mostly in the evenings after busy days of preaching and healing and growing verbal disputes with the Jewish authorities, but gradually our confidence was reinforced and we knew that with our own experience of mission work and Jesus' incredible presence that we would succeed.

It was just then that we received terrible, threatening news, we were returning back to Peter's house in Capernaum as we entered, Peter's wife greeted us in floods of tears, through her sobbing she told us that a boat had just come in from Magdala with the news that John the Baptist had been executed on the previous evening in the dungeons of the palace of Herod Antipas in his desert fortress of Machaerus on the East side of the Jordan.

Part 15

The Death of John the Baptist

Jesus stopped where he was, he seemed to be riveted to the ground, his face glazed over, he was not looking at anything around him, it was as if none of us or the house or anything else existed, he stayed like that for what seemed like a long time. We were all waiting to see his reaction. Suddenly, with this dramatic news, what had seemed to all of us like vague threatening forces circulating round us, like vultures, had become very real, very close, very dangerous and potentially spelled imminent disaster for Jesus, for ourselves and for our families. What were we to do? Was this the moment to attack? Clearly a great injustice had been committed, although we only found out later just how sordid the circumstances were. One option was to follow John's example and to publicly denounce the criminality of this murder just as he had exposed the sinfulness of the Antipas marriage. Was this the moment to withdraw? To flee from the naked exposure of power that Antipas had over the lives of his subjects and the careless self-interest that guided his use of this power. Should we rally the common people who had shown such loyalty to John and to Jesus and force Antipas to change his ways and accept Jesus as the Emmanuel and use his power for good rather than evil, so that we could show how God works to recover even the most cruel and sinful man such as Antipas. What would our reluctant families and friends say now? It looked as if their predictions, that this would all end in tears, was coming true, we had joined the mission but it was too dangerous to go on. I could just hear them "If it was just you men it would be bad enough but what about the rest of us your wives and children and parents and all your wider family, knowing Antipas we could all be rounded up and sold into slavery!" Already we had to cope with the guilt we felt for having deserted them and now we were exposing them to mortal danger. Was it fair, was it reasonable to expect these innocents to be put at such risk? All these thoughts and many more rushed through our minds, to the extent that we could almost hear the soldiers disembarking in the harbour and marching into the town to arrest us all! It was the first time that we felt real fear of the consequences of the mission we had been forced to join. We really started to feel that we had been hijacked into a project and were building up excuses why we should not be arrested or punished, it wasn't our doing we were just by-standers who went along with the idea to see how far it would run! Our confidence was draining out of our feet, we had totally forgotten that Jesus had warned us that we would be subjected to exactly this sort of pressure and that we must have faith that God was our defence and that his power was infinite and exceeded beyond imagination the puny human power of this evil man Antipas. All that had gone, we were not just ready to run away but also ready to desert this man Jesus, at the very moment when we should have been rallying to his support and boosting his confidence! When we talked among ourselves, later, we found we were all thinking the same things and were dreadfully ashamed that we could instantly become cowards and deserters to this cause that Jesus continually declared was to change the world. All these thoughts passed through our minds in seconds, the Devil is a fast worker if he sees a chance.

Jesus, he told us later was praying for John's soul and thanking God for his life and dedication and self-sacrifice to his duty as 'the herald crying in the desert to prepare for the coming of Emmanuel' predicted by the prophets of long ago. He was asking God to forgive the perpetrators of this crime because they did not know what they were doing. The few seconds passed, Jesus turned to us and said with absolute confidence, the time for my real confrontation with the powers of evil is not yet, so you have no reason to be afraid, God is with us and he is our strength and protector. "Who, I ask you, can succeed against us". He then turned back to the household, who were all waiting to hear what we would do. He told them that this murder was a demonstration of the power of darkness and evil at work in the world and although it might seem invincible, God had ordained that the devil's power was to be broken and that God had given Jesus this task, this was His mission. We were all to trust in God, we had already seen the power of God in miracles of healing and the control of the physical world and had heard him teaching about the real will of God for his people. Of course it was a very sad day, John had been a courageous man and had died because he would only accept God's truth in the world and openly challenged the morality of a spiritually sick and sinful family. It was a certainty that John would be remembered to the end of time for his courage and devotion. Antipas would also be remembered but as a warning to all rulers and governors that power corrupts the soul and drives individuals into their own private hell on earth. He told us all that he was confident that today, when Antipas recovered from his drunken stupor of the previous evening, his remorse would be dreadful, his anger with his wife and daughter would be without bounds. He knew that his desire for status, his lustful attraction to his own daughter, his stupid self confidence had led him in one awful moment to kill God's messenger, a present day prophet. He was Jew enough to reflect on the consequences to the kings of old when they committed such a crime and would expect those consequences to be implemented sooner rather than later. He would know that he had just written his own destiny and his own death warrant. Jesus told us that there was no way that he would countenance repeating such a crime so we were not to worry that he would treat us cruelly and he repeated the time is not now for the final confrontation. We only half understood what he was saying; he had restored our confidence and we waited to hear what was the next thing to be done. We were not a little surprised after these words that he continued by saying that the forces of evil were at work, they would try to cease this moment and it would be prudent to temporarily put ourselves outside Antipas' reach and proposed that we continue our work in Herod Phillip's territory on the east side of the Jordan. These two half brothers hated each other Antipas had stolen Phillip's wife! It would be impossible for Antipas to organise an extradition. We would only stay for a short time, the impulse to act against us that the devil might manage to generate, would soon dissolve as other more pressing problems were imposed on Antipas and his evil band.

So we spent the rest of the day resting, but with Jesus 'resting' was a stimulating experience. Somehow we divided up into small groups and although the talk started innocently about the weather or the family or the work we used to do it always ended up that we were talking about the mission. The problems that occupied us most were first, the overtly stated 'final confrontation' that Jesus frequently referred to, the question was what was going to happen, generally we concluded that this would be when the authorities were forced to recognise Jesus for what he was, the Emmanuel! Perhaps then, when God revealed his glory we, his loyal disciples would receive our reward. Then the other serious problem was that he kept reminding us that we would change the world and this seemed to imply that we would do this on our own! If there was some master plan we had absolutely no inkling what it might be, but we all knew that when we tried to understand what was happening or to interpret, to Jesus, our understanding of things that had happened we were always wrong. It seemed that the whole understanding of Emmanuel that we had been brought up to understand was wrong and that there would never be a resurrection of the Jewish state to some position of power and supremacy and that Emmanuel was coming to the whole world and not exclusively to God's "chosen" people. More alarming than that idea was that the redemption of Israel, it seemed, was nothing to do with any political or economic recovery of vaguely remembered Glory. It was, we all felt, inconceivable that this little band of twelve could achieve anything at all let alone change the world, with or with out God's power. Even after witnessing so many miracles and listening to His explanations and his teachings and his parables we still could not bring ourselves to commit our lives to God to put our total trust and faith in him. Jesus seemed to know what was going on, perhaps we were more uncertain than usual because of John's execution, he circulated among these little groups and gave us understandings and insights into these problems. He was always so confident, so cheerful, so attentive and so encouraging. I never once heard him say anything like, "I have told you this fifty times, will you ever understand?" He once did chastise us all by saying "You of little faith!" but generally he was sympathetic to the dramatic shift in our mindsets that we were being asked to make. When I look back to those days I am humbled by the inadequacy of our performance, but equally I am amazed that Jesus knew that if he could turn us round to face a new direction then changing the world could be and would be achieved. As the afternoon wore on into evening and we could hear the welcome sounds from the kitchen we came together as one group, we prayed together for John, for our families and for ourselves and for the lepers and all the others who had received a life changing experience. Then as it started to get dark Jesus told us this little parable, "You are the light of the world, who would light a light and put it under the bed, or who would light a light and then put it under a bowl, no a light is for all to see it is set on high so that it spreads to all the corners of the room. The darkness in the room can not resist the light, the light is always more powerful than it. Even the smallest light fills a darkened room." Again I say to you, "You are this light of the world. You must shine in the world so that men will see your good works and glorify God because of them." Then he explained what he meant, the darkness in the world is the evil and sin that pervades everything, everyone and everywhere. The light is the message of God's love, of God's forgiveness, of God's redemption and his promises of peace and eternal life. This light when it confronts evil will always overcome the evil. "You will proclaim this message of salvation to the whole world and although many will turn aside from your message enough will understand and will accept this light that changes the world." As we turned towards the house the evening was well advanced and it was almost pitch dark, there was no moon and it was a cloudy evening, and there shining out of the kitchen door was the single light of a lantern, shining like a beacon in the darkness to show us the way home to comfort, security and peace.

The atmosphere at the table was sombre and quiet, quite clearly everyone was very anxious about the news of John's execution and were concerned for their own safety and the safety of their loved ones. Jesus opened the meal with prayer he asked God for his blessing on us all, he thanked God for the life and witness of John, he asked God to guard and guide us through these troubled and dangerous times and to give us the strength and courage to persevere in the work we had to do. He reminded us that we were doing God's work and God would not be thwarted or deflected from his intentions so we should have no reason to fear. I don't remember if anyone questioned him, his air and demeanour were of absolute confidence and he talked to us all about his adventures and our adventures and the whole atmosphere gradually became positive and confident. Eventually the women, who took their responsibility for caring for our physical needs, very seriously, told us it was high time we were all in bed and so we retired, many of us still with deep anxiety about the future despite Jesus' assurance to have faith and confidence. The next morning the twelve of us were all up and about at first light, the air was like nectar, the blue of the sky was unimaginable, birds fluttered and called in the bushes around the garden and peace reigned supreme. Peter, who he admitted had not slept well, suggested that we pray. Many people joined in with their own prayers and thoughts but the main thrust was about our personal security, an inclination to deny or at least question Jesus' authoritarian confidence that we were doing God's work. Gradually we became despairing, every where we looked there seemed to be powers raised up against us which pushed us continually to the conclusion the it really was not going to work and we had best give up now! We all knew that we were failing Jesus, some one asked where he was just when we needed him to boost our confidence. Of course we knew he, too, was out on the hills somewhere praying. We asked God for his strength, we asked God for his guidance, we asked God to send Jesus back to us. Nothing happened we became just more and more disillusioned as we prayed and raised our problems to God instead of them being eased they became more and more acute. We all had experienced our individual prayers being answered, it had been one of the most dramatic features of our missionary expedition and each of us thought that we had learnt how to clear our minds of the non-essentials, to concentrate, to listen to God and to trust in his finding the way forward for us to follow. Now nothing seemed to work, always our minds were deflected back to the implications of John's execution and the myriad of gloomy possibilities that it had for us and for our families. The Herod family were well known for their tyrannical response to any one who criticised them or threatened in any way their power and that was just what Jesus was doing. Now Antipas had the taste of blood he would probably search out Jesus and would eliminate him and all his adherents. What were we to do? We were probably in too deep to escape his wrath and this had all happened because we foolishly responded to Jesus calling us to restore Israel. All those people who had doubted our sanity would be proved right, we had been mad to even contemplate such a mission. Worse than that we had seen very quickly that Jesus had no real intention of directly confronting the powers in the land, the only people he seemed to care about were the social outcasts, how could such a rabble defeat the power of Rome. Eventually we went in to breakfast and were confronted by our families saying the same things, we were lucky we were with our families, what, we asked our selves were those other families in Bethsaida and Cana and Nazareth saying to each other about their men-folk who had abandoned them. What about all the people who had sworn allegiance to Jesus and had tried to convince their neighbours and their synagogues of the truth of his message, how would they fare when Antipas launched his offensive against us all. Depression was now turning to demoralisation and doubt, then it turned to bickering and argument, factions were developing, people stating their intentions and challenging Jesus as our master and leader. I know that I was praying desperately for Jesus to return to us to show us the way, to give us the courage and confidence to see God in all this anxiety. He didn't come, we had a miserable breakfast of disputes and anger, followed by a more miserable morning when we all felt deserted. Where had he gone? What was he doing? He must have recognised the distress we all felt the previous evening he must know that we needed his leadership now more than we ever had before! Lunch time came and went, it was now being mooted that he had recognised the whole mission had failed and had actually left. There was a growing undercurrent of resentment and some were talking about desertion and picking up the pieces of their old lives. We had never been left this long. Had he met with some accident, was he ill? We kept trying to remind ourselves that he had told us that he and we were doing God's work and God would not let us down, but even these words seemed to have a hollow ring. Mary, his mother told us that he had left after dinner the previous evening and she had not seen him since, of all the people she was the one who was calm and confident. She kept assuring us that he was the Emmanuel, announced from before his birth, that God had protected him and nurtured him all this time and would not leave him now. He was, she assured us, fulfilling the scriptures and quoted the prophets and the psalms to reinforce her conviction but the confidence she gave us was short lived. Then quite suddenly he was with us again, nobody saw him arrive he was just there as one of us, the relief was immense. Everyone crowded round him asking all sorts of questions and some being critical about his absence. Others asked him how we were supposed to cope without our master in such a moment of crisis. He listened to all we had to say, he was patient and attentive, he showed no sense of disappointment or surprise at our out-pouring of worries.

When we had calmed down a little, he reminded us of our lack of faith in the boat on the sea during the storm when we had been convinced that all was lost. He had tried to show us then that God's power was greater than anything in nature, he had told us that we had to have faith that we were doing God's work and that it was not in God's plan that we should be destroyed before we had hardly started. The devil had come between us and God and we had such little confidence in God that we could not see it was the devil at work and had fallen for his wiles and despaired. The devil is very cunning and uses all our frailties to drag us away from God by exaggerating our worries and confirming our unbelief. We have to learn to combat the devil at his own game, we have to learn to recognise the devices of the devil and be on our guard against them and we have to pray to God for the strength to resist the temptations put in our way by the devil. That was on the boat, now we had another problem and another example of our lack of faith, commonly seen as panic! The start was the news of John's murder, all our thoughts were for our own skins we only saw the dreadful spectre of Antipas searching us out to torture and kill us and our families. This is again the devil's work, again exploiting our lack of faith, he had taken such power that we could not pray, all our powers of concentration our faith, our trust had been undermined by our self-delusion instigated by the devil. As we had failed to get relief by prayer, our faith was further eroded, we began to believe that prayer did not work, and that despite our common and individual experience that it did work. Then we began to undermine our confidence in Jesus, just because he was not there we began to think that he had deserted us. We began to question whether he had lost his nerve and abandoned the whole project, what level of faith and loyalty was this? Then we listened to our families who were only too ready to give up and return to the comfortable life they had known and they too further undermined our confidence in Jesus and God! Then we started to argue among our selves using our energy and confidence to squabble rather than to support and encourage each other. So we must see that the devil had been winning all the way, and what would have been the outcome if Jesus had not returned. We were by now very ashamed of our performance because we knew that the answer we had to give was that we would have abandoned the whole project, and we also knew that then the devil and all his powers would have won and we would not be able to change the world and darkness and sin and evil would continue to rule. When he was with us and we felt his power round us, his analysis of our behaviour was like a sword piercing through us.

Then he asked us to try to examine what had really happened. First we had the news of John's murder, a dreadful event! Second we had ignored John and concentrated on our selves. Third we had chosen to forget all the promises that we had from God backed up by experience of the truth of these promises. Then we set about arguing among ourselves. Finally we are about to capitulate, the situation was only saved when he returned and used his power to fight off the devil. These were serious lessons that we had to understand and learn from so that the next time we would recognise the devil at work and beat him with the weapons Jesus had given us. We must be sure that the devil would attack again and again.

"Make no mistake", he assured us, "you were chosen by God to defeat the devil and the devil himself will use all his guile and deviousness to try to thwart the will of God by leading you into sin."

Then he led us away towards the sea and the harbour. There he sat down on a bollard and talked to us. He told us that our experience and his of visiting the towns and villages had shown that the people were hard hearted and could not and would not accept his message of a new relationship between God and man. He was ruthless in his criticism and condemned the people and their leaders for being deaf and blind to the urgent need for them to accept a new way. The only thing that the Jews wanted was political power to wreak revenge on their enemies. Despite his demonstration of God's power, despite the teaching, despite his explaining the historic importance of the Jews dedication to their one God they were incapable if comprehending the new message from God. So having tried and having given the Jews a chance, another way would be developed and the plan to "change the world" would be fulfilled. The message would be broadcast to all nations but to achieve this we had to better understand the power of God and his love, the discipline that was implied in God's love and that, as the prophets had foretold, the Son of Man would be raised before all men as the witness for them to see. He told us that in the morning we would set of for the region of Ceasarea Philippi and would spend some time there, most of our time, he told us, would be in learning a deeper understanding of God and his intentions for men and the world. He told us that we would understand how the new message that he proclaimed was consistent with the prophecies of old but gave men a new relationship with God which would dramatically and permanently change the world for the good of all men, believers and non-believers alike. This was God's great plan and there was nothing that could interfere with its final implementation; sin and the devil may delay the implementation but in the end the power of God's love would overcome all opposition through the witness and evangelism of ordinary men.

Part 16

Ceasarea Philippi

We were all, I remember, very depressed when we assembled in the morning. We had prayed singly or in small groups for God's guidance in this next stage of our adventure but we all felt that it was a bit like running away from the enemy. Jesus attitude had been changed by the result of his personal solitary mission and the results of our missions and this change had been reinforced by the news of the murder of John. It was clear that the mission to Galilee had not produced the results that Jesus expected and that now a new direction was being initiated. His demeanour had changed he was still confident, he was still cheerful and determined but, when I look back, I am sure that he already knew what the final climax to his mission to men had been determined. The atmosphere was one of intense urgency, even more than when we went from town to town with Jesus proclaiming the good news and healing the sick and disputing with the Scribes and Pharisees.

After breakfast we bade farewell to our families and set off up the field paths towards Chorazin. There were about twenty of us, Jesus and the twelve he had chosen, Mary his mother and her daughter, Mary Magdalene, my wife and Mathew's wife and a couple of servants. The weather was balmy, the harvest had been brought in and the fields looked bare, the orchards still had their fruit and the olive groves were bearing their second crop. From the field path we looked down into villages and farmsteads and could feel an air of relaxed satisfaction that all was well and that the winter would not bring starvation and sickness as it so often did.

As we walked Jesus used the time to teach us by parable and by using nature as a demonstration of God's creation to show us his magnificent infinite power. As we passed along the edge of a wheat field he gleaned an ear of corn that had been dropped by the harvesters, he called us round him and asked us whether any of us could see God's power in the seeds of corn. I have to admit that we were taken aback by the question, to us it was just an unremarkable wheat seed there was nothing special about it, so he told us these parables. The first parable was that the seed of corn, could do nothing unless it was thrown into the ground to die but then out of its death new life would appear. The lessons to be learnt from this were several. For instance he said that if the seed is the word of God, the new message he was bringing, then we could not keep it to ourselves we had to sow it in the ground of men's minds for the new understanding to be realised and accepted. Or, the seeds potential could be seen that this one seen when it grew and ripened would produce a new enlarged crop perhaps sixty or even one hundred new seeds and if these were planted another sixty or a hundred seeds would come from each of those seeds, and so on, so that in a very short time, only a few seasons, the "death" of this one seed would produce an untold, uncountable number of seeds. He told us, that he is like the first seed, bringing his message of God's love and forgiveness, we were the next seeds, the first harvest and we had to "sow our seeds", that is to proclaim the new relationship with God, and they would bear fruit. The message he brought was so new so important so understandable that in a very short time the word would spread and we would have changed the world. But he said the seed could just be kept and although it still had the potential to produce many more seeds nothing would happen if it was not sown into the ground. Then he told us another parable that we had heard before, about the sower and the seed falling on the path, in stony ground, among thorns and in the good ground, he reminded us that we must not be disappointed if not all the seed produced a worthwhile crop. The work of the Devil would drag people away, some who had heard the word fall back into their old ways. What we had experienced in the past weeks had been that many people had accepted his word and had started to live a new life but then they gradually fell back into their old ways and failed to love God and failed to love their neighbour, the result was that they had gone astray. There was good seed producing good results, for instance the work our families were doing in Capernaum and Bethsaida to support the families of those who had been cured to maintain their faith in God, there was the family in Magdala who were showing great determination to further God's word, he reminded us that we had news that the woman who had touched him in the crowd was now the centre of an ever growing community who supported each other in need. But the vast majority of people who had come face to face with the reality of God through contact with Jesus had given up and fallen back into the old ways, Many of them because they were threatened by the Pharisees and the Rabbis with excommunication if they continued to promote the arrival of the Messiah in Jesus. Another example of the seed and its relevance to our mission was the existence of the need for a proper relationship with God that lies latent in all men and waits, this is the seed that waits for the word to germinate just as a seed will germinate in the soil. So the potential for men to hear and receive the word is available to us but we have to proclaim the word to allow the germination of the seed in each man to start. The other thing that he told us was that of course the seed may germinate and start to grow but unless it receives water and the warmth and light from the sun it will not grow. This nourishment comes from God and it is so with people, unless they get spiritual nourishment from God their faith will wither, for this reason we must pray to God and listen to God we must recognise God in the actions of other people and we must support each other with encouragement and correction. "This", he told us, "is my task now, but it will soon be your task. God does not come but he sends, he has sent me and I will send you and you will send others. You are God's seeds in this sinful world and you will bring forth sixty or one hundred fold and send out more seed into the field but then you will be the nourishment sent by God to nurture the next crop, once the word has been planted it will grow and grow until all the world has heard it." We were amazed so much teaching to be obtained just from a single wheat seed!

So we went on and after a while Jesus stopped again and plucked a flower from the hedgerow, he turned to us and said, " Here is God's creation!" He told us to look at it carefully to see, not just to look, the beauty of the arrangement of the leaves and the petals, the regularity of the design, the intricacy of the delicate inner parts, the colours of the petals, the latent seed pod, the pollen and the stamen, the perfume exuding from the centre. "What", he asked us, "could we learn about God from just this flower?" Well, we said, we were not sure. Of course it was beautiful, but after all it was a flower and flowers are beautiful and of course its perfume was intoxicating but that was as flowers should be, and of course we knew God had created it so it was special in that sense. Jesus agreed with all this but then said that we should recognise that nothing that man ever had made, or ever could make, could match the perfection of this flower and every other flower and every other living thing. God's designs were perfect, there was nothing superfluous, there was nothing out of place, every part had its purpose. What is important to man to understand is that these flowers and all the creation round us is a demonstration of God's infinite power after all there were thousands and thousands of different plants, thousands and thousands of different animals let alone the innumerable number of insects and fish and trees and birds each one made to the same perfection to fulfil its purpose. God had made them all, but God had also made man and his intension, as with this flower, was that man should be perfect to fulfil God's purpose. Man had by his sinfulness frustrated this intension and the world was now filled with evil, men had lost their way to God and it was his purpose to show them for the

227

last time the way to God and to his planned perfection, a perfection more beautiful and complete than the flowers of the field or the birds of the air. The purpose of Jesus' mission was no less than to change the world so that man could take his rightful place in God's perfect plan and we were chosen and charged with propagating this message to all men every where. Peter, who was always very practical asked him how this was to be done, after all he said between them they had some Greek and some Latin, but there were all the other languages of all the races of the world how could we tell them this saving message. The answer was very surprising!

Jesus said in reply to Peter, " The power will be given to you when the time is right and you will find that the word can be spread to all nations. You always ask for the practical solutions to your perceived problems, you have to learn to have faith. Do you think that God will send you out into the world with the urgent message of forgiveness and God's love and not have considered the practical details of how that will be done. Of course he has the plan for that detail as he has for all the other matters some of which you can understand but most you can not and never will understand."

Peter was quiet for a few minutes and then asked, " How do you know all these things, how is it that when we ask what seem quite sensible questions, and we are grown men, that you always tell us to have faith? We do find it unsettling that we are setting off into the unknown with no plan that we can understand but we must just have faith!" It was the first time we had heard Peter talk so boldly, but we knew he was stating what we all felt and several others asked similar questions. I think that Peter's boldness was grown out of a sense of doubt that had been with us all ever since John's execution and reinforced by another growing feeling that Jesus was leaving Galilee in fear of Antipas which could be construed as a lack of his confidence in God's infinite power. So Jesus walked on a little way and then sat himself down on the grass and when we had all gathered round and settled on the ground, he answered Peter's question.

"Oh you of little faith! How many times and how many ways do I have to explain to you the power of God and his plan for me and for you in the world. Have I not shown you God's power in action? Have I not given you that power? Have you not found that you can use that power? But still you doubt God's power. Do you think that because you have cured people and preached to people, because you have seen water changed to wine and five thousand fed from three small fishes that that is the extent of God's power or that you have problems that are beyond God's competence? Do you think that God is unaware of the powers of evil at work in the world? He knows more about evil and the plotting of the devil that you can or ever should know. I tell you most sincerely that the only part of God's plan that you need to provide for its completion is "faith"; absolute faith in God's power and providence and to show that faith to the world, and then you will change the world. So you have to learn that the answer, God's answer, to all your doubts and anxieties is "Have Faith", and with that everything you need to fulfil God's will, will be provided and much more than you could ever expect." We did not know what to make of this, for instance Peter commented, "It takes time to learn to speak another language, it takes time to travel the world, it takes time to talk to people to make them believe in the message of God's love, how can we twelve do all this?" Jesus looked stern now, "Peter" he said, "I don't think you were listening when I told you about the seed, can you not see that once you make someone believe he will tell others and convince them, they will then convince others and each will hand on the truth in his own language. So there is no need for you as individuals to learn many languages, God will see to it that the truth will be spread, but you have to sow the first seeds and for this purpose you were chosen and for this purpose I am teaching you. Now do you all see that this simple question about language shows your lack of faith but I have used it now to show you just how simply God will provide a solution. Now you understand the solution, I think you will agree that it is quite clear, but it was not clear until I told you. You will have to learn to accept that you do not know the answers to the problems facing you, but perhaps you will sometimes remember how shallow your faith was when you concerned yourselves about Languages!"

Instead of getting up to continue our journey he stayed where he was and after a little while he asked us if we could see another lesson from this discussion about language. The response was, I am sure an uncertain silence, what else could there be the matter had been resolved and we thought we had a better understanding of the way God worked these things out, so what else could there be? Our confusion was quite obvious to Jesus, he listened to our attempts to find other meanings and eventually he stopped the chatter and told us that we had to concentrate our minds and energy on the important things of life. He took us back to the flower, he said "Remember the flower we used to talk about God's creation; well I tell you Solomon in all his splendour was never dressed as beautifully as that flower. God took that much care over a flower that is here today and tomorrow is gone, ask yourselves, how much more care will he take of you. He made you in his own likeness, he has brought Israel through all its history of rebellious sinfulness and tragic failures, he will not desert you even if you desert him. To live a full life man must look to God to provide the wisdom and guidance he needs to achieve a close relationship with God. To do this you have to learn to recognise the important things in life, these important moments are when your soul is at risk, when the devil is most aggressive and when you are most vulnerable. It is at these moments of crisis that you have to call on God's power, when you have to have faith in that power and when you have to have the courage to tread the path of the righteous, the difficult and dangerous path which is the only way to fulfil God's purpose. So now this business of the languages, you understand now that God's plan provides a straight forward solution, what is much more important is not the language but what is to be said. So you see there are two levels of problems to be solved the most important is to pray, in faith, for God's power to say the right words and if you do this you can be sure that God will not shrink from providing the solution to the problem of language. You have to learn to see the real deep requirement of the moment and not to be distracted by the superficial fringe issues of the moment."

Peter was quick to join in " So its like our fishing, there's no point in worrying about the sandwiches if we go without the nets!"

"Exactly so, I couldn't have put it more succinctly myself!" was Jesus reply and I think we had all learnt another lesson. So we set off again feeling that despite our early failures we had perhaps begun to understand some things.

We stayed on the West side of the Jordan we had long since passed Chorazim on our left side nestling in the fold in the hills, we could see the great paved Roman road to Damascus and then on to Antioch and the provinces of Asia running parallel to us in the low country beside us. Sometimes we could see camel trains, perhaps they were taking our fish paste, plodding along the road and occasionally there was a horse being ridden at speed and kicking up a huge dust cloud, no doubt this was some urgent message for the Romans in Damascus. It crossed my mind that perhaps what Jesus had just been teaching us was before us, here we were with the task of changing the world, just a small group of unimportant men and women plodding along the field paths but with God's power all round us and there below us was a messenger taking a message to the greatest power mankind had ever witnessed, one day the roles would be turned! Eventually we came to the pass in the hills where the road crosses the Jordan just south of Gadot and we dropped off the hills and made our way to the township. Our purpose was to avoid attracting attention as we were still in the lands of Antipas and we did not want our movements to be reported back to him. We stayed on the paved road only for about half a mile and then took to the hill paths again, to our surprise Jesus didn't take the direct route out into Philip's land where we would be reasonably free from any threats but set off directly north to Gadot. This place is only a small farming community and a very mixed population of Jews and Greeks, but everyone was making a living from the soil. The place had an air of comfortable prosperity, the fields look well tended there were flocks of sheep and goats on the hills around, the houses looked well kept and there was a new synagogue.

We were not so alarmed as we had been in the past, when Jesus walked up to a front door and confidently knocked, after all we had done much the same on our own travels, Philip reminded me of our first experience and we had to smile at the memory. We were terrified when the door was opened by a Roman, he wasn't in military uniform but he was dressed in the expected clothes of a Roman house servant. What, we thought, have we done now? We shall be immediately reported to the military authorities, arrested and sent back to Tiberias to be imprisoned and eventually in all probability executed just like John. Disaster was upon us what were we to do, there was a general move to retreat or at least be positioned where escape might be possible. Jesus was not in the least anxious he passed a few words with the servant and was then invited inside, an invitation he accepted without the least hesitation. So now what were we to do, should we escape while we could or go on with Jesus and all get caught so that the mission was certain to fail, with our hearts in our mouths we followed where Jesus went quite sure that this was the end. You could not imagine our surprise and relief to find that we were in the courtyard of the home of the Centurion whose servant Jesus had cured that day on the beach at Capernaum. The man was in fact a proselyte, he had accepted the Jewish religion and despite his professional duties was leading an exemplary life. He had sent his servants regularly to listen to everything that Jesus had been saying and to report back on all his deeds. He had accepted the new way, he had shown his love for God and his love for his neighbour. The new synagogue we had remarked on as we entered the village, he had paid for, out of his own money he had paid for the digging of new and deeper wells to make sure the water supply was reliable and pure. He had encouraged the town to contribute together to provide a sewage system under a paved road through the middle of the village. By making the people see that if they worked together to help each other there were many things that they could achieve which separately were not possible. A new oven for bread making had been built and everyone took their turn in collecting fuel, whether it was for their bread cooking or for others. A new wash-house had been built, this was a revolution, the stream through the village had been diverted through a roofed building where it passed through a pond, and then out to rejoin the stream. The women of the village took their clothes and washed them, in the shade, in clean running water and all together to chatter and help each other. The men were now working as a co-operative, instead of selfishly guarding their tools, their seed, their workers and watching others struggle, they had agreed that, in order, they would plough all the land together, they would sow all the land together, they would tend the growing crops and harvest them together as a communal endeavour. They had found the results were dramatic, the harvest was held in common and the taxes were paid in common, although they didn't let the tax collectors know what was happening. Every farmer had his share and nobody went hungry. They had a surplus that they could sell or exchange for things the community needed. We now began to understand why this village looked so much better than everywhere else. Here we could see that loving God and loving your neighbour was a practical, worthwhile exercise, and that God was smiling on their endeavours. Surprisingly, they told us that babies don't die like they used to, that people and animals don't go sick like they used to and that nobody was poor, there were no beggars and there were no thieves, there were disputes but, probably because of the wash house they always seemed to be resolved amicably. Well it seemed like a little bit of heaven on earth. The centurion, who was on his last tour of duty had decided that he would retire here but he wanted to try to put Jesus words into a real life situation. He knew he had the organisational skills to make things happen, he knew he had the money to pay for things to happen but he wanted to see what happened when everyone pooled their physical and spiritual resources together for the common good. It worked, what is more people were happy, co-operative and secure. Just as Jesus had promised, greed and envy and self interest had been replaced by mutual love for each other, nobody saw this as a weakness to be exploited, everyone contributed for the good of themselves and their neighbours. They did, we noticed, have one advantage their was only one Pharisee in the village and he had been prevailed upon to be part of this new way and not to continually point out that the "law" was being broken here, there and everywhere!

We were all made most welcome, the man who had answered the door to Jesus was the very man who he had cured, he told us that when the master came home he was totally confused but decided there and then that his household would adopt the new way that Jesus was teaching. He did this quite publicly and because he was such an important man and had such power every one joined. Of course there were those who joined in reluctantly but as they saw that he really meant what he said the enthusiasm was infectious and the achievements were amazing. Clean shirts everyday for instance! We all settled in and were shown where we would sleep, the women went off to the kitchen and met all the household and helped prepare the meal, the evening was drawing in and soon we were all sitting together for a splendid festive supper. I suppose because the Roman army is like that, Septimus, the centurion, made a speech to welcome us all, he used very flowery Latin, some of which we understood but then he spoke in Galillean and we all felt much more comfortable. For a foreigner he spoke our strange dialect quite well! Before we ate he asked Jesus to bless us all and the food we were about to eat. Jesus stood among us and blessed us, he asked for God to care for this household and the village, he asked God to support them in their work together and he asked them never to forget that everything they had came from God and none of it was of their own making. He then blessed the food and we all set to and enjoyed the food and the company.

The next morning after, we had breakfasted, we set off for Ceasarea walking on the little used field paths and most of the time we avoided crowds, occasionally we could look down over the Jordan Valley onto the 'Kings Road' on the far side. We could see camel caravans plodding along the way and people in little groups with their bundles of belongings or baskets of produce with children dashing about among the grown-ups. We saw the cloud of dust thrown up by a Roman chariot driving north as fast as his horse would go and wondered what message was so important. We were relatively at peace and pleased to be separated from the rush and bustle on the road. It gave us time to talk about the many things that had happened in the last few months among ourselves, Jesus used the time to explain some of the issues that were causing him concern.

The most significant was that the Jews, that is the ordinary people, were prepared to accept that Jesus was a great prophet and that he must have God's power with him but they were not prepared to change their ways. Although they readily accepted that they were sinful and only through repentance and leading a life of love of God and love of their neighbours could their souls be redeemed, they were not changing their ways. He concluded that their sinfulness was so deep seated and so continually replenished by the scribes and Pharisees that they could not recognise the evil that was abroad in the land and respond to his call for repentance. This then raised the problem of the response of the scribes and Pharisees and the leaders of the synagogues, everywhere we were met with hostility. It was only when Jesus was teaching and healing in the open with large crowds or in the security of a home were people prepared to open their hearts and confess their need for forgiveness. In public there was little evidence of any retained conviction of people to change their way of life. It was quite clear that the power over the mind of the people lay with the Pharisees. This power was exercised, not through convincing the rightfulness of their intentions, but by exerting intense social pressure on people to conform to their standards by continually referring to their interpretation of the Law of Moses as God's interpretation. Their sanction was the authority they claimed to declare individuals to be sinners and thereby excluded from the synagogue and from the Temple if they did not conform. This socially divisive, subversive pressure was reinforced by neighbours acting as spies and tell-tales to the Pharisees and this environment ensured that to "Love your neighbour", let alone your enemy, was an unattainable commandment. The reality was that the scribes and Pharisees held such control over the people that it was only at the risk of great personal sacrifice and social exclusion that any individual could disobey their laws and regulations and accept Jesus' new interpretation of the Law in particular to "Love your neighbour". Jesus' continual overt breaking of the law, particularly of the Sabbath, his open association with sinners, and his authoritative and damning response to the Pharisees when they challenged him was intended to show the people just how far they had been led away from the real will of God expressed in the Law of Moses. It was to show the people that there were answers to the apparent power and assumed holiness of these men that Jesus goaded them into confrontation.

It was strange, after all they had all heard what John the Baptist had predicted and what they saw with their own eyes and what they heard with their ears was exactly what the prophets of old had predicted. John had attracted such crowds that his message of repentance and urgent expectation of the arrival of the Messiah, did not go unheard and despite his murder his disciples were still strong in their conviction that the time was now. Despite all these endeavours it was quite clear that the mass conversion of the Jews of Galilee was not going to take place however much effort was applied. I think that the reports we all brought back of our endeavours at evangelising confirmed to Jesus that there had to be another way. The power of evil had to be confronted and the guardians of the power of evil were the scribes and Pharisees. There is no way that they would willingly forgo the power and the status and the wealth that they extracted from the people without a fight. The reason that they were the power of evil was that they actively diverted people away from God, they made all their own petty regulations about food, about cleanliness, about the Sabbath, about social status, about religious status, and all the rest of their paraphernalia more important than God's love and God's forgiveness. The tendency of religious ceremonial and dogma becoming more important than the message of God's love has to be continually avoided. Otherwise the result was that everyone spent all their time trying to obey their strictures, and watching that their neighbours did so too, and at no time worshipping in true reverence the God who had promised so much as his chosen people. Of course this was not a universal situation and Jesus gave examples of people who did see the right way and managed within the "legal" constraints to worship God as He wished, but to the majority the generally accepted view was that the outward forms of behaviour were the only needed criterion for a perfect relationship with God. It didn't matter then what people were saying in their hearts or that they behaved sinfully but within the minutiae of the Law. The system was steeped in hypocrisy, Jesus set about exposing this hypocrisy and put himself in a head to head confrontation with the religious leaders. The problem that we faced as we walked gently towards Ceasarea was that the people had not responded to the challenge, they had enjoyed the spectacle of the miracles and the healings and the arguments with the Pharisees but they had not "seen with their eyes nor heard with their ears" and certainly they had quickly drifted back to their old ways. Our own families efforts in supporting the families of Capernaum who had been cured of sickness and who had joined in when they set up centre for feeding and clothing the poor and the beggars had found that people didn't want to change their ways despite the blessings they were receiving. Worse than that they all felt exploited, they found people were coming into the town just to see what free hand outs were being provided. Greed and envy seemed to be the most outward expression of any spirituality. It took a great deal of personal commitment, prayer and mutual support to keep on with the work. High in their minds was always the parable of the Good Shepherd who risked everything for the sake of one lost sheep!

Despite our problems we were all feeling quite encouraged because for the first time we were working to a plan. Jesus told us that we would stay a while in the area of Ceasarea and he would teach us many things that we needed to know, before we set out on the next stage of the adventure which was to go to Jerusalem to proclaim the word. We were all very excited by this plan because we could see that Jerusalem was where Jesus would show God's power and He the Messiah would restore Israel to its former glory, would destroy its enemies and force the world to accept the great God 'I AM' as the one true and only God! And we, we band of very ordinary men would be there to make sure it all happened and we would, of course, replace the present holders of power and influence. So we could see that in a very short time our lives would be transformed and we would become the rulers of the world, we would be sent out as Jesus representatives to every corner of the world to enforce his will, just as the Romans did! Everything looked very positive, we had seen his power at work and we were convinced that he could achieve anything and everything, our expectations were high and our optimism was unquenchable. We spent time among ourselves talking about the new order, about the power we would wield and, yes, about the comforts that we expected to enjoy and that our long-suffering families would enjoy.

At the end of the day we came to a farmstead, it was really a large estate, it consisted of orchards, with apples and plums and oranges and pomegranates and lemons, extensive vineyards with lines of trained vines disappearing into the distance. There were olive groves with their silver grey leaves as tufts across the hill-sides and wide open arable fields for growing wheat and barley. Then besides this there were pens for what looked like innumerable sheep and goats and cattle. There was an air of self-satisfaction about the estate, all the buildings, and there were many, were in good repair and new ones were being added. There was noise and activity everywhere, people were busy at work keeping the organisation functioning, it really was very impressive. It was a bigger operation than any of us had seen before and we thought that perhaps Jesus had brought us here to show us just what the Kingdom of God could look like if we got it right.

Much to our surprise, although we should have been accustomed to it by now, Jesus was welcomed with open arms. There was a great deal of teasing and joking, gradually we were all introduced and we found the Jesus had come to work at the farm when he was a boy. He told us that his father Joseph had decided that he should know more of the world than carpentry and had arranged for an exchange of sons with the manager of the farm who was some very distant relative. Apparently Joseph had met his cousin when he had come on a trip to Mount Hermon buying timber for part of the rebuilding of Sepphoris, anyway the exchange was arranged and Jesus had worked here for a year and a half learning all about the art and problems of agriculture. The boy who had gone to Nazareth for his eighteen months learning carpentry was now the estate manager, the owners were absentees in Ceasarea, so he really was in charge!

Our little party hardly noticed among all the family and the workers, we were given beds to sleep on and all the comforts we could imagine. When we were settled in we met with Jesus who took us on a conducted tour of the farmstead, he talked with great knowledge about all things we saw and answered our questions about the operation of such a large concern. He knew all about the seasons, the fertility of the soil, the interactions between all the different sectors of the business to ensure that nothing was wasted and that nothing was exploited beyond its capability. The whole thing was very, very interesting, and it seemed to us that we were being shown all these things for a real purpose. Little did we guess that Jesus was enjoying the demonstration of a good relationship between God and man and used this to explain many things to us later. Then after we had returned to the farmhouse itself he told us that he wanted to pray and that he would go into the fields alone and talk with God! He told us he would be back in time for the evening meal and that we should take full benefit of this moment of calm. So off he went and very soon had disappeared into the heat haze over the fields.

So now we were left to our own devices, none of us had any experience of farming all our work had been in fishing or commerce or administration so we were interested in these new surroundings and spent a happy few hours talking with the workers about the way that a large estate actually functioned. We discovered that absolutely nothing was wasted, product that was not needed for human consumption or animal consumption was returned to the soil; the waste from the animals was returned to the fields; the fields were rested, just as we needed our rest; one crop never followed the same crop, and land which was becoming tired even with this care was put down to orchards or olives or vines. Nobody was idle, there was always be the next job waiting to be done, even if the animals and the land had been cared for there was the continual need for maintenance of the buildings, these were so extensive that a fulltime carpenter-cum-mason was at work making good and making new as was needed and could be afforded. They sold their product mainly to the towns close by, but the majority actually went to Ceasarea, a city of great consumption and no production. They supplied special food for the Jews and then different food for the gentiles, mainly Greeks and Roman, military personnel and administrators. Of course these people were not usually Romans from Rome but had been drawn from all over the Roman Empire and their food requirements had introduced many new crops to the estate, brought in from as far away as Spain and Gaul and Cappadocia.

After spending some time with the farm and all its interest we coalesced together and excitedly discussed our prospects, we were generally very impressed that Jesus seemed to have come round to our way of thinking and that we had to show God's impressive power to the authorities in Jerusalem and through them effectively to Rome. I remember how we talked with such confidence about what we were going to do and how we would exercise power, there were I seem to recall only two of us who were not so sure that we were right in our thinking. The first, was Thomas, who told us very eloquently that we were forgetting all that Jesus had taught us so far about love, about how we should love God, love our neighbour and more importantly that we should love our enemies. He said that while he listened to us he heard just selfishness, and aggression and revenge and seeking power to control the rest of the world. Had we already forgotten the first prayer that Jesus had taught us? He asked! We had been taught that God was no longer a vengeful judgemental God, he was a God so loving and caring for each one of us that we could call him Father. We prayed that His Kingdom should come on earth, did we not see that that was a Kingdom of love and not of power to control and exploit and limit the potential and freedom of others. Of course by now we all knew Thomas and how he was always unsure and we were very surprised how adamant he was that we had got it wrong and how clearly he expressed his verdict. Someone said that it was impossible to think that just by love for each other the world would get healed from its present state, what about all the people who didn't join in with the idea of love, wouldn't they just exploit our "weakness". Somebody said quite fiercely that we should all have learnt by now that impossible was no longer a word in our vocabulary and that we clearly didn't understand what was happening. He didn't offer an explanation, he was just confirming that none of us understood and we all began to feel frightened as our confidence began to collapse. Then Matthew joined in, he said that he had listened to our conversations over the last two days, just like Thomas, and he had only heard views expressed that we would replace the powers of the princes and principalities, but Jesus kept telling us that we would change the world. He said that to him that meant that things would not be the same, we would not be a replacement we were to be something totally different. He told us that he did not leave his work for the tyrant in Rome who demanded the exploitation of everyone just to glorify himself and his minions to become the minion of yet another tyrant. He told us that he left everything because he knew that self and possessions, were a prison that he had to escape and what Jesus was saying and doing was showing us the way to escape, not a running away and hiding escape but a giving, forgiving and loving escape. He told us that he didn't expect it to be easy, he told us that he expected it to be confrontational that we had to expect to be rejected and abused and excluded by the present system, he had become used to that after all he hardly had to remind us that he had been "a tax collector and sinner". He then told us that he had begun to understand that we should not expect to understand God's plan or purpose; that God would provide us with just the amount of resources as we needed and part of that resource was how much we needed to understand. After that we had to have faith and confidence that all matters were in God's all-powerful hands, if that sounded like a cop-out it was all he could cope with so far, but he did not think that our visit to Jerusalem was going to be anything like the ideas that had been discussed among us.

We had never heard such a long comment from Matthew, he had become one of the less vocal of the group but now what he said was a real challenge to us all. Someone asked what he did expect, he said that he thought we had to live today as best we could and that tomorrow was in God's hands but he did expect that we would see a clash of power between Jesus and the Jewish powers in Jerusalem, he had no way of telling, and neither did we, what the outcome would be and we should pray to God that whatever the outcome may be He would bring us safely through, if that was His will, and that he, Matthew, was committed to submit to God's will and Jesus was the only man who had shown us how God worked through love and faith. Well we were suitably impressed, we all felt that Matthew had perhaps a better understanding than we had, he quickly told us that he did not understand but he did have faith and that was all, he also had a sure hope that God would provide everything else as he needed it. The discussion bounced to and fro between us, but there was certainly less talk about what we were going to do and more recognition that we were in God's hands and were totally dependant on Him and that he would decide what we were going to do.

Then people began to drift away, either alone or in twos or threes, it seemed as if the challenge that Thomas and Matthew had thrown at us was too much, it was too concise, it was too threatening perhaps people really were ready to quit. Later I discovered that everyone had a common feeling not of despair but of needing to talk to God; to ask his forgiveness and to re-confirm that we were going on with his power beside us and with Jesus to lead us to where ever and what ever that might be. I know I went off and found a corner of a field where I was quite alone and there God found me, I became aware of His presence, and it was that same still small voice of calm which Elijah had experienced and that Moses had experienced; all my fear and anxiety evaporated and I knew that we would submit to God's love and that we would never turn aside from the path we were on no matter what the price.

As the sun started to go down we all reassembled at the farm house, the smell of cooking was delicious, all the women had been working, and talking, in the kitchen and the yard preparing vegetables, cooking bread, roasting meat and making delicious sweet dishes. We were a large group, there were about twenty of the "Jesus" group but then there was the farm compliment as well, I lost count at about thirty or so of them, interestingly everyone ate together, the men the women, the servants and the slaves; there seemed to be no distinction, dishes of food were passed around for people to help themselves and there was no recognisable pecking order. The atmosphere was relaxed and there was a lot of teasing and banter about the happenings of the day, the little anecdotes of problems and successes were openly discussed and resolved. Then when the meal was nearly over the farm manager called for a little order and told everyone what the plan was for the next day. He nominated people to jobs, mentioned some special tasks that needed attention and then asked for God's blessing on their endeavours.

When he had finished he introduced Jesus, of course every one knew who he was, he explained mostly to us how the close relationship had been forged many years before, that they had heard something of the great things that Jesus had been doing and saying and he asked Jesus if he would like to talk to them now. A hush of expectancy came over the assembly and all eyes were on Jesus, there was some jostling for a good view and then quiet.

"A sower went out to sow and as he sowed some grain fell among the stones and some fell among the weeds and some fell along the path and some seed fell on good ground. The seed germinated and put down its roots, the seed that was among the stones shot up quickly and then in the heat it withered and died, the seed that fell among the weeds also germinated but it was choked and died, the seed that fell on the path did not get a chance to germinate because the birds came and ate it, and then there was the seed that fell in the good ground, it germinated put down its roots and prospered and yielded a great crop for the sower and his master."

"The story I have just told you explains that the seed is the message I am giving you and have given to many. Some will hear it with enthusiasm but will fall away as things get difficult, some will find the pleasures and anxieties of this world too demanding and will be unable to follow the word but some will hear and understand and will change their ways to God's way. It is for each one of you to decide, but the matter is urgent, you have heard about John the Baptist who was the last great prophet who warned everyone that the Emmanuel was at hand, well, I tell you the time is now and I am the one who was foretold of old. So now I will tell you another farming story that explains the urgency."

"There was a man who owned a large and successful farm, every year he seemed to prosper, more and more, his barns were full and his flocks multiplied, he became very confident that he now had control and that anything he did would prosper. So after he had had a discussion, just like yours, he decided to build some bigger barns. He gave the orders and the old barns were pulled down and the new barns were built twice the size that had been pulled down. The project was completed just in time and as the harvest was being brought in the barns were finished and ready to receive the bounty. The farmer sat back and said to himself 'Well, what a success you have made, you can now sit back and enjoy the fruits of your labours your barns are full and the future is secure' That very night God called for his soul and he died! 'What good was all his wealth and possessions then?' I tell you this, you must store up treasure in heaven, not on earth, treasures in heaven are gained as you obey God's commands from your heart before you even consider the treasures on earth. The man who has great wealth on earth has to be sure that he remembers that it was God that provided the wealth and it must be used for God's purpose, once a man becomes arrogant and thinks that it is by his hands that he has the wealth he will forget his God and fail to love him and will certainly fail to love his neighbour and then although he may feel that he has gained everything he will in truth have lost everything."

"Now before we go to our beds I will tell you one last story and this is the story of the 'Good Shepherd' There was a shepherd who had an hundred sheep, he knew them well and they knew him, when he called them they came, he provided them with good pasture, he gave them a safe fold to sleep in every night, he looked after their scratches and injuries, when they were born he was there and he was there when they died. He was a very good shepherd. Then one day as the sheep came to the fold at night there was one young sheep missing, he checked again but it was so this one sheep was missing. So he closed up the fold and as night came on he set out to find his lost sheep. Well, you all know just how dangerous it is to be out in the dark and alone in these hillsides there are wild animals, there are robbers and brigands, there are unseen potholes and ravines where a man can easily fall and be injured. He knew all these dangers but he set out because this one sheep was lost and had to be found, eventually after a long and dangerous search he

241

found the sheep stuck fast by its horns in a bramble bush. The poor sheep was frantic, it could hear the roars of the wild beasts, it had no friends to comfort it, it had injured itself in its struggle to escape, but it was still alive. The shepherd released it from the briar he cut away the thorns that were holding it and he hoisted it onto his shoulder and walked home, rejoicing. He had found and saved the one sheep that was lost.

I am the Good Shepherd, I am sent by God to bring salvation to the lost, the outcast and the sinners, to show them that they are as valued in the sight of God as any other person and that God is there to offer forgiveness and redemption of sins for those who will accept his word and lead a new life loving God and loving his neighbour. But you see the time is now, you are stuck in the thorns and you can be saved but now is the time to come back to the loving embrace of God, and I am the Way."

The gathering had been absolutely absorbed, even the smallest children were quiet and attentive. Jesus' voice had a calm confidence and certainty, nothing he said seemed extraordinary or outrageous even when he was condemning the very basis of the Jewish understanding of God's purpose. His statements were produced as if they were a straightforward, unarguable consequence of the whole of our national history and that it was not possible to see it in any other way, his statements were the truth, the whole and absolute truth and there was no alternative but to accept them. On this occasion, with this audience, the setting of the agricultural parables that he used were completely familiar to his audience and the implications behind the apparent every day situations were also clear. We had heard the Good Shepherd story many times and with many audiences but this time there seemed to be a special sense of the possibility of a new life. Many of the people there were servants and labourers and slaves, their prospects in life were almost zero, generally society treated them not as people but as things. The message of hope in the stories made these people take notice. When we left Capernaum we had walked out of a primarily Jewish society and into a mixed society of Jews and Arabs and Greeks and Romans and they all seemed to be represented at this meal and all were listening to Jesus. The gentiles among the assembly had never heard anyone talk as Jesus did, it took them a little while to understand that everything he was saying had multiple layers of meanings and that quite clearly below the surface there was a message so revolutionary that they could not believe it. The most amazing idea was that we should love our enemies. How could we love our enemies, people who misuse us, people who destroy our hopes and aspirations, people who

242

publicly be-little us, people who bully us, people who undo our hard work, people who physically abuse us and eventually people who will kill us? This is not possible, the natural, human law says a tooth for a tooth and an eye for an eye, how can we possibly care for these people who treat us so badly and show them God's love; the questions kept coming in a torrent from every quarter. Eventually Jesus raised his hand and replied, as best as I can remember something like this. "Who in this room can claim that he is sinless?" There was an embarrassed silence. "I tell you that God loves everyone of you, you are the lost sheep in the story, you have wandered away from God's will, you have abused his love and his patience, you continually break the Ten Commandments, you take pleasure in finding ways of avoiding the consequences of your sinfulness and you think that God doesn't know. Well he does and he still loves you. So if God can love you as sinners and send help to you and to give you resources like this very successful farm and all the other good things you enjoy, how can you return this benefit by not caring for all the people you are in contact with even if they are your enemies. You must be sure that this commandment that I am giving you is not the same as the commandment in the law, that says "You shall not do your neighbour any disservice that you would not like to have done to you" That is a negative attitude, God looks to you to go out of your way to do good things to your neighbour, just the sort of things that you would like somebody to do to you." This commandment is not an easy yoke, it is difficult enough to satisfy with people you know, your friends, your colleagues or your relatives; it is much more difficult when the people are complete strangers who you find in need and even more difficult with people who are your enemies, but it is God's way! Through this way is the route to happiness and peace of the soul and a sure way to heaven."

Then our host asked why Jesus was against wealth and suggested that the farmer building new barns seemed to him to be a good husbandman and reaping God's reward for his hard work. He said that he was a good farmer and felt that he was satisfying his master, the land owner, providing employment and security for all the people he saw around him, providing food and other products for the people who lived in the area and after all God charged Adam with the care of the world and to use all the resources for his good. Quite clearly the man felt that the story was a rebuke of him in particular, and farmers generally, and was upset at such an overt criticism in return for the hospitality he had shown to his old friend and his party.

Jesus listened to the complaint very attentively and then responded; wealth in itself was neither good nor bad, the problem was that the way men look at wealth and the impact that it has on their souls that is good or bad. What the story tells is that if the acquisition of wealth becomes the principal driving desire of a man he will forget that he is first and foremost God's creature and that first and foremost he must love God and not his possessions. He must see his possessions as a way of serving God and not for his own egotistical satisfaction. We all see men around us who are acquisitive who become grasping and greedy, who want more and more and more, who never even contemplate that God has given them everything they have and that they should be concerned to give to others, to relieve their poverty or need, and to show to them God's love through generosity. The warning is that none of us know the time of our death and once we are dead it is too late to change our relationship with our neighbours and too late to change our relationship with God. There is an urgency for men to come to God now, while there is time and it is this urgency that has to be impressed on the world. He told us all that it is the most difficult thing for a rich man to do; that is to see his wealth as just God's good grace for which he is the custodian to make sure it works for God in the short time that he is responsible for it.

Then someone asked, "Who are you to be telling us these things, some of us here remember you as a spotty youth who came to work on the farm. Nobody would suggest that you weren't a willing, cheerful, quick witted lad who was always cheerful and never caused any bother, but now you are here telling us we should ignore the rabbi in the village and the Pharisees and the scribes who have taught us all we understand about God and accept what you say. Why should we?" Jesus immediately recognised the anxiety that he had caused, on the one hand he had offered an attractive way of living and a more personal relationship with God, on the other, it was a way that had deep personal significance. How could they show the love that he was proposing to sinners and gentiles without risking the wrath of the Pharisees and the probable exclusion from the synagogue by the elders for breaking the law?

We were amazed that any one, just an ordinary worker on the farm, should ask such a profound question! Even the Pharisees and scribes, although they had alluded to the question and had accused him of being in league with the devil, implying that that was the source of his power and authority, had not openly shown the challenge that Jesus was making to our society and to the religious authorities. For a few seconds there was silence every one was waiting for Jesus and he was clearly considering how he would reply. I must say that I had never asked the question myself, at the moment on the lake side when he had challenged Peter and I, it didn't occur to me to question his authority and within only a day or so it was quite clear that his authority came directly from God. We were fortunate, we had Jesus with us all the time and when we were challenged by the powers of the synagogue Jesus was always there to respond and defend us. We were not left on our own to defend ourselves and it was this problem that the questioner raised very clearly. Any one who accepted his word and began to live by it would inevitably be on a collision course with the earthly religious authorities and would have to face the consequences on their own without Jesus to defend them. Everyone knew that only being accused of being a sinner by the scribes or Pharisees put a man and his family outside, excluded from the synagogue, shunned by their neighbours, the power that was exercised to ensure that people conformed to the dictates of these controlling groups was overt and covert and it was a brave man who would subject himself voluntarily to such sanctions.

Then Jesus started to speak, firstly he said "My authority comes from God, you will have heard of the healing of the sick, hundreds and hundreds of the sick, you will have heard of the miracles of water turned to wine, of the feeding of a crowd of five thousand from five small loaves and three small fishes, you will have heard of the calming of the wind and waves; all these things I have done but they have been done by God's power working within me. If you have not seen and heard these things there are twelve men here who will witness to these marvellous things. I have told you that I bring a new message to you, a new commandment, I have not said it is to be easy to obey this commandment but what I tell you is the truth. This truth is not disguised or shrouded in ritual or procedures or structures or organisations, this is the truth spoken by God to every individual who will listen. The whole of history as been waiting for this moment and it is here and now and it is urgent, the prophets foretold the coming of the Messiah; the Messiah who would save the nation and restore it to its rightful position, the Messiah who would bring God's blessing on all the people not just to Israel but also to the whole world. The last and greatest of these prophets was John the Baptist who declared that the promised Messiah was here and demanded the people to repent and be cleansed by washing in the River Jordan to be ready to receive the Messiah, and I AM The Messiah."

"But this is only part of your question" he went on " You are really telling me that I am asking too much by suggesting that you should repent and accept the new commandments, to Love God and to Love your neighbour, well I tell you that this is the only way to heaven and to live eternally in God's house, **you** have to decide what value **you** put on

your soul and if **you** value eternity then **you** will obey my commands. The decision is **yours** and nobody else's

Now I will tell you two more stories before we all go to our sleep.

The Kingdom of heaven is like this; a man found a great treasure in a field and instead of lifting the treasure he covered it up again and went home and sold everything to buy the field. Or again the Kingdom of heaven is like this; it is like a merchant in search of fine pearls who on finding one pearl of great value, he sold everything he had and bought it!

These two very short stories show you that there is nothing that a man should not do to enter into God's kingdom, there is no sacrifice or persecution or tribulation that he will not endure to achieve this prize. Be sure that there is a high price to be paid by those who will attain eternal life!"

There was an air of muted disappointment at this pronouncement; Jesus had made it quite clear that the message of the Messiah was not at all the message that we had all been taught to expect. The new King David was not going to come as a warlord leading his people out of slavery into everlasting freedom and security from their enemies. Gradually people drifted away to do the last jobs of the day and then to go to bed. Jesus sat and watch them go and then turned to us and said that for many people the price was just too high and they could not "sell all they had", possessions, he reiterated were the distraction to men from their real needs. So we went to our beds wondering whether our assessment of the planned visit to Jerusalem really had anything to do with the price we had already paid!

The next morning at breakfast our host told us that what Jesus had said in the evening had kept him awake all night but he had decided that he would have no slaves or bondsmen all would be released now, today! He said that he hoped that he had been such a master that they would want to stay to work on the estate and he hoped that his neighbours would see that he prospered using labour that was free and not bound to him. He also said that he would abandon the system of hiring casual labour on a daily basis but would instead employ his need for workers on a permanent basis to give them a sense of the worth that he placed on them and there-by some reflection of the worth that God placed on them. He had already ordered the mason to build good quality dwellings on the estate for at least 10 families whom he knew would now become established on the estate. We were all very impressed, quite clearly the talk that Jesus had given about the rich man and his barns had been very direct. We asked him how he would explain these changes to the estate owners, he said he had absolute power on the estate and that the owners were interested in the general running of the business but their main interest was in the income that they received. He went on to tell us that his anxious tossing and turning during the night was just about this problem, but that he had decided that God had spoken to him directly through Jesus and that it would be a cowardly excuse to hide behind the owners opinion when he knew that he should do it now. He told us that he was sure that giving the workers their freedom and their security would make them better workers and they would see that their work was rewarded by God through the estate's prosperity.

He then told us that there was more work for us in the barn and it wasn't threshing, despite our intension of staying "incognito" the word had got round the local district and there was a crowd waiting for us. Well, what a crowd it was, there were over two hundred people; they had come to see, they had come to listen and they had brought their sick to be cured. As we stepped into the bright sunlight of the farmyard from the cool darkness of the kitchen we could hear an excited hub-bub from the great barn. So we walked the few paces and as we entered silence fell on the crowd, the noise was replaced by an air of electric expectation. Somebody had thoughtfully brought a milking stool and the people had arranged themselves sitting on the ground in an arc facing the empty stool so that when Jesus sat down there they would all be able to see and to hear. On reflection I think our host had sent to his neighbours to tell them that Jesus of Nazareth was staying with him and that this was a chance in a lifetime to see the man who had become so famous in Galilee. So they had come, the land owners, the farm managers, their labourers, their bondsmen and their slaves and they had brought their wives and children.

Jesus, was, as usual very cheerful, we had had a stimulating breakfast that climaxed with our host's announcement that he had heard the commandment from Jesus to love his neighbour and had recognised his neighbour without needing prompting. Now was another, unexpected, opportunity to extend God's words of love and reconciliation to more people. Some of the people Jesus recognised from all those years before when he had stayed at the farm and he mingled among the people greeting them and asking after others, it was a very happy and warm reunion. We of course had got used to this amazing man who had created so much excitement and disquiet and uncertainty would behave in an ordinary simple human way, he did not put on airs and graces, he did not expect to be reverenced or privileged all he ever wanted was to be with people and part of people. But for

247

many of the people in this intimate and secure environment this was a remarkable sight, this man who was the nearest thing to a prophet, like Elijah, that they could ever expect to meet, and really never had expected to meet was just like them there was nothing threatening or awesome about him. He smiled and chattered and sympathised and listened and laughed; and this was the man that rumour had said was the Messiah, the new David, the promised one who would restore Israel, it was totally unbelievable! What they had expected was a champion, a man of great military might who would galvanise the Jews into a mighty conquering force who with God beside him would defeat all their enemies. Eyes were jammed wide open, mouths fell open and said nothing all heads turned to him and followed his every movement and ears took in every word and every intonation. We had seen it before but it was dramatic in this confined space in the barn full of people how Jesus dominated everything and none could possible ignore his presence. Then after a little while Jesus saw the stool and went over to it and sat down, the company had left a polite separation between themselves and the stool but Jesus first remarks to them were totally unexpected. "Oh, please let the children come to the front and sit close to me. In years to come they will be able to say to their grand-children, 'I was there at the farm when Jesus talked to us, and will be proud to retell the story of today for the thousandth time.'" So all the children came and sat on the straw at his feet, their eyes never left his face and it seemed to us that he chose his words just for them.

So he told them stories, special stories all with many depths of meaning, but stories that young minds could understand and old minds could relate to, their experience of life and their knowledge of the sacred texts that were read to them at the synagogue or for the men they had learnt by heart at the feet of their rabbi. He told them about the Good Shepherd, he told them about the Labourers in the Vineyard, he told them about the talents, and he told them about the invitation to the marriage feast of the king's son and finished with the story of the Foolish Virgins at another wedding, the children loved the stories they could see the wit and drama of the situations. I could feel the grownups getting uneasy as they saw the darker highly critical sub-plots of the stories and of course this was exactly what Jesus intended. Having taught them by parables he then taught them directly, he told them that he had come to show them the way to God, that the old way through the Law had been contaminated by men and made it a vehicle for their own pride and status and that the message of love and caring and forgiveness had been lost. He told them the time was now to repent to ask for forgiveness and to start a new life. This new life had to be led by God's ordinances these were "to love God with all your body and soul and to love your neighbour", this ordinance was not an easy option because it demanded that they must stand aside from the ways of the world and adhere to the ways of God. Somebody in the assembly asked, "Who is my neighbour?" Jesus replied with the story we all now knew well about the Good Samaritan, when he had finished there was silence when they all realised how far they were from that standard of love. He then told them that God was a loving, forgiving, tolerant God, he was not the vengeful, judgemental, cruel and uncompromising God that they knew, God wanted to extend his blessings to all men and each individual had to decide how he would respond to the invitation to eternal Life.

Then he told them that he was the Messiah, the reaction was noticeably mixed, some were relieved that they could acknowledge his message from God others were completely bewildered and disbelieving. Maybe two hours had now passed, we could all see that people were getting tired, they had walked a long way early in the morning and had then listened and concentrated on the most amazing sermon that they had ever heard, aimed, as some of them could see, at undermining the whole established basis of their society and worse, the relationship which they, as Jews, had with God.

Then some one said, "We have brought our lame daughter to you because we believe that you can heal her! We have heard that through God's power you can cure the sick, we need your help, nobody else will help us. What will happen to our sweet child when we die? Is it God's will that we should be so troubled, this God that you say is full of love and caring?" Jesus said to them, "Bring the child to me!" they struggled with the poor pathetic thing she was all twisted and misshapen, she could not stand, her face was twisted and she mouthed words which could not be understood and she dribbled! The gathering moved aside to let the family through looking with horror on this faulted being, they did not want to be associated with it, they did not want to be contaminated by it and they did not want to take any responsibility for it. Eventually when they got to Jesus they laid their precious little bundle gently on the floor and waited expectantly. Jesus waited as well, the crowd had become agitated, because of the message Jesus had given them, but also at the shame and disgust of seeing this travesty of God's creation and convinced that this was entirely the result of sinfulness. Then gradually a quiet was restored and everyone looked to Jesus, it had been the child's father who had first challenged Jesus, but now it was the mother who spoke, all she said through her tears of anguish, embarrassment and anticipation was, "Jesus of Nazareth, we know that you have helped many people who were afflicted with many sicknesses, help us we beg you, we plead with you for the sake of this little lamb who is hurting. We know that this is not a sign of God's love but we know that through your power we and all these people will see God's love here and now!" This for a Jewess was a long public speech and we were all very impressed, Jesus lent forward and said very gently "Your faith has made your daughter well." And to the child he said, "Little girl, you can get up and join the other children here with me!" Without any hesitation the child stood up and came and sat with the others as Jesus had said, she immediately started to chatter and smile and turn around to talk with others round her. Her parents were now in floods of tears of unimaginable joy, they fell on their knees in front of Jesus and thanked him and thanked him and thanked him, the assembly were stunned into silence. A sense of fear seemed to have overtaken them, here was a power that they had never conceived of before, in front of their own eyes a dreadfully crippled child had been instantaneously restored to good, normal health just by a few words, it was amazing, it was perplexing. If this man could do that what else might he do?

Then they gradually gained some sort of confidence and others brought their children and relatives to be healed, Jesus only asked of each, "Do you believe and have faith that through God's power I can cure you?" The healing went on for a while and the assembly was continually being surprised and amazed and gradually recognised that God's amazing power was there in action right there among them. People dropped to their knees and prayed, people sat staring in total disbelief at what they were witnessing and nobody moved they sat or stood transfixed.

Then Jesus said to them, "You have witnessed God's power at work and this power is available to mankind to all who believe in me. I am the Good Shepherd, that I told you about just now and I have come from God to recover the lost sheep of Israel. For those who believe in me, confess their sins and follow my commandments, is the promise of eternal life. I call each one of you by name, each one of you has to decide if you believe or not, if you accept this, then the prize is yours; if not you are lost and cannot be saved from eternal damnation. Be sure that the promises made by God to your forefathers are still good, I have not come to undermine the special relationship between God and the Jews, but it was not and never will be a blanket redemption for your sins just because you are the sons and daughters of Abraham. To achieve the prize is an individual personal commitment to God to live by these two Laws, Love God and Love your neighbour, and these two Laws summarise all the Law and the Prophets."

He then stood up and blessed them all and set off back to the house. We did not follow, not because we shouldn't, but because they stopped us; they all wanted to talk to us about our part in this incredible man and his mission. They asked us, How could he speak with such confidence, such authority? Where had he learnt these things he said? Who was his teacher? Why was he here and not teaching in the Temple? Of course we could not answer the barrage of questions, all we could tell them was that he had chosen us and that we were convinced that he was the Emmanuel who would save Israel. We told them it was a great privilege to be so close to such a man and that although we had forsaken our homes and businesses we expected to be rewarded eventually. The visitors and the farm workers gradually dispersed and then we were left alone in the quiet of the barn. Our old insecurity was flooding back. What was it that Jesus was doing? He seemed to go out of his way to undermine the very basis of our national identity! Why should he choose to tell this particular gathering that their relationship with God was not the security they thought it was? Why should he undermine their confidence in God's covenant with the Jews? The promised Emmanuel was to restore the Jews to their rightful position as God's favoured nation and the most powerful and influential nation on earth! Yet Jesus was now implying that the Emmanuel would demand individual personal commitment to these two Laws and that that was all that he was intending to do. Where did that leave us? Why did he need us at all? Why did he just get up and leave when peoples' real questions were just coming out? Where was he now? So we left the barn and came out into the bright sunshine, the women were waiting for us, they told us that Jesus had gone away into the fields to pray and that we would be staying on the farm for another night but would move on in the morning. They told us he looked very tired when he came out of the barn and didn't speak very much, they thought he looked very distressed and anxious as if his confidence was undermined. You can imagine this news really cheered us up and once again there were those who really were ready to abandon the whole mission. Peter was great he said that he was staying and that nothing would convince him to do otherwise. He reminded us that we had to have courage, to have confidence that we were doing God's work and that God would protect us. We had to recognise that we were the pupils and Jesus was our master and that we were foolish if we thought that we should understand everything! If we did know everything then why should we need a master? Was it not part of our role to support and encourage Jesus? How could we even think to desert him at every little upset we perceived? Well his pep talk did us all good and then we got the scent of lunch and everything seemed better!

(As a small diversion, about thirty years later I was passing that way again, of course the world had been turned on its head and Jewry had seen its demise in the fall and sacking of Jerusalem, I was made most welcome and the family were proud to show me that the milking stool that Jesus had sat on was still in its place and that people used that corner of the barn as a sort of sanctuary when the matters of the world became too frenetic and they needed to talk to God!)

So we all went in to lunch, to start with it was a quiet gathering, I think that we were all nervous to talk about what we had experienced that morning, quite clearly it had been a dramatic exposure of God's power, quite clearly Jesus was an exceptional person. If his message of forgiveness and love and caring and service was as important as he made it and as urgent as he made it, we all had to change. When faced with the clarity of his pronouncements we all saw by contrast how far short we fell of his ideal for mankind and so we needed forgiveness and we needed mercy if we were to even aspire to the model he presented. Whatever our previous assessment of our own position or performance may have been when we were confronted by the demands that Jesus made on us we knew how far short we fell. The twelve of us and the few others who were making this journey with Jesus were used to watching him and listening to him, but today the teaching and healing in the barn and then his sudden departure had made a new and profound impact on us, the farm congregation were still in deep shock at what they had witnessed. Then suddenly he was there, nobody saw him come in he was just there among us; and just as suddenly his infectious confidence and joyfulness lifted everyone's spirits.

The conversation around the table that had been sombre suddenly became enlivened. Jesus wanted to know what was happening on the farm, he had seen men working in the vineyard and was told that they had found some disease on the vines and were cutting it out to avoid the problem spreading and spoiling the crop. Then he asked why the sheep were being separated, he was told that now was the time for the lambs to be separated from the ewes otherwise they would not produce lambs for next year, they always did this now and before the rams were allowed back with the ewes they would all be sheared. This job of shearing had always been and always would be done by a band of specialist sheep-shearers who went from flock to flock around the locality, it would be more than a month before they came which would give the flock time to produce thick fleeces. There was lot of banter and argument going on among the servants and although we had heard some snippet's Jesus stopped to listen to what was being discussed. The meat of their discussion was about who was most important now they had been granted their freedom. Our host looked a bit exasperated and embarrassed he looked at Jesus and confided in him, "I was concerned that this might happen, before I changed things everyone was content, I mean they knew their place, now they are like chickens deciding the pecking order anew. One trouble is that you really cannot give people a little freedom, it's all or nothing, and then the trouble is that when you have given people freedom you never know where it will stop." Jesus said, "I think that that is a good example of how God looks at mankind and perhaps is a warning to everyone of the upset that I am telling the world to choose. God is giving men the freedom of choice to be free from sin or to be enslaved by sin. The laws that were given to Moses were to set men free but men have used them to ensnare themselves in the law. From God's view He sees mankind running around worrying about the "pecking order" and this they suppose is their real relationship with God. Now I tell you there are only two laws and they release men from the web of the old law but it allows men more freedom to decide continually whether their own, individual actions words and even thoughts are good or evil. To have a close relationship with God is not about "pecking orders", it is about the choices individuals make day in and day out as they are faced with life's problems. If these choices are made to show God's love to the world then all will be well for him and for the world." Our host said that when things were very heated in the morning he almost reversed his decision to release everyone who was bound to the estate but had resisted the temptation. Jesus told us that the freedom that God had given to mankind would never be withdrawn and that God loved the world in a way that they could not understand now but one day they would, even if, from man's view there seemed little evidence of men loving their neighbours or their God.

I think John joined in at this point and supposed that one serious problem these people had when being suddenly presented with their freedom was to understand that their individual freedom only had reality when they recognised the responsibility that gave them for ensuring other people's freedom and that reinforced Jesus demand that we love each other and in that way we gave our fellows their freedom and in return were given our freedom by them. Well it was all getting very intense and although the understanding was needed, we also needed to relax. We were relieved when Peter asked where the delicious fish paste had come from, this complete diversion was welcomed while we digested what we had just heard. Peter of course knew very well that it was Galilean, and was delighted to be told that it came from our company in Capernaum. This led to a long discussion about fishing as an antedote to all we had heard about farming. We discovered that trying to explain about fishing to people who had mostly never seen the sea and certainly never understood the niceties of nets and currents and winds and shoals and bates and sails and all the other niceties of fishing was difficult. Eventually, Matthew, who had joined in to start with, realised that most of the gathering had either left the table or had gone to sleep so he tactfully suggested that we all went for a walk to shake our splendid lunch down. Peter was just a little hurt when this proposal was adopted with enthusiasm, he felt that his beloved industry could never be boring!

The next morning we set off on the final stage or our journey. We continued on the field paths and because we were close to the desert there were very few other travellers. We still got glimpses down into the valley and the main road to Damascus, but we felt remote and detached from the traffic hurrying north and south. Jesus walked at his usual brisk pace but stopped every now and then to allow people to catch up and for us all to rest. These moments were very welcome, not only was the sun hot and the air drifting in from the desert very dry but there were always interesting conversations among small groups which could be shared among us all. I remember one in particular and it all started with a comment from Peter. He and some of the others had been talking about the mission and wanted to know how far the Kingdom of God stretched.

So under the shade of an acacia he asked Jesus, "You have told us that we are chosen to change the world, to bring salvation to the lost sheep, tell us does this salvation extend beyond the Sons of Abraham? Do we include Gentiles in the saved? Or is the message just for the Jews who are lost, and not just sinners but the lost tribes who betrayed the Lord and worshipped the god Baal?"

Jesus reply was profound, "God love extends to the whole of his creation. The Jews have ignored the imperative that God gave them. They were charged to bring the knowledge of the one true God to all men. The Jews have made their knowledge of God an exclusive right to Jews and to Jews alone. God instructed our forefathers on the way to attain a permanent reliable and holy relationship with God. Had they followed his rules they would have prospered and the world would have recognised that it was their relationship with God that provided prosperity and would have adopted the same relationship with God. They failed to do this and were subjected to many, and frequent, tribulations. Many good and faithful men were sent to them as prophets to show them how far they had wandered from God's purpose and the consequence that would befall them, but these men were at best ignored. The message has not changed and the purpose has not changed, we are now given the task to do what the Jews have failed to do and that is to bring the message of God's love to all people. God's love is available to all but it can only be seen when mankind responds and that response is 'to love God with all your heart and mind and spirit, and to love your neighbour as yourself.' The response is not from kings and empires it is only from individuals, each individual has to decide how he will respond to the challenge, but enough will respond truly and this is the seed that will grow and change the world. Peter, you have to start somewhere, God has had a special relationship with the Jews for hundreds of generations, the Jews know and understand a great many things about God, Jews are spread all over the world and so it is right and proper that the Jews should be the first to be challenged by God's special message of God's love and the forgiveness of sins. You must be sure, all of you, the message is not exclusive to the Jews it is inclusive to all mankind!"

Then Thomas asked him, "How will we do this? We are only twelve! We have no training! Every time you are out of sight our confidence disappears, people start talking about giving up and despair seems to overtake us! The moment you come back all is well and we are sure that all will be well! But you can't be with all of us all the time, wherever any one of us happens to be! When we went out to preach, on your instructions, we may have behaved with confidence but in reality the whole experience was a failure, nobody really listened. Of course they wanted cures for their sick, but they didn't want to know about the sickness of their souls! So how are we going to do it?"

There was lots of nodding of heads and grunts of agreement. Peter tried to rally the flagging spirits by reminding us that we had already decided that these ideas were the work of the devil and that we had to have faith in God that he would, as Jesus had told us, provide the resources to undertake his work, whatever and whenever those resources might be needed. That none of us seriously contemplated abandoning the mission, we all knew we were doing God's work and that Jesus was the Messiah, didn't we? I quite expected Jesus to reiterate to us what he had said many times before, that accusation, that challenge, that question and yes, that condemnation "Oh ye of little faith!" He didn't he was very gentle with us, I think now as I am writing this that he already suspected the trauma that we would be facing soon and wanted to show us how much he cared for us, how much he sympathised with us and to give us confidence in himself.

Jesus then said, "You are being asked to do something

extraordinary, something nobody on earth had ever been asked to do before and that nobody would ever be asked to do again. That must bring with it just the sort of uncertainty that you are experiencing. But remember, as I have told you often, you did not volunteer for this task, you have been chosen by God, you had been commanded by God. There were plenty of records of the experience of others that God's command could not be avoided. Abraham, Noah, Isaac, Moses, Saul, David, Jonah, Jeremiah, Elisha, Elijah and all the prophets had had moments of despair, of doubt, of trying to avoid the command, by running away, by thinking up excuses and then finding that God always called them back to their task. He assured us that we were in good company. But we had a special advantage that these men of old were not granted, we had the Messiah to guide us and protect us and show us by example what incredible power was available to us as a group and to each of us individually. We should take courage from the example that these great men left us. They had stood firm and fulfilled God's will entirely alone, they were frightened, they were unsure, they had no idea of the outcome, as we know what happened to them, and they faced the isolation of pronouncing exceedingly unpopular news to kings and princes and to a whole people. They were ridiculed, they were persecuted, they were hunted down as criminals, they were imprisoned, they were abandoned, they were friendless, they were starving and yet they held on to do God's will. They were convinced that the word of the Lord had given them a mission to fulfil; nobody else believed them and still they kept to their command. With such a company of examples how can you consider running away and hiding when you have the Messiah here with you? God has moved on, this is the last chance for mankind there will be no more prophets! God's will for mankind is being made absolutely plain, there can never again be any lame excuses, there can never again be the excuse of waiting for the Messiah, there can never again be the claim that Israel is blessed above all others, Israel is blessed and so are all others." "You, my precious little band," he told us, "You are chosen to be the messengers to the world that the Light of God's truth and love has arrived and it will shine in the darkness of man's sinfulness for ever and it will never be extinguished." Jesus was explaining things to us that we could not yet understand and we felt entranced by his words and his presence, we felt relieved but we all knew that the doubts would return as soon as his back was turned. I think he understood this.

Instead of leaving his teaching there he went on, "Fear not I will never leave you, I will always be beside you wherever you are and whatever you are doing. My spirit will live on whatever happens and that you will feel it round you, protecting you and encouraging you. My spirit is always available through prayer, you must learn to pray and to practice praying, through prayer you can communicate directly with God and just as importantly God can communicate with you. I have told you before and tell you again prayer doesn't have to be in a special place or on a special day or at a special time or facing a special direction or after you had washed or after you had dressed in special clothes or used special words or followed the priests or the rabbis. Prayer is available to all believers, all the time and there are absolutely no preconditions. I am telling you these things so that you can be assured God's power and his spirit were with us and would stay with us for ever."

When he stopped it was like the world had stopped, we could not comprehend what he was saying all this emphasis on "forever" what did he mean, how could he give such assurances. The only promise we had ever heard like that was God's promise to the Sons of Abraham and Jesus was making the same promise to us and then extending it to the whole of humanity. Was this man really more than the Messiah, he had forgiven sins, he had healed the sick, he had raised the dead, he had stilled the sea, he had walked on the sea, his miracles were amazing and frequent and now he was giving us promises that surely only God could give. We were all completely bemused, we needed time to digest this lesson and Jesus could see that we had had sufficient so he suggested that we went for a short diversion together, he said he had rediscovered a small oasis in the desert hills to the east and he would like to show it to us. So off we went, what started as a gentle stroll ended up as stiff climbed up the rocky hillsides above the spring-line and into the arid desert after nearly an hour of scrambling among the hills we saw below us in a hidden fold an almost perfect oasis. It was a circular pool of clear, mirror like water surrounded by many shrubs and palms, it looked perfect. When we had made the descent, from our vantage point, we found the water was sweet, the palms were full of ripe dates and there seemed to be an aviary of small bright birds calling to each other. We were all entranced by the place none of us really had any experience of the desert, even the Jordan Valley road to Jericho and Jerusalem was not in the wild dry hills, the place of desolation and despair so the walk we had just finished was a new experience to us all. The surprise was to find such an idyllic point of refreshment and comfort.

Jesus studied our reaction and then said, "I have brought you here because this place is like a parable. The desert was the world, its despair, its apparent hopelessness and the oasis was God's promise within all the misery it was there and available to us all. The hard climb we had made was the same as the struggle that mankind has to escape from the sweet attractions we are tempted to by the worldly temptations of the Devil. Here we have an understanding of God's love, but we have to return to the desert, that is the world, full of sin and disgrace and shame and cruelty but we know that the real world as God wants it is as this oasis and we know that it is always here as our knowledge of God is always with us."

We had left our route and could not stay for long in this ethereal paradise and had to retrace our steps back to the path and then head north again. Eventually we dropped off the hills down to a pasture and there under the shade of a mixture of acacias and figs were the rest of our party just waiting to refresh us with the most delicious and unexpected picnic. We were left wondering how did Jesus know that we would be needing his teaching at just that point on the journey, how did he know that there was an oasis just where he needed it and how did the women know in which pasture to prepare the picnic. We were all left with only one conclusion, "God works in a mysterious way!"

After lunch we set off again at the usual brisk pace, and having recovered the watershed followed paths which seemed to us to twist and turn to join and then separate to pass near but never through villages and hamlets, Jesus was our guide we knew only that Caesarea was the destination. All the time in the distance we got glimpses of the snow capped Mount Hermon, the source of the River Jordan, it got bigger and bigger as we got closer, we hardly noticed that we were gradually climbing always the path kept just above the line of springs that tumbled down the hill sides. The sun was very high and shining on our backs, we were relieved that we were now walking in woods among dappled shade. It wasn't long before we began to notice the chill in the air and then quite suddenly in a clearing in the wood we saw below us the new city of Caesarea Philippi. It was dazzling in the sunshine, it was beautiful, the buildings were all new and white, grand palaces built of dressed stone hewn from the quarries in the hills behind us. There were Temples of the Grecian style that we knew from visits to the Decapolis cities and Sepphoris. We could see the people coming and going on the paved streets, horse drawn chariots taking people up and down, ladies being carried in litters and protected from the sun by slaves carrying shades. There in the centre of the town we could see the baths where we knew wealthy Romans, Greeks and Jews would be taking their ease. We stood and watched for a while and then with no comment Jesus moved of up the pathway, clearly we were not going into the city, it was a contaminated place just like Tiberias. So we walked on, still climbing, through the rich and ancient forest as it had now become with huge trees all round us, and the path weaving its way between them and quickly disappearing from view. Then suddenly there was a band of men standing on the path barring our way. Peter, who was always prepared, started to draw his sword, I don't know why he always seemed to have a sword, and stepped forward to be beside Jesus! There was a moment of high tension we did not know what to expect and then Jesus called out "Hello Jonathon, God bless you, thank you for coming to meet us but it wasn't necessary you should know I would never forget the way." So Jesus had done it again! Here we were in a foreign country and he has friends, not only that but somehow unbeknown to us he has warned them that we are coming, when we are coming and which path we were using, it was incredible but he kept doing it! So then there was a great round of introductions and greetings and eventually we set off again and in a few minutes we came to a clearing in the forest and there was a substantial house and timber everywhere! There were stacks of freshly felled trunks and there were stacks of split trunks, there were finished planks, everything was marked with paint on the ends, different colours and different patterns there were heaps of bark and heaps of chippings and shavings there were men cutting and swinging axes and adzes and there were mules hauling logs and wagons. There was business and noise and shouting all round us! Jesus clearly loved it, some of us had witnessed occasions when he had cast a critical professional eye over a piece of furniture or a door. Some times we had caught him staring at the floor and then realised that far from being deep in thought about the mission he was looking carefully at the timber and its joints perhaps even recognising the carpenter from the tell-tale way in which each individual used his tools or completed his task. He told us once that carpenters were like potters, their mark on the work they did was there forever.

The owner of the estate heard us arrive with the escort he had sent and came out to meet us, this was Jonathon's father an elderly man but still very fit and clearly a strong physic, he reminded me of Zebedee although this man was taller and his shock of hair had gone white. He had a broad friendly open grin and welcomed us with open arms as if we were all old friends. We should have been confused but we were now used to welcomes like this from complete strangers and knew that eventually Jesus would explain to us how he knew these people, so we accepted their generosity and entered into the open, friendly atmosphere. We were led into the house where the women, met the hostess who was charming, and they all disappeared into the kitchen amid a lot of chattering and laughter. We were then shown into a large

259

hall with a high arching wooden roof beautifully constructed of cut and sawn timber, nobody, not even Jesus, had seen any thing so grand before. We were used to Roman buildings but they were all of brick and stone with massive walls and semicircular arches supporting flat roofs using timber as rafters, their buildings gave an atmosphere of doom and repression and foreboding. This building on the other hand was light and airy and it seemed to soar into the sky, it seemed to liberate your being, there were shuttered windows at intervals along both sides between the arching timbers which joined in pairs along the length of the hall; the gaps between each of these arches was filled with overlapping planks of sawn and planed wood parallel to the ground and running all the way to the apex they were beautifully fitted and there was no possibility of drafts or rainwater getting in; the whole building was mounted on a dressed stone foundation raised above the ground level and outside that was a ditch which allowed rainwater to run away from the building. The end walls were magnificent they were plain fitted timber rising straight up from the floor to the apex, high up there was a shuttered window with a little gallery so that the servants could open and close the shutters, this allowed light to flood into the space below, at ground level there were double opening doors. The end walls were painted white it, made the whole space glow from the light streaming through the shutters. We all assumed that this was a barn for storing crops until we looked at the floor, at each end where the doors were you entered on to a stone flagged area and then the centre of the room was covered in timber planks, quite clearly this hall was not a barn, a dirt floor was all that that warranted, and this was far too grand. We were reluctant to ask what was its purpose and it wasn't until sometime later that the owner explained that the whole building was an experiment to try to convince people that good buildings could be produced in timber, and that they did not have to be stone!

We were amazed, as everyone who saw it must have been, it was totally new and totally different. Then Jesus said that, Nathan, the owner had invited us to stay with him for two or three weeks where we were securely remote from any threatening authorities and from the daily distractions that had demanded our time and energy. Nathan explained that this splendid building was for our use, he had arranged that the east end would be a dormitory and the west end a messing hall, his household would supply all our needs, but if there was anything we needed we should ask. He then told us that there were only two special house rules. The first was, please, don't wander off into the woods, for fear of being lost or eaten! The second was, please, don't wander about in the yard where all the work is going on, timber is very heavy and many a good man had been accidentally crushed! Otherwise we were free to do as we wished. We all agreed that the rules seemed eminently sensible, being lost, eaten or crushed didn't seem to be worthy ends for any of us. After this introduction our host said that for tonight we were all to eat with the household in the main house and we would be summoned when it was ready then he left us alone.

Jesus was immediately inundated with questions and we all wanted to be answered at the same time; so we sat down and he told us why we were here and what we were going to be doing. First of all he told us why we were here, it was that we had to be prepared for our task and that two things were distracting us all and preventing our being properly trained. These two things were that the daily attention of crowds of people was taking all our energies, even when we tried to escape we were pursued. The first issue, he told us that he was very concerned that we should not become a sort of circus act healing the sick was not an end in itself the important thing was that through healing people should be focused on the love of God and the message of forgiveness and a way to eternal life. If this message was not being received then the healing was at the risk of being seen as some sort of magic and magic is the work of the devil. The second issue, which we had to understand was that the forces of evil in the world had seen the success of Jesus presence in the world and were determined, if it was in their power, to destroy God's intentions. We were continually hounded by scribes and Pharisees, the Temple authorities had sent spies, to report to the high priests what was happening and to undermine what he was saying and doing. These men were not interested in the message they were only interested in ensuring that others did not hear it and if they did that they should not believe it, in short they were acting as the devil's fifth column. The forces of evil had to be defeated and this would be completed in Jerusalem, which was our next destination after our stay here and we would be there for the Passover. In the time available we had to learn many things, we had to understand many things and most importantly we had to have our faith reinforced so that whatever may happen we would always trust God.

Then he turned to the question of how he knew about this retreat in the forest. He told us that he and his father, and more lately he and his brothers, had been coming here to buy timber for years, in fact as long as he could remember. So, that was why he knew the paths so well, why he knew the place for lunch, why he knew where the little oasis was and why he had known about the farm, we thought he had only visited when he worked there as a boy. He explained to us that the best

<hr/>

timber was Lebanese hill and mountain timber, it grew straight and was harder than other timbers. Most of the wood used in Galilee was either local wood from the hills of Galilee or came from Judea, probably because they grew more quickly in these warmer districts the wood was softer and more knotted and never such long straight pieces. Joseph, Jesus' father had set up a business separate from his carpentry that was to trade in timber, this allowed them to bring Lebanese timber all the way from Mount Hermon to use and to sell to other carpenters around Nazareth by buying in bulk. That way he got a good price here and defrayed the haulage costs over a large quantity, of course this part of the business was risky and was only possible using the Roman roads that ensured a speedy and secure passage of goods. So over the years they had got to know this "woodsman" well and he was delighted when through James, Jesus' his elder brother, an approach was made to see if we would be welcome.

As far as the building was concerned, Nathan had been talking about this project for years, he wanted to find a way of increasing the use of wood in buildings, and here was the result a demonstration building for all to see and it must have many advantages over stone buildings and even mud brick buildings in many circumstances. Jesus felt sure that there had been some thing special that had happened to stimulate Nathan to realise this expensive project just now and that no doubt we would be told about it as time went by.

Then there were many other questions and we were still there discussing all sorts of things until it was nearly dark when we were summoned to dinner in Nathan's house.

Nathan had a large house, constructed, as you might guess, almost entirely of wood, the main room into which we were shown had tables and benches to accommodate about thirty people. From this large room through a curtain was the area for the women and then the kitchens. To minimise the risk of a kitchen fire, they were actually in a separate building some distance from the main house. All the men assembled to eat and were seated as was the custom with the most important people at the head of the table and progressing downward to finally the two youngest sons who were just twelve and fourteen and so accepted among the company of men. It was interesting that Jesus, as was his habit, waited patiently to be seated by the host who then distributed his guests among his family so that everyone could converse in small groups round the table instead of all having to wait on the conversation at the head.

Nathan's family consisted of his father, his father-in-law, both of whom were venerable old men and shown great respect, then there were Nathan's two younger brothers and then all the grand sons; there must have been a good dozen of them! They were a fine set of men, clearly used to hard physical work in the forests, they moved with a grace which comes of perfect fitness, their skin was without blemish and their eyes had a bright sparkle and they all looked alike. It was some of these fine young men who had met us with their father in the forest earlier in the day. So the meal started, it was splendid, dish after dish of delicate flavours and robust sauces, meats and vegetables, fruits and breads and delicious wine; it was remarkable that only fifty miles north of our homes their should be such a new and unexpected cuisine. With such a band of hungry mouths the food disappeared almost as soon as it arrived and the kitchen was kept very busy until we were all done. Then, as we relaxed with that comfortable feeling of being well fed, the conversations started, until then there has been almost silence apart from grunts of appreciation.

The little group that I sat with consisted of one of Nathan's brothers and half a dozen assorted cousins and four of us, the first question we were faced with was, "Who is this Man?" They explained that even in this far away corner of the nation they had been hearing for many months stories of Jesus of Nazareth, the amazing words he said, the way he argued with the Scribes and the rabbis and the Pharisees, the wonderful stories he told, the miracles: feeding 5,000 from five loaves, turning water in to wine; but mostly of the cures for every illness and disease that ever contaminated mankind. Every one joined in telling what they had heard! Peter was with our group and asked them if they had also heard of John the Baptiser, and of course they had, so he said that John had been sent as the herald of the Emmanuel and that he, John, had recognised Jesus as just that Emmanuel at the Jordan and in fact although we had not understood it at the time we, that is Peter and I, had actually witnessed this moment of recognition. Then Jesus had disappeared for months only to re-appear in Galilee, as an itinerant preacher going from town to town and village to village preaching a new message. That message was of God's forgiveness of sins and of God's love for mankind, the whole area was soon buzzing with excitement. The impressive thing was that this carpenter who was well known and respected for his skills was suddenly proclaiming with a confidence and authority, that nobody could understand God's message to mankind. Peter then continued that we were just ordinary folk like them, only our business was fishing and theirs was forestry. He then recalled for them how we had been about our business when Jesus appeared and said, "Follow me!" Well, he explained, he didn't just say, "Follow Me!", he actually commanded and demanded that we followed

Him. We had no option, what is more, we had no time to tell our family or our friends what we were doing, in fact we didn't know what we were doing but, we now know that we were setting out on the most amazing journey that anyone could possibly imagine. He told them that Jesus' instruction to us had been to learn from him because we were going to change the world! So, he concluded, everyone has to decide for himself whether he will be part of this mission or not, but if not then his future is indeed bleak, whereas if he will then Jesus promised eternal salvation. They were dumb struck and we were very impressed that Peter could summarise what had happened so succinctly. The questions came thick and fast, we were able to confirm or deny the reports they had received by word, we were able to retell to them some of the stories, we were able to confirm that we had been given power to cast out devils and to heal the sick and that we had all done these things on our own, throughout the whole of Israel. We tried to transmit to them the sense of urgency that we had felt and accepted that the time was now and men had to decide.

Then somebody asked, "Why, if the matter was so urgent, had we come to this outpost of Jewry and not gone to Jerusalem to deliver the 'Good News' to the doctor's of the Law and the priests in the Temple. Or why were we not raising an army to destroy the gentiles in the Land?"

I suddenly found myself saying "The time is not yet come for Jerusalem, we know that God's plan has to be worked out in every detail, we know that we have to meet the doctors and the priests but only after many other things are completed. We have come here because there has to be a time of preparation, a time of prayer, a time of learning, a time of consolidation and we have to be isolated from the distractions of the world for a while for this preparation. As for an army, well, we have the strength of God with us, you know how he sent fire from heaven to Elisha when he prayed, just think what power is available to Emmanuel if he determines to use that power, we do not need an army. Think also of the power that he gave to David when he slew Goliath, or to Joshua when he destroyed the city of Jericho, or to Gidian when he defeated the enemies of Israel. And you ask where is our army!"

The questioner was amazed, frankly so was I! After a pause I went on, "We are charged by God to change the world and we feel perplexed and frightened, but then we have so many examples of men who did change the world and who were just as unsure and afraid. Abraham heard the Lord and left his father and mother and all that he loved, because God said go where I show you, do as I say and I will form out

264

of you a new nation. Is that not changing the world? Moses spent years running away from the work that God had for him to change the world, he made every excuse he could to avoid the task, but in the end he trusted God and without him the Jewish nation would not exist, and without him the Jewish Law would not exist, is this not changing the world? Well we don't know what the outcome will be of the work we are doing and will be doing but we do know that because it is God's work it will change the world! The fact that we have left our homes and families makes us seem to be special but everyone has a duty to do the work that God has ordained for him. It may not seem important and it may not seem that anyone will notice and it may be dull and monotonous but it is the work that God has given and so it has to be done for God and it may also change the world."

By time I had finished saying this the whole table had stopped talking and were looking at me, I was so surprised I just stopped, I had nothing else to say and wanted somebody else to join in but for what seemed an age nobody did. Then Jesus came to my rescue.

"And so," he said "Andrew has just shown you that he is doing God's work! He doesn't know what the outcome of what he has just been saying to you all will be, but he does know that he has opened your eyes to God in your lives and perhaps now you have heard that you will change the way you work. Others will notice and they will change and so on and so on and just those words will have changed the world. On the other hand you may all be interested and do nothing and then Andrew's words will not have changed the world, but I know, and he knows that he will say the same thing again and again and again to thousands of people, as long as there is life in his body because it is God's work he is doing and it will change the world!" Now there was only one discussion at the table and it centred on Jesus.

Somebody asked, "So what do we do, now, today, tomorrow morning?"

I thought Jesus was going to tell them a parable but he didn't, instead he said "You have the Law of Moses, obey that and the world will be different! When I tell you to obey the law I am not telling you as the scribes and the Pharisees tell you, I tell you to listen to the actual words of Moses and do that. But I can help you with a summary of the Law and it is. You have to love God with all your spirit, with all your strength and with all your mind and then you must love your neighbour as if he is yourself, if you do this you will change the world. I am sure you would all agree that if everyone did just that the world would be a very different and a much better place. In fact God's Kingdom would be here on earth and the sins of Adam would be absolved. This charge I give you is not an easy option, but those who are determined can bring a little bit of God's Kingdom to earth."

So after a short silence while we all tried to absorb that, Nathan asked,

"Well tell us how do you think being a forester and timber merchant fits in with all this? God may be there in the forest somewhere but for us it is just work and very hard and dangerous work too. Some times I wonder if our bit of the world is not God's Kingdom but the devil's kingdom!" There were lots of murmurs of agreement and nodding of heads, and we were also interested to hear what Jesus would say because we knew the power of God when storms changed the calm Sea of Galilee into a raging demon, but most of the time God didn't seem to have had much to do with the daily round, it was much more about taxes and the cost of nets and down to earth practical things. Jesus replied to Nathan by first reminding him of the first of his two parts of the summary of the Law and asked us all to think about where worshiping God might be involved in cutting down the forest. Somebody said that he always thought of God when he smelt the perfume of fresh cut wood. Another said he always saw God in the beauty of the forest when he stopped to take his breath and looked around. Then someone else said that he saw God in the amazing result of the work of men's hands in taking a raw log cut down in the forest and crafted into all manner of products that were needed by carpenters and furniture makers. Nathan's father joined in and said his praise of God was that he had always produced enough profit to employ this large family and many other hired hands and to give them a good life. It was surprising how many ways there were that people saw God and praised God in the work they did, I have recorded a few but there were many more that convinced the whole room that there were many ways in which they could praise God in the work they did. So Jesus then suggested that perhaps we could think about the way we could show our love for our neighbour in this dangerous business. The conversation went to and fro, there were suggestions about better working conditions, care for the elderly, care for the sick or injured and their families the estate providing housing for its workers and many others but then Nathan chimed in that all these ideas were fine except the business had to make a profit to exist and provide what benefits people already gained from their work. If he provided all these benefits the business might not survive because the costs would have to be passed on to the customers and there were always plenty of people willing to steal his customers already. He said that all these things had to be done gradually and that there were many other calls on the available finances that were about ensuring the future and so ensuring the jobs the business provided. Then Jesus stopped us and said that although the discussion was fascinating and very instructive it missed the point, the point of God's love is about the souls of men, their bodies are important but much more important was their souls. So then we had to try and understand that and think of ways in which the business could obey the command 'Love thy neighbour's soul'. Now there were less suggestions, so Jesus told us that all the things that had been suggested may have an impact on peoples souls but as a secondary consequence of looking after their physical needs, for instance they were relieved of the anxiety about the consequences of sickness or old age and this allowed them to contemplate God with more confidence. But what could be done to satisfy their soul, then we talked about how people actually interact, how do we communicate with our words, our faces, our bodily behaviour all these things send messages to the listener that are far louder than the words. They actually communicate from one person to another how they each project and perceive their worth to the other; what God tells us is that he loves us all and he loves us all equally, so we should value the people we interact with as equals in the way we value them as individuals. Quite clearly there has to be some structure to enable a great enterprise like this timber business to function, but that didn't mean that the overseers could lord it over the men that the foremen should belittle people just because they had a perceived position of power and authority or that they should treat people just as things. They would not like to be treated as things, none of us do and that is what God's love should do, it should stop us ever thinking about other people as things and not as God's children, just as we want to be treated. So he concluded if we could all treat everyone we came into contact with, as especially God's children we would change not only this business but the whole world! We were stunned, it seemed so straight forward, so easy to do, there was no need to decide how to use the money the company had there was no financial cost and it could be done now. So then there was a lively discussion mainly centred on why it wasn't like that already. One of the sons, I seem to remember he was called Jon, said that the yard would be surprised if he went about grinning and asking "How are you?" to every one he met. Jesus said that unless such comments were genuinely meant from his heart they would be recognised instantly as a sham. So he suggested that perhaps if Jon involved people in deciding how the work was to be done, who was to do what and with whom and issues like that and really took notice of what people said and used their ideas and gave them the credit for their ideas then he might see a change because this way he was talking to a man's soul. People, he told us, have God given talents and it is our duty to use those talents to our very best doing the work he has chosen for us, it is as much a sin as theft or even murder for one man to so use another man that he is unable or unwilling to use the talents God has given him. One of God's great gifts to mankind is our ability to talk to each other, and so we can organise great endeavours like this timber business. This requires people to do things, so there has to be a structure of people telling other people to do things, you have noticed that we are all, generally speaking, being told what has to be done and telling other people what has to be done. It is important to remember this obvious fact but then we have to be careful that we are not ourselves stopping the people we are telling what to do from using all the talents God has given to them. Poor Jon had looked very hurt when Jesus said he might stop shouting at his people, he hadn't said that at all but we had all seen him in the yard barking monosyllabic orders to men who dashed here and there trying to meet his commands, giving an air of great activity and chaos. So he was relieved to find the teaching move from the particular to the general and started to nod in agreement, no doubt thinking about how his boss treated him. The room went quiet for a while and then conversations started again, around us it was all about this astonishing view about God's love which most people had admitted seemed to them more like a national insurance policy for the Jewish nation than any thing that would actually effect the way they did their jobs. After a little while I looked down the table to see that Jesus had quietly slipped away, I knew he had gone to pray and in a little while suggested it was time we all went to bed. We thanked our gracious host and found our way back to the hall, to find beds laid out on the floor ready for us to sleep!

The next two or three weeks were spent talking and listening and debating, gradually we began to understand some things; but we didn't know how much more we had to learn. Jesus taught us about God's love, he taught us how we had to show that love to those around us he gave us many, many examples of how we failed to grasp opportunities, how we were blind to other peoples needs and full of our own needs and concerns. He taught us how to listen and how to see deeper into people; to understand their real needs or the real question they were asking. He taught us how to use the question of one man to answer the questions of many. He taught us that we had to treat all men equally, if a man asked what may seem a simple or even an apparently stupid question, part of our demonstration of God's love is not to put him down but to answer his question honestly and humbly and to use the occasion to explore some other feature of God's presence and God's

268

love. He always listened to our conversations and joined in to correct us to show that the way we were talking and reacting was showing to each other a lack of listening and that his was a demonstration of our lack of God's love for each other. Gradually the lessons were learnt and we found we could talk easily knowing that we would not be taken at face value but that the others would be concerned at our concerns. He sometimes used parables but always he then explained the meaning, the deeper, hidden meaning that only those who knew God could devise. We tried to use parables as well but our attempts never approached the skill that Jesus had in choosing an everyday situation of great familiarity and turning it into a lesson about men or about God or about heaven, even now, in my old age, although I have tried and tried I fail continually. Jesus ability with parables is one of the most enduring features of his teaching crowds because the message was available at every level of understanding and perception. But these discussions though memorable and important pale into insignificance when compared with the incredible sessions that Jesus clearly set aside to teach us about God and particularly to show us how God is totally different in everything from men. I know that these teachings have already become the famous "Sermon on the Mount" and are being circulated wherever followers of Christ meet together. Some of the topics we remembered were what a few of us had heard on that day of rest at Nazareth when we sat and admired the view East to the Sea of Galilee and life seemed rather less threatening.

I want to just tell you about the one great lesson now called the Beatitudes or the Blessed. The whole experience is still very vivid in my mind; it had become our habit after breakfast to meet together in a sunlit glade a little way from the timber-yard where it was remote from the noise of the workers although we could hear them as a background of human activity. The air was heavy with the scents of the trees and the flowers, we were surrounded by the songs of birds, mountain birds we did not recognise and the buzzing of insects, the air was crisp, not cold, but it had a sharpness that you only experience in the mountains. Since then I have been in many mountains and every time I am reminded of this particular day, when we were hidden away from the world in the forest above Caesarea. We felt secure being with Jesus, secure among ourselves and oblivious to the dramatic adventure that was to engulf us all in the next few weeks and months. We were innocents in an evil, hostile, vicious world, how much Jesus knew or suspected I cannot say, he was full of confidence and enthusiasm and he showed us all that his way to God was exciting, joyful and sure. Not for him the dull reverential, penitential rituals of the rabbis and

Pharisees, to him always finding God in the world in new ways was exciting and fulfilling. We were sitting on the warm dry forest carpet of pine needles and waiting for him to start and to our surprise instead of being ready to launch into the explanation of a parable or some other discussion he was very quiet and still. It was as if he was listening as if he was unsure and hesitating as if he were looking for inspiration, we were all very attentive. This was a new Jesus we had not seen before and we wondered what would happen next, then he started to teach and what we heard was the most beautiful and profound poetry we had or ever would hear. I spell them out here for you as I remember them and as I have repeated them so many times since.

Blessed are you poor: for yours is the kingdom of God.

Blessed are you who hunger now: for you will be filled.

Blessed are you that weep now: for you shall laugh.

Blessed are you when men shall hate you separate you from their company and reproach you and cast out your name as evil for the son of Man's sake. Rejoice in that day, and leap for joy: for behold, your reward is great in heaven: for in the same manner did their fathers to the prophets.

We were absolutely amazed! What Jesus had just said was a complete and absolute contradiction of all that we had experienced in life.

It was the rich who had slaves and servants and clothes and houses and security. It was the poor who had nothing who had to scratch and scrape enough each day to live and yet Jesus was saying they were blessed when quite clearly the rich had blessings in abundance. It was the rich who were received with honour and respect in the synagogue, it was the rich who walked haughtily and for whom everybody else made way; everybody wanted to be rich. It was the rich who could bribe the tax collector, it was the rich who could pay for prayers to be said for his soul, it was the rich who were buried in exotic and expensive tombs, it was the rich who made it quite clear that they had bought their way into Abraham's Bosom; everybody wanted to be rich.

What could possibly be less blessed than a hungry man, the wealthy who always had enough to eat seemed much more blessed, God never seemed to make the blessed man go hungry. Who will feed the poor? The law requires the hungry to be fed but it never happens; those people who are desperate are given enough to just keep them alive and they stay hungry and desperate.

Why should weeping be conceived as a blessing? How can sadness and distress be a blessing? It made no sense at all! How can anyone be happy and laugh when the tragedies of life over take them? When a small child dies or a parent dies or other close relative or friend dies, will we be happy; nobody can stop death and nobody can stop the sadness of the loss of loved ones.

The final challenge to rejoice when we are ill treated for God's sake seemed like madness, our God is all powerful we should be calling down the curse of God on the perpetrators of such ill treatment, why should God not protect his elected people instead of watching them being abused by his enemies? Yet Jesus is commending us to accept and even welcome such ill treatment, to never resist, to accept anything that anyone cares to do to us and be respectful and obedient, it is not possible. How can the world be changed by such submissive behaviour, the world is changed by confrontation and war; if you don't fight you will be annihilated. So how can Jesus recommend this as the way to change the world? It is all right talking about rewards in heaven but we have to defeat the evil men of this world before heaven is a consideration!

These are not just my words, we were all totally amazed at such comments and predictions and explanations of God's expectations of us and for us. We had accepted our mission with Jesus to "Change the World", we had all learnt that there were sacrifices to be made to achieve this end but now he is telling us that all we can expect is poverty, hunger, sadness, and abuse and somehow that will change the world! Jesus must have anticipated the reaction that his words produced, he must have seen our shock and disappointment and so he produced another set of predictions. As an antidote he pronounced these great warnings to the world;

Alas for you who are rich; you have had your time of happiness.

Alas for you who are well fed now; you shall be hungry.

Alas for you who laugh now; you shall mourn and weep

Alas for you when all speak well of you; just so did their fathers treat the false prophets.

When he had finished we all started to question him. How could this

271

be? Why should he give such a depressing forecast of God's will for mankind? How did this relate to the other things he had told us about God and his kingdom, for instance, God's love and God's forgiveness?

So he stopped us all to expand on what he had said. "First", he told us, "you must understand that the things I am teaching you are things of the spirit and are not of this world. Many will hear these words and think that they refer to this world and then they cannot understand. They will interpret what I have said as foolishness, just as you have been thinking and saying. So let us look again and think about these words as relating to our spiritual nature. The first commendation is: 'Blessed are the poor: for yours shall be the kingdom of God.' It is important to understand that the poor, in spirit, are those who realise their need for God and forgiveness; without this recognition of need men cannot even approach a proper relationship with God. But for the man who puts away all the trappings of the world and its pomp and dignity, its segregation and exclusivity, its greed and ambition, its hatred and exploitation and realises that his only refuge is God's love and forgiveness for his soul, he will enter into God's kingdom with all the benefits and blessings that I have been showing to you. There is no other way! Unless a man humbles himself, in the eyes of the world, he cannot receive God's blessing, and the only way is to listen to my words and to believe them and to live them all day every day. I say to you again I AM the way the truth and the light nobody can come to God except by me.

So the next commendation is: 'Blessed are you who hunger now; for you will be filled.' This commendation is not about hunger for the food we eat, this is about the hunger of the soul and what the hungry soul is searching for is goodness and righteousness. Men search to satisfy their soul, they follow any fashion or philosophy that happens to have some attraction, they become intensely involved in their business be it fishing or farming or forestry or the synagogue or like the lawyers about the law or the Pharisees about adherence to the rules of the law or the rabbis in their studies they are all searching for the food of the soul and that food is goodness and righteousness. All these pursuits are temporal and they are limited by man's limitations and folly and so they are poor purveyors of the food of the soul. Men become distracted by sin, they make their enthusiasms idols, they make the activities exclusive and become proud and so forget to love their neighbours and forget to love God. I say to you unless you follow my words and do my commands you will not be satisfied, but if you do, goodness and righteousness will be yours in abundance. I AM the only way, I AM the truth and the light; there is no other truth and no other light than me, those who do not heed my words will live in darkness and they will not be filled.

So what about those who weep, who will be comforted? Remember this is all about the spirit, those whose spirits are so distressed that their very spirit weeps, those who are lost whose sinfulness has overtaken them, those who can find no comfort in their lives and have lost all contact with God, those who can only see a future of sin and darkness and regret and spiritual death. I am not exaggerating, there are many, many people who live their lives with this burden, they can see no possible escape, they know that they are lost but there is no one to lead them, they can see no light anywhere to guide them to God and to peace and joy. The Jews know in their hearts that they have strayed but when they try to return to God the blackmailing of the scribes and Pharisees pulls them back. I have told you many times that the new way of love, love for God and love for each other, is the only way to God, but you and the leaders of the Jews can read this in the writings of the Prophets. Isaiah has told them but they will not listen; now I am telling them and if they will not listen, you my faithful friends will tell them again and they will not listen. Then you will tell the whole world and enough will listen to change the world. The Jews will be left behind as an interesting backwater of religion that has been made redundant. The message to those who weep is that now they are comforted, now they can leap for joy; God loves and cares for each one of them individually and God gives freely and repeatedly his loving gift of forgiveness. The only commitment that God asks is that they individually believe in me and live their lives according to my words. Compared with the burden of sin my burden is light, it is the burden of rejection by men and of exclusion from the world's distractions, but compensated by the all surrounding embrace of God's love. Now they can see because a light shines in their souls; they know that they can be saved, that they can reject the life of sin and shame and look to a loving caring God. This is their own individual God and they need no priests or temples to defend Him or hide Him. They know that they have within themselves the power to interpret God's will and do not have to accept the views of weak and sinful men to interpret the Law for them. I repeat I AM the way the truth and the light and only through me can men come to a proper relationship with God."

We sat dumbstruck, we knew that Jesus was a prophet but now he was claiming in effect that he was equal to God. This seemed like blasphemy, nobody had ever made such a claim; all the great leaders of the nation had only claimed to be either a servant of God, or a messenger of God or appointed by God. We had seen his great works and had heard his words, witnessed the miracles of healing but we had never thought that he was other than the Messiah and that all these amazing works were to persuade people to join his cause for the restoration of the Jews. Now we were faced with his claim to be equal with God; we would all be charged with blasphemy; the punishment for that was death! It was just as well that we were secreted in the woods in the remote north of the country and there were no eavesdroppers. These words of Jesus were rebellion indeed but not the rebellion we had thought of, this was directed at the Chief Priests and the Sanhedrin in Jerusalem. We suddenly began to feel like conspirators, so now we understood why Jesus had brought us out of the sight of the Jews. He knew that the Greeks would take no notice of us and neither would Philip unless we caused trouble. Jesus knew that he could tell us things in private that could not be said in public, the time was not yet ready! How wrong we had all been we had all thought that we had left Galilee partly for fear of Antipas and partly because Jesus thought we had failed; there was no indication of failure now, he claims to be God. The pause for these thoughts was probably only a few seconds, we all felt it and talked about it later. We had a sense of foreboding of disaster gathering round us and that it was too late to escape, fear began to well up within us, even panic; blasphemy was a very serious crime!

Jesus had paused for breath but with great effect and now he continued. "Finally" he said, "we have to think about the final commendation. You will remember this, 'How blest you are when men hate you, when they outlaw you and insult you and ban your very name as infamous, because of the Son of Man. On that day be glad and dance for joy; for assuredly you have a rich reward in heaven; in just the same way did their fathers treat the prophets.' I tell you quite clearly; those who will promulgate my words will be punished by the authorities, both spiritual and secular. You are already anxious because you are beginning to understand the profound nature of my mission, which is now your mission. This message to the world will overthrow the powers that exist today. It will over throw all the powers of the world to come and cannot be resisted because it is God's plan. I am here not speaking my words, I am speaking God's words and God cannot be diverted from his plan. Powers will come who seem to follow my commandments but they will fail because they will fall to the temptation of self confidence and forget whose authority they have, when that happens they become evil and are doomed! You have to understand that this is to be expected.

I repeat, I AM the truth, I AM the way and I AM the light.

You must always remember this, to the end of the age

Part 17

Jerusalem, written by John

Andrew has told you something about the incredible experiences that we, that is the twelve, and many others lived through in that first stage of Jesus mission to mankind in Galilee. I have read through his manuscript and recommend it, there were so many things that happened, always totally extraordinary and totally unexpected. Everyday was an adventure in itself, we never knew what to expect and Jesus used every opportunity however casual and ordinary to show God's love at work in the world, or to show how sin was preventing men coming to God. He proclaimed forgiveness of sins to those who repent and have faith, the comfort and consolation that this brought to the people was instant and dramatic. He managed to see peoples' sinfulness not as punishable but as forgivable, to help people to lift themselves out of the pit of despair and see that the love of God was there, even in the pit, to save them. Well Andrew has written a lot but it is only a fraction of what could be written and now I have taken up the task of telling the next part of the story. A story that is dramatic like no other story, a story that ends in God showing to man his infinite power, love and promising that it is available for our use to do his work on earth. We were alternatively elated, overwhelmed, bewildered, disappointed, frightened even terrified, confident and ashamed at our lack of understanding and faith. Unbeknown to us, as we set out on this journey to Jerusalem, we were to be involved in the most dramatic demonstration of God's power in the unending conflict between good and evil.

I think that perhaps I should make a short introduction about my background and why I feel that I can recount this stage in God's revelation of Himself to man.

To the family fishing partnership of Jonas and Zebedee our most important market for fish products was the Jordan valley. We were at a disadvantaged with our competitors, due to our location at Capernaum, on the northern coast of the Sea of Galilee compared with the fishermen in the south, as this added to our transport costs. But over the years we had developed a reputation for quality and service that allowed us to sell our products at premium prices, in fact our products were considered to be the very best available. It had taken a lot of effort to win this accolade and we took great pains to protect our reputation. We spent a lot of effort in training our workers in the skills they needed to ensure the quality was maintained. Only the best quality of the catch was used; all the herbs and spices involved in the pickling and curing processes were carefully selected; only the very best packaging and presentation were used. We had developed very good relationships with our suppliers and although we paid more for their best products we found that this added to our status in the market. We had sole agents in Jericho and Jerusalem, who took regular large volume deliveries, the demand was continuous throughout the year and had made a stable basis from which to grow the business. When I was about twenty I assumed responsibility for these customers and so made frequent visits, three or four times every year, to negotiate new contract arrangements and to deal with any problems that may have occurred. The agents had become family friends over the years and I knew that I was always welcome on my visits, and came back to Capernaum with all the latest gossip and news, from the capital. What the Sanhedrin were doing, what the Romans were doing and of course an update for years on the building and finishing of Herod's Temple.

The Jewish faith demanded absolute loyalty to Jerusalem, every Jew made it a lifelong commitment to make at least one visit to the Holy City. There were always Jews from foreign lands in the city; they came from all over the world, from every corner of the Roman Empire and also from the lands to the east. There were colonies of Jews in the great cities of the remnant of the Persian Empire and countries beyond. God's plan for the propagation of His word had been laid down over many generations, the prophets of old had told the Hebrews and the Israelites to extend their knowledge of the one true living God throughout the world. They had failed in this task by keeping this truth to themselves by their determination to avoid contamination from gentile races, but this very exclusivity had kept them available as a means by which the of the knowledge of Jesus Christ and His refreshing covenant would eventually flow through these widely dispersed communities even if they failed again to recognise the message as the fulfilment of God's plan.

I usually came back to Capernaum full of news from lands far away and little known to any of us. I was also able to make business contacts that gradually developed into trading arrangements so that our preserved fish products became known and demanded in countries north, south, east and west of Galilee. I also got to know on a personal basis many of the important and influential people at the centre of the political scene both sacred and secular, which allowed me access to places to which other visitors were generally forbidden. My trips were usually down the Jordan Valley to Jericho and then up through the hills to Jerusalem. I usually returned by the same route avoiding the alternative return route through the hill country to Nablus, it was still wild country full of robbers and cut-throats and if you managed to steer clear of those hazards you then had to negotiate your way through the hostility of the Samaritans. Even after nearly a hundred years the Romans had not managed to bring their security to this route through the hills!

Jericho was a very wealthy city with beautiful streets and palaces, Herod had built grand palaces and impressive civic buildings to show off to his Roman visitors but even before him the Greeks had built many beautiful temples to their pagan gods. Although it was really in the desert, tucked under the edge of the hills of the Judean wilderness and facing east across the Jordan valley at the northern end of the Dead Sea its bountiful springs ensured that palm trees were abundant and provided not only the best dates and oil in the whole of Israel but also provided shade from the fierce desert sun. The wealth of the city was not based on dates alone but on the Balsam trees that produced the very expensive balsam oil that was exported throughout the Roman Empire and to the Arabs to the east. So Jericho was not only, as it claimed, the oldest city in the world, but also the most prosperous in Israel. The old tyrant Herod, father of Antipas and Philip and builder of the Temple and many other wonderful works, willed the city and its revenues to his widow and she lived there in opulent luxury for the rest of her days!

Jericho was a delightful haven of prosperous tranquillity, which I always left reluctantly knowing that Jerusalem was a turbulent city full of noise and tension. The climb from the Dead Sea to the ring of hills around the city was always long and tedious, the road winds like a serpent up through the wilderness, sometimes in the spring there is some green on the bare rounded hills but that is rare. There are no trees or even shrubs, there are no streams, there is no habitation, it is a most "God forsaken" landscape, we always made the journey in a convoy of travellers for defence against the risks of bandits and bad weather, we were always very pleased to see Bethany on the final ridge from which we knew we could look across to the Mount of Olives which had a commanding view of the City of God itself. We usually stopped in Bethany over night and the next day plunged down the hills into the city to be engulfed by the noise and the crowds. It did not seem to matter at which season I was there it was always crowded, just walking in the streets you would hear, above the general hub-bub, every language of the Roman Empire and many, many more. The temple itself was a great draw to Jews who had a duty to visit at the great feasts, but it had become a tourist attraction, one of the wonders of the world! Its reputation for grandeur and opulence had spread everywhere so many visitors were there just to see the huge works that had been undertaken to provide this magnificent House of God. Hopefully they would be duly impressed by our one God compared with their many; hopefully they would spend plenty of money in the guest houses and taverns which seemed to be everywhere while they gawped at the huge blocks of granite that Herod had used to make the vast rectangular platform on which stood the Temple itself, with its magnificent courtyards and porticos and elaborate colonnades. When you looked at the building it seemed to be just made of gold and every Jew agreed it was a fitting symbol for our God, even though Herod had nearly beggared the nation building it!

So after that short introduction, on with the adventure!

The day came when we were to leave Capernaum, after we had rested from the adventure on Mount Hermon, we expected to be away in Jerusalem for a few weeks, but even so there were tearful farewells and we were eventually relieved to be off. We had spent a few days encouraging our families and preparing for the journey. We, that is the brothers Zebedee and Jonas, were fortunate that we were actually at home, the other members of the group had to send messages to their families and while we were in Capernaum we had many visitors from these families. During our stay Jesus' family came to visit, they were alarmed at what their brother was doing, they even accused him of being possessed, they accused him of having no concern for his mother or the rest of his family. They challenged him to explain why he, who they knew as a skilled carpenter and senior man in the family should abandon his duties and set of on a 'mad-cap' adventure that was bound to fail and would almost certainly bring disaster on them all, They pleaded with him to give it all up and come home to the comfort and security of the family in Nazareth. He listened to them and then told them that this was his mission in life that He was doing God's work and there was no possibility of his denying the task that God had set before him whatever the cost to himself. He assured them that they were safe and would come to no harm. He tried to convince them of the good news he was bringing to the world but they would have none of it, to them he was just their brother. How could he be bringing God's word, they had known him all their lives and could see nothing special in him, what they could see were risks to themselves and their livelihoods. It really was as far as they were concerned a big family row and eventually they stormed out and went back to Nazareth, all except Mary his mother and the one sister who had been with Mary all the time. Just one brother stayed with us and became an important leader and organiser of the church in Jerusalem, that was James, like all the rest of us he had been totally convinced of the message and in the middle of this row he had heard the truth and like us could not leave Jesus.

The atmosphere was very tense it seemed that everyone realised that this was a very important stage, if not the final stage in Jesus mission. We all felt that we were about to face a confrontation with the authorities at the Temple and that this confrontation would decide the success or failure of our mission. We had absolute faith that Jesus and our God would protect us. We knew that Jesus could convince anybody and everybody of the truth and justice of his message, even the scribes and the Pharisees were astonished by his power of argument and the profound impact that his healing and miracles had on people. Many had become followers of the new leader that had appeared amongst us and accepted him, as we did, as the Messiah, sent by God to save the nation. Still more of these religious men, however, were confrontational and continually accused Jesus and us of flagrant disregard of the Law and particularly the Sabbath Law. They continually laid traps for him, traps to be able to substantiate accusations of blasphemy, but they failed. We knew, and I recognised, that many of these learned men were from Jerusalem and that they would carry the news of Jesus' counter arguments back to the Temple and the Sanhedrin. He was so outspoken and direct in his criticism of the authorities that we expected to be spied on and everything that we said and did would be known in the capital. We hoped, that Jesus would temper his directness to encourage these powerful men to see the truth and become convinced of the changes that had to be introduced. I am sure that deep down we did not expect such a change, and we wondered among ourselves what we were about to witness. We all anticipated that in the end Jesus would defeat the existing deeply sinful religious authorities and that he would become the supreme King of the Jews and would exercise his authority with justice and mercy. We hoped that the Romans would see that this change was to their advantage as it would dissipate the groundswell of hatred aimed at them as the violators of the Holy Land of God's Chosen People. We all held this view despite Jesus continually telling us that it would not be like that, we chose to ignore his many predictions that his Kingdom was 'not of this world', and again his frequent dark predictions that he would be killed before his Kingdom could be seen on earth.

So with very mixed feelings we set sail on one of the company boats, due south from Capernaum to the outfall of the Sea of Galilee into the River Jordan. There we disembarked and sent the boat home with the skeleton crew, hoping that it would not be long before we met them again. Our party numbered about twenty, there were the twelve and Jesus, Jesus' mother and his brother James, who had become attached to the group, Mary from Magdala, Andrew's wife and several serving girls and one or two dedicated men who had received special blessings from Jesus and were determined to stay with him whatever might befall. We set off at a leisurely pace using the tracks that followed the meanderings of the Jordan River. We passed through lush meadows and forests, well managed fields and orchards; these paths were well used by Jews travelling from Galilee to Jerusalem on pilgrimages to the Temple and by many business men making their regular visits to clients in Jericho and Jerusalem, just as I had done so many times in the past. There were other routes on better roads used by the military and the rich in their litters and with their entourage of servants and guards to protect them from bandits. The Samaritans never came this way they always stayed in the hills moving from village to village, seeking protection and succour in the security of each community along the way. The route we were taking was familiar to us all, many times had we been to the temple at the great feasts in our younger days. We knew where all the rest houses were along the way and debated as we went which one would be the best to stay at for lunch or the night. These establishments provided for visitors to stop for meals or overnight and if they became too full they expanded into the pastures around them. They were always jolly places with lots of people to talk to, to exchange news and to catch up with the latest gossip. There were always people you knew, or at least who had friends or acquaintances in common, there were people coming north with news from Jerusalem and others, like us, going south. The route was so well used it was very secure there were always people just in front and just behind and a regular flow of people passing in the opposite direction, despite this we had come armed, several of us had swords and we all had stout staffs. I can not remember any planning about what to take but I think we were all nervous about what might happen to us either on the way or in Jerusalem. We joked among ourselves about being a small army of God, but in the event we didn't need any protection on the journey. Our progress was slow; we were frequently stopped by other travellers when they realised that it was Jesus of Nazareth who was in the party. The news seemed to have travelled up and down the river valley, parties coming towards us knew he was there; parties caught up with us having heard from people going north that he was in front of them. The rest houses seemed to be ready for us, there were always beds and food ready for our arrival. Everyone was very excited and there seemed to be an assumption that he was going to Jerusalem as the Messiah to claim his kingdom. We had difficulty keeping the crush away from Jesus, and our progress was very slow, many of the travellers stayed with us or turned round to return to Jerusalem with us and we soon became a throng. From time to time Jesus would stop and talk to the people nearest him, his words were transmitted to the whole party. We overheard people translating his words into many languages; the crowd consisted of many people from many lands, and not just Jews. Sometimes when Jesus spoke in the Aramaic dialect of Galilee you could almost hear the ripple of translation in the crowd, just as if the words were a pebble dropped into a pool and the ripples it caused spread among the listeners. He tried to make them understand that he was going to Jerusalem to bring God's message of love and peace and forgiveness to those who repent and follow his teaching. The Jews were generally familiar with the thrust of Jesus message, what was surprising to us was just how intently the gentiles in the crowd listened, clearly the message was saying something very new to them and when they could they asked us just who this man was and where had he learnt such revolutionary ideas. Despite Jesus' best endeavours to prevent the Jews in the throng becoming over excited, the expectation was maintained, among everyone, that he was going to Jerusalem to declare his rule and restore Israel to her former glory.

When we stopped for lunch or to rest for the night he taught the people with his amazing parables. We had heard many of them already but we had to listen carefully because he could and did easily slip in a new twist, a subtle alteration that made the story more interesting but made the underlying meaning more difficult to devise. We spent a lot of time discussing the meanings of these parables and frequently Jesus had to come to our aid. Even now we still discuss them and find even deeper meanings, particularly now that we have the benefit of hindsight and a wealth of experience of God's work in the world. We actually had very little time with Jesus on our own, there were always crowds of people pressing in on us, and on the few quiet moments someone would always arrive with requests for help or healing or guidance. It was quite normal for a Pharisee to challenge Jesus on what he had said or how he interpreted the Law and more especially who he was! We seemed to go to bed later and later as we proceeded towards Jerusalem and to get up earlier and earlier to find some peace to pray to God for strength and guidance before the pressures of the day crowded in around us. It was difficult even to eat, everywhere we stopped there was a welcome with food prepared for us but there was never anywhere to hide away for a few minutes relaxation and re-creation. The women were very good at shooing people away to give us some space, but generally Jesus was pleased to talk with the crowds, he had favourite remarks when we got too exasperated, "For a little while yet the light is among you. While you have the light walk in the light, the man who walks in the dark does not know where he is going!" or "Let them that have ears, hear!"

As we approached Jericho the crush became more and more intense, the air of excitement and anticipation was almost tangible, people just wanted to get close enough to see his face and to hear his voice, mostly they did not stay long enough to hear what he was saying. It was quite clear that most people only wanted to be able to say to their friends or relatives that they had been so close that they could hear and see; everyone expected him to become the next great leader of the Jews and that this would be their only chance to get near to him. We felt privileged and proud that we were there right at the centre of these historic moments, people from the crowd came to us and to ask for help to get close to him or even having a brief interview with him. Even though we could do nothing we felt important just being asked, and expected that this would be the norm once Jesus had convinced the powers in the Temple of his rightful position as the Messiah, that long awaited Emmanuel.

We stayed for about three nights at Jericho; Jesus seemed reluctant to press on, we were all encouraging him to move quickly while there was so much euphoria and enthusiastic support. We thought it would be better to convince the Temple, with the backing of the population. How little faith we had! What impertinence to think that God needed human support to achieve his great plans, but of course we didn't know the plan. I'm sure we would not have believed it even if Jesus had explained it. We spent the time in Jericho mostly in discussions with Pharisees, scribes and priests, most to them were clearly very wealthy and living comfortable lives in the luxury and peace of Jericho. None of them seemed to have any interest in the poor, the cripples and the beggars who were abundant even in the midst of all the wealth. They were the cream of Israel's intellectuals and treated their religion as an exercise in ritual,debate and logic and not remotely connected with the world of the ordinary people. Their example was that it was the rich and respected who had God's attention and that was demonstrated by the blessings that they displayed proudly to the whole population. Jesus always turned the tables on them as they tried to trap him in their webs of cleverness. They were wrong-footed and forced to accept that their arguments were unsound, he could quote chapter and verse of the law to them and contradict their protestations. His consistent thrust was that God, was a God of love and forgiveness, and that His concern was to help people find the way out of their sinfulness. The severe God of punishment and retribution was a mistaken concept and all the trappings of public worship, intended to placate this tyrant, were a human creation and had distracted men from the truth and ensured that God was remote and unapproachable. He not only rebuffed their traps with inspired arguments and answers, but he taught them in parables. The Good Shepherd, The Sower and the Seed, The Good Samaritan, the Wicked Servant, The Prodigal Son, The Talents, The King's feast and The King's Vineyard, The Wedding Feast, to many of these listeners the import of the hidden message was not so difficult to devise and they recognised just how deep was the criticism of their religious practice. It was clear that they had some grasp of the message because most of them became very angry and abusive. There were some who were impressed by the debates and the parables and talked to us very sincerely about the message, we began to recognise the reality of the 'sower and the seed'. In fact later after the great events in Jerusalem many of these men joined us as convinced adherents to the message that Jesus brought to the world, so 'some seed had fallen on good ground'. This short interlude in Jericho, gave us a contrast between the priests and rabbis of Galilee who were, generally, humble well-intentioned men of the people who were doing their best to show God to their allotted flock. On the other hand these men of Jericho showed such arrogance and pride and haughtiness, it was as if they had achieved all this status and power by their own endeavours and nothing was God's gift. It was interesting that they initially approached Jesus, with superior condescension but quickly found that he bettered them on every point they raised. They were amazed and perplexed by the incisive arguments that Jesus used; all their schooling and experience had never been put to the test as it was in their confrontations with Jesus. They found it incredible that this apparently simple carpenter from the almost unheard of town of Nazareth should have such perception, understanding and unexpected grasp of the Law and its interpretation, after all it had taken them all their lives and continuous study and they were worsted by him on every point they raised.

We were, as Andrew has told you, by now convinced that Jesus was the son of God and that he was the Messiah, we had absolute faith in him and were not the least surprised that he had no trouble countering and overturning the arguments of these experts in the Law. We had seen him totally destroy the vain-glorious arguments and assertions of the Pharisees sent from Jerusalem, and knew that he would produce unexpected arguments to counter these experts; and he did! What did concern us was any accusation of blasphemy, this was the most dangerous accusation because the punishment was stoning and could be instituted just by a crowd getting wound up by some agitators. The questions that would lead to such accusations did not arise, so challenges to Jesus about "Who are you?" "From where do you derive your authority?" "How can you forgive sins?" were not raised and we all felt relieved that these obvious questions had for some reason not been part of the debates. It was surprising, after all they knew about the miracles in Galilee, the healing of the sick, even the curing of lepers, his pronouncement of forgiveness of sins and they would have known about the acceptance by the crowds that this was the Messiah. We were greatly relieved and, among ourselves, concluded that Jesus had realised just how provocative his claim to be the Son of God would be and that almost certainly it could lead to his death! We remembered that when Peter declared our conviction he instructed us not to broadcast that knowledge, clearly He was well aware of the consequences if the authorities heard such a claim.

After three days in Jericho Jesus decided it was time to move on and we set off towards Jerusalem on the road through the wilderness. But before we continue on the adventure there was one incident just as we left this magnificent, affluent and opulent city which I must tell you about, it had a profound effect on us at the time and has continued to do so on all that have heard it since. The incident started unremarkably, we had just left the city and were surrounded by crowds who we knew would come someway with us, when we heard behind us a man shouting out 'Jesus of Nazareth' over and over there was a sense of determination in his voice, almost of desperation. Jesus somehow heard this one voice among all the others round him and stopped to see who was calling him, and there was a young man running as fast as he could from the city gate so we waited and when he arrived he fell at Jesus feet and panted out his question. 'Good Master, What should I do to inherit eternal life?' Jesus was clearly impressed by this direct and sincere question, he looked down at the man with a kindly understanding of his dilemma. In his familiar way, instead of replying directly he countered the enquiry with two questions of his own. 'Why do you call me Good? No one except God alone is good. You know the commandments: "Do not murder; do not commit adultery; do not steal; do not give false evidence; do not defraud; honour your father and mother." ' But Master,' he replied, 'I have kept all these since I was a boy.' Jesus looked straight at him; his heart warmed to him, and he said, 'one thing you lack: go, sell everything you have, and give to the poor, and you will have riches in heaven; and come and follow me.' At these words the young man's face fell and he went away with a heavy heart; for he was a man of great wealth. Jesus looked after him as he went back towards the city and then he turned to us and said with a sad voice, 'How hard it will be for the wealthy to enter the kingdom of God!' We were all taken aback by this statement after all the young man seemed to have blessings in abundance, as usual he seemed to understand our confusion and repeated to us, 'Children, how hard it is to enter the kingdom of God! It is easier for a camel to pass through the eye of a needle than for a rich man to enter the kingdom of God,' This reiteration of the penalty of wealth on earth just added to our discomfort, he could tell that we all believed that it was the wealthy whom God had blessed and it was the wealthy who could keep the Law and the wealthy who could relieve the suffering of the poor and widows and could resist the temptations to sin, 'So who,' we were asking ourselves, 'can possibly enter the kingdom of God?' Jesus again could read our thoughts and gave us the affirmation he had given us many times before, 'For men it is impossible, but not for God; everything is possible for God.' So now we were even more confused because he was telling us that whatever we did we would not justify our acceptance in heaven, and that it was God and only God who made acceptance in heaven possible. It was Peter who broke the silence which had overcome us all, 'Jesus Master,' he said, 'We have, at your command, given up everything we had and held dear to become your followers. Are we not eligible for entry into heaven? You have just told that wealthy young man that he could achieve eternal life if he gave up all he had and followed you, that is what we have done but now you are telling us that is not enough and that we have no way of earning the gift of eternal life?' Now Jesus knew that Peter was expressing all our anxiety and misgiving; he promised us that everyone who made the sacrifice of possessions and family for His sake and the sake of the Gospel would be rewarded in this life many times over and would achieve eternal life. This helped us to overcome our concerns, but then he added the rider 'and persecution also'. He had told us many times that persecution was what we had to accept as his followers but none of us thought this was to be worse than the problems we had seen of being excluded from the synagogues and being publicly accused by the Pharisees of not keeping the Law, of being shunned by our friends and family because we met with sinners. It was unlikely, we had learnt already, that his words and actions would not stir up a reaction from the authorities; we were on our way to Jerusalem to sort the problems out and all would be well, we had faith in Jesus that he could not be defeated. He had just confirmed that our reward on earth would be substantial and after He had won over the authorities in Jerusalem we would become important people in the rebuilding of Israel.

For Jews making a pilgrimage to Jerusalem, as we had all done many times in the past, this was the joyous completion of a hazardous journey, we knew that when we had climbed this road we would come to the Holy City, David's City and God's House on earth. This time however as we walked on following Jesus on the hot dusty road, skirting the base of the Judean hills on our right and the wilderness on our left, our confidence gradually slipped away and we began to doubt that we could achieve a reconciliation with the Jewish authorities at the Temple, it seemed to us as we got nearer and nearer to Jerusalem that the risks of a disaster became more and more real. The road to Jerusalem winds its way up through the east facing wilderness, it is a desolate place, there are no trees, except after rare showers of rain the hills are devoid of even a blade of grass, there is absolutely no shade from the hard sun shining in a cloudless sky. There are no birds, nothing to give any indication that there is life on earth. There are interlocking hills all round separated by deep precipitous ravines worn by the very occasional torrential winter storms. Once you leave the flat desert of the Dead Sea there is nothing but hills, piled up one upon another, all the way to Jerusalem. These hills are smooth and rounded, they are cut by horizontal narrow rings produced by the flocks of sheep and goats who are continually searching the hills for some nourishment, guarded and guided by shepherd boys. These boys are the rare signs of life, there are no villages, there are not even isolated farms in the steep sided valleys between the hills; all is desolation. As we walked up the steep road rising from the Dead Sea to The Judean heights above Jerusalem we were mindful of all the references to the wilderness in the books we had heard from childhood in the synagogue. We remembered Jesus telling the parable about the man set upon by robbers and rescued, not by the Priest or the Lawyer, but by a Samaritan! The hiding places for brigands were everywhere. We were not afraid of being attacked because we were a large party all walking together, a man on his own would be at risk, despite the rule of Law and security that Pax Romana had provided.

It is a long hard walk and we eventually arrived at Bethany very late in the afternoon. We knew that we would be staying with Lazarus and his sisters, we had visited them several times on past visits to Jerusalem. Lazarus was a well-to-do merchant and was very well known and respected in the city, his house was always welcoming and comfortable, the family were among those already convinced of Jesus mission and his two sisters Mary and Martha always provided us with a resplendent feast, however big the party was. So it was on that day, the door was open, Mary was waiting to meet us and behind her was Lazarus to welcome us to his home, we were tired and hot, the servants brought water for us to wash and wine to refresh us and quickly the strain of the journey subsided as we talked and listened to Lazarus' report on the state of affairs in Jerusalem. He was so well connected that he knew most of the happenings in the city and was particularly determined to make sure that Jesus knew what a dangerous mission He was undertaking. He told us that the Sanhedrin were determined to destroy the mission by whatever means they could, they knew that Jesus was coming to Jerusalem and had set informers to tell them what was happening, they had paid spies to report to them everything that was said and to identify the people with Jesus.

We had all become familiar with the inevitable presence of scribes, Pharisees, doctors of the law and sometimes even members of the Sanhedrin; in Galilee where ever we went they were there; asking difficult tricky questions designed to trap Jesus into some culpable response; denouncing His teaching as being contradictory to The Law; challenging His right to cure the sick through the pronouncement of forgiveness; and questioning the very reality of the miracles that He produced, even suggesting these were the work of the devil! These people had undoubtedly been reporting back to the authorities in Jerusalem throughout the period of missionary work in the towns and villages in the north and would now be very apprehensive of the impact that Jesus would have when he eventually arrived in the Holy City. We had found it hard, as his band of disciples, to understand why there was such antagonism to Jesus amounting almost to fanaticism. Every time there was a confrontation they were put to shame, however carefully they prepared their ground Jesus always managed to turn the tables on them, either by cogent logic or by asking them a relevant question that left them without an answer. Always his answers were directing the questioners and the large crowds of listeners to an understanding of God's love, a love that is not of this world but is of God's infinity. He continually asserted that God is Love; that nothing any man can do, however sinful he may be will separate him from this love and that forgiveness of sins was readily available to all men. He emphasised that the strict adherence to the Law as promulgated by the scribes and doctors of the law and advocated by them as the only way to God, actually ensured that men could never achieve the right relationship with God. Looking back we were perhaps naive to expect that they could re-assess their whole understanding of the Law; they had all been trained to see the world as established Judaism. The great revolutionary message he brought was 'that access to God was by an individual through prayer, repentance, forgiveness of sins and obedience to the two great commandment, love God and love your neighbour'. This was a direct challenge to the whole Jewish religious belief that, because of the promise given to Abraham and the covenant given to Noah and through Moses, the Jews were a chosen sacred people and that they had God to themselves as a nation, that the individual only had to meet the rules of Jewishness to be part of God's 'elect'. The only conclusion from Jesus' pronouncements had to be that the ritual and power of the Temple no longer held any sway, that in fact gentiles as well as Jews had the same access to God. This was a direct and overt challenge to the accepted power structure of Jewish society that it was bound to generated confrontation, fear and hatred among the holders of power, while the poor and disadvantaged saw it as a way of re-arranging the distribution of power both religious and political and economic.

The Sanhedrin and the other power groups, even when they were confronted with the clear fulfilment of the prophecies regarding the expected Emmanuel, they could not understand, they were deaf and blind to what was happening. They were imbued with hatred and fear and were intent on finding some way of destroying Jesus or at least damaging His reputation and undermining his message. We were perhaps naïve as well; we had learnt from Jesus the meaning of his new message, although the full impact was still to come; we expected that the crowds in Jerusalem would recognise Jesus and by popular demand force the authorities to accept his message and establish his rule in the land! What our friend Lazarus reported to us did not in any way sound as if the authorities were about to capitulate, it sounded more likely that they would do anything and everything they could to destroy Jesus, and us, by whatever means came to hand. Lazarus knew Jesus well enough not to try to persuade him to change his plans, he only reported what he had learnt from his friends in high places, to warn Jesus and perhaps to congratulate him as well that he had made a real serious impact on the authorities and to be for-warned was to be for-armed. I remember Jesus listening to Lazarus and questioning him about his sources and which of the many factions in the Sanhedrin were saying what, but he did not show any signs of anxiety, it was as if he not only expected this news but would have been surprised had it been otherwise. We, the twelve, on the other hand were once again surrounded by fear and doubts; our comments were much more to reconsider the sense of a direct frontal

289

attack on the establishment, perhaps we should delay until after the Passover Festival to make our intentions clear in a less charged atmosphere when the authorities would perhaps be better able to listen and understand what the Love of God really meant to the daily living of everyone. There were those who would have been quite happy to withdraw back to Galilee and wait for a quieter time. We all reminded Jesus that we had been reluctant to make this journey at this time and that we should re-assess the risks before we went any further. Jesus response was exactly the same as he had told us many times before; we were working to God's plan not our own; God had brought us this far, he had brought us through many difficulties and like Jonah we were not able to avoid his demands. Furthermore he told us all that we were agents of God's love to mankind and that we were to play a critical role in demonstrating this incomprehensible love to the whole world for all time. None of us understood what he was saying but he had such confidence that we eventually conceded that we had to see the project through to the end, whatever that may be!

As I remember, he also introduced another aspect of the human response to God that had not, until now, been shown to us, this was part of Jesus' clear understanding of our deeply held anxiety. He told us, again that we and all men were continually tested by the forces of evil, the devil and all his works. The weapon that we had to combat the devil was faith and faith was shown by a determination to stay with God's plan, to never let human plans supplant them. He reminded us of the sower and the seed, the parable we had heard very soon after we had been called to his mission. There were four areas of ground that the seed fell on and most of it fell among the weed seeds and had to grow in this hostile environment. The truth is, He told us, that taking God's path was never the easy option, we had seen and suffered from the abuse and exclusion of our fellow Jews, we had been threatened, we had been hounded and had traps set for us. But we knew as well that always God had protected us and that as long as we kept to God's plan no opposition had been successful and no powers of man had been able to divert us from the path. But we all as a chorus said that we had always needed Jesus' presence at the moment of doubt to show us the way. He now told us that an absolute requirement of his disciples was the determination to hold on to that which is good and true whatever the circumstances, whatever the apparent consequences or threats of consequences. The world is an evil place and men are only too pleased to do the devil's work and this policy of his is to ensnare men into a cycle of sin from which there is no escape except through the love of God. When this message is pronounced to men the devil has to respond otherwise his hold on men will be lost and he will demand greater and greater sacrifice from those who have the message of God's love to proclaim. What is true is that the devil's policy is eventually bound to fail because it is through the determination of the proclaimers of the message and their acceptance of great sacrifice that others see the Love of God at work and recognise this as the true way. God's only weapon in this battle for men's souls is love, the response that we have to give to God is faith, it is this faith that is the weapon that men have to enable them to continually combat the devil and all his works.

Then he told us that there were many sins, that breaking the Law had defined many of these sins but there were more, like gluttony, or drunkenness, or greed, or envy but the one sin against God that was most damaging was sloth. Sloth is like a cancer it is not just idleness it is an attitude of having given up, an attitude of being unconcerned, an attitude that will not volunteer to face the difficulties, an attitude of letting someone else do the work or complete the task, an attitude that will not go the extra mile, an attitude that puts self in the centre and pushes God to one side, an attitude that tells God and men that you do not care, an attitude that says that it is all too difficult and that God had better find someone else to fulfil his plans. Now he said to us, "Is it not sloth to think that because our dear friend Lazarus has given us an appraisal of the situation in Jerusalem we should just run away?" The reason that sloth is the most damaging is that sloth ensures that nothing will ever change and that the evil that surrounds us cannot be defeated and that the devil has won! But God is LOVE and love sees the needs of others and puts them before self and puts God at the centre and love is the fulfilment of the Law. It is love that defeats all sin, and it is love that defeats sloth. "Now", he challenged us, "Who will stay the course with me? Because it is God's plan that we go to Jerusalem and there sin and the devil will be finally conquered!" Everyone there swore to continue and to follow Jesus wherever, he led, we were sure that he was the Messiah and Peter had only a few days before affirmed that we also knew that he was the Son of God. Failure and defeat or retreat were not words in the Jesus vocabulary and with him to lead us all such thoughts were impossible. He instructed us that our reaction to all and every situation must be thanks to God, if we really have faith in his infinite power then we must thank Him for his love and protection that has brought us this far. We must subdue any feelings of disappointment or failure and put our trust in Him and re-dedicate our selves to accept his will in all things, to recognise that any human sentiments that we may feel are actually the work of the devil and he will continually try to wean us away from our faith and trust and confidence that God is our shield and protector. Thanks to God is the foremost defence we have to the temptation of the devil, it lets him see that, like Job we put our trust absolutely in God and will continue to accept his will and not usurp it with our own will.

Everyone at the discussion was amazed, suddenly we saw how another piece of the well learnt studies of our Holy Scriptures, was re-interpreted into a new positive and active relationship with God by Jesus.

Lazarus' house maintained a welcome to all travellers and the news of Jesus' imminent arrival had been circulating for days so that instead of coming to a quiet comfortable home we actually arrived to a huge crowd. It seemed as if half of Jerusalem had come out to greet the Messiah, all along the main street of Bethany there were people waiting for a sight of this saviour of the nation. There were shouts of 'Hosanna, to the new King David', shouts of support and asking for blessings, 'Blessed is he who comes in the name of the Lord'; everywhere there was excitement and expectation of great things to be enacted in the next few days. The popular support was intoxicating despite the warnings we had heard, despite Jesus continually warning us that some dramatic confrontation was about to be played out, we were drawn into this atmosphere of confidence and felt that with this level of support then nothing could possibly threaten the success of the pilgrimage we were making to God's Holy City and that we with Jesus were about to change the world. We were convinced that we were to see the fulfilment of Isaiah's prophecies that 'all the wrongs of the world were about to be put right' by the power of Jesus. Our enthusiasm was at such a pitch that we pressed Jesus to continue our journey without delay.

Jesus, on the other hand and quite uncharacteristically, showed no urgency, we stayed in Bethany for nearly a week, it seemed that he wanted the authorities to have every opportunity to prepare for his entrance to the city. Every day crowds of people made the walk out of the city to come and see Jesus, to listen to his teaching, to be cured of their sicknesses, to receive forgiveness of their sins. People swore to support our mission when we came to the city. They saw in Jesus, just as we did, the possibility of the restitution of the Jews to their rightful position of power as God's chosen nation. They saw the opportunity to throw off the yoke of Rome and to punish the corruption of the religious leaders. Looking back on those few days it was quite clear that nobody looked at themselves as sinful, we saw all the faults in those around us and particularly in those of any position of authority. We did not recognise that they were just a reflection of our own sinfulness, we did not understand that to change the sinful man-made system we lived in needed the change of the heart of all men not just the rulers. I doubt, if people had understood this need there would have been quite such a level of enthusiasm; for a man to change his heart is much more difficult than for a man to demand that others change their hearts! Every day, from dawn till dusk, Jesus was teaching and healing, he did not seem to tire, he took little food or rest. When we tried to protect him from the crowds to let him rest he told us in no uncertain words that 'Now is the time and that the time was short, soon it would be too late for Him to teach and heal and bring souls nearer to God.' Jesus had an air of peaceful confidence, he clearly knew exactly what he had to do and how he would do it, nothing disturbed him, he exuded love and compassion to all the people who came to him, he never tired, he never became irritated, every question he treated with sincerity and used it to explain his message or to expose the misunderstanding or insincerity of the questioner. The atmosphere around him was hushed and attentive, nobody wanted to miss a word he said or the questions he was asked. Away from his immediate vicinity small groups formed and dispersed as people came away to tell others what was happening. Despite the huge crowds of many hundreds of people there was no pushing and aggression, most people were in a state of bemused shock as they heard that salvation was for the individual to achieve and was not a birthright for a nation, there was no scapegoat; that their sins were their responsibility; that strict adherence to the letter of the Law was not a way to heaven if a man did not have God's love in his heart; that the only way to heaven was to accept that Jesus was the Son of God and that His way was the only way.

The days were exhausting, the twelve of us were in great demand and spent our time explaining what we understood of God's gifts of forgiveness and his love for mankind, but we were very much second best and we knew it, the only voice they really wanted to hear and the only face they really wanted to see was that of Jesus himself. Every morning and evening Jesus, went away to pray, as Mary had told us, he was up long before day break by himself; he always returned full of confidence and cheerfulness. We had learnt to pray and observed the same routine but until Jesus came back at breakfast time we were consumed with doubts and anxiety. The anxiety was very debilitating; we worried about His health and stamina, no normal man could keep up the level of public exposure without cracking; we worried about the enemies that were, we knew, circling around us waiting to find reasons to destroy Him, and us; we were worried about our reception in the city, all our hopes and expectations lay in the restoration of the true faith and if that was not to be what would become of us all. In the evening it was the same, the crowds would gradually thin out and then we would go back into the house where the smells of a meal greeted us, either Martha or Mary were there to meet us with a welcome refreshing drink of wine or water, we all collapsed with exhaustion. Jesus, after taking a drink, would excuse himself and disappear to pray for an hour or so and always returned just in time for the evening meal fully restored and full of chatter about the days events. He was the best company at the table that any host could ask for; he kept everybody included in the conversation but when he was speaking to you as an individual it was as if there were no one else in the room. If the current topic began to lag he always had a question to ask us or made a challenging comment to change the subject. The women who in other company would not have been seen were welcomed and included; it was interesting that he treated their views with the same regard as anyone else's. When somebody commented on this to Him he re-emphasised that in the sight of God there was no difference between men and women, slave or free, Jew or Gentile, rich or poor, sick or whole, Pharisee or sinner all were equal and all were worthy of His love. He reiterated that they were worthy of our love, in fact it was our duty, if we loved God, to show them the same respect that we would show to the most important person we knew.

The days passed by, I can not remember how long we stayed at Lazarus' house on this visit, the days just became blurred, the crowds never stopped and then one morning Jesus announced that we were going to move on into Jerusalem. As usual there was no preparation after breakfast we set off towards the city, down across the Kidron valley and then up into the city. The story has been written by others, the crowds the shouting the excitement the palms being waved and the patient donkey who took Jesus into The Holy City of God. The Son of God came into the City of God.

Despite our deep misgivings about the trip to Jerusalem this unexpected triumphant entrance into the city dispelled all our worst fears. It was clear that the popular acclamation of Jesus as the Messiah, the Son of David, as he was greeted, could not be resisted and the authorities would have to concede that Jesus had come to restore Israel. There was no resistance by the Sanhedrin's police or by the Romans and we progressed, slowly, towards the Temple in a sea of people pressing in all round us. Most people were only able to get a glimpse of the 'King riding on a Donkey' a few got near enough to throw their cloaks under the animal's feet, all was excitement and welcome it was an amazing experience! Eventually we arrived at the gate to the Temple and Jesus dismounted and walked into the courtyard, he walked towards the moneychangers and the sacrifice sellers and then disaster struck. Without hesitating Jesus walked to their tables and with great energy born of burning anger he turned their tables over scattering their money and the doves and pigeons and shouted at them that they by their greed and selfish interests they had desecrated God's house. His exact words were 'You have turned my father's house into a den of thieves!' now the authorities did act they tried to arrest him but the crowd was too great, the guard retreated for fear of starting a riot. Then the priests and others in authority demanded of Him, in front of the crowd, 'By what authority do you disturb the temple court like this?' He did not reply to their demand but countered their question with His own question, he asked them how they viewed the baptism by John, that is John the Baptist who had been executed by Herod Antipas, whether his baptism was from God or from man. They were confused and dumbfounded by this challenge and they could not answer him. So he told them he would not answer their question, they were furious but could do nothing. So, then, he told the people several parables all of which were easily interpreted that the authorities had abused their responsibilities, that they would destroy anyone, even the Son of God, who presumed to criticise their behaviour or challenge their power. But each parable ended with the overt threat that they would be destroyed by God's judgement. Having heard these stories the authorities decided that they had to find some way of trapping Jesus into making some statement that they could use to bring him to their justice. So at an early opportunity they posed a trick question to him thinking that whatever answer he gave they would have the evidence they wanted to subject him to the rigours of the Roman Law. The question was this, 'Is it lawful to pay taxes to Caesar?' This was a question that the Jews themselves found impossible to answer but clearly if Jesus said 'No' then this would be seen as a revolution against Rome and the punishment would be swift and terrible, if he said 'Yes' then the Jews themselves would be offended and his popular support would quickly vanish. His answer is well known and is to this day a remarkable analysis of the situation his questioners had prepared for him. He rounded on them, accused them of hypocrisy and then asked for a coin which he examined and when the Pharisees and the crowd had confirmed that the likeness on the coin was Caesar he told them 'Give to Caesar that which is Caesar's but at the same time give to God that which is God's' the answer was astounding and the Pharisees were left with no reply. It is an answer that we must all adhere to and obey both parts. The second part is more demanding than the first; it is a direct reference to obedience to the law of Moses and specifically 'Though shalt love the Lord your God with all your heart, with all your mind, with all your body and with all your strength, and thou shalt love thy neighbour as thyself!' The whole crowd knew that this was impossible they knew that the continual sacrifice of animals was a desperate, but failed, attempt to avoid the wrath of God. The debate continued at a furious pace, He asked them about their understanding of the Messiah, about the resurrection of the dead, about the Law and they were confounded, to the extent that these experts in the Law and their beliefs were put to shame and they could think of no way to trap him. Then he told the crowd openly that these men, their religious leaders, were no more than a den of vipers; that these men, who set out to be his tormentors, had no ability to hear his message through their deaf ears and blind eyes. He spelled out just how evil these men were and that they would receive their just punishment from a just God on the Day of Judgement. The crowd was spellbound and hung on his every word, in all the time we had spent with him we had never heard such an attack on the authorities although in the past he had been very critical of their failures, He had never been so condemnatory.

We had listened in awe to his performance and were proud to be associated with His criticism, but gradually we became aware of the enormity of what he was doing. We had assumed that he would persuade them of His right but instead he attacked and attacked and attacked, again and again. Now we became alarmed and frightened, these men held the reins of power and we knew that they would do everything they could to destroy Him, and, with Him, we would also be destroyed. We tried to dissuade Him but He could not be stopped, He showed no fear or anxiety, He was absolutely confident in all He said. His confidence spread to us and when people from the crowd asked us why he was being so critical we told them that the Son of Man was here to claim His rights and to recover Israel to God. Eventually we left the Temple precincts and then Jesus talked to us about the future, he told us that all the state structure of the Jews would be destroyed and that even the Temple itself would be destroyed, we could not believe what he was saying and asked him when this would happen. He gave very clear predictions of the circumstances and we now know that what He said was the truth. The Temple has been destroyed and even the Holy City itself has been destroyed and deserted but that was many years later. When it happened we all called to mind that day of confrontation in the Temple courtyard. Many other things had to take place before that time and I must tell you about some of those things to make you understand and believe that this man was indeed the Son of God.

To our surprise instead of staying in the city that had welcomed him with such enthusiasm he led us back to Bethany, Lazarus and his sisters were there to welcome us and were very excited and alarmed by what they had heard from others and from our report of the day's happenings. Jesus talked to us all about the consequences, that he would be taken and would be executed, I don't think anyone believed it! But he was sure and told us that we would withdraw from Jerusalem for a while but that in a few days we would return. The next morning He announced that we would go back to the Jordan where we could be alone and He could teach us more of the reality of God and the work we had to do to change the world. None of us understood what he was doing but we tried to rationalise what would happen and concluded, among ourselves that he realised that the authorities needed time to understand that he had confronted them with and to give them time to repent and amend their ways. Certainly, despite His prediction of His final destiny, we hoped that He would show us how we should govern Israel and this new government would convince the world that it could change for the better by following his Gospel of adhering to God's commandments and that his message of love was to all men. We set off back down the road to Jericho but when we reached the valley floor instead of turning north he led us south.

As long as men could remember this road had always been a camel track used by caravans bringing spices and other valuable merchandise from Arabia and further east, having come through the fabled city of Petra. Now it was a Roman road but built by Herod to bring supplies and materials for his Summer palace at Masada. There were many places to stay along the way but Jesus took us to the oasis of En Gedi, where there was abundant fresh water and where we could relax away from the crowds. Since Herod's death, and the removal of his inept son Archelaus, the Palace was little used and the busy traffic that had once frequented the road had almost disappeared; this was certainly not a route for pilgrims or tourists. It had now reverted to its past, seeing just a few camel caravans, that rarely stopped at En Gedi, as they made their way to Jerusalem or Jericho and then north towards Galilee.

We had hoped that we would be able to relax, but Jesus seemed to be driven by a determination to utilise every available moment to talk to us, to teach us and to admonish our lack of understanding and faith. We all needed a rest after the excitements of the journey from Galilee, the stay at Bethany and the confrontation in Jerusalem. We were exhausted from the sheer pressure of frenetic activity all day very day, but Jesus did not seem tired, just determined; we rose early for prayer, then after breakfast, Jesus taught us and questioned us, after lunch we went for a walk and Jesus continued to talk to us about God and His infinite perfection and infinite power and about man's folly and sinfulness and wayward ways. Mostly he tried to explain to us how the forces of evil were at work in the world, how insidious these forces were, how, even when men knew they were falling short of God's standards, they could not resist the sweet temptation that Satan presented to them. He told us how these forces were real and that they were determined if it was possible to stop Jesus proclaiming His message of salvation from Satan's trap that was available to all men Jews and gentiles alike. He warned us continually that the struggle would be fierce, that blood would be shed and that He would have to sacrifice Himself for the battle to be won. He told us that His sacrifice was necessary, that with this final sacrifice the Devil would be beaten once and for all, death, that is spiritual death would be finally overcome and eternal life was the prize he had to deliver to mankind. The grace that God would give to those who believed in Jesus and obeyed His commands was available to all men; all men included sinners both Jews and Gentiles. As no human being could be free from sin it was only through God's grace that men could be delivered; this is the true and profound example of God's love towards His creation. He warned us that we had to be strong, to stand firm and to maintain that faith that he had demonstrated to us, that faith which knows that God is in control and that all matters are in His hands.

It was during these talks that He told us about His own temptation after John had baptised Him, how the Devil had offered Him power over the world if He would worship him, the temptations he explained to us were all temporal, human satisfactions, like power over nature to satisfy His needs; political domination of the world; great physical achievements expressed as destruction of the Temple and its miraculous reconstruction; and his personal safety. All the seductive powers that men sought, to control and dominate their neighbours and to accumulate great human assets to satisfy their greed. He warned us that we must always be on our guard against these seductive pleasures, that resistance may seem easy but the devil was a clever operator and packaged his temptation so that it looks harmless but they always have a deadly seed contained within them. He warned us that we must be careful to see the devil invading the good that men do to turn it to his advantage, the plans of men are always flawed by the ease with which the devil can pollute them, it is only through God that perfection can be achieved and that perfection is not available to men. He told us time and again that fear is a trick of the Devil, and that fear is only effective when our faith has been destroyed, it was when situations are threatening when we don't know how we will succeed or even survive that faith will ensure that God's will, will be done.

As I now look back at these last few days of Jesus earthly mission I have to admit that we twelve still saw the future as one of a glorious political victory over the religious powers centred in Jerusalem that would introduce a new religious and political order with Jesus as the pivotal source of God's love and power to change men's hearts and minds. That, from this change in the way Israel was governed, the rest of the world would follow and that the devil would be defeated. In his defeat would disappear all the consequences of man's sinfulness, the cruelty, the exploitation, the uncaring, the lack of love, wars and armies, the greed, the envy and the exclusion of men from access to God. We were convinced by these conclusions that were entirely of our own fabrication and showed, in the light of the events that were unfolding, just how far we were from having real faith in God and how we continually put our ways before God's ways even when Jesus was absolutely clear in the preparation he gave us for the turmoil of the next visit to Jerusalem. It surprises me that He was so patient with us, he told us again and again what was going to happen but we did not hear Him; we were deafened by our own self interest and conviction that we were about to receive our reward, a reward couched in human terms of political power and prestige. We never guessed that we were about to receive a reward, a spiritual reward, that Jesus would earn for us, which now gives us faith, confidence and power to change the world and the works of Satan cannot prevail against this power.

We had only been in the desert for three days when a messenger came with the news that Lazarus was sick and likely to die. We all expected Jesus to abandon His stay and return immediately to Bethany to cure His well loved friend, but He didn't. When the news came he was quite calm, he talked to the messenger, a trusted servant of the Lazarus household, and then sent him back saying he would come but not just yet. In fact it was four days later that we set off back to Jerusalem. When we finally arrived in Bethany it was quite clear that Lazarus was dead, the whole village was in mourning, we were told that he had died three days earlier and had been placed in his tomb these three days. As we approached, the news of our arrival went forward to the house and his sisters came out to meet us, they were very distressed, they had hoped that when Jesus got their message would have returned and would have saved their brother; after all he had cured many others who were not his friend or even his acquaintance so how could he ignore their plea for his help. Their disappointment had boiled over into anger and betrayal, they accused Jesus of failing them in their moment of need and now it was all too late and the most important person in their lives had been needlessly taken from them. He had not even given them the assurance through their servant that all would be well as he had done on other occasions to complete strangers and even to gentiles, how could he treat them so? Jesus listened to their out pouring of grief, he seemed to understand their accusations and anger, he was very upset I'm sure that he was moved to tears. What, we were asking each other, was there to be done? Our only response was to shrug our shoulders and say we were sorry but that's the way life is and we all had to accept it, there was no alternative. Then much to our surprise we heard Jesus saying, 'Take me to the tomb!'; it was only a short walk and when we arrived He commanded that the tomb was opened! Nobody ever opens a tomb, the appalling smell of putrefying flesh is more than you can stand and anyway there could be no good purpose. Eventually at His insistence the tomb was opened, the smell was dreadful but He ignored that and shouted into the tomb, 'Lazarus come out!' The whole crowd went totally silent, I think everyone stopped breathing, what was happening how could Jesus talk to a dead body, how could he call him by name it was ridiculous everyone knows that dead bodies can't walk and certainly dead bodies can't hear! Then in the silence we heard a rustling sound and out of the tomb stumbled Lazarus still cover in the winding clothes he had been buried in. Now the silence turned to fear, this was a ghost come from the after life a terrifying apparition; but Jesus, in His most commanding voice, ordered the clothes to be removed and some brave men went and un-shrouded Lazarus who was revealed live and well although slightly wobbly. Now all eyes turned to Jesus, who was this man who had power even over death?, who could command a corpse to rise and walk?, who restored a dead man, already well decayed, to his family in health and full of his previous faculties?. Such power had never been seen before it had never been conceived as even a possibility and yet we had seen it, but not just us, the village was full of visitors come to mourn with Mary and Martha and many of these people were influential men from Jerusalem, Pharisees, Sadducees, members of the Sanhedrin and Judges of the People, besides business people and other citizens there as friends of the family. Nobody asked Him now, who he was or by what authority he did things or said things, nobody challenged his power to act; every one was dumbfounded, what they had witnessed was beyond understanding except that this man really was the Son of God, with power beyond all human concept.

Gradually people moved away, quietly and reverently, Jesus and the Lazarus family moved off towards their home and we followed some distance behind, all of us covered in confusion. As we gradually thought through what we had seen we concluded that this was a planned overt demonstration of God's power, publicly demonstrated through Jesus, to convince the authorities that he was a man not to be trifled with and that if they did so they would have to accept the consequences that clearly could be terrifying. The rest of the day is only a dim memory, I think that Jesus and the family stayed close, we twelve almost kept guard until the crowd eventually dispersed late in the evening and then we slept, wondering what this man was that we were so involved with and whose power we had witnesses many times but had now been demonstrated in a way beyond any comprehension. The next morning, one of great joy in the Lazarus household, we twelve met together and prayed. We prayed that God would increase our faith in his power to change things that seem unchangeable, to remove our fear of the unknown and our fear of the future, but we all knew how weak we were in the presence of God as shown to us in this man, Jesus. The future looked very threatening, we felt hemmed in by forces being organised by the Jews to stop Jesus. Forces that were to us unassailable, we regretted ever having set out from Galilee, we recalled that we had argued hard with Jesus not to make the journey or at least to delay the journey until the Passover festival with all its crowds and tension was over. He had told us that this journey was God's plan and that we could not resist it and what was more we should not resist it or even consider resisting it, and because it was God's work we were doing all would be well. So we had come to Jerusalem, we had hoped that after his triumphal entry into the city and his confrontation in the Temple, He had realised just how powerful the opposition would be. We had taken comfort when he retreated to the desert but now on his return He had made such an overt and public demonstration of His power that the opposition were clearly determined to stop him at any cost.

Then Jesus arrived and listened to our fears, His response was as usual, 'O you of little faith, Every time the road gets difficult or there are threats that you perceive all you do is worry yourselves into a state of abject anxiety and all that you have learned is forgotten. I tell you again, we are about God's work and he will ensure that we can complete the task. What you have to remember is that God's plan is not your plan and His intentions are not shown to you at once, they are revealed gradually as the task is fulfilled. When this work is complete you will understand and you will receive the power you need to continue God's work in the world.' His confidence spilled over us and our doubts and worries evaporated, we were left feeling such poor disciples because yet again our faith had been shown to be so weak.

So we were restored and enjoyed a hearty breakfast; after which Jesus announced that we had to go back to Jerusalem. Despite all he had said to us only minutes before we were gripped with fear and anxiety, he looked round the room at us and rather sadly said 'Can you not understand that God IS with us? I tell you God is with us and that gives us power and courage to achieve the impossible and it is in Jerusalem that the impossible is to be achieved.'

When we came out into the courtyard we were confronted by a huge crowd who cheered and waved and clapped, the word had spread like wildfire and it seemed that we had no need to go to Jerusalem, Jerusalem had come out to Bethany to greet us and to see this man who had power greater than death itself. Jesus walked towards the crowd and it parted and we followed on behind Him and as He went through the crowd it turned and followed on, cheering and shouting their enthusiastic support for this "Son of David".

Progress was slow but eventually we entered the city and because the streets are so narrow it seemed almost as if we were alone and had been deserted by the crowd, unless you turned round and saw them following, or looked up and saw people crowding in windows and on roof tops. Jesus was intent on going directly to the Temple and when we arrived the crowd burst in and the outer court became a sea of humanity, surging this way and that all trying to witness was happening and what was being said. Jesus sat down on one of the benches along the colonnade that separated the Court of the Gentiles from the inner courts where only Jews were permitted, and started to teach the people. Somehow very soon there were many teachers and lawyers and Pharisees and scribes and all the other groups of the ruling class surrounding us and listening and questioning, Who He was? What authority He had? Why He thought He could challenge the Law? What was this power He had to cure people of their ills and even raise people from the dead? Was He not just a simple carpenter from Nazareth who was causing a great disturbance and encouraging people to break the Law of Moses and to eat with sinners? He answered them in many ways, by parables by counter-questioning the questioner, by disputing the very foundation of the beliefs that underpinned the questions, but there were always more questions. Sometimes he was very direct in His criticisms particularly when the dispute was about the role of the priests and the leaders, He frequently referred them to their duty as 'good' shepherds clearly showing that they were not 'good' at all. When they used the written word in the scrolls He showed that their arguments were hollow because they did not understand that God is a God of love and that they did not understand what God's love was. When He told them that He had come to fulfil the Law not to destroy the Law and that He came with God's specific instructions he was accused of blasphemy and there was an attempt to stone Him, but the press was so great that He easily slipped away.

The whole atmosphere was full of challenge and I cannot, now, remember what happened exactly when; the confrontation in the Temple was over three or four days each of which was charged with high tension and high drama. What was happening, and we felt it then as much as I can remember it now, was that the authorities were becoming more and more alarmed, not only at the ease with which their best brains were put down by this 'unlettered' prophet but that the crowds were openly hostile to the authorities and the risk of serious civil unrest against them was continually growing. The authorities were continually trying to find ways to use what Jesus said to trap Him into blasphemous statements so that they could legally arrest Him and put Him out of circulation and if possible to put Him to death but they could find nothing. The Feast of the Passover was growing nearer and nearer, Jesus seemed to be determined to use every day to the full, He was clearly trying to persuade His listeners and his interrogators that they had to change their relationship to God and to each other and that the matter was urgent the time was now, there was no possibility of delay, they must hear and understand what he was saying and that He spoke the truth and that his truth was the only truth. Many people were convinced and swore allegiance to His way but many more failed to see that they must change. In particular His insistence that the rituals and regulations about the observance of the Sabbath were fabrications and that the exclusive attitude towards sinners advocated by the Pharisees totally contradicted God's love for His creation, they were stumbling blocks that many could not overcome. These attitudes were woven into the very fabric of the Jewish society and there were serious social and spiritual penalties imposed by the 'Law', that is man's Law, for those who transgressed.

The Feast of the Passover was approaching, the city and the surrounding countryside was crowded with visitors from all over Judea and Galilee and from all over the world. Jews had been spread throughout the Roman world and even beyond its frontiers. The strife of the Jewish nation over many centuries led to the dispersion of Jews due to enslavement in wars and of course the great exile of Nebuchadnezzar had transported may be thousands of Jews to Babylon and when they were permitted to return to Palestine many had declined and stayed where they were. Even when only a small settlement of Jews took root in a particular place they were often persecuted and fled to other places so extending the nation far and wide. The Jews maintained their sense of a special people where ever they went, this meant that they did not mix with the peoples they lived among, they kept themselves separate in their religion, their eating habits, their observance of the Sabbath and their marriage, Jews only married Jews. They were persecuted as convenient scapegoats by political leaders and were easy to identify because of their separateness from the rest of the population. Because they were good businessmen they prospered and were envied by the local populations, their wealth and business acumen was the underlying cause of persecution forever. For Jews wherever they were their 'specialness' was represented by the Temple at Jerusalem, they paid the Temple tax and they had a duty that, at least once in their life-time, they would be at the Temple for the Passover. Every year Jerusalem became the focus of a huge migration, for weeks before and after the festival the population doubled and it was impossible to find somewhere to stay unless you had special friends and had made prior arrangements; if not you had to look for accommodation in the towns and villages in the surrounding country side.

We asked Jesus what he wanted to do for the Passover Feast and He told us we would celebrate it together and that we would find suitable accommodation in the city. So it was that we met in 'an upper room'. The requisites of the Law spelled out very specifically the cleansing preparation that has to be made for the feast both for people and the house, it also spells out the way the food is prepared and the exact menu for the meal and all the ritual that must be followed. The most important part of the ritual is the readings from the ancient books and although most of us knew the words off by heart it was with great reverence and ceremony that all the words were rehearsed. So once again we met for the feast and all the procedures were carefully observed, not a single syllable was missed not a single ritual was curtailed or missed and the air of prayerful reverence was maintained throughout. This ceremony is an annual reminder to all Jews that the Lord, their God, the only God, rescued their forefathers from slavery in Egypt and after many trials and tribulations brought them to the Land of Canaan, the land promised to their forefather Abraham. The ritual demanded the slaughter of 'a perfect lamb without blemish' whose blood was the protection of the people; through this repeated sacrifice the Jews knew that God would protect them from their enemies as long as they obeyed His Law, 'The Ten Commandments'. This then was the 'covenant' between God and the people of the Jews. The ceremony is a family affair, it is partly to confirm family ties and partly to educate the next generation in their 'specialness'. We were almost all miles from our families and as we listened to the words and watched the ceremonial our minds were with those we loved dearly who we knew were doing exactly the same thing at exactly the same time, it brought feelings of joy and sadness. As the meal progressed we began to relax and to put aside the fear and anxiety that had haunted us ever since we left Galilee. It was a shock when at the end of the meal Jesus told us that one among our tightly knit group was about to betray Him to the authorities, it was incredible we were all so convinced that this was the Messiah and that we were His special chosen group who would 'change the world'. How could one of us jeopardise the whole project when success was just within our grasp? There was a deathly silence and then Jesus challenged whoever it was to get on with it, now, and with that our brother Judas Iscariot rose and without a word or a look left us forever. We were stunned!

Then when the shock had died down Jesus told us that he brought a 'New Covenant', that this covenant was not just to the Jews but to the whole world and he instructed us that we should have a new ritual among His followers. In total silence we listened as he blessed some bread left over from the meal and then broke it, He told us that this represented His own body that would be broken for the sins of the whole world and to bring forgiveness to sinners, then he said that He was the perfect sacrifice, that the sacrificing of animals was finished. He took and blessed a cup of wine and told us that we should all drink of this cup, He told us the wine represented His blood that would be spilled; it was the blood of a new covenant between God and all mankind. He then charged us that whenever we, or those who believed in Him, had this special meal together we should say and do these thing in remembrance of Him.

We were stunned, we could not believe that after all the success He had achieved in Jerusalem the adoring crowds, the skilled arguments he had had with the Scribes and Lawyers he was once again predicting that he was to die. To calm our anxieties He talked to us repeating many of the lessons he had taught us in the past he reminded us of the power that he had shown us, we had at our command and He warned us not to be afraid. He repeated that encouragement that we had heard so many times, 'Do you think that our heavenly Father is going to let disaster overtake you before you really start the task of changing the world, be of a good courage, God is with you and will protect you.'

I suppose we were a bit encouraged but I felt sick to the pit of my stomach, every time we had had this sort of conversation with Jesus he always said that this was not the time, this time he did not say that, we knew when we came to Jerusalem that He was going to confront the authorities and that that was very dangerous, and now He had just sent Judas off to betray Him. Our experience to date told us that when Jesus said something it would happen and we were greatly alarmed for Him and for ourselves. We all felt that somehow we had to protect Him. Peter started to protest at His apparent acceptance of His imminent death and said he would never leave Him. Jesus looked at him with sad, rather tired eyes and said 'Peter, I tell you that even you will deny me publicly before the cock has crowed twice tomorrow morning.' The rest of us were dumbfounded, Peter of all people, he was so loyal, so protective, so strong, so confident. If he was not reliable what hope was there for the rest of us. Without more ado Jesus got up from the table and told us we should go and pray together in the garden in the Kidron Valley called Gethsemane.

The story of that fateful night has been described in detail many times and what turned out to be a major crisis does not need repeating in detail here but I will tell you about how I saw the events unfold. I was in many respects a privileged observer because through my business contacts I had access to the inner workings of the High Priest's Palace and the Court.

After the arrest in the garden of Gethsemane we all fled, we all wanted to find safe houses; there were many supporters of Jesus in Jerusalem but we could not be sure who would provide a safe haven if the authorities decided to have a purge of the known twelve adherents. We were frightened that Judas, having betrayed Jesus, would not stop at betraying us and revealing the safe houses to the authorities. We knew that we were all well recognised, we had been seen with Jesus every day since we came to the city, many people had talked to us about our lives with Jesus and how we were chosen to be his disciples. The worst thing was that we were all Galileans and we had an easily recognised accent, I'm sure that some would disguise the accent by speaking Greek, Jerusalem was full of visitors and there were many strange foreign accents and foreign languages to be heard but even with that protection the coarse Aramaic of Galilee was very distinctive. It was difficult to decide whether to get out of the city and risk being recognised first as a stranger and then as a disciple or to stay inside the city in the hope that we would be indistinguishable from other visitors. Without any comment we all went our own ways, it would have been foolish to stick together as a group and we would certainly have been an easy target had the Temple authorities decided that they should arrest us all or as many as they could. So we ran! I think this was perhaps because we had an inflated view of our importance at that moment to the Jews. The truth was, from their point of view, that there was only one person that had to be stopped and that was Jesus himself, none of us had ever made any public utterances, none of us had claimed any special power or relationship to God, and in particular none of us had in any way challenged the power of the State. The authorities would have been quite right to expect that without Jesus the whole revolution that was being fermented would collapse. I am sure that we felt exactly the same but we could not be sure that we would not be sought out and punished for our closeness to Jesus. So we ran and hid!

I spent some time mingling with crowds, purposely not speaking to anyone, it was late at night and dark so it was fairly easy to be almost invisible, I thought of seeking refuge with some of my business friends but decided that I could not be sure of their loyalty and that anyway it was unfair to ask them to take the risk of arrest on my behalf. I ended up with an urgent desire to see what was happening and made my way to one of the back entrances to the High Priest's palace and quite easily was admitted as a well known and respected supplier of fish products, once inside I could move about easily and quickly found my way to the Sanhedrin Chamber where Jesus was being held and questioned. Everyone knew that the court could not sit at night but here they were trying Jesus, all the rules of the court were being completely ignored, trumped up charges were being proposed and abandoned, false witnesses were being called but they could not find any reliable proof of wrong doing, Jesus was being abused verbally and physically; the anger, aggression was almost tangible. Jesus just stood there in the middle of this sea of hatred, he looked from one to another of his abusers with his look of disbelief at their behaviour even with a detached interest as if he knew that nothing that they could do now would to change God's intentions for the final acts. There was shouting and insults, a demand now, there and then for a demonstration of the power he claimed; nobody was interested in any thing he might have said, it just seemed a competition among them to see who could invent the most extreme accusations. It was "a kangaroo court", the sort of exhibition of the evil power of a totalitarian state acting against the individual, which has been used since time immemorial to put away anyone who dared to accuse the state of any excesses. Eventually the High Priest, Ananias, he was not even the High Priest he was a past High Priest, a nasty self interested, money grubbing politician who called for silence and asked Jesus directly, "Are you the Son of God?" Jesus replied "I am." Well that was what they were looking for, that was blasphemy and the sentence was death, they needed no corroborative evidence this was a public personal admission of guilt.

307

Not a single person there even considered the possibility that he was telling them the truth and that this was their last chance to avoid the catastrophe that was about to overtake them, even though the consequences for them took a few years to come to fruition. Jesus demeanour did not change one bit, I'm sure he saw me in the shadows, I felt His gaze continually as if to say "You are my witness against these wicked men." When Ananias had pronounced the sentence of death the place went mad, they all marched round Jesus, spitting in his face and slapping him about the head and face, they were behaving like badly behaved school boys bullying a boy who could not or would not defend himself. Nobody came to his aid, nobody questioned the legality of what they were doing despite the court consisting of the best legal brains in the land, nobody attempted to stop the brutish behaviour of the "victors". The state had won! On reflection later I thought it was remarkable how frightened they were of this simple carpenter from Nazareth. They were really alarmed that the message of his gospel was a revolution and that they would be swept away if they did not stop it now, all the power, wealth, status, pomp and security that they had accumulated from the existing system would disappear they would loose all control and they would not allow that to happen. Perhaps some of them knew that he was the Son of God but could not contemplate just what that meant except their own destruction.

So they sent Him to Pilate and the cross!

The final act of the tragedy was the reaction of the people to the travesty of justice being played out before them and which had they wished they could have stopped. Jesus asked his accusers why they had not arrested Him in the Temple; day after day he had been there teaching and debating with the scribes and teachers of The Law and yet only one feeble attempt had been made to restrain Him. The reason, both He and they knew, was because the people would have stopped them and defended Jesus against any attempt, so he was arrested in secret in the night and then He was tried by a 'kangaroo' court sitting, illegally, in the middle of the night. In the morning the Sanhedrin set about stirring up the crowd using every technique they could muster, rumours, bribes, threats, innuendos, false accusations and enough people were infected by these lies that a crowd, who could so easily have demanded Jesus' release, turned on Him and demanded His death. When Pilate offered Him freedom, the crowd who were now being agitated by the Sanhedrin, demanded His blood and the release of a murderous revolutionary. This was a clear demonstration of the Devil at work; the Devil knew that this was his only chance to stop Jesus and His mission of Forgiveness and Love to mankind. Well he thought he knew, what was actually happening was that God was manipulating the Devil to fulfil the plan that Jesus should be the one, final, satisfactory sacrifice for the sins of the whole world and that by this means sin, death and the Devil himself would be defeated. The sinfulness and unreliability of mankind is demonstrated no better than by the fact that this same crowd had not long before welcomed Jesus into the city as the 'Son of David', the Messiah and now they were rejecting the very person whom God had sent for their redemption.

As I watched I could only see the person of God being rejected, just as the prophet Isaiah had predicted. This man who had chosen me a sinful ordinary common Galilean fisherman, this man who had tutored me to understand something about the reality of God, this man who had cared for me who was the best friend I had ever had and would ever have, this man who I had witnessed performing miracles of healing and caring, this man who had shown that He had control of nature, this man who had rewritten the Law and re-set Man's relationship with God, this man who I had witnessed Transfigured before us and who talked with Moses and Elijah, this man who was the flawless expression of God's love for mankind was being murdered by mankind. One of His last words as He died was to pray for His persecutor's forgiveness, because "They did not know what it was they were doing."

At that moment I had no idea, and neither did any of the other players in this tragedy, that we were witnessing an epoch changing cataclysm that changed the world for ever, that this apparent moment of failure was in fact the moment of triumph and that God's plan was being fulfilled. The Sanhedrin had their moment of satisfaction, I felt despair disappointment that my ambitions for power and influence were destroyed and a yawning need for an answer to the question WHY?

This was a great moment that will be remembered forever, the key action that changed the world, but I am continually reminded, day by day, that the actions we take, the things we say, the way we respond to people also changes the world. Like Jesus we have a responsibility for the future and we will only make a better world when our decisions are made to fulfil God's will and not our own selfish needs!

None of the other of the Twelve were anywhere, we were all terrified for our own safety so we had all fled. I watched the action and then followed in the crowd as Jesus was led to His execution, it was dreadful! This man who had caused nobody any harm, on the contrary He had extended God's love to everyone was being punished with the most cruel, shameful and agonising sentence. Many people jeered at Him, but some were very quiet and many were in tears as He passed by, they knew that what was being done was wrong but the sentence had been passed and there was nothing that could be done to reverse the process and so He died the most horrible death ever devised by man.

I was sure that as soon as the Passover was complete there would be a witch hunt to find and arrest all His friends, I could not leave Jerusalem on my own so I stayed in hiding moving quietly from one safe house to another hoping that I would not be noticed. Gradually I heard of others who were similarly trying to avoid capture if we were to be hunted. Eventually we all met together, almost by accident, and the discussion was then what to do next, most people were ready to return to Galilee where at least the power of the temple was less threatening and we had family and friends. We talked about restarting our old lives and admitted to each other that the expectations we had that Jesus was the Messiah and that He would change the world had come to nothing. We talked about the evening only three days earlier and the message that Jesus had given us then, we determined to obey His command to remember Him when we broke bread together but we didn't really expect the group to hold together. We remembered how His last talk to us was all about being positive, caring for each other, aiming to be the servant and never the master, how love was the greatest power in the world and that was God's gift, finally he had promise to protect us what ever happened and that we would be given power to take His message to the ends of the world. As far as I can remember, in this time of gloom and foreboding, none of us recalled His most dramatic promise,

"That in three days He would rise from the dead!"

Part 18

The New Life Written by Peter

I am Peter, Peter is the name Jesus gave me many years ago, my family name is Simon and I was the second son of Jonas, a fisherman who lived at Capernaum on the northern coast of the Sea of Galilee. You will know something about me from the words my older brother Andrew has written and the words that my best friend John has written let alone what my dear, long dead, father wrote many, many years ago.

John finished his part of this amazing story with the profound words:

Jesus promised that in three days he would rise from the dead!

We were all in total despair! Then, when we discovered that no one had been arrested, our courage gradually recovered although we were still very frightened of the authorities and nervous about what they might do next. On the second day we heard that Judas had committed suicide. We were all very sad that a man who had been our friend and companion throughout our travels with Jesus should have been the crucial element in his downfall and death. However now he was dead we were sure that no more information could be leaked to the authorities and that our friends were able to offer us safe havens without undue risk. So we felt that we could meet together as long as we were careful. We were all ashamed that we had deserted Jesus just at his greatest hour of need; we all admitted that we had fled and hid. John as you have read had enough courage to stay close to the action and so was able to tell us what he had seen and heard of the trial and the execution. The only people who had any courage at all were the women-folk, they had stayed and witnessed Jesus in agony on the cross, John had stayed for a while but then fled in terror and despair. The women, about six of them who had come from Galilee with us, had stayed right to the end and after Jesus had died had helped to prepare his body for burial. One of Jesus' followers, and convinced that Jesus was the Messiah, named Joseph from the city of Arimathaea in Judea, had persuaded the Roman authorities to let him take the body away for burial according to the Law of Moses. He had reserved for himself a tomb cut into solid rock and he and the women organised that there he was buried. They had just finished all the rituals when a band of soldiers arrived and told them that they had orders to seal the tomb and to stand guard over it until they were relieved. The women all fled, they had no idea what was going on, but despite their great love for Jesus they were very frightened to be near any form of authority either Jewish or Roman.

My own story is one of shame and will be told for all time. Jesus had predicted in front of all my friends, while we celebrated the Passover together, that I would deny Him as my friend and master before that dreadful night was out. I was being my usual show-off, self-confident, arrogant self and had became angry at the very suggestion and swore that I would stay and defend Him to the end. When the police came to arrest Jesus I did try to protect Him, I had brought my sword with me expecting that things might get violent but Jesus told me not to fight, so all that was left was flight! I ran away but not very far I kept in the shadows and followed the police to the High Priest's Palace. There I thought that in the dark I would not be recognised but would be able to hear from the servants what was happening. It was there that, despite my strong assertions of bravery, I cowardly denied Him, not to any threatening authority but to a little slip of a girl who accused me of being one of Jesus' followers. She thought she recognised me and from my accent knew that I was a Galilean, she may well have only wanted to comfort me. Then the cock crowed and I realised how Jesus' prediction had come true I was so ashamed, I just fled and hid myself to grieve for my weakness and pride. It was a full day before I could bring myself to look for the others. We all had tales of deceit and cowardliness to admit to each other at least then I didn't feel that I was the only one who had failed Him.

What we didn't understand then was that all the disasters we had seen and heard were part of God's plan. It was a salutary awakening for us all when we did understand that God is still controlling the affairs of men even when the situation seems to us to be totally disastrous; we then reminded each other of how often Jesus had told us to have faith! It was some time before we began to grasp what had actually happened on that dreadful night, the perpetual warfare between Good and Evil had finally and permanently been won by Good.

We did not know what to do but we stayed together for the whole of that night and early in the morning our courageous women folk decided that they would visit the tomb. We men, knowing that there were soldiers there, were too afraid to go with them but stayed together hoping that the women would not get into trouble. We certainly did not have the courage to even try to protect them, but the authorities did not take women seriously, they were of no consequence so we expected that they would not be ill-treated. We spent our time in weeping and talking together mainly about how all our hopes and expectations had now come crashing down and that there was little to be done but to pack up and go home and try you pick up our lives where we had left them before Jesus had demanded our allegiance. The fact that Judas was His betrayer made us nervous about each other; I know I kept looking round at this group of men who had become close, intimate friends, who had shared so much together in Galilee. I suppose that we all were thinking to ourselves, "Well if one of us could have betrayed our master there was a reasonable probability that some one else would betray the rest of us." Somebody managed to get some food and so we were eating a very miserable breakfast when the women came rushing into tell us that the body had been stolen, the tomb was empty! Now without any thought for our own safety, John and I jumped up and ran as fast as our legs could carry us to the tomb. Fortunately it was still very early and there was nobody about otherwise we might have been arrested for disturbing the peace! The tomb was empty, the great stone that closed the tomb had been pushed aside, the seals were broken and the soldiers had all gone! We looked inside the hand cut cave and as our eyes became accustomed to the dark we were astonished by what we saw. There was no corpse, but what was more extraordinary was that the funeral winding-clothes that had wrapped the corpse were there, lying just as if they had wrapped a corpse the bandages covering the head were separate from the bandages that would have covered the body! It looked just as if the body had been slid out, there was no sign of any disturbance. Our minds and hearts raced, what could possibly have happened; were we at the right tomb? But nobody would leave the winding clothes inside an unused tomb; if somebody had stolen the body, why would they strip it and then fold the clothes so perfectly and carefully? There was no explanation! Then we realised there were two young men in white sitting in the tomb, we had to rub our eyes to convince ourselves, we were sure that they were not there when we first looked in, one of them said to us quite clearly; 'Do you not remember that this Jesus that you are looking for told you before he died that on the third day he would rise from the dead and would join you again. It is so and you will see him again soon.' With that they disappeared and we were left in the empty tomb! We looked at each other in total amazement mixed with disbelief. Was it true? Jesus had raised several people from the dead before our eyes, the most recent was Lazarus and we had hardly believed that miracle although we knew he was alive and well, but who had raised Jesus himself from the dead? We did remember that he had predicted that he would return to us but it was impossible! Our minds were in a whirl, what our eyes had seen and our ears had heard made no human sense. We stayed rooted to the ground for several minutes and then reluctantly, in a state of total confusion we left to report to our brothers what had happened. We wanted to believe that the misery of the last few days might be turned to joy, we wanted to believe that the message we had received was true but all our instincts and experience told us it could not be; we knew He was dead, we knew He had been buried, all this had been witnessed by dozens if not hundreds of people and yet it might just be true. Jesus had performed many miracles that would have been deemed impossible, His power to change men's understanding of the limitations of the rules of the natural world when confronted with the power of God had confronted us many times, so perhaps it was true. He **had** calmed the storm on the Sea of Galilee! He **had** walked on water! He **had** fed 5,000 with a child's picnic snack! He **had** made a blind man see! The list of miracles over nature was almost endless but this was entirely different. What if he really had risen from the dead?

When we got back to the others and told them what we had found, at first they were dismissive and totally disbelieved what we told them, gradually they began to wonder if it could really be true, just as we did, the atmosphere among us was one of total confusion, anxiety mixed with hope, joy mixed with sadness, disbelief battling with a need to believe, every one was quiet and unable to express their inner confusion. The question then came; 'Should we tell any one else?' we knew that if we did we would be laughed at, if we didn't then how would we explain how the body had disappeared? Something had to be done, Jesus had a large following of loyal supporters and they would expect us to say something! We did not know what to do, the risk of being laughed to scorn was uppermost in our minds, it was possible that there had been a hoax and if we said anything the hoaxers could then produce the body and then what would we be able to say? So we decided to wait, it now seemed the cowardly thing to do but then it seemed the most prudent. We spent the rest of the day wondering and hoping and praying. Then late in the evening two of our disciples arrived, the knocked urgently on the door of our safe house and eventually after ensuring their credentials we let them in. Their news was dramatic! They had decided to walk to Emmaus, like the rest of us they were depressed and hoped that their walk would cheer their spirits. On the way they were joined by a stranger who joined in their conversation about the disaster that had overtaken us in the last three days. The man could not understand their sadness and fear, he then explained to them that all the happenings were predicted by the whole of the Jewish peoples experience as God's chosen people. He explained how the stories from Abraham Isaac, Jacob, Moses, Samuel, David and all the prophets were a prelude to this Jesus. That Jesus was the Messiah, the Saviour of the World. They were very surprised by the understanding this complete stranger had, they said that they felt that their eyes had been opened to the almost unbelievable patterns that were there for all to see. If they had eyes to see! They asked their fellow traveller to stay to eat with them at an inn and then when the meal was served He took the bread and blessed it just as He had on the night that He was betrayed and suddenly they realised that this unrecognised stranger was in fact the risen Lord! They were overcome with confusion and then they realised that He had left them! Without eating their meal they left the inn and hurried back to tell us the amazing news that indeed he was risen, truly risen. He talked, He walked, He laughed, He handled physical objects, this was no ghost this was unmistakeably a man, they had no suspicion that it was other than a man and when he blessed the food they had absolutely no doubt that this was Jesus. We were dumbfounded; the two were bombarded with questions and answered them all with absolute conviction. We were all busy talking and asking and debating, the noise was nearly deafening, this was what we had so wanted to hear and yet we could not really believe what we were being told.

Then suddenly, without anyone opening a door, Jesus was there, right there in the middle of the room! He looked just the same, His clear bright, happy, and confident, eyes were smiling at us just as they always did. His smile was the same enthusiastic, loving smile that we had all longed to see again in the last three days and here He was! We were dumbstruck, was this a ghost? Were we all suffering from some mental aberration? Then He moved, He walked just as everyone walks, when we looked He was breathing just as everyone breaths; but our minds said this man is dead; what we are seeing cannot be true. Then He spoke, His voice was the same calm, soothing voice which had calmed our anxieties so many times in the past all he said was 'Peace be with you all. My peace I bring to you.' There was no sign of any distress from the terrible torture he had suffered, He didn't look tired or tense, He didn't sound as if he had been subjected to any ill-treatment in fact he looked better than he had since we left Galilee. All the accumulated tiredness of the weeks leading up to the execution had gone and He was just as He had been in those exciting days, which now seemed so long ago, when we walked in the green hills overlooking the Lake. Nobody moved, nobody breathed, we were frozen to the spot.

But there was no sign of panic or terror just blank amazement. My mind was in a whirl, I was fighting with my senses but the overall sensation was one of relief; Jesus had foretold us that He would be killed by the Jews and He had told us that on the third day He would rise again and here He was, apparently just as He had been, as if the last tragic days had never happened. I wondered whether I would receive another of His accusative reprimands that seemed to happen to me so frequently in the past. I could not erase from my mind that I, of all His disciples, had denied Him just as He had predicted I would and all the disciples knew it. They had never mentioned my failure; they could not be critical everyone had deserted Him in the Garden of Gethsemane when Jesus was arrested. I suppose that it might have been quite natural for us to fall on our knees and worship Him but nobody did. Then Jesus said "Look it really is me, here are that wounds I suffered, you can see they are still raw. But now I am returned to you for a while so that you know and believe that death has been conquered and that the evil of men and the devil cannot succeed in My Father's plan for mankind. This is the sign that God's love is all powerful and this is the message that you have to broadcast to the whole world that those who believe in me and do as I have told you will have eternal life with me in heaven." When He had said this we were all convinced and believed! We daren't ask questions and there were many spinning through our minds, our anxiety and fear and wonder gradually transformed into joy. Sublime, unlimited joy, joy that gave us an inner peace and that peace has never left any of us since. We were sure that now we could change the world, nobody could deny the power of God and would have to listen to the Gospel of love and forgiveness. Then just as he had come he was gone!

We all asked each other, "Was it real, had we really seen Jesus?" We all confirmed that we had seen the same thing, we had all heard the same words and had all felt His peace envelope us. Now we had no doubt we had to tell the world and we started with the people who had supported us and had accepted Jesus' teaching. The news spread like wildfire, as soon as we told a few it seemed the whole of Jerusalem knew, floods of people went to see the tomb and not just people who had been His supporters. Scribes, Pharisees, members of the Sanhedrin were among the throngs of witnesses to the empty tomb. Of course there were many disbelievers, who said the body had been stolen or that this was not where He had been buried, but the vast majority were convinced and many came to us to assure us of their conviction that this was indeed the Son of God!

Through his contacts in the Temple, John heard that the Chief priests and the Sanhedrin were called to an emergency session to decide what was to be done. They were now well aware that the mob who had called for Jesus blood could easily turn on them; they realised that Jesus had predicted the destruction of the Temple and the mob might just do that if they were convinced that their rulers had executed the Son of God; they knew that the Romans would deal severely with any civil unrest and they knew that if that happened their hold on power would be lost. We quite expected to be arrested for putting round 'scurrilous rumours' that would disturb the peace; the emergency meeting went on for hours. The factions within the Sanhedrin accused each other of unlawful actions, of failing to consider the outcome of their actions, of self-interest, of manipulating the people to achieve their illegal intentions. The hearing had been a 'Kangaroo court', it had operated at night and was not legally constituted; the chief priest was accused of forcing through his wish to have Jesus killed and had abused all the rules of justice and the process of law that had been so carefully developed over hundreds of years. Eventually they decided to do nothing, they decided that anything they did was more likely to reinforce the news. They hoped that the excitement would die down in a few days they relied on the knowledge that at the festival time the city was mainly populated by pilgrims and they would leave in the next day or so. Then they expected that the notion that Jesus had risen from the dead would be seen as a fraud. There were many of them who remember only too well that Jesus had only very recently and very publicly raised Lazarus from the dead and were very anxious that they should not attempt to quash the news as it may be true! We were all on edge when the Sanhedrin meeting broke up without any action being taken, just in case there were to be any reprisals, friends provided us with 'safe houses' so that we could not be easily arrested. We met together every day to break bread just as Jesus had instructed us to do and frequently Jesus was there among us; then there were other occasions when He appeared to substantial crowds of people and many, many people were then convinced of the truth of His resurrection and that He was the Son of God, the long awaited Messiah. Some people were disappointed that, although they knew now that Jesus was the Messiah, their heart-felt desire for an avenging David was wrong and that the real Saviour of the World came preaching love and forgiveness from God to man and that His kingdom would be established when man gave love and forgiveness to his fellow man!

When Jesus was with us he taught us many things, things that we would not have understood before the crucifixion and resurrection. He told us about the temptations He had suffered in the desert after John had baptised Him in the River Jordan. He released James and John and me from our promise of silence about the transfiguration we had witnessed while we were at Caesarea. He showed us that everywhere in the holy texts predictions of His coming were to be found where they had been hidden but now they were quite clear. He reminded us, many times, of the hostile reaction that would be the response to our broadcasting the message He had entrusted to us, but He assured us that He would provide the strength and courage to withstand the works of the devil. Just as God had provided all the courage and power that Moses had needed to confront Pharaoh, or Elijah had needed to confront Ahab and Jezebel. He explained to us that the message, which is so simple and so clear, was in man's terms a direct assault on all the established systems of society and undermined the pretentious 'authority' of the 'powers temporal'. He forecast that this hostile reaction to His commands would be repeated generation after generation until He came again! Man cannot resist the temptations of the devil, He assured us, unless they have been given the grace of God and have faith to put their trust in Jesus and so to live out their lives obeying His commands. He reminded us that He had forecast that the temple would be destroyed in three days and then rebuilt, now the three days had passed and in reality the whole fabrication of temple worship and animal sacrifices was at an end. He had made the one and only perfect and satisfactory sacrifice for the sins of the whole world, that is all the sin past, present and future. He had shown that God is available everywhere and cannot be 'imprisoned, in a man made structure, either of stone or of rules and regulations made up by men! He explained to us how the terrible experience of the trial and execution were necessary and part of God's intention so that the fulfilment of the prophets, for instance ' he was sent like a lamb to the slaughter, without complaint' and many others. The lesson for us and for all mankind, that we have to learn, was that, as long as we had real faith in God we too could face the same dangers and sacrifices with confidence and that in fact we would face them with a sense of inner peace and completeness, knowing that we were fulfilling God's perfect will.

A new age had been declared by the death and resurrection of Jesus; there was the time before Jesus and now the new time after Jesus; man's relationship with God had been redefined; the power of death had been destroyed through the one final and complete sacrifice; God was offering His grace to mankind to provide faith, hope and love and the forgiveness of sins if they accepted the message of His Son Jesus Christ the Messiah.

We stayed in Jerusalem for about two weeks, then Jesus told us that He wanted us to go to Galilee and that He would meet us there. We were all relieved to be able to leave the city which still represented a threat, our hosts were getting very nervous too, safe houses are only safe for a short time. We all wanted to go to visit our families. We knew they would need a lot of help to understand that the crucifixion was not a failure and that God's work would go on. We had with us the great news that Jesus had risen from the dead, but we didn't know how that would be received. We anticipated that our families would be delighted to see us, relieved that we had avoided imprisonment or worse. They would undoubtedly be hoping and that we would now abandon all the ideas of changing the world and return to our jobs as fishermen, tax collectors and all the other worldly tasks we had previously occupied to earn a living. We, on the other hand knew that our mission had only just begun and that now we knew that the 'Good News' of the resurrection would really change the world. We knew that our task was to spread the knowledge of this new beginning for mankind to the whole world. What was a disaster and foolishness to the world was, in fact, the wisdom of God in action! There was no possibility of any of us settling down to a previous life, too much had happened, we had all changed and were determined that we had to travel the width and breadth of the world and that we would never again have the comfort of a settled, orderly, safe life style again. We had to follow Jesus' example and become nomadic preachers convincing as many as we could to accept the commandments of Jesus; to love God and to love each other! To show that through His death and resurrection He had given proof that He was the Son of God and that a new order had been launched for mankind. We didn't expect that when we told our families of our plans they would be pleased. On the contrary we expected to have to accept that they would be hostile to the very idea that their nearest and dearest would now be leaving home for ever and that all the aspirations that we had once anticipated, of rewards in this life in the form of political power and influence, wealth and social status had died with Jesus on the cross. We were all convinced that our reward would be an everlasting reward in heaven, that is what Jesus had promised and what He promised, we knew, would be fulfilled!

So that afternoon we went up to Bethany to see Lazarus and his family. We had been to see them several times and had discussed the new situation with them. This time they were very welcoming and wanted to know the details of all the 'appearances' of Jesus and how the community of believers were coping with the perceived threat from the authorities. The visit was one of celebration rather than despair. We all knew 'that God was with us, so who could be against us.' The next morning set off on the journey north to Galilee, retracing the way we had come only a few weeks previously. We remembered how unsettled we had been how concerned for Jesus' and our safety, now we knew that Jesus was the Messiah but we were unable to express this confidence. We were frightened of being arrested by the Jews and frightened of being ridiculed by the people for having followed a failed prophet who had been crucified. So we travelled quickly and kept ourselves to ourselves, we found that we were not recognised; without Jesus we were just ordinary 'invisible' travellers. Once or twice we had sympathetic comments in the rest houses on the way, such as 'We were sorry to hear about your friend, such a nice, gentle man, such a charming voice and what great stories, but he did criticise the Temple and that's not on really, is it?' We felt depressed that all the effort, all the sacrifice, all the expectations had ended up as a 'five day wonder' and yet He still expected us to change the world. We all knew that we would feel better in Galilee, but we also knew that there would be much more personal abuse from our neighbours, many of them would have expected to gain from a 'successful' Jesus who had wrested the power from the Sanhedrin and been a new David. Jesus had told us to meet Him in Galilee so that is where we were going. Even that was surprising and we began to doubt whether we had actually seen Jesus risen from the dead. May be we were just running away from the truth that all we had expected from the Jesus experience was finished. It had been an amazing experience but we had to put it behind us and get on with life. We all agreed that we were better men for it and that we would set an example to our friends and families and to our business contacts and hopefully people would recognise that we were different and maybe they would also recognise that that was because of our Jesus experience. Not much return on effort and not likely to change the world! Then there was the problem of His power, we had all experienced it, in fact we had all found that we could heal people, but without Him we did not dare to try in case the power had been lost and we looked stupid. We reminisced about our discussions on how we would run the country and the world when God gave us the power and then looked at ourselves a disconsolate band stumbling back to our homes expecting to be met by 'We told you so!' It was just like that, of course our nearest family were pleased to see us back, but generally people were only too pleased to show us the error of our ways and when possible to make sure that even though we may have thought we were something special they knew all along that we were just ordinary people just like them.

When we got back to Capernaum, home for five of us, everyone else stayed as well, Jesus had just said He would see us in Galilee although He was not specific where in Galilee it seemed most likely to be Capernaum which had become His adopted home. James, when he heard a discussion like that, got quite cross with us, asking, "Have you forgotten already that Jesus is the Son of God and that concept of place and time were human and not divine. Had you so quickly lost the sense of wonder, fear, excitement that we had experienced only a few days earlier when Jesus appeared among us and that these appearances were totally unexpected and totally beyond our comprehension. You have to expect to meet Jesus anywhere and at anytime and in any circumstance. Had you forgotten that Jesus had told us that 'I will be with you always.' that means everywhere and all the time!" This justified reprimand certainly stiffened our courage but we soon drifted back into lethargy, hope seemed to desert us. Where? We kept asking each other, where was our faith? We remembered Jesus asking us the same question, we couldn't answer it then and we couldn't answer it now. We reminded each other of His confidence that God was with us and would not let His plan to change the world stumble, but still we all knew that we had lost the courage and confidence that we had with Jesus to guide and protect us. We were disheartened and depressed. Eventually, after two or three days of this debilitating atmosphere, I had had enough and told them that I was going to go fishing to show myself and everybody else that I had not forgotten how to earn my living. Every one said they would come too, fishermen and non-fishermen alike, so we borrowed a boat from the family business and although it was a bit crowded set out that evening for a night's fishing. Well, if you want to be depressed go fishing all night and catch nothing, our spirits were pretty low when we set out and as we were coming in to shore they were at rock bottom. We expected to be met by all the doubters saying things like, 'Have you heard Simon bar Jonas has been on a wild goose chase and on the way he has forgotten how to fish!' We were tired and fed-up the wind had dropped and we were having to row the boat into the beach and with all the people that was difficult, tempers were getting short, we must have looked like a real bunch of amateurs. Then we hear a man calling to us from the beach eventually we made out that he is suggesting that we throw the net out on the wrong side of the boat. Our reaction was, as you would expect, we had toiled all night, we were experts, though a bit out of practice, and this busy-body landlubber is giving us bright suggestions. He obviously didn't understand fishing and boats, you can only fish off the port side of the boats, the starboard side has all the steering gear and rigging there is no space to fish from that side. Andrew looked at me, I looked at James and James looked at John, that was all we wanted helpful, useless advice at this stage of the trip. The rest of the 'passengers', who also knew nothing about fishing or boats, said 'Go on, nothing else has worked you might as well try it.' The man on the shore was becoming very insistent. Eventually much against our better judgement we cleared all the gear out of the way, without anybody falling overboard and cast the net over the wrong side of the boat. We were hoping that none of our fishermen friends were watching this extraordinary behaviour, the boat flopping about in the sea, lots of people shouting, clearly we were behaving like a bunch of school boys, not grown men who had earned their living for years by fishing these waters. The net paid out very evenly and then went taut, our immediate reaction was that we had snagged some thing on the bottom then the net would be lost and how would we explain that to the family? Then we couldn't believe our eyes the sea started to boil with fish and big ones; we started to haul in but the weight was too much for us and we knew that if we tried any harder the net would tear. There was nothing to do but to hold the net as it was and start rowing for the shore, it was very hard work but eventually we got into shallow water and I jumped in to pull the net onto the beach. I had been a fisherman all my life and I had never seen such a catch, there were literally hundreds of fish and all of them full grown, the size that got premium prices, it was a bonanza. Then somebody on the boat cried out that man on the beach is Jesus. I looked up and there He was; He was smiling with delight and called to us to bring some of the fish as he had a fire and we should all have breakfast there on the beach. We were beside ourselves with delight and made haste to beach the boat and join Him at the fire He had lit. We were once again amazed at Him. How did he know there were fish and so many fish just within our reach? How did he know we were fishing just there? How did he know we had toiled all night and caught nothing? The answers didn't matter, all our embarrassment evaporated, all our doubts disappeared, all our misgivings and despair were instantly forgotten. Our master had returned to us!

He was so pleased to see us all, He asked how we had been and we had to admit that we had been depressed and demoralised, that without Him we could not see how we could possibly do what he wanted us to do. We told Him about the reception we had found in Capernaum from friends and families that had made us feel failures. We told Him that our loss of courage to demonstrate God's power, we had not attempted to heal the sick that were brought to us and the town became hostile and threatening. He listened attentively, of course we had to learn that He knew it all already, he was not disappointed or disillusioned. So over breakfast he told us that it was only that we had lost our faith; that the devil had found a weak spot in our defences and had exploited his opportunity. He reminded us of the many times this had happened before and He reminded us how we had rejoiced in Jerusalem when we knew that He had risen from the dead. He promised us that He was with us always and we did not need to see Him to know that God would protect us and guide us, but we must have faith! He asked us about our prayers and we all told Him that we had been praying fervently for His help and guidance but there seemed to be little response. So, He asked, why do you think you came fishing here, to this beach, this morning? Had not this been an answer to your prayers? Were you safe? No serious problems had beset you, had they? Even our families, although disappointed that their ambitions had not been fulfilled, had welcomed us home and shown us the love that a family will, even to its wandering sons, was not this an answer to our prayers? We have to understand that God answers all our prayers, but that sometimes the answer has to wait for some other matters to be settled and very often we get an answer we don't expect and even don't like; but we should be sure that an answer will come when we pray in faith because God has the problems before Him before we ask and has the solution planned before we ask, the key to prayer is faith in God's love and God's infinite power.

Then He talked about the catch, He talked about Jonah and Moses and Elijah and compare our reluctance to obey God's command with our arrogance in assuming that we knew better than God, was just like those great heroes of Jewish history and that eventually when we did God's bidding all was well and the results of our action was far greater than anything we could possibly imagine. Well perhaps we could be excused we argued we did not expect God to be a super fisherman. Jesus seemed delighted with the humour of this reply and told us that we had to expect God to be there in all sorts of situation, and that he was a super everything! We had to see God in everyone we met because He would use anybody, literally anybody, to bring His commands to His people, and to bring His solutions as well. Remember Ramases Egypt's Pharoah who delayed but could not keep the Hebrews captive when God had decided they were to be free, remember the shepherdboy David who became the great king of Israel chosenby God and dedicated by Samuel, remember the swindler Jacob who became Israel the unlikely father of the nation and now remember the Sanhedrin who had executed the Son of God and were unwittingly the instrument of God's plan to save mankind. Remember how in His ministry Jesus had used people continually to demonstrate God's love and God's power. He told us that we had to humble ourselves to do God's will and to accept that we were just part of God's plan for humanity and that there were an infinite number of other people who would be used to achieve His intensions. To do God's will we had to pray and we had to listen to God telling us what to do, He gave us His assurance that when we did God's will all would be well, He smiled very kindly to us and said softly but firmly, "Even when it all seems like a disaster and total failure." He said that we as a bunch of unremarkable fishermen and business men should not be surprised at the assortment of men and women who would be used by God to further His will. We had a responsibility to listen very intently to the things people said to us and never to dismiss any one because they don't seem to meet our expectation, it may well be that they are a messenger from God! He warned us that we had to learn to discern those people from the others who were wreckers sent by the devil to damage or delay or distract us from God's real purpose, but even these people had to be respected because out of their evil intents can come opportunities to show God's love and power to the world. He reminded us about His response to the business of tribute or the judgement He was asked to make on the woman caught in adultery. These questions had been traps set by men with evil intentions but we should remember that they had been exploited to show a right relationship between man and God. He talked to us for what seemed like hours but then he set a challenge directly to me.He asked me if I loved Him, three times He asked this and I began to get anxious. Was He reminding me that I had fulfilled His prediction that I would deny Him in His moment of need? What could I say to express my self-disappointment my utter shame and regret? As he asked me the third time I wondered if I could ever satisfy Him. The rest of my brothers were alarmed, was some terrible retribution about to be sentenced on me? Eventually he seemed to be satisfied that I really did love Him despite my public failure to show it and then He commanded me to feed and lead his sheep. The atmosphere suddenly relaxed, we had all felt that we were without a leader and now Jesus had decided that I should take this role. Somebody was nominated to make decisions about how we used our resources to fulfil God's will. At the same time I was minded of His words at our final Passover meal; "that he that was first should be last and that to follow him was to serve his fellow man and not to command him". I wondered what his command would mean and my mind suddenly went back to that room in Nazareth many years ago when a young girl had been challenged to an apparently impossible task by the archangel Gabriel and like her I promised that with God's help I would feed and care for His sheep.

With that He was gone!

So they all looked at me and asked 'What now?' So I suggested that we took the catch up to town and distributed it among the poor and needy, that tomorrow we returned to Jerusalem because it was from there that we had to start the task of changing the world. I was surprised at my own words and so were the others, they told me afterwards that I exuded confidence that this was God's will for the next stage of His plan and what they needed most at that moment was confidence.

I think the family had decided that we would probably be leaving and they had arranged a sort of farewell dinner party for us all at the farmhouse on the hill. It was a very warm and happy occasion but tinged with some sadness and apprehension about the future. We were all confident that we were doing God's work, it might be difficult, it would probably be dangerous but we knew that God would protect us and provide for us. Our families were not so confident and I think they really expected this to be the last time they saw any of us as we returned to Jerusalem where Jesus himself, who to them was the ultimate demonstration of God's power, had been executed most horribly. All our protestations that Jesus had risen from the dead, that the tomb was empty, that we had seen Him many times and so had hundreds of people in Jerusalem and that all these thing confirmed that He was the Messiah just as the scriptures had foretold and He had told us would happen all this was listened to politely but not really believed. They quite expected that the next thing that they would hear was that we also had been executed as rebels or that we would come home again having learnt some hard lessons at the hands of the chief priests. They had to admit that they were surprised to find men setting out to almost certain death should be so cheerful and confident. It was very difficult to say good-bye to wives and children and parents, they were tearful, and so was I, but they accepted that there was nothing they could say or do to dissuade us from our plan.

Somehow they had heard about the treachery of Judas Iscariot, we asked them to make sure they contacted his family and try to explain to them that what he had done was out of a deep misunderstanding of Jesus mission to mankind, it was borne out of his disappointment that Jesus was not a David and that His kingdom was one of peace not war, of loving inclusion not hateful segregation. It was true that it was an awful thing to have betrayed the only man who could change the world but without the crucifixion there could be no resurrection and there could be no fulfilment of God's plan for the recovery of mankind from the pit of sin into which men had fallen with Adam. I never heard whether they did talk to them, I hope so they needed comfort more than many.

So the next morning we set off, back to Jerusalem this time a smaller party. There were the eleven of us; and Mary Jesus' mother and Jesus' brother James, my wife, Mary of Magdala and several younger women. The women said that they came to make sure we behaved ourselves and to make sure we ate and slept properly and to help with the work to be done, they were all absolutely confident that we were doing the right thing and were very supportive and encouraging. If anyone felt down hearted they were the first to remind us that Jesus would have told us to have faith in God and all would be well and so it was. James, Jesus' brother, had become an unflinching supporter of Jesus message and ministry, he had been with us in Jerusalem and had seen the risen Lord and he wanted to be with us and to help to change the world. What he did for the infant church in Jerusalem in the next months and years ensured that it was well established and never wavered from the command to make the message known to everyone.

We arrived back in Jerusalem, having stopped one night in Jericho and one night in Bethany, to find that great things had been happening in our absence. The news of Jesus resurrection had acted like a catalyst and every day more and more people were committing themselves to Jesus. They came bringing their worldly goods to give to the church. When we left we had appointed several of the disciples who had followed Jesus from Galilee to Jerusalem and some of the disciples from Jerusalem, charging them to Break Bread together daily as remembrance to Jesus as He had told us and to care for the orphans, widows and the sick with what ever funds they had available. Their success had been dramatic there were now several hundred disciples meeting daily in safe houses dotted around the city. Every day people came with gifts of food and of money, they came to pray and to listen to the disciples recounting the story of Jesus life and to hear his parables and his teaching, but mostly they came to hear again and again the news that He had risen from the dead and that death was no longer the final terrifying consequence of life but that eternal life was available to all who believed in Jesus, who confessed their sinfulness and followed His commands.

Those were exciting days, I can remember so clearly the enthusiasm of the people. The city was still full of visitors from all over the world, east, west north and south, within the Roman Empire and outside the Roman Empire. All these Jews wanted to know all they could about Jesus, He was being hailed as the Messiah and if that was the truth they had to know to take this news back to their families and friends. Every day we were surrounded by crowds wanting to hear the news; the fact that He had been seen alive after He had been shamefully crucified as a common criminal or rebel, forced people to take notice. We made sure that these Jews who would spread the word had the full story about His life and his message to the world. Even if they did not believe that he was the Messiah we wanted them to take the word back to their homes for others to hear. The name of Jesus of Nazareth in this way spread far and wide very quickly. God works in a mysterious way, I am convinced that God prepared the world for the visit of His son, He generated the great power of Rome and its sophisticated system of communications through roads and seaways, the skill of their soldiers to build and maintain roads and bridges and to spread law and order, the Pax Romana, all this prepared so that His message of a new order for mankind could spread unimpeded throughout the world. More than that He had ensured that an international language had arrived allowing peoples of different nations to speak and understand each other. The language He chose was the delicately subtle language of Greece that had developed a special ability to disseminate man's ideas and thoughts in a way that none of the other available languages could do. This language had spread and been accepted in place of Latin the language of the conquering Romans even among Romans themselves. He had thousands of years earlier chosen the Jews as His Chosen People, He had charged them to spread the knowledge of His greatness and power and blessing to all people but they had never fulfilled this responsibility, they were insular and exclusive. He had given them His promised land, the land of Canaan positioned at the cross roads of the world so that the whole world would see His power at work among this people. To further His plans He forced them into exile to show how a people dedicated to Him as the one God showed courage and loyalty even under extreme persecution. To recover the momentum of his plan He restored them to Canaan and rebuilt Jerusalem and the Temple. To further His plan He made the Jews a wily acquisitive nation who populated the whole of the world with colonies of traders and businessmen all of whom held fiercely to their religious peculiarities that set them apart from other people and the people they were living among. Again, despite persecution, these Jews were loyal to their inheritance. To further His plans He demanded that all Jews maintained a practical link to the centre of their faith, every man had to pay his Temple tax of half a shekel every year and it was beholden on all Jews to make the pilgrimage to Jerusalem as often as was possible and at least once in their life. Through His prophets He had promised them a Messiah who would restore them to a status of respect and power

327

remembered in David and Solomon. So, slowly but surely, on a time scale and with patience outside man's understanding all the necessary details were put into place for God to demonstrate His love for His creation. Now, this comprehensive communication system of people and roads that He had so carefully prepared was being put to His purpose: to promulgate the news of Jesus of Nazareth, His life, His death, His resurrection and His message to mankind throughout the world. The news would spread like a wild fire to the whole world, and it did! You who are reading these words have heard the Word! We, the apostles, have spent our lives, as have many others since then, travelling the world telling people the good news and teaching them the way to lead a new life walking in God's holy ways. Through God's good grace and His infinite power over the affairs of men we were able 'to change the world' and fulfil Jesus' instruction to us. But I am jumping ahead of myself there are other matters that I want to tell you about.

So we came back to Jerusalem and were immediately totally absorbed in the activities of the new converts who continually arrived at the numerous and now well known 'safe' houses. There were the poor, the destitute, the sick, the repentant sinners all the debris of society, as well as many wealthy and 'sophisticated' 'educated' men and women, Jews, Greeks, Romans and many other nations visiting or resident in Jerusalem. We reminded each other, when there was a brief moment of calm, of Jesus parable of the king's feast, how the king had commanded his servant to go out to the hedges and ditches to bring the poor and needy to His feast. We had nothing to give them, or so it seemed but somehow every day we had enough, people brought food, they brought clothing, they came offering hospitality to these drop outs, they brought money. These were not the dregs of society these were the wealthy merchants, lawyers, scribes and priests, these were the people who had conspired together to destroy Jesus and now realised their mistake and had to do something to remedy their actions. Many people came with anonymity, others were quite open but all were humbled by the events of the last few weeks. All wanted to do what they could to follow Jesus' command to love their neighbours and had been reminded just who their neighbours really were. The daily exchange of people in need being satisfied by people willing to give became a happy, cheerful chaos but it quickly became clear that we twelve could not manage these exchanges and we had to appoint some deputies to share the work. We wanted to use these opportunities to teach the word of God and not to be ensuring that peoples' physical needs were being met, it was important that everyone understood that it was God's mercy that was being dispensed. After a lot of thought and prayer and discussion we appointed a group of young men all convinced of God's purpose and gave them the task of managing these daily exchanges. It was at this time that James, Jesus' brother, showed his amazing gifts of organisation everyday he went round from house to house arranging for surpluses to be moved to satisfy needs, he ensured that money was distributed so that it was available to meet the needs. He quickly knew everyone and was known by everyone. The result was that requests for help came to him and we were relieved of those tasks and could teach, console, pray with and for the people. We quickly discovered they were all "poor in spirit" and now were being "blessed". They desperately needed God's comfort through Jesus promise of forgiveness of sins. Although we were all very busy we made sure that we met every day to break bread as Jesus had instructed us in remembrance of His death and resurrection and the New Covenant between God and mankind, that he had given us.

We were doing this on the morning of the feast of Pentecost when quite suddenly we were overwhelmed by a sense of a presence, it gave us a feeling of peace and comfort and power, it was as if we band of very ordinary men from Galilee were being elevated to a position of special purpose, as if we were being granted a special relationship with God to enable us to have absolute faith and confidence and never again to doubt God's power and Jesus' promises to us. It is impossible to describe, but we now know that when a man really comes to know Jesus he experiences this blessing that we received that morning and that has stayed with us ever since through all the difficulties and dangers we have faced and still face today. We were so amazed at what had happened that we rushed into the street and proclaimed God's message to everyone, many of them were equally surprised as somehow we were speaking in their own languages. Later that day I was reminded of that day long ago when I questioned Jesus as to how we could spread the word to the world when we only spoke Aramaic, I suspect that he was chuckling in Heaven as he watched us begin to understand the power of God. This empowering spirit of God gave me the courage to publicly address the population of Jerusalem. It was an opportunity that was derived from the accusation that we were drunk who had received this blessing, I quoted to them the prophet Joel's words; that they were witnessing the day predicted when the Lord would come. I told them the truth about Jesus and exposed their guilt; that they had conspired together to murder the Son of God, the Messiah. The effect was dramatic and over 3,000 were convinced of their need for repentance and forgiveness and were converted and baptised. We all were convinced that we were invincible, all those doubts and fearfulness that had undermined us throughout our travelling and witnessing Jesus' mission had evaporated. We continually reminded each other of His response to our fears, 'Have faith in God your Father who cares for you.' It was an extraordinary feeling of peace and power and great joy we knew then that we were able to do God's will and that we really would change the world. It is a sensation that has never left me, I still feel it today, many years later, and I am sure it will stay with me until He calls me home or He returns in Glory to proclaim His kingdom on earth and to use His analogy 'To bring His sheep safely into the fold of the Good Shepherd'. It is this courage that has given us the confidence to preach to Jews all over the world and show them that Jesus is the fulfilment of the prophecies from the whole of our history and many have come to believe. It is this courage that has extended our preaching to the gentiles and bring them to the same belief in God's love and forgiveness to those who repent and follow Him and that the reward for this belief and transformation is eternal life. This is the power that Jesus promised us before He finally left this physical world. He promised us that He would never leave us and that He would send us a "comforter", a spirit of power and confidence, a spirit of courage, a spirit that would support us through troubles and would enable us to proclaim the Gospel always and that is exactly what He has done. We have confronted great dangers from the devil and the world but we know that He is there with us to guide us, guard us, feed us and to keep us safe to fulfil His will. Immediately after the crucifixion and even after the resurrection we were not sure that we had retained the power that Jesus had given us to heal the sick, after the gift of the spirit our confidence returned. We preached and taught in the Temple everyday, part of our ministry was the healing of the sick who came in droves to find some relief from their sufferings. We followed Jesus lead of confirming the faith of the plaintive and asked for a commitment to change their lives to follow Jesus' teaching. The healing caused a great deal of excitement and it was probably this as much as anything that brought many converts to the cause, it also ensured that the Sanhedrin could not ignore our activities.

Eventually we were all arrested and thrown in jail. During the night while we were singing and praying an angel came and opened all the doors, charging us that in the morning we should resume our habit of being in the temple precincts spreading the good news of man restored to God. That morning there was a real kafuffle and eventually we were re-arrested and brought before the court. We were questioned closely about what we were doing and on whose authority we were preaching.

Well that was just the opening we wanted and we reminded the presiding priests, lawyers, Pharisees, Sadducees and scribes that they had connived together to murder the Son of God and that we were ensuring that the people knew His message of love, forgiveness and eternal life. We told them that we were preaching this message and demonstrating how the law and the prophet all were a fore-runner to Jesus who had come as the fulfilment of the promise that God had given to Abraham. They were angry and confused, we knew that some of them were already convinced of these truths but others had closed their minds to what they were seeing and hearing everyday. The end result was that we were instructed to cease 'spreading these dangerous rumours', to which we replied that we were subject to a higher power than their's in this matter and could not obey them. They could find nothing to condemn us and as the people were seeing the healing of the sick everyday, they were frightened to take any action against us, so we were sentenced to be birched, a minor treatment compared with Jesus' suffering and sent on our way. This was the first whipping that we received but have now become used to this sort of punishment from authorities who can not accept that the life, death, resurrection and ascension of Jesus has started a new era for all mankind.

It is surprising to us, and to many, that the peace and joy that the spirit provides stays even when we are called, as He was, to give up our lives for His purpose. The story of the stoning of Stephen, one of our ordained deacons, who died praising God and blessing his persecutors, is well known, not least because it was Saul, now Paul, who was there giving official blessing to this murder. The other early martyrdom was James, John's brother and a life long friend of Andrew and mine who had witnessed all the adventures we had with Jesus as one of the twelve. Although we were greatly distressed by both these deaths, and many since, we rejoiced in their witness and in the knowledge that they had been received into Heaven. The attitude of the Jews began to harden towards us when the Sanhedrin realised that their policy of 'Leave well alone and it will all calm down and disappear.' clearly was not working. We were making so many converts that they decided to clamp down on us and began a reign of terror against us. It is interesting looking back on the decision they had made and the conclusion that they should draw if the Jesus cult did not wither away; that conclusion should have been by their own argument that Jesus really was the Son of God and that they had to make amends for their crimes against Him. However that was forgotten and James was taken onto custody and on completely false trumped up accusations was beheaded on the authority of the Roman puppet king Agrippa. It all happened in less than 12 hours. They had clearly decided that they would destroy the adherents and advocates of this new relationship with God and that the easiest way was to destroy the leaders, we were all well known and made no attempt to hide, as we had done in the aftermath of Jesus' crucifixion. We were daily in the temple praying and teaching without fear of the authorities so we were easy to identify and to arrest and I was the next to be taken into custody! I expected to face the same fate as James and prepared my self by prayer, to be ready to take whatever opportunity came to once again preach to the authorities the message of Jesus. Because there had been the earlier remarkable escape, when all the disciples left the jail together, the authorities had me chained hand and foot to a soldier either side and I was incarcerated in the innermost prison cells. So I spent time praying for strength to face the tomorrow's problems, whatever they may be and talking with my guards, telling them the good news. They were not interested but I thought they might one day remember this night. At about midnight there was an earthquake, it was quite violent there was dust and rubble every where, somehow or other I was free, the guard seem to have gone into a trance the shackles that held me came undone and an angel, yes, an angel in shimmering white clothes, commanded me to get up and follow him. There was no difficulty in leaving the jail all the doors were ajar and the guards were in a trance. As soon as were outside the angel disappeared so I made my way through the silent deserted streets. Thinking about it now I remember noticing that there was no sign of an earthquake; earthquakes are not uncommon but even so each one usually causes some panic and everyone rushes out of their houses to see what damage has been done, but the streets were deserted. I made my way to the house where I was sure that the faithful would be praying for me. The girl who answered the door was so surprised that she forgot to let me in! When eventually the exited girl did open the door everyone was amazed at my story and concluded that God was not going to let the temporal powers destroy the man he had chosen to lead His church and to feed His sheep. It was a miracle! I never got to meet Agrippa, and I really had prepared a great sermon for him. I would have told him about the attempts that his grandfather the wicked Herod the (so called) Great had made to destroy Jesus at His birth in Bethlehem. Many years, later Paul met his son, another Agrippa, and presented him with the facts about Jesus and His gospel of forgiveness and eternal life. Paul was under arrest but claimed a Roman citizen's right to be tried by The Emperor, that device got him to Rome to spread the word.

Although the ten of us, who were left from the twelve, were not molested seriously after my miraculous escape the authorities stepped up their policy of persecution; they made life very difficult for anyone they caught who professed belief in Jesus. There were beatings, executions, imprisonments, confiscation of property, loss of employment, exclusion from synagogues and many more draconian measures. The result was that there was a general exodus of converts from Jerusalem and they took The Word throughout Judea and Galilee and to further parts of the world where some people had friends or relatives and felt safer away from the vindictive power of the Sanhedrin. If the policy of the Sanhedrin was intended to suppress what they saw as a dangerous sect, their policy of repression and persecution had exactly the opposite effect. We knew that the many visitors to Jerusalem were carrying the gospel to their homes around the Roman Empire and beyond, now this emigration from persecution was reinforcing and accelerating the spread of the good news, God had used the wickedness of these Jews to His own ends 'to the ends of the world'. Despite their serious endeavours, the authorities could not stop the church expanding. There seemed to be an unending stream of people drawn to the message that Jesus had proclaimed. Mostly it was the poor and needy, the sick, the orphaned and the widows and there were lots of them! Every time the authorities made public examples of people by floggings and executions they could not stop them declaring their love of Jesus, their undying faith in His love for them and that they knew they were going to heaven. The result was that even more were attracted to this new way of living. There were also many of the aristocrats and the wealthy, the Pharisees and even the Saducees who came to believe and trust in Jesus. These men came with their whole household and their servants and their slaves everyone accepted that there was no difference in God's eyes between rich and poor, master and servant or slave, old or young, man or woman. We all accepted that in the sight of God we were sinners and that it was only through the love of Jesus and His interceding on our behalf that we were spared the rightful just consequences of our sinfulness. Any assets that came to us were used for the relief of the many. Most of the assets were human beings, it was remarkable how people came together and willingly gave of their time and energy and skills to demonstrate that God was at work among us. It seemed that whatever we needed to do we had the skills, right there within the congregation, available for us to use, there was never any talk about payment, or about who was in charge or responsible, the needs were clear, as they still are, and it seemed that then things just happened. There was a continual expansion of the houses that were welcoming people and giving them shelter and food and clothing and comfort. The accumulation of the food and clothing was particularly impressive, nobody accumulated any thing that they did not need it was just passed on to where there was somehow known to be a need. There was a continuous flow of gifts, mostly anonymous. We never knew how we would deal with tomorrow, we were never anxious about it, we were confident that God would supply and He always did! And, be very sure, He still does and He will continue to ensure that His kingdom on earth will never be frustrated by the lack of resources.

The ten of us spent a lot of time in the Temple precincts, teaching and explaining that Jesus was the fulfilment of God's plan for mankind, to show people how all the books of the founders of Israel and all the books of the prophets were in fact anticipating the arrival of Jesus on earth. That His very fate was to be expected, that all these writings were actually God inspired and show the world just how mankind drifts into chaos and anarchy as sinfulness takes hold in any and every society. The story of the Jews warns them and all mankind that God will exercise His judgement and Justice when men ignore His rules for society enshrined in the Ten Commandments and that ignoring Jesus new covenant between man and God underwritten by Jesus' self sacrifice as a final once and for all time sacrifice, oblation and satisfaction for man's sinfulness ensuring that God's mercy is available to all who follow His life and obey His commands. These realities came as a real revelation to most people, the Jews have always assumed that they had a birth right to a safe relationship with God and that the gentiles were debarred from any such salvation. To hear the word proclaimed to all men was a challenge to the very basis of the Jewish nation and many found this impossible to accept but as I have already said large numbers were convinced and changed their lives to follow Jesus' commandments.

The story of the Church is one of continual expansion, the need is just as real today as it was when we started, we have made our contribution and after us many more are doing God's work. We were the privileged few chosen by the Son of God himself to help Him to start the process of 'Changing the World'. Now many come with the same privilege of being chosen by God to do his work. The work must go on, for the world always needs changing as men continually fall victim to the Devil and his works.

I am now an old man, I have travelled widely throughout the world bringing the Gospel the Good News to people wherever I went, lately I have been writing to my friends and I leave you with this belief.

You are **ACCEPTABLE** to God; you are **VALUED** by God; God makes you **CAPABLE** of doing His work and you are **FORGIVEN** your sins by God.

You are the ones chosen by God, chosen for the high calling of priestly work, chosen to be a holy people, God's instruments to do his work whatever that may be and speak out for him, to tell others of the night-and-day difference He made for you - from nothing to something, from rejected to accepted.

The End, or The Beginning.

Book List

This book has been born, partly, out of many years of reading many books about Christianity. About the historical, political and religious background to Jesus mission. I offer a very limited list of books that I have found particularly helpful and instructive.

I apologise to the authors, still living, for not asking their permission, they will I hope be satisfied that they have inspired another Christian to write to help others come to Christ.

The Bible

William Barclay, 'The Daily Study Bible Series' of New Testament commentaries.

'The Bible Speaks Today Series' of commentaries on The Old and The New Testaments.

Tom Wright, The 'For Everyone' Series of commentaries on the New Testament.

Floyd V Filson, 'A New Testament History'

Sean Freyne, 'Galilee, Jesus and The New Testament'

The Penguin translation of Josephus, 'The Jewish War'

J S Proctor

Born in Bristol in 1938, third of a family of seven children. Educated at Bristol Cathedral School, followed by an apprenticeship at Bristol Aeroplane Co. leading to an HND in Mechanical Engineering and then a one year postgraduate study at Imperial College gaining the DIC Diploma.

Worked for nearly forty years as a senior manufacturing manger and company director in the Steel Tube Industry and the Steel Wheel Industry. A demanding profession that was primarily about the encouragement and direction of the managers and workers available, in the many plants involved, to greater and greater performance achievements. He accumulated experience not only in England but also in Germany, France, Italy and America.

These experiences progressively convinced Proctor of the deeply spiritual nature of the work he was doing, already a committed Christian he endeavoured to recognise his, and every manager's, responsibility of the very soul of the people who relied on his decisions and behaviour. The result is this book that shows how Jesus taught by demonstration and by teaching his small band of 'God Chosen men' who changed the world!

His preciously published work is a management hand book intended for both young and mature managers and based on his experience. It is entitled 'The New Manager'

Lightning Source UK Ltd.
Milton Keynes UK
UKOW05f1418050114

223990UK00004B/325/P